COLUSA COUNTY FREE LIBRARY

P9-DVE-643

THE AFFAIR

THE AFFAIR

A NOVEL

Alicia Clifford

Doubleday Large Print
Home Library Edition

ST. MARTIN'S PRESS ✖ NEW YORK

COLUSA COUNTY FREE LIBRARY

This Large Print Edition, prepared especially for Double-day Large Print Home Library, contains the complete, unabridged text of the original Publisher's Edition.

This is a work of fiction. All of the characters, organiza-tions, and events portrayed in this novel are either prod-ucts of the author's imagination or are used fictitiously.

THE AFFAIR. Copyright © 2012 by Alicia Clifford. All rights reserved. Printed in the United States of America. For information, address St. Martin's Press, 175 Fifth Avenue, New York, N.Y. 10010.

ISBN 978-1-61793-704-0

**This Large Print Book carries the
Seal of Approval of N.A.V.H.**

COLUSA COUNTY FREE LIBRARY

For Rumi, with love and gratitude

ACKNOWLEDGMENTS

Thanks to my mother, Alice Mary, for once more remembering for me what it was like to live through the Second World War; my daughter, Sasha, for excellent advice and reassuring me that I really had reached the end of the novel; my friend Lizzy for giving me the benefit of her experience on being an army child sent out for summer holidays to Africa in the late 1950s; Peter for advising on army matters; Caroline for telling me about makeup tricks in wartime, and for sundry other nuggets of useful information; two more friends, Nelly and Lily, for various advice on the unnamed country in Eastern Europe where they were born; my agent, Bill Hamilton, for unfailing support and encouragement; and everyone at St. Martin's Press, especially Sally Richardson and my wonderful editor, Charlie Spicer.

THE AFFAIR

CHAPTER ONE

**If perfect understanding can exist be-
tween two people, each bound by different pasts and set in distant shelves,
might not all magic be possible?**
Appended to undated shopping list
(*bone from butcher, coffee, tuna,
matches*).

The day after the death, a large exotic insect was noticed in the sitting room of
Parr's, where members of the family had
gathered to discuss funeral plans.

"You might like to know, Mummy, there's
a socking great beetle on your picture."
Robert sounded angry, but only because
he was stressed and fearful. There was a
list in front of him because his approach to
any challenge was to reduce it to a series

of columns. He'd got as far as "Hymns." For the time being, grief had been marginalized.

His seven-year-old niece Bud, with her keener eyesight, corrected him. "It's not a beetle. It's a moth." She'd been stroking her grandmother's limp hands, staring imploringly into her empty eyes. But now, as if giving up, she rose and approached the picture Robert had indicated.

"Leave it," cautioned Sarah, as her daughter climbed on a chair. Her voice was very soft and careful. As she kept reminding everyone, just because Bud seemed fine, that didn't mean anything. She'd been staying with her grandparents when her grandfather had suffered a fatal heart attack, soon after supper was served. It was she who had telephoned her parents, even as the resident nurse was still absorbing the situation. "Grandpa has passed away," she'd announced in an astonishingly composed voice. (Nurse-speak, of course, because nobody in Bud's family referred to death like that.) And now, as if all that hadn't been traumatic enough, she was forced to witness the effect on her adored grandmother.

For all their efforts to behave normally, the family were frantic. For years they'd resented the costly invasion of nurses and caregivers; but now they'd have offered any amount of money if their mother, Celia, would only return to her former self. Why couldn't she see the death as a mercy, like everyone else? She was only sixty-three—years younger than their father had been—but now seemed bent on following him to the grave. She wouldn't eat, wouldn't speak. But of course the marriage had been famously happy, and his long illness had only brought them closer.

Then Bud shocked them all by announcing, voice shrill with excitement: "It's him! The moth's him!"

"Oh please!" thought Margaret, closing her eyes. She knew it was not acceptable to criticize a sibling's child, but this was too much. Bud had behaved commendably in frightening circumstances, but she should never have been allowed to sit in on the funeral discussion.

For all her usual indulgence, even Sarah seemed at a loss how to react. And before anyone could stop her, the child made

things worse. Her attitude became con-
spiratorial, almost loverlike: "He's come
back because he's really really worried
about you, Gran!" Suddenly she let out a
shriek. "Look! He moved his wings! He
heard me! He's saying yes!"

Celia had been staring into space with
that dreadful new apathy, like a travesty of
the daydreamer they'd grown up with. "Off
with the fairies again," their father used to
tease. But suddenly, to their very great relief, she was back—kind and warm and
engaged. "What a perfectly wonderful
idea, darling!"

Margaret (who was good on nature) said
tersely: "It looks like an elephant hawk moth
to me. But it's not possible. Not in January."

"It's Grandpa!" Bud crossed her arms
and glared at them.

"Grandpa . . ." Celia echoed, sounding
bemused; then she gave a delighted smile
as if inviting everyone to join the game.

Her children exchanged exhausted, uneasy glances—what was this madness?
Then they believed they understood. They
were pretty sure their mother didn't sub-
scribe to the myth of reincarnation any
more than they did. No, this had to do with

applauding in a grandchild something she'd failed to find in them. They'd no imagination, as Robert would cheerfully admit. "Not a smidgeon," he'd say on behalf of them all, sounding exactly like his father. "We're doers, not thinkers." And once he'd demanded, sounding a little aggrieved: "Who wants to sit in a room on their own, putting a lot of invented people through their paces?" Celia was the only writer in the family—and good luck to her!

Actually, Bud didn't believe in reincarnation, either. She'd no idea where the suggestion had come from. But the magical effect she'd achieved now provoked an extraordinary reaction in her mother and aunt and uncle. Without conferring, they plunged into making fools of themselves. It was a measure of their concern. They'd have done anything to stop Celia from sliding back into that terrible despair.

"It's funny because he loathes that picture," observed Margaret, who'd never have come out with such silliness if her new husband, Charles, had been there. It was a dingy old oil painting of half a dozen horsemen straggling over a vast plain, which her mother had found somewhere.

The family had always assumed their father disliked it because the riders were disorderly and going nowhere and therefore bound to annoy a former soldier.

"Why's he sitting on it, then?" asked Robert, mouth twitching as he imagined describing the scene to his wife, Mel. He ran a hand over his pink, worried face, like smoothing it out. "Would he *want* to come back?" he murmured a little tactlessly.

"He'll be worrying that we won't arrange things properly," said Sarah. "He's keeping his beady eye on us all." Unlike Margaret, she longed for her husband to be there. Whoopee had a wonderful sense of humor. He'd have adored watching the Bayley family make fools of themselves.

Bud shrieked: "He's wearing his specs!"

"So he is!" agreed Celia because, by now, she'd risen to her feet and crossed the room a little shakily to examine the moth, too.

The two of them were behaving as if they were the only people in the room. But when Bud began crooning, "Dear little Grandpa!," the others came to their senses.

"That's quite enough!" said Sarah, unusually sharply.

However, Celia was still staring at the

moth. Earlier, she had failed to react when "Onward Christian Soldiers" was suggested as the first hymn. But now she said, sounding brisk and anxious to wrap up the meeting, "Perhaps 'Jerusalem the Golden' might be better."

The strange thing was that the day after the funeral, the moth vanished, never to be seen again. "Daddy's last inspection," Robert called it—as a joke, of course.

It was a turning point, they came to understand: the moment their mother shook off the seductive tug of death and chose, instead, the pleasure of watching her grandchildren grow up. Also—and here was the astounding part—she would at last become a real writer.

Nearly twenty years on, keeping each other company on the eve of her far sadder funeral, Margaret and Sarah recalled that extraordinary demonstration of the power of the will.

"If that hadn't happened . . ." Sarah began.

"Well, this wouldn't have," Margaret responded a little sharply as if her sister had stated the obvious.

"Why didn't she warn us?"

Margaret shrugged.

They'd been over this already. Was it their fault—as Margaret was indicating with that helpless, irritated gesture—that their mother hadn't warned them what to expect after her death? Or was it possible that modest woman had never guessed? The family was in shock and yet, to the outside world, had to pretend otherwise.

Sitting at their mother's table in her kitchen, halfway through yet another bottle of good wine from her cellar, the sisters still expected her to enter at any minute, bent and diminished by age, but still curious, still amused, still possessed of a remarkable memory. "Oh good!" she'd have said in her courteous way, "that Sancerre needs drinking" (though it had been kept for rare dinner parties). She'd have joined them to listen to the wind moaning down the chimney, bursts of rain spattering the black windowpanes like tears. She'd have smiled at Robert's lists pinned everywhere, his complicated plan for when the mourners came to the house after the funeral the following day; the sound of his voice from his

father's old study next door as he practiced his address, stopwatch in hand.

"I'm not going to speak about my mother
as a writer," Margaret and Sarah heard
him boom. And then he stopped and began again. "I'm not here to talk about my
mother's writing. Others far better qualified than me have already done that . . .
Oh, damn and blast!"

The sisters exchanged smiles.

"Others far better qualified than *I* have
already done that . . ."

The house still held her flavor, like a
vase just emptied of flowers. Staring at a
diary pinned on the wall, so poignantly
empty of spindly blue writing after August
10, they still expected to hear the irregular
tap of her stick, the gentle humming of a
wartime tune (as if part of her pined for
that terrifying era). But it was strangely
comforting to feel cross with her. Of course,
she should have prepared them!

However, the truth was, her writing had
been ignored within the family. Their father
had set the tone. "Mummy deserves nothing but praise for the way she keeps at it!"
he'd marveled, but almost in the same

breath confessed very apologetically, "Not my sort of thing, I'm afraid." So they'd never read her books, either. Looking back, it seemed to them that their mother had colluded in this. "Froth," she'd once laughingly described her work. And so it happened that when, at age sixty-four, she wrote a novel that attracted critical attention, they failed to take account of that, too, though it was the first to be published under her real name.

Now they stared at photographs of her in the newspapers and re-read the lengthy obituaries and longed to be able to check with a simple phone call that the person given such prominence and their mother were the same. According to a top-ranking literary novelist, who'd started all the fuss, the woman who'd begun by writing romances had transformed herself into "a sculptor of the human condition; a writer of enormous passion and truth." The tabloids had seized on the story, too, with excruciating (and inaccurate) headlines like, "The eighty-year-old who wrote porn." It added spice, of course, that she'd been married to a distinguished soldier. But at least everyone had stressed the happiness of the marriage—the only bit to come as no surprise to the family.

In widowhood, Celia had taken to working in a spare room at the top of the house, which was kept locked. But now, with leisure to explore the house (which had, after all, become theirs), her children discovered it had been converted into a proper writer's den with a good supportive chair and an expensive word processor and built-in bookcases bursting with reference books as well as numerous editions of her novels. "Did you know Gran could use a computer?" Sarah had asked her daughter, Bud, only to be told: "We set it up for her." Sarah wanted to ask more questions but was afraid of appearing foolish.

The room was extraordinarily messy. There was paper strewn everywhere, much of it yellow and crisp with age. There were letters and bills and notebooks and diaries and newspapers. It seemed amazing that anything finished had emerged from such chaos, let alone critically acclaimed novels. "I *must* sort this out," Celia had been heard to remark worriedly only a month before, as if she sensed a dark presence stalking her, just out of sight. She'd died suddenly in her bed, leaving the junk un-touched.

There came a soft tapping on the kitchen door and the sisters exchanged looks.

"Only me! I'm not interrupting, am I?"

Robert's wife, Mel, had ostensibly come to make a lemon and honey drink lest he strain his voice before the funeral. How-ever, they guessed she was longing to confide in them about her own problems. "Oh well . . ." she kept saying, but with less and less optimism.

"Oh dear," said Sarah when she'd gone. "It's all so impossible, isn't it?" And that was the closest she came to saying that however much she and Margaret might privately sympathize with their sister-in-law, their loyalty would always belong to their brother. But they'd no time for others' troubles. Grief was working magic. Sud-denly it seemed irrelevant that one of them was happy and the other was not. For the first time in years, they were getting on.

Margaret rose from her chair and opened the fridge to retrieve the half-empty bottle. She paused for a moment, admiring their work.

It was living through the war, they understood, that had made their mother so bad at throwing anything away. They'd removed a bowl of malodorous stock, a soggy half cucumber corseted in plastic, a leatherlike slab of cheese, some shriveled mushrooms, a carton of rotting cream, a box of eggs date-stamped two months before, a few squares of nut chocolate with a white bloom on them and a cling-wrapped single portion of some dark wet vegetable, possibly cabbage. Even the butter was off. After they'd washed and disinfected the fridge thoroughly, they'd filled it with food brought down from London: cartons of fresh sauces to go with boxes of fresh pasta, French cheeses and salads and soft fruits and juices. However, meals kept appearing on the doorstep, shyly delivered, usually early in the morning. Only that day, they'd discovered a big Irish stew and a chocolate cake on the porch, together with a note: "Please accept this as a token of our esteem. P.S. No need to return casserole dish and plate immediately. Jim and Nina Barton ('Greenslade,' just past the crossroads, first house on your right)."

"It seems a shame to waste this," said Margaret, slicing herself a piece of the cake, which was quite dry and crumbly with a very sweet soft topping, as if it had been made from a packet. The young people had rejected it. They were extraordinarily fussy about food.

"Why do people always assume the bereaved are hungry?"

"It's the only way they can think of to be helpful. I must say, it was wonderful not having to cook for everyone this evening."

The entire family had descended for the funeral. Sarah's daughter, Bud, and Robert's son, Guy, the greatest of friends, were out walking and talking in the dark lanes. Robert's daughter, Miranda, who was newly pregnant, had retired to bed. "So sad!" she kept murmuring to herself because Celia would never meet her first great-grandchild now. The teenagers, Margaret's Theo and Evie, were in an upstairs bedroom with Sarah's son, Spud, who preferred their company though he was almost thirty now. There was a crash from overhead, as if a piece of furniture had been overturned, followed by barking and whining from Celia's old dog, Oscar, who was alarmed but excited by the glut of company and still searching for her.

"So good she could stay in her own home till the end," said Sarah, very positively.

Margaret nodded. "With all her marbles."

"Fit as a flea."

"Apart from the knees and the eyes."

"She was really really lucky!"

"So were we."

Sarah started sobbing. "Where is she?" she asked, like a frightened child.

Margaret shook her head, unable to speak.

"She's still in us," said Sarah, making an effort. "And our children. And she'll be in our children's children, too—if there's any world left for them by then." She forced a smile. "She's in Miranda's baby. Suddenly, that makes sense. That's *true* immortality."

"You think?"

"Oh, far more than any books!"

But the reality was that outside a small circle of people their deaths would pass unnoticed. Their only fame would be as a footnote to their mother's: "Celia Bayley is survived by a son and two daughters."

Life had become extraordinarily dramatic. Thick bundles of letters from strangers arrived every day. The telephone rang constantly with requests and inquiries. Journalists turned up at the door, unannounced, with camera crews. Only the day before, Robert had given an interview to a local television station, and nobody watching his assured performance could have guessed that he hadn't read a single one of his mother's books. But it upset them, nevertheless, when people outside the family wrote about her with such authority. What did they know?

The kitchen door opened and Margaret's husband, Charles, came in. "Ah, cake!" he commented, sounding as if he was trying to make a joke but managing merely to convey a kind of awkward disapproval.

"I only had a bit," protested Margaret, instantly on the defensive.

Sarah wrapped her arms around herself, like making a private comparison.

"Where's Whoopee?" she asked. Everyone in her family had excruciating nicknames. Her conventional, inhibited relatives suspected it was purely to annoy them. Whoopee called Sarah Crinkle (though no one had ever wanted to ask why) and his children Spud and Bud. The most Robert

had ventured (sounding pompous and embarrassed) was that it was ridiculous to
go through the performance of choosing
pleasant names like Stephen and Emily
for your children and even holding expensive christening parties, when they were
almost immediately going to be called Spud
and Bud. Plus it was bound to attract attention, he'd added, missing the point.

"I've just left your husband in the conservatory," Charles responded, sounding
prickly and offended.

Sarah guessed Whoopee had been up
to his tricks again. Charles usually took
care to avoid his brother-in-law's company,
but she and Margaret had made it clear
they didn't want to be interrupted and Robert was absorbed in buffing up his address
in the study and nobody was allowed into
the sitting room because it had been
vacuumed and tidied for the funeral. She
couldn't help smiling as she pictured the
scene in the freezing conservatory: wary
Charles buttoned into his three-piece suit,
her handsome, casually dressed husband
seeming innocently curious as he sought
opinions on such matters as immigration
and the wars in Afghanistan and Iraq. If

that had failed to provoke the response he was after, he'd probably attacked parents who sent their children to private schools. Naughty Whoopee, who knew exactly how to press the right (or wrong) buttons. She asked: "What's my darling husband doing, anyway?"

"He said he had to make a phone call."

She was astonished. "Whoever to?"

A roar of laughter, almost immediately suppressed, came from the young people upstairs. It was like hearing an audience start to applaud before a piece of music had finished, and it sent a small shock wave through the gathering in the kitchen.

Bursting with people, yet painfully empty, the house had cast off the melancholy that had so oppressed them on arrival. It was like a last feverish performance because, once the funeral was over, the clearing would begin.

Singing started above: some kind of rap song. It seemed awfully inappropriate. Margaret recognized the overexcited voice of her daughter, thirteen-year-old Evie, the baby of the group. Perhaps she should put a stop to it? Then, in her emotional state, she fancied she heard her mother protest very faintly, "Oh, let them!"

It was ridiculous, of course. Death was final. So why did she have the strangest feeling that her mother was still with them in spirit? Almost as if there was something in this world—or this house—that held her back from moving onto the next.

CHAPTER TWO

When I die, I don't want my family to mourn. I want them to use the occasion to throw a big extravagant party. I know I've been truly blessed, and it should be celebrated.

> Shaky writing. Apparently one of
> the last notebooks. No date.

Bet Parker watched Robert climb the steps to the pulpit looking grave and determined and self-conscious and felt the same deep thrum of protectiveness as she had when he was nine years old. She and Priscilla Forbes-Hamilton were trying to make themselves comfortable in cramped pews with rocklike hassocks jostling their feet and nowhere to prop their sticks. At eighty-six, Bet was an unwilling expert on funerals and familiar with all the tricks and traditions to seduce mourners into believing this wasn't really the end—the gallant hymns and thoughtful prayers and uplifting music. But that first glimpse of Celia's coffin beneath its trembling sheet of flowers had been dreadful. This time, a truly beloved person had gone and there could be no softening it. The old photograph of a young woman reprinted on the service sheet only intensified her pain.

Once upon a time, when that photograph was taken, there'd been wedding after wedding, one friend multiplying into two with luck, and no funerals at all. As the youngest of their threesome, Celia had been the first to marry and, sixty-five years later, Bet could remember every detail of the hasty ceremony: Frederick's head gleaming like a dark conker in a ray of cold sunlight, someone dropping a book on an uncarpeted floor as Celia whispered her vows, the odd mixture of relief and sadness on her mother's face when the registrar pronounced "You may kiss the bride." November 1944, and the tail end of the war, but it seemed like yesterday . . .

Funny to remember the whispered doubts

she and Priscilla had shared back then. It was all so quick and Celia was only seventeen to Frederick's thirty, and he was far too glamorous to be faithful. Those two had been lucky, Priscilla had once suggested, as if a successful marriage depended more on chance than faith and hard work.

And here was the sixty-two-year-old son of that marriage, like a faded carbon copy of his handsome father, crushed by sadness like them all but rising to the occasion because he had a splendid character, as Bet well knew. As she waited for his confident mellifluous voice to fill the church, she fancied for a moment that he *was* Frederick, about to extol his beloved Celia.

But Celia's husband had been lying outside in the cold graveyard for years. And besides, Bet reminded herself, the Frederick she was remembering so fondly had vanished long before his death.

All the obituary writers had stressed Celia's conventional, upper-middle-class background, which, they implied, had been an unlikely birthing ground for what they described as "a passionate and original voice."

It had begun to rankle with Robert. What was so wrong with "conventional" and "upper-middle-class"? It seemed to him that his family was being mocked for its very strengths. So, most uncharacteristically, he made a last-minute decision to give a new opening to the much-rehearsed address tucked inside his jacket. He'd seen the photographers at the entrance to the church, which meant there were bound to be journalists with notepads inside. "Reptiles," he thought, though all his dealings with the press had been most amicable. He'd enjoy confounding them.

He'd read somewhere that an effective way of ensuring attention when giving an address was to pause significantly before beginning. Robert waited for as long as he dared—several seconds, which felt like eternity—while observing the sea of increasingly puzzled faces beneath. There was beloved Bet next to Priscilla, his mother's other old friend; the family lawyer, Rodney Cartwright, who'd inherited the job from his father; the newish, youngish doctor. But all these others? He'd no idea his mother had had such a wide acquaintance. He thought he recognized the odd famous face. Wasn't that an actor in the fourth row? He dared not look at his wife, Mel, who knew nothing of his decision. Perhaps even she, so devoted, was beginning to find him dull.

He took a deep breath, then bellowed with all his might: "DO AS YOUR FATHER TELLS YOU—IMMEDIATELY!"

The effect on the congregation was everything he'd hoped for. He paused again, before making his voice so soft that the deafer members—still quivering with shock—had to strain to catch every word. "Mummy was the gentlest of people, but what Daddy said was law. Oh yes!" He relished the chuckle of comprehension that rippled through the church. "As you all know, they were a supremely happy couple."

Then, satisfied he'd made his point, he put on his spectacles and began to read the speech everyone had been expecting—about a remarkable life rooted in solid, old-fashioned values, the fine example of selfless love that had been set at the end, and so on and so forth.

"Lovely address," Priscilla told Margaret, back at Parr's. "Dear dear Robert. Celia

never shouted like that. Still . . . pwetic
license, or whatever they like to call it."

Margaret was thinking that nobody spoke
like Priscilla anymore: that way of lazily
snarling out some words, clipping off others, like a parody of old BBC English. She
could see her nephew, Spud, listening with
an incredulous smile playing over his lips,
saw him mouth "pwetic" like tasting some
exotic delicacy.

"And d'you know, darling," Priscilla went
on, beaming, "I saw you come into the
church and I thought to myself, '*What* is
Celia doing here?'"

"Celia *was* there!" Bet snapped, and
Margaret saw Priscilla put out a knobbly
freckled hand as if she understood only
too well what had provoked the temper.

"Do I really look like my mother?" Margaret doubted it but found comfort in the
comparison. She was enjoying talking to
the over-eighties, who had immediately
commandeered the only really comfortable
sofa. Skin-and-bone Priscilla with her
tissue-paper skin and drunkenly penciled
eyebrows, her hair puffed into a transpar-
ent white loaf; and dear Bet, plump body
straining against her clothes, chin as prickly

as a man's. They still laughed like girls and used slang picked up during wartime service in the Wrens well over half a century before. "Sling over the wardoo," Bet had just requested and when Priscilla instantly passed a jug of water, Margaret observed them exchange a look of triumph.

Unlike Bet (who didn't need to), Priscilla was catching up on family news. How old was everyone now? Were husbands behaving properly? Were children satisfactory? However, she asked all these questions in an incurious, amused kind of way: almost as if, for her, being in a noisy house packed with different generations was like visiting a foreign country.

Bet rose with difficulty from the sofa and headed for the food. She felt as if she was bearing the pain for the whole family and absentmindedly piled far too much on her plate. She bit into a sausage roll and it released a shower of greasy crumbs onto the bosom of her much-used black suit. "Yes, yes, yes, I'm revolting!" she thought crossly, as if agreeing with some unseen, critical presence. "But once I had men coming out of my ears, and now one more person has gone who can remember it."

She was deeply thankful Priscilla was still around. Time had leveled their once great differences. On this saddest of occasions, they'd shared the journey from London, once falling into hysterical giggles at the sight of a man in a woolly hat. "Mustn't get pissed," Bet had cautioned as they drank gin-and-tonics at the bar in the train to give themselves strength for the ordeal to come. "*Chère comrade,*" Priscilla had called her after the second, in memory of their wartime adventures and, momentarily, a pale pretty girl had seemed to metamorphose. But it was only the alcohol, of course. Thank goodness they'd tanked up because nobody was refilling glasses—hence the water, which they usually avoided.

Predictably, Priscilla snapped open her crocodile skin handbag to ensure her return ticket was safely in there, even though they wouldn't be leaving for hours. Then, infuriating Bet all over again, she assured Margaret with her trademark radiant, batty smile: "Celia would adore all this!"

"They're drinking too much," Robert warned his niece Evie. Operation Post Funeral had kicked off the moment the family arrived back at the house. Each grandchild had been given a printed timetable setting out his or her part in the proceedings minute by minute, commencing with parking duty and coat duty. But now a problem had arisen, except that Robert didn't believe in them. "There are no problems, only indecisions," was one of his favorite sayings.

He'd thanked everyone for coming to the funeral, murmuring "See you later?" to a well-judged selection. But it now seemed as if the whole congregation had turned up at the house—more than twice the number he'd calculated. "Yes, yes, yes!" he'd responded testily, whenever his sisters had warned him he wasn't ordering enough wine. It was obvious that bottle duty would have to be extremely carefully managed. "We must get everyone except family eating," he urged Evie, only to be confronted with another dilemma since there was a corresponding shortage of food (his fault, too). To make things worse, he could see that Bet had already made a big dent in the sausage rolls. "We're going to have to bring in portion control. Where the hell are Bud and Guy? They know they're on grub duty."

"Shall I get Spud to help?" Evie asked, indicating her cousin, who was lounging in one of the armchairs that had been plumped up for guests, flicking peanuts at his grandmother's dog and making a mess of the painstakingly vacuumed carpet.

Robert glared at her for asking such a ridiculous question. Spud had smashed a valuable decanter the evening before out of sheer carelessness. In Robert's view, he was lucky to have been entrusted with parking duty, but that was only because they were stretched to the limit. "I'll have to put Miranda on grub duty." Suddenly, he felt like bursting into tears. There were too many pressures and, to make it worse, he couldn't even have a drink. He was retiring in a week and, despite insisting to everyone how much he was looking forward to it, could feel only dread. It was like a rerun of seven years earlier, when he'd been required to leave the army, except that now he was quitting paid work for good. At sixty-two, he had high blood pressure, and after the stroke that had felled his father, everyone was insisting it be taken seriously. Then there were his manifold responsibilities as head of the family. And finally, dwarfing all the rest, there was the ferocious though silent row that had erupted between Miranda and him. He blinked rapidly. What had *possessed* his beloved daughter?

Then he pulled himself together. "From now on, don't refill glasses till they're empty," he barked at Evie like a commanding officer. "And find more jugs. Put water everywhere."

Bud paused to light two cigarettes in the dark lane that led away from the house and handed one to Guy, just as she'd done as a teenager when the pleasure had been about defying parents. The distant chatter and laughter from the house seemed obscene against the deep peace of the night. They passed a neat sign made by Evie that read "Parking" and had a big arrow pointing the way into a field where numerous cars had been left. It looked chock-a-block and ramshackle. It was difficult to imagine anyone negotiating a way out.

"Smoking is an unacceptable habit," observed her young cousin, Theo, who had tagged after them, having efficiently dispatched coat duty. At fourteen, he had the serious, fussy mannerisms of his father, Charles. "Anyway," he reminded her, "you're meant to be on food."

"We *don't* smoke," Bud retorted. "And we don't want to be lectured on passive smoking, thank you very much. And people are perfectly capable of helping themselves to sandwiches and sausage rolls." She added even more crossly, "Anyway, who asked you to come along?"

She was deeply thankful for her other cousin, Guy, though. Their friendship had survived a barrage of mockery from her father. Guy was dull and a swot, according to Whoopee. But Guy was a success now, which he found infinitely more irritating.

He was exhausting, as a father. He'd enjoyed a rich miscellany of careers, none of them profitable, and pretly much all of them had ended badly. His latest job as an estate agent (which he loathed) was hanging by a thread, for once due to outside circumstances. "Who needs safety?" he liked to say, though his wife, Sarah, had worked as a secretary for the same insurance company throughout their marriage, taking the major part of supporting the family. His son, Spud, who considered himself a poet, had become a supermarket shelf-stacker in order to concentrate his mind on his art and was commended for integrity. Bud, on the other hand, was mercilessly mocked for building up a decent career in public relations.

He was wrong about Guy, though. As Bud had always appreciated, Guy was a rebel, in his quiet fashion. And now he was reinventing himself, as if he'd studied the family with the intention of being as different from them as possible. Guy wore expensive, beautifully cut suits and lived in a rented penthouse flat where all the furniture was new. If he heard an interesting or funny story, he'd pass it on only once for fear of repeating himself. The night they'd arrived for the funeral, he'd driven to the nearest town, Guildford, for a takeaway Indian meal for all twelve of them, despite being told it was a criminal waste of money and there was already masses of food. His father, Robert, had said this three times (while thoroughly enjoying his tikka masala).

Guy had just confided to Bud that, unlike the rest of the mourners, he'd been appalled by his father's outburst in the church. It had so clearly been a distress call.

Theo remarked: "I wonder what'll happen to the house."

"If Gran's not there, I don't care," Bud snapped.

"There are no 'ifs' about it, Bud, I fear," Theo corrected her in his maddening fashion. She guessed it was a clumsy form of flirting. Often she'd catch him watching her, as if mesmerized by her sophistication.

"Inheritance tax'll take most of it anyway," said Guy, sounding uninterested. He found the whole concept of inherited money archaic, he'd informed Bud on the way down. But with a high-profile job in banking, he made plenty himself. He'd given her a lift from London in his new Golf, parking it next to his father's dusty old Volvo like making a statement.

"A few months ago, it would have been worth a great deal more, of course," said Theo in a bored yet confident way. He was only parroting his father, who'd invariably add that nursing bills must have consumed any savings.

"What exactly are you saying, Theo?" said Bud, making her voice very threatening.

She saw his instant terror. She knew very well that he hadn't meant it would have been a good thing if their grandmother had died before the property crash; could even appreciate that the strange snort he let out had nothing to do with amusement. But she let him suffer because she was miserable, too, and needed to talk to her favorite cousin in private.

She threw down her cigarette. "Coming?" she asked Guy pointedly and watched with uncharacteristic heartlessness as Theo turned and crept back to the house, ripping up a sheaf of cow parsley on the way.

"Sorry," she muttered, too late. "But, really!"

She and Guy fell in step together. Before them, the pale lane striped with a toothbrush of grass stretched ahead between clumpy black trees. They walked in silence for a while, and then Bud went on, voice quite toneless as if she was only stating facts: "She promised to give me a sign, but where is it? I'm waiting, Guy."

He was the only one in the family she

could talk to in this way. The two of them had often stayed with their grandmother as children, absorbing her strange take on the dead. They were everywhere, she'd maintain. She wasn't afraid, she'd say with a strange laugh. Quite the reverse, she welcomed the company—and the hope. "Supposing your house burns down?" Guy had once asked. "Will the spirits disappear then?" Their grandmother had made a face (but only because the week before she'd absentmindedly left a packet of dog biscuits to smolder on a hotplate and it had been a near thing). Then she'd said passionately, "That could not be" and quoted from a writer called William Faulkner: "The past is never dead. It is not even past." After that, in apparent contradiction, she'd told them: "Thank goodness I write books—otherwise I wouldn't be able to remember any of it."

"I can't bear to think I'll never talk to her again," said Bud and a tear trickled down her cheek as she remembered her grandmother's affection, the curiosity more precious than any gift, the special relationship they'd enjoyed. "She didn't belong with us," she went on, looking up at the dark bowl of sky, even though there was no question who'd held the family together.

She heard Guy clear his throat as if he longed to come out with words of comfort, but couldn't.

Then a strange thing happened. In her misery, she thought she heard someone whisper: "I'm still here for you, but from now on think of it as half a conversation." It was so real—so exactly what her grandmother might have said—that it was almost impossible to believe her spirit hadn't just hastened past.

Had Guy heard it, too? A second later, he said: "Dad'll be going bananas. We'd best get back."

Feeling guilty about her offhanded response the evening before, Sarah was making a special effort to be nice to her sister-in-law. It wasn't hard because they all loved Mel. Brought up in an army family, too, she was perfect for Robert, even if Whoopee had rather unkindly dubbed her "the cart-horse" because, though nice enough looking, she was a far cry from the exquisite blondes he'd once pursued. It was just as well she was sweet-natured, thought Sarah, because Robert was showing himself at his most maddening, bossing everyone around. What was more, the wine was about to run out, just as they'd all forecast, but she was fighting the temptation to crow.

"I'd no idea Celia knew so many people," said Mel. "See that couple over there? They're beekeepers. They were just telling me she used to go and talk to their bees!"

"That explains the honey," said Sarah, remembering the jars of cloudy liquid gold found in a kitchen cupboard. She squirreled away the item about the bees to amuse Whoopee later because, despite their long and happy marriage, she still fretted that she wasn't interesting enough for him.

Mel continued in the same bright determined vein. "I'm trying to get round to talking to everyone," she said. But Sarah could see that she was watching her daughter, Miranda, who was cutting a quiche lorraine into minuscule slices while chatting to a group of elderly neighbors waiting patiently with empty plates. Miranda was smiling, of course—she smiled all the time now. Sarah saw Mel make an involuntary

movement, as if she wanted to bound forward and whisk her daughter away before
she said too much. As Robert saw it, Miranda had concocted a devilish plan to
bring shame upon the whole family.

At thirty-seven, and a top-earning ac-
countant, she was still single, with no known
boyfriend. "She's got time," Robert and Mel
had insisted because it was what parents
said nowadays (even though Mel had given
birth to both her children in her twenties).
But Miranda was more pragmatic.

When she'd broken the news of her
pregnancy to her parents, she'd wanted
nothing more than their blessing (because,
after all, she could provide everything
else). "*I'd* have been happy," thought Sarah
because, unlike Whoopee, she was longing to be a grandparent—and in fact Mel's
immediate reaction had been delight. But
then Robert had demanded details. As
soon as the words "Internet sperm donor"
were out, he'd put both hands over his
ears and stamped from the room. Ever
since, he'd ignored the pregnancy. But the
baby was growing every day, straining a
contented marriage and souring relations
with a beloved daughter.

By contrast, Celia's attitude had been remarkable. "It's Miranda's life," she'd insisted, adding to Robert's silent fury, "She's a sensible girl." She'd mentioned biological clocks, too; and, once, that ancient woman born long before the sexual revolution had been heard to murmur, "What century does he imagine he's in, anyway!"

"Oh, I miss her!" thought Sarah, remembering all this. She was longing for a drink, but since that was out of the question, she looked round for Whoopee to cheer her up.

Left on her own momentarily, Bet was absorbing the scene from the sofa. Thank God her hearing was holding up, though the eyes were beginning to go. What a shame, she thought, that this party couldn't have been held when Celia was alive, because the whole family was there and, more to the point, making such efforts to get on.

She could hear Charles reprimanding Theo in his fond and fussy way. "You stink of cigarettes! If you've been smoking . . ."

"I wasn't!" Theo protested immediately. "It was Bud and Guy!"

Charles was an excellent father, thought Bet, and a good husband, too, even if Margaret was incapable of appreciating him. "Bitter," thought Bet, who could tell when a man was suffering. But she found it impossible to blame someone she loved so deeply. "Not her fault there's no chemistry," she'd once remarked to Celia, who'd listened without comment, as was her habit. "Bed's the problem there, if you ask me."

Margaret had married when everyone was convinced she'd left it too late; and, in her early forties, she had given birth to two children. If anyone believed Margaret was cold, thought Bet, they'd only to watch her with Theo and Evie. Thirteen-year-old Evie reminded her how beautiful Margaret had once been, though that opinionated, bossy child saw to it that her looks were never the first thing people remarked on.

Now, *there* was a happy marriage, thought Bet, looking at Sarah and Whoopee, though she conceded that he must be exhausting to live with. Even now, he was trying to convince some complete stranger he was a clinical psychiatrist (a favorite trick of his in company he considered dull).

Not content with that, he had his hand on Sarah's bottom and was caressing it in full view of the guests. Bet was remembering the serious, dutiful child she'd known. Whoever could have guessed Sarah would marry someone like Whoopee? But he was very attractive. Even though Bet didn't like him much, she was forced to admit that.

"Aunt Bet?"

"Yes, darling," she responded, smiling into Robert's anxious face.

"Is it going all right?"

"Like clockwork," she assured him.

He looked pleased. "You think?"

"Mummy would be so proud of you."

His eyes slid away, embarrassed. "Where's your glass?"

"Oh, I've had masses to drink," lied Bet.

"It's nearly time to light the bonfire." Then he looked stressed because even something so simple required organization. "I've put Guy in charge."

Bud always found it impossible to explain her family to outsiders because it was so disparate. At one end of the spectrum, there was deeply conventional Uncle Robert, with his army discipline, who said grace at meals; at the other, her charming irrespon-sible father who was capable of milking even a funeral for laughs.

Her heart sank a little when he turned up in the field, saying he wanted to take his turn at bonfire duty, but really, she knew, because the grandchildren had gathered there and he loved the young. To her further dismay, he was the only per-son at the funeral who appeared drunk, and indeed the one member of the family who wasn't dead cold sober. He must have laid in a secret cache of alcohol—probably in the boot of his car.

"No pyrotechnics," he warned them all, stumbling over the word.

"Ha-ha!" said Evie, who was behaving with mature responsibility as she fed the fire with branches.

"NO JUMPING THROUGH FLAMES," he bellowed suddenly because, unlike Guy, he'd been delighted by Robert's out-burst in the church. A wonderful new joke had been added to the not exactly crowded family collection.

Evie giggled. "Oh, be your age!"

"YOU'RE ONLY AS YOUNG AS YOU FEEL!" He slapped her lightly on the bottom. "THAT'S WHAT I ALWAYS SAY!"

Bud's brother Spud was seated cross-legged on the turf, staring into the fire. They'd nothing in common. And Whoopee hadn't helped by playing them off against each other, heaping praise on Spud's meaningless poetry while scoffing at her "bizarre need for security," as he put it. But she adored her father. She'd forgive him anything.

However, she could tell from the tight look on Guy's face that Whoopee was getting on his nerves. He didn't take kindly to his own father being mocked.

Perhaps Whoopee realized he'd overstepped the mark. Next thing, he appeared to have accidentally lost his footing and was rolling toward the crackling fire while Evie shrieked and even Spud, who should have known better, looked alarmed.

He stopped just short of the flames. And then he staggered to his feet, appeared to slip, and repeated the whole performance while Evie and Theo yelled at him that he was pathetic and immature.

Even Guy was smiling by the end. That was the thing about her father, thought Bud. He was a life enhancer. Whatever the circumstances, he could make them laugh.

The wine had run out a long time ago. The grandchildren delegated to washing-up duty had begun clearing away glasses and plates, and at last people took the hint and started to leave, whereupon another problem arose. However, it proved a godsend for Robert, who'd been dreading the end of the evening. As the guests kissed the rest of the family good-bye, they could hear him booming away in the distance as he masterminded the unraveling of the tangle of cars Spud had brought about in the parking field.

"A beautiful service," Celia's publisher pronounced—not the original one, of course, who'd taken a chance on a young wife more than sixty years before and whose firm had been bought out long ago. This publisher was smart and sought after—and delighted by her inheritance. "I'll be in touch," she promised as she left.

"Beautiful . . . triumphant . . . memorable . . ." Such powerful, evocative words were murmured as the evening wound to a close. It occurred to Margaret that "sly" was missing, because the truth was, her mother had deceived them all. But for the extraordinary posthumous attention, these decent, ordinary people might have continued to believe she'd been just like them.

And then Priscilla imprisoned her in an astonishingly powerful embrace. Did every good-bye feel to her as if it might be the last? Or was all physical contact prized when you were old and alone? Margaret cast a desperate glance at her sister, but she was absorbed with Whoopee, whose dark suit was, for some reason, covered in grass.

"I loved your mother, darling."

"I know you did." Margaret could feel her whole body stiffening in response to this surfeit of emotion.

"We went back to the year dot. I even met *her* mother once. What a bizarre evening *that* was!"

"Really?" Margaret was watching her sister brush Whoopee down, both of them giggling like silly children. "He's drunk!" she thought.

Priscilla wheezed into Margaret's neck

like a pair of worn-out bellows. "She didn't talk about those days. Oh, I don't blame her, darling. It was because of him, of course—she did it for him. But d'you know, I always did think of her as one of us."

"Of course," Margaret responded, though she had no idea what Priscilla was talking about.

To her very great relief, she was released. Then Priscilla did something strange. She nodded solemnly and drew an imaginary zip across her mouth from left to right, leaving a smear of magenta on one cheek.

It was time for bed. But some of them wandered down to the field for a last look at the bonfire, whose fierce, crackling authority had sunk to a brooding glow. In a few hours, there'd be nothing left but a pile of ash. Sarah and Margaret wept in the darkness, crushed by the symbolism.

Suddenly, there was a loud whoosh from somewhere outside their circle and then they were all under attack from a manic force that exploded into a hundred brilliant lights and fizzed and banged and darted erratically round the field for what seemed like ages and came so close to

Evie—like shaking a fist—that all her sassy self-possession vanished and she burst into hysterical weeping and clung to her mother.

Then, just as abruptly, the frenzy ended with a damp hiss.

Miranda's smile had vanished. "We might have been . . . we could all have been . . ." She put her hands over her flat stomach.

"Who would do such a stupid thing?" demanded Bud.

"Yes, who?" echoed Sarah, glancing at Whoopee a little anxiously. But to her great relief, he appeared as outraged as everyone else, as if he had at last decided to become a full member of the responsible, dutiful family he'd mocked for years.

Evie had a torch and they found a telltale stick buried in the ground some twenty yards from the fire. Obviously, someone in the group had sneaked away to set off a large rocket. The fuse had smoldered undetected in the thick grass, allowing plenty of time to get clear.

In the absence of Robert, Guy took charge. "I'm going to get to the bottom of this," he warned, casting an ominous glance at his male cousins.

However, in Bud's opinion, Spud was too immature and self-centered to have planned such a thing; and much as Theo liked attention, he was very law-abiding.

But whoever set off the rocket had surely done it with the best of intentions, as a last spectacular tribute to the woman they'd all adored. It was just sad that instead, after terrorizing her beloved grandchildren and her unborn first great-grandchild, it had fizzled out ignominiously in a puddle of mud.

CHAPTER THREE

A strong weight-bearing cane is required to take some of the load normally used by the afflicted leg. Canes should be employed by the hand opposite the injury or weakness. This may appear counterintuitive, but allows the cane to be used for stability in a way that lets the user shift much of their weight onto the cane and away from their weaker side as they walk.

Printed advice on using a walking stick, found in study, with note scribbled on back: *I totter between this world and the next, unsure which direction to lean.* Almost certainly written in the days following F. B.'s death, so post January 7, 1990. Very shaky writing.

"There's pheasant pâté," Sarah informed Margaret before she'd even crossed the threshold of Parr's. She was speaking very fast, as if this was the only way to endure coming back. "Whoopee did the picnic. Well, he advised me what to put in. There's walnut bread and goat's cheese and raspberries and cream. I am *so* lucky!" She clutched her basket of food. Then her eyes filled with tears. They were fixed on her mother's gum boots, patterned with mud and ancient spiderwebs, still standing upright in the hall.

At that moment, they both became aware of a few muffled sepulchral bars from Pachelbel's Canon and Sarah's sadness vanished. She laughed as she rummaged in her untidy handbag, pulling out a lipstick, sunglasses, tweezers, and a small trowel for removing plants. She explained the joke. "It drives Whoopee nuts when operators put him on hold and he's forced to listen to that stuff. Last week, he changed my ring tone to 'Spring' from *The Four Seasons*. He says if someone had told Vivaldi that one day his music would make people want to strangle him, he might have thought twice about writing it." She'd finally located her mobile. "Hello, darling. Yes, I'm at Parr's. Just got here this minute. I'll be all right, promise . . . Sort of." Her voice wobbled. "Okay, ring me later. Love you, too . . ." She giggled a little hysterically before adding, like one of the operators Whoopee detested, "Bear with me," and Margaret heard his mock angry voice clacking down the phone, miles away in London.

"We'd better get started," she said, though Sarah had only just arrived and it was nearly one o'clock and she could think of nothing nicer than tucking into the picnic. Her expression hardened as she thought of her good-looking brother-in-law and imagined her sister's life filled with fun and jokes, and a marriage that must have been like a door opening. She wouldn't see her husband, Charles, for a couple of days now but still felt sour and mean, as if it was no longer possible to cast off the person she'd become.

She'd arrived at the house half an hour before Sarah. The leaves on the Virginia creeper that had rampaged up the red bricks all summer long were already beginning to yellow and float off and spatter the long grass. The place looked as if it had been empty for far longer than a matter of weeks. The telephone started to ring while she was still fiddling with keys, but had stopped by the time she got to it. There was no answer machine, for which she was grateful. She didn't think she could endure to hear a recording of her mother's voice—a last trace of her physical presence, like the wispy trajectory of a departed airplane written across the sky. She'd dialed caller ID, to learn that the number had been withheld. Her immediate reaction was to assume it had been a journalist, though on reflection that was unlikely now. The newspapers had become dominated by party conferences and tension in the Middle East. It was as if the obsession with a demure octogenarian had been a piece of summer madness.

Once, the house had taken its tone from her beloved, bossy father, who'd applied army discipline. No sleeping late; no loitering inside in fine weather; no moaning or feebleness. Though clever, he'd been no intellectual. At times of stress or difficulty, his solution had been to go for a brisk walk or play a strenuous game of tennis. The cruelty was that for the last twenty or so years of his life—immobilized and silenced by illness—he must have conceded there was a case for self-pity and depression, after all.

And after his death, Celia had spent years there alone, crouching over her desk, even in the hottest of weather. She'd not let her brain atrophy, like so many old people. She'd sat in her study under the roof, concentrating hour after hour, while arthritis danced through her bones and her eyes ached, writing the books that would make her famous. And when the work was done, the house had come alive with voices: the radio chattering throughout the night, louder and louder as the years passed and hearing dwindled.

"It's so quiet," Sarah marveled, remembering the journalists who'd pestered them for days, the camera teams who'd filmed the house and the neighbors, and once even their mother's old dog.

"You sound as if you miss them!"

"Well, I miss talking about her."

"We can still do that," Margaret responded a little helplessly.

"And I miss talking *to* her." A tear fell on Sarah's jumper.

Something in Margaret recoiled—as if she could no longer summon up comfort for her sister, who was so blessed. She thought, "I still miss Daddy," but she said very briskly, "I'll light a fire, shall I?" Without waiting for an answer, she went outside to the woodshed, which she found piled to the beams with kindling and logs. This evidence that her mother had so confidently anticipated another winter caused a spasm of grief. She paused for a moment in the half-light to compose herself. When she returned to the house, she was unnaturally positive. "Shall we eat in front of the fire? If you could find some plates and glasses, and maybe a cloth . . ."

Sarah went off obediently.

The wood was insufficiently seasoned. But, even in her late fifties, Margaret couldn't shake off her upbringing. It wasn't until she'd wasted half a box of matches that she went in search of fire lighters.

"I need a drink," Sarah confessed. Her hand trembled as she poured wine from the bottle she'd brought up from the cellar—a fine Merlot, Margaret noticed, too good for a picnic. And then she staked a claim. "I've always loved that," she said, indicating the Venetian mirror that hung by the door, age freckles spattering its glass. "She told me I should have it."

"Really?" said Margaret very sharply because she'd earmarked that piece for herself.

The family had not yet met with the lawyer for the reading of the will, but understood that, even supposing the house could still be sold at a good price, there'd be little left. Like so many women of her generation, their mother had seemed uninterested in money and, after the huge nursing bills for their father, there were bound to be debts. As for the division of chattels, she'd seemed confident they could arrange it among themselves.

Sarah said, like pressing a tiny red "sold" dot on the mirror: "Whoopee and I went to Venice on our honeymoon."

"I see."

"Don't look like that!"

"Like what?" But Margaret thought bitterly, "That is so typical of how she gets her way!" She coveted the elegant old chaise longue, too. Would her sister now inform her that she and Whoopee had once embraced on it? "Why don't you want that instead?" she thought, glowering at a green velvet armchair where she'd once sat during a momentous conversation with her mother.

"Have the mirror, if you want," said Sarah suddenly, adding, to Margaret's astonishment, "What does it matter?" A tear fell.

"Are you sure . . . ?" Margaret began, though she'd wanted the mirror badly enough a moment before.

Sarah mopped her face. Then she said something unexpected. "Do all men have affairs?"

Margaret gave her a sharp glance, suddenly wary.

"I wouldn't know," Sarah went on. "I'm such an innocent. Remember, I was married at nineteen."

"Yes," thought Margaret, compressing her lips in the way that had changed her face over time, taking away its dreamy generosity and making her seem mean and judgmental. "Weren't you lucky?"

And then, in an instant, everything changed. The famously uxorious Whoopee was having an affair. It transpired he'd dropped this bombshell the day after the funeral as he and Sarah were enjoying supper at home and she was anticipating the usual enjoyable dissection of the family. "My love," he'd called her before slipping in the knife.

"He says he still loves me but he's not *in* love with me anymore." Sarah sobbed as she relayed the awfulness of this. "He wants to be honest."

"Whoopee?" Margaret had never been more surprised in her life. Whoopee who, even at his mother-in-law's funeral, had been unable to keep his hands off his wife?

"He's very good to me," said Sarah, just as she'd done on so many occasions before. "I'm so lucky!" Only now there were tears in her eyes.

"Who is it?"

Sarah's face contorted. "Some twenty-something! She's younger than Bud! How dare she! He wears a wedding ring, doesn't he?" She blinked away tears and, astonishingly, the anger morphed into tenderness. "Poor Whoopee, I suppose you can't help falling in love!"

"What rubbish!"

"Is it?" Now Sarah seemed very anxious to get her sister's take on her matter.

"Of course you can!" Margaret could

feel her voice rising, her heart pounding, as emotions she hadn't thought about for years returned. "The minute you see it happening, you run away. That's what you do if you value your marriage. And you leave the girl alone. She's a child! *She* doesn't know what she's doing!"

"Oh, doesn't she?" protested Sarah savagely. "He says he's tried to give her up but she won't let him!" She chewed her lip. "Also, he says it would feel antilife. Mummy's death really affected him, you know."

"How dare he bring Mummy into it!"

"Don't blame Whoopee. He's so hard on himself!"

"Well, good! I've never heard of anything more outrageous!"

"At least he told me."

"And that's being kind, is it?"

"I'd rather know."

"Well, *I* wouldn't!" Margaret added: "I'm glad we're down here. You need to be away from this."

"So he can see *her*?" Sarah's hand shook and she spilled a little wine on the rug.

"You can't stop them meeting, even if you're there," said Margaret as she poured salt on the stain. "You need to think about this. Why should you put up with it? You're in a powerful position, don't forget. Whoopee depends on you utterly."

"Does he?" asked Sarah, tears filling her eyes. "Do you really think so?"

"You know he does. You're the bread-winner. Besides, Spud and Bud would never forgive him. Even he couldn't be such an idiot as to let you go."

It was a mistake.

"What do you mean, 'even he'? The family have never liked him!"

"That's not true," said Margaret. "So long as he made you happy."

"He feels you look down on him."

"Oh, rubbish! For what?"

Sarah pursed her lips as if the family had made it quite obvious. Whoopee's background had been very much more humble than her own. Then she said, "You probably think it was him who let off that rocket the night of Mummy's funeral!"

"It never occurred to me," Margaret re-sponded, genuinely taken aback; but in retrospect, it seemed obvious—the firework less of a tribute to a mother-in-law than a personal celebration of freedom from mo-nogamy. "Listen," she went on, reminded of why they'd come to the house, "it's good we've so much to do. It'll take your mind off things."

"Oh, I wish!"

Margaret was thinking of how their mother would have reacted to this tale of a man who involved his wife in his every reaction to his affair, using her—of all people— as a sounding board. She'd have turned away her head in distress as the story proceeded, and her hands might have twitched as if she longed to slap him. But not a word of criticism would have passed her lips.

"At least he told me," Sarah kept repeating, as if Whoopee should be commended.

For most of her adult life, thought Margaret, her sister had been made to feel beautiful and special. Now the same man who'd performed that magic had packed up his box of tricks to use on someone else. Was it the first affair? Thankfully, the question didn't seem to have occurred to Sarah.

The house telephone started ringing, and instantly her mood lifted. "I'll get it!"

Of course it was Whoopee again, thought Margaret coldly. He'd love to be talked about: he was without shame. "Have you told her, Crinkle?" would probably be his first question.

But she was wrong. "I see," she heard Sarah say, voice very flat. "What exactly is this about?" Then there was a long pause. "I'll have to speak to my sister." She put her hand over the mouthpiece. "It's some girl. Says she's a journalist. Says she came back here after the funeral."

Margaret frowned. "Bloody cheek!"

Sarah smiled faintly. "She's in the village. Says she wants to come and see us."

"Whatever for?"

Sarah shrugged because it was surely too late for another obituary.

"Well, she can't!" To be fair, Margaret couldn't fault the conduct of the press during the surreal period leading up to the funeral. Nevertheless, it made her extremely uncomfortable to think of a journalist moving among them, uninvited and incognito. She said: "Tell her to get lost."

Sarah whispered, "It might be nice to talk about Mummy."

"Really?" Margaret could tell where the day was heading. More alcohol would be drunk and Sarah would sink deeper into distress while continuing to defend

Whoopee. It was an exhausting prospect. Besides, there was no way they were going to make a start on the house. She found herself agreeing: "Okay, tell her to come for tea."

"So she lived here all on her own?" The visitor, whose name was Jenny Granger, was absorbing her surroundings with intense, almost embarrassing interest, and, for a moment, they tried to see the familiar sitting room through her eyes. With the curtains drawn and the fire now settled into a glowing mass it was cozy, and the lighting was pleasantly soft unless you wanted to read a book. Even so, they noticed a couple of stains—tea? the dog?—on the seat of the big yellow armchair; also, the walls, with their mix of traditional and modern pictures, badly needed repainting. The low ceiling was stained by smoke from the fire. But Jenny had been here before, of course: she'd said so.

"She liked being alone," said Margaret, sensing criticism. She got up to put another log on the fire. The truth was, none of them had seen their mother enough, but that was mostly because she'd seemed absorbed by her writing, and consequently undemanding. How different from other people's elderly parents. It had made any time spent with her unusually precious. But Margaret hesitated to try and explain all this to a stranger.

"I can understand that. The house has a lovely feel about it, as if it's seen a lot of happiness."

Margaret and Sarah exchanged cautiously pleased glances. They'd forgiven Jenny for gate-crashing a private family do—her description, not theirs. "I feel awful," were almost her first words. "I know I shouldn't have come. But you were all so lovely. My only excuse is that, after that wonderful service, I couldn't bear to leave."

"It's some girl," Sarah had told Margaret after listening to that soft, hesitant little voice on the telephone; and, on opening the front door, she had believed for a moment that she saw a young person waiting outside in the dusk. It was because of the shoulder-length fair hair cut with a fringe, the anxious round eyes, the slender almost anorexic body, the very short skirt, the opaque black stockings ending in little ballet shoes. It was only after Jenny had stepped into the well-lit hall that Sarah realized she was in her late thirties, or possibly even early forties. But they couldn't remember her at the funeral at all.

"Did you ring earlier?" Margaret asked suddenly.

Jenny shook her head. Then she took a sip of tea and ate a morsel of the rather stale fruitcake they'd found in a tin. When she finally spoke, it was with childlike enthusiasm. "I'm ashamed to say that until all that publicity about your mother, I'd never heard of her. But now I've read all her novels. Correction—*devoured* them! They're so fresh—even the early ones written under a pseudonym. And by the end . . . My goodness! She wrote like a young girl!"

The sisters were silent. They still hadn't found time to read the books, nor had they discussed this. As for the idea of their white-haired, breathless mother writing like a young girl . . . for some reason, it made them cringe.

"My Waterstones was reordering for the third or fourth time. You must be so proud!"

"Oh, we are!" Sarah agreed.

"Do any of you write?" Jenny asked, and being subjected to that shy but intense interest was like having a searchlight turned their way.

Margaret shook her head immediately, but Sarah said a little self-consciously, "My son's a bit of a poet. Nothing published yet, but fingers crossed."

"No writers her side of the family?" the journalist pursued, as if the information about Spud had passed her by.

They shook their heads once more.

"You know, in spite of all the attention, I have the feeling that perhaps nobody's captured the *real* woman . . ."

Margaret made a dismissive face. "Oh well, newspapers!" She added, like shutting a door: "Our mother was a very private person."

"I believe you," Jenny assured them. "You must have thought at times, 'This can't be her we're reading about!'"

"Well, yes!" Sarah looked astounded by the perceptiveness of this.

"*We* knew her better than anyone else," Margaret pointed out, sounding cold and off-putting.

"Of course!" Jenny agreed. There was a moment of awkwardness before she exclaimed: "That's them, isn't it?" She'd twisted in her seat to gesture at a black-and-white photograph in a gleaming silver frame and it was somehow obvious to the sisters that she'd been waiting for the chance. She probably assumed the photograph had always stood on that table; but, in fact, until the funeral it had been kept in one of the upstairs bedrooms. It was Sarah who'd brought it down, like dressing a stage set, and Margaret had rubbed away the tarnish.

"The day they got engaged," said Sarah.

Jenny got up. "Do you mind?" she asked with her shy smile, though she was already bearing the photograph toward a lamp. She studied it for what seemed several minutes—their impossibly glamorous father, their adoring child-bride mother, posed against the trunk of a tree with an imposing white façade in the background. "Wow! Where was it taken?"

"The house where our mother was brought up," said Margaret.

"Far Point, it was called," Sarah supplied helpfully.

"Looks vast. Did she have brothers, sisters?"

"No, she was an only child. Her father died when she was five."

Jenny made a sympathetic face.

"The obituaries didn't go into it," said Sarah, "but he was wounded in the Great War. He was something of a hero."

"So she lived there with her mother. And servants, I assume?"

Sarah nodded confidently. "Lots. But most of them went off for good when the next war came along, though Daddy once mentioned an all-purpose housekeeper who stayed. He was billeted there at the beginning of 1944. He was quite a bit older than Mummy, and already a decorated officer. He was involved in the D-day landings. A lot of the landing craft set off from the beach there and he helped with the planning. Very hush-hush. He never talked about it. But Mummy told us the whole area was cordoned off for ages. No one could get in or out without a pass."

Jenny's attention shifted to a second photograph, which had always been on display. Taken many years later, it showed their father bristling with decorations, their mother in a long white evening dress and diamonds. Behind them was an elegant mantelpiece with an exotic flower arrangement in place of a fire. The young people in the engagement photo had become a formidable team. "My goodness! He was a general, wasn't he?"

"Yes, that was taken in Nigeria." Sarah went on eagerly: "It was such an adventure for us, spending school holidays there. We felt very special."

"I expect you have lots of pictures, don't you?"

Sarah burst out laughing. "Masses! There'll even be proofs somewhere that were never returned." She explained: "My mother was incapable of throwing anything away. You would not *believe* the amount of junk!" She glanced up at the ceiling, as if picturing the mess out of sight. "It's why we've come down, actually. To sort it out."

"So you're selling the house?"

"Maybe," said Margaret, with a warning glance at her sister.

"You've been very patient with me," Jenny told them. "I'll come to the point. I feel it's time for a proper appraisal of your mother."

"Which means?" Margaret demanded.

Jenny twisted her hands together as if embarrassed. "I write profiles," she told them in her childish little voice. "You may have read some? I've worked for the *Independent,* the *Guardian,* the posher Sunday papers . . . But for some time now, I've wanted to tackle something more substantial. I suppose I've been waiting for the right inspiration."

"So this wouldn't be just a profile?"

Jenny looked almost distressed. "I'm talking about a *biography.*"

"Oh, I don't think so," said Margaret immediately. She looked to her sister for support, but Sarah was holding the engagement photograph and staring at it with an unhappy expression.

"The fact is," Jenny continued, "this whole story has caught at the public imagination, and I don't think it's going to go away."

"It seems to us that it has," Margaret replied, and, to make the point, she took the photograph from her sister and replaced it on the table.

"It may seem to have," Jenny corrected her gently. "But just because it's no longer in the newspapers doesn't mean it's forgotten." She added quickly: "Nor should it be. I think your mother *deserves* proper recognition—but for that to happen, you need to be involved from the start." Her voice dropped, became sad and knowing. "I've seen it so many times. A family rejects the idea of a biography. Then, all too soon, an unauthorized one appears, an irresponsible piece of work they find deeply upsetting. Whereas a sympathetic biographer, working closely with the family from the start, can produce something everyone's proud of."

"Sarah?" said Margaret a little sharply, like calling her sister to attention.

But to her dismay, Sarah murmured dreamily: "Perhaps we owe it to Mummy."

"It's entirely up to you," Jenny told them gently. "All I'm asking at this stage is that you think about it. And if you come to the conclusion that it's a good idea for us to work together, well, perhaps I could even make your job a little easier." Her eyes fluttered upward just as Sarah's had done a short time before. "You say your mother never threw anything away?"

"Nothing!" Sarah laughed. She seemed

to be enjoying herself now. "Not even supermarket bills! She'd use them as scraps. You could be talking to her about something absolutely ordinary—what to have for lunch, for instance—and suddenly she'd get that distracted expression. She had to find something to write on—anything! Once I found a torn-off bit of cornflakes packet and it had, 'Frances mistrusts good looks' scribbled on it! But she just laughed when I asked what it meant. It's probably still up there, along with all the rest. She *was* going to tidy up. But she never got round to it."

"They seldom do," said Jenny, but so softly that both of them thought they must have imagined it. "If you like, I could advise on what should be kept."

"You mean you just want to go through our mother's stuff!" said Margaret coldly.

A moment later, she was horrified to be taken literally.

"That would be wonderful!"

"We'll have to talk to our brother," Margaret muttered.

"Of course!" Jenny responded, as if this was only sensible.

The meeting was over. They were easing

themselves out of their chairs when, to Margaret's dismay, Sarah suddenly said: "Wait!"

She watched helplessly as her sister went to the big desk in the corner and pulled out the wedding album. More joy frozen in time, because nobody dared produce cameras for divorces or funerals. "See?" she said, turning the pages. "The wedding was very quick. Daddy said he wasn't going to let a lot of murderous Huns interfere with their happiness."

"November 15, 1944," Jenny read out loud. Then she studied the old photos: Frederick in his officer's uniform, Celia in a knee-length cream dress draped over her bosom and hips, a tiny flat hat perched at an angle, posed on steps outside a building.

They'd always made Margaret uncomfortable. It was because of an almost tangible aura of sex—not something she cared to associate with her parents. Her father looked strangely relieved as if, right till the last minute, he'd feared his child bride might take fright; but he needn't have worried because Celia appeared dazed by bliss. However, maybe the album had embarrassed her, too, because, for as long as Margaret could remember, it had been shut away in a drawer.

"So they didn't marry in church."

"Caxton Hall," replied Sarah. "Don't they look happy?" Her voice wobbled ominously, and Margaret understood that she was still hoping for an introduction to her own story. Then she pointed at a middle-aged woman in the background. "That's Mummy's mother. And those two girls there are her best friends, Bet and Priscilla. They both made it to the funeral, bless them!" She gave Jenny a mournful, meaningful look. "Weddings! We all believe we're going to live happily ever after."

"Your parents did," Jenny pointed out.

"They were lucky," Sarah whispered.

"I envy that generation," said Jenny. "Terrifying times, right? The threat of occupation, death just round the corner, real hardship. . . . But the truth is, our lives are flat, by comparison. When I think of the passion there must have been then!" She gave a little shiver as if the word unsettled her. "Oh yes, they were lucky all right!"

Margaret frowned as she thought of her mother's life: a privileged upbringing in a beautiful place, a famously happy marriage to a distinguished soldier, exotic travel, this lovely house to come back to, children and grandchildren. And as if that wasn't plenty, there'd been a long career with critical acclaim at the end, like signing off with a flourish. True, she'd had to cope with the illness of her husband, but she'd loved him and to Margaret, locked in her miserable marriage, that compensated for everything.

Jenny asked almost shyly, "Was it love at first sight?"

"Pure Mills and Boon," Sarah told her with a sad little smile.

Margaret made a face because there was no doubt their parents' meeting could have come straight out of the romances her mother had once written, and, of course, they'd gone on to live happily ever after. But it was also true—though never acknowledged—that for the children of the marriage it had often felt deeply lonely.

CHAPTER FOUR

The most valuable thing that can happen to a writer is to find himself in the position of an outsider, with other people believing he doesn't exist.

                    No date. Black notebook.

In 1933, when Celia was six years old, she and her mother moved to Far Point. Though not enormous by the standards of country houses, it was the biggest she'd ever seen: a house arranged so oddly that for a long time she believed it to be two separate ones. Suddenly, the only screaming was distant and unthreatening and came from white birds freewheeling over the sea. She'd been removed from the old life so abruptly that very soon memories acquired the patchy unreality of old nightmares.

It wasn't until her seventies that details of her early childhood returned. Not just the constant uncertainty about what her father would do next, but the mashed-potato smell of the weekly wash boiling away in the copper and the silvery trails left on the wooden draining board by the slugs that had squeezed in and out of the kitchen during the night, and the stench of the outside latrine. It was ironic to recover such squalid memories in a high-tech age when she forgot from one minute to the next where she'd left her glasses. Unwelcome smells, which had imbued her whole childhood, had almost ceased to exist by the twenty-first century. But though life was sweeter with aerosols and deodorants and plastic bin-liners and exhaust fans, it was duller. It was a lot safer, too. There'd been no contraceptive pill in her day; and, tragically, young men and women had died from polio and tuberculosis. "Ah me!" Celia would sigh, looking back over the century that had galloped ever faster as it petered out.

Far Point, some hundred miles from London, was without history or real style. But its position made it special. The big, two-storey, white-painted villa with green shutters was set high above the sea in a belt of pines, its front shaded by a huge lime tree dominating a graveled courtyard, its balconied and veranda'd back looking over the water to the long low outline of the Isle of Wight in the distance.

"We could be in France," Celia heard her mother grumble when they first saw the house. Her response was to leap up and down with delight. The train journey had been an adventure in itself: miraculous to watch houses stream into fields and woods and people become cows and sheep. She'd bounced around the carriage, testing one seat after another, while her mother had sighed and frowned in a corner. And the magic hadn't stopped!

"Silly, of course we're not in France!" What Helen, her mother, had really meant was that the house was even more remote than she'd feared, as well as peculiarly foreign-looking. She was exhausted by years of caring for a mentally ill husband; crushed by mounting debts and, finally, the loss of their home. She was unable to see this as a fine new start. She could only think that in a matter of minutes, she

was going to have to make the most humiliating readjustment of her life.

An old friend had learned of a staff va-
cancy in a house she knew and offered to
put in a word to the owners, Sir John and
Lady Edith Falconbridge. "Look how you've
managed," she'd pointed out.

Helen had been more shocked than she
could remember. "But I can't become a
housekeeper!"

"Listen, this is a real chance!" Her friend
had proceeded to tell the dreadful tale of
an ex-ambassadress friend, reduced to
scrubbing floors. The truth was, plenty of
women who'd never expected to work for a
living were being forced into service, their
safe landscapes demolished by war and
the Depression. And Helen had agreed in
the end, of course, because there was no
choice.

Everything about their new home seemed
to offend her: even the sea at the bottom of
the garden, making a sound like someone
sighing over and over again through brown
paper. "It's damp," she said with a shiver.

"That's going to be a problem, too," she
snapped when the five-barred wooden

gate dragged on the gravel drive as they pushed it open.

"Doesn't matter." Even at six, Celia was an expert soother.

"That bush needs a good prune," was all Helen noticed about a ceanothus with beautiful fluffy blue blossoms. And "Shame it takes the light," was her verdict on the magnificent lime tree in the courtyard.

The house had two doors. Years later, Celia would remember her mother hesitating between a simple, black-painted one to the right and a much grander glass-paneled one, with a porch and potted bay trees, on the left. Then, a plump girl in an apron emerged from the door on the right and beckoned them inside.

Celia noticed that her mother dropped her surly attitude as soon as they were taken to meet Lady Falconbridge. She hated to hear her spoken to coldly and see her so timid and quiet, but couldn't know of the discomfort the other woman was suffering. For, despite the appearance of wealth, Lady Falconbridge perceived herself as déclassé, too. Her husband had been foolish with investments, and consequently the far grander house inherited from his father had had to be sold. Despite its lovely situation, Far Point, with a handful of staff, was a comedown, and Lady Falconbridge was already regretting the decision to take on Helen. The new housekeeper, with her refined way of speaking, seemed like a dreadful portent.

After the short interview, the maid, who introduced herself as Ella, took them through a swinging furry green door into a whole hidden section of the house. Whereas the much larger Falconbridge section had been chilly and formal and lightly scented by wax polish and dried flowers, the one they now entered emanated a warm, robust energy and the smell of boiled cabbage and sweat. It was much noisier, too, partly because rugs had given way to balding linoleum.

Celia studied her mother's face for clues as they were introduced to a person called "Cook." Cook appeared to be a woman, as she wore a flowery pinafore over a stout, waistless body and her sausage-shaped legs were clad in thick lisle stockings that ended in black lace-up high-heeled shoes like a pig's trotters. But her pale heavy face bore the shadowy muzzle of a mustache and beard and she spoke in a harsh, deep voice. In the background, another person, unmistakably male in muddy trousers, was seated at a big scrubbed wooden table slurping tea from a mug. He barely looked up when introduced as Mr. Peters.

"Just the one?" But from Cook's disapproving expression, it was obvious that even one child was too many. She showed them a little room leading off the kitchen. It had a small round table covered with a patchy gold oilskin cloth under a hanging lamp decorated with a fringe of dark red beads. There was an ancient wireless perched on a shelf next to a copy of *Mrs. Beeton's Book of Household Management.* This was the office from which Helen would run the house. It was a mark of her seniority over the other servants, and Celia sensed her soften.

She was less satisfied with their bedroom. "Like a cupboard! Who do they think we are?"

It was true it was cramped and bare. And, instead of facing the sun and the sea like the back of the house, it looked onto a forest of pines and a mass of bracken some three or four feet high. Celia imagined all the hidden things that might creep through that jungle, waiting to pounce. More cold linoleum covered the floor. The skimpy curtains were unlined and the room was freezing and the tiny fireplace was choked with soot. Thankful not to be sleeping alone, she put her arms around her mother's waist and, as if suddenly remembering her, Helen kissed the top of her head.

"We'll manage," she said briskly, as if it was time to put away the bad humor. "Which bed would you like, 'just the one'?" Then she started unpacking their suitcases.

Helen was an attentive mother. She dosed Celia with syrup of figs once a week to keep her regular, and checked her hair for lice by combing it over a piece of brown paper, and very occasionally and mortifyingly stuck a hairpin up her bottom to hook out threadworms (afterward behaving as if nothing had happened). But mostly she treated her like a younger sister, confiding thoughts and reactions as they cuddled together for warmth in one of the two hard beds at night. Cook—who seemed to have no real name—could get ratty when the pressure was on; and Ella, the maid, had a nasty tongue; but Mr. Peters, who was the head gardener, seemed a good enough sort. Sir John Falconbridge was quite kind, Helen whispered, adding a little puzzlingly that she wouldn't want to be left alone with him. Then she fell silent because it didn't need to be spelled out that angular Lady Falconbridge, with her expensive but dated clothes and her cold discontent, was the one to fear.

Celia couldn't understand her mother's dismay about the way they lived because, as far as she could see, their side of the house was much more interesting. There was a drama to life behind the green baize door which, combined with its undercurrent of jocular subversion, was very bracing. By contrast, all the Falconbridges seemed to do was eat four times a day, occasionally taking a slow turn along the seafront or around the garden. At regular intervals, their two children, Albert and Hermione, both older than herself, came back from boarding school for holidays, when they would play with children from surrounding big houses. Celia would study them from a

distance as if they were wild animals—
Albert wiry and bright-eyed, Hermione
stocky with frizzy hair—and sometimes pass
them in the drive and long to speak but end
up hanging her head. The food changed
when they were around. Cook made more
jellies and trifle, and, once, Albert came
into the kitchen and thanked her for making chocolate cake—but mechanically, as
if he'd been ordered to, keeping his eyes
averted from her pale, bristly face. Cook
was delighted; she talked about it all day.

All meals had to be served on the dot—at
nine o'clock, one o'clock, four o'clock, eight
o'clock—on a trolley that clattered over the
bumps in the rugs on the way to the dining
room (or at teatime, the drawing room),
even as the grandfather clock was chiming
out the hour. Celia couldn't understand why
this extreme punctuality was so important,
but it explained the panic in the kitchen.
Cook was on a perpetual short fuse. You
always knew what the menu was because
while furiously chopping and boiling and
baking, she'd growl it under her breath, over
and over again: "Pilchard pâté, chicken
supreme, steamed roll . . . pilchard pâté,
chicken supreme, steamed roll . . ." She

was extraordinarily efficient. Celia loved watching her fit in everyday tasks like cutting biscuits from a sheet of mixture with a down-turned tumbler, or folding and punching dough before flipping it into loaf tins to rise. Each meal dispatched to the dining room was a triumph because the range was so temperamental. However carefully it was attended to during the day, it always went out at night, and one of the duties of Ella, the all-purpose maid, was to relight it in time for breakfast, which meant getting up at five. The distant sound of clinkers being riddled out with a poker was as punctual as the first chirrups in the trees. Ella grumbled, of course. Did the Falconbridges have any idea what was involved in getting their porridge and kippers to the table on time?

Life as a servant was never going to be easy for Helen, with her refined ways, and keeping aloof from the grousing only added to the resentment. Celia ached for her mother, knowing her vulnerable heart, and once was dismayed to overhear Ella giving a cruelly accurate imitation.

And then, one evening, during a particularly hectic run-up to dinner for important guests, the other servants' attitude changed.

The roasting tray slipped as it was being removed from the oven and a big leg of lamb tumbled onto the tiled floor, and instantly, as if he'd been waiting his whole life for this opportunity, Mr. Peters' mongrel, Sparky, bounded through the open backdoor. Cook bellowed "Roast lamb!" for, even as they watched, frozen by horror, it was being removed from the dinner menu, and it was five minutes to eight and what would happen if there was a yawning gap between cream of artichoke soup and fruit trifle? To make things even worse for Cook, Helen, the housekeeper, had seen the whole thing and was bound to report carelessness to Lady Falconbridge. Who could blame her, after the way she'd been treated?

But as they stood there helplessly, Helen slammed the backdoor, cutting off Sparky's escape route, and then she grabbed the snarling dog by the scruff, wedged him between her knees, forced his jaws open and wrested the greasy joint away. "What the eye doesn't see," she commented with astonishing coolness as she handed the meat to Cook. Then she checked closely for dog hairs as, carving with a trembling knife, Cook arranged overlapping slices in a serving platter, garnishing it with the usual generous sprinkle of gritty parsley.

The drama was replayed all evening, with every terrifying what-if explored.

"Could've bit your hand off, Helen," said Ella. She added a little mystifyingly, "Let sleeping dogs lay is what I say."

"He weren't laying," Cook corrected her with a shudder. "One minute more," she went on in her harsh, mannish voice, "and he'd've been out in them woods with my meat, taking his time."

"What the eye don't see," Ella repeated, as if still tickled pink.

"*We* ain't out of the woods yet," Mr. Peters announced ominously. He paused for maximum effect: "There's always supposing Sir John or Her Ladyship or one of them guests in there contracts the distemper."

Finally, to more uproarious laughter, Ella assumed the composed, subservient expression she'd worn when trolleying the meal into the dining room. The staff didn't dine off leftovers that evening, though there was plenty of lamb. Cook made them a big omelette: one of her mushroom and cheddar cheese specials.

The incident turned Helen into a respected and integral member of the group: a party to the gossip and the jokes. And there was plenty to laugh about.

When salad was on the menu, Lady Falconbridge would insist the shredded lettuce and sliced cucumber and tomato be served au naturel. It was because she didn't trust her precious olive oil to the kitchen, Mr. Peters suggested with a sniff; but Cook disagreed, even though it was kept in a locked cupboard in the dining room. You had to be a lady to mix a "Contynental vinny-grette," she'd tell the other servants, mouth twitching with sardonic amusement; and then Ella would act out Lady Falconbridge taking up her prized spoon and fork made of olive wood that matched her Italian salad bowl, measuring imaginary ingredients before crooking her little finger and raising the spoon to her lips to taste.

Sir John Falconbridge would take full credit when visitors complimented him on the garden, as if it were he who had envisaged a long crimson splash of rhododendrons and the subtle pastel hues of the herbaceous borders, while Peters, his head gardener, had merely obeyed orders. However, Mr. Peters seemed more entertained than offended. After all, didn't Sir John react in exactly the same smug, unsurprised way when someone admired the sea view? "Thinks he's God Almighty," Mr. Peters summed up, puzzling Celia (who took things literally). "Bless him!"

When the staff joked about the Falconbridges, Helen would look down at her lap, though her cup sometimes trembled against her saucer in her hands. That was how Celia knew Ella had mocked Sir John, though her words had made no sense at all. A moment before, she'd been talking about doing the laundry. The next she was addressing the head gardener, a cheeky glint in her eye.

"I were sorting his Lordship's long johns, Mr. Peters, and I thought for a minute you'd run your muddy tractor over 'em." She added most affectionately: "Bless him!" Then she and Cook and Mr. Peters burst into ribald laughter, and Celia heard that tinkle of china from her mother's direction.

There was little that escaped the sharp

eyes of those servants. They could trace their employers' actions, step by step in the seclusion of their bedroom, by the garments dropped on the floor, the pale face powder smudging the glass top of the dressing table, a ghost of Coty's La Rose Jacqueminot hanging in the air. They knew more personal things, too, like the month Lady Falconbridge finally stopped menstruating. And, of course, they were aware of how the Falconbridges talked when they believed themselves alone because you became invisible when you served.

It was at Far Point that Celia first became aware of the privacy and independence of the mind. The staff wore deferential masks behind which their rebellious, impertinent thoughts darted unchecked—even her mother, who'd always stressed to her the importance of truth.

Celia resented the bolster of land on the other side of the Solent, though her mother assured her that France lay far out of sight beyond the next horizon. She was fascinated by the notion of a separate country where people spoke in another language. Maybe they talked about ideas and dreams, unlike Cook and Ella and Mr. Peters. The kitchen was like a mouse's cage, Helen had once remarked, though Celia had no idea how she knew.

She felt shortchanged by the island in another way. Without its calming presence, the sea would be far wilder, with waves rollicking all the way across the Atlantic before crashing in a fountain of spray. She'd imagine them before she went to sleep and change the narrow pebbly beach into a swath of soft golden sand.

Far Point was a terrifying place at night when she lay alone in bed on the upper floor, listening to the distant clatter from the kitchen and waiting for her mother, who was still in her little office, where the beads hanging from her crimson lamp cast shadows shaped like elongated beetles. The pines outside swayed and moaned, and she knew that, beyond the closed door of her room, the long rugs in the corridors were heaving and rippling like snakes.

"It's all right!" she kept telling herself, but to no avail. She was so frightened that she became convinced she was drifting away from herself and the appalling notion came to her that, any minute, she'd be looking down on her own body, huddled under the blankets. She wanted to run downstairs to her mother, but she was imprisoned on all sides.

Then—in this state of almost catatonic terror—she believed she heard her own words spoken out loud, very soothingly, in a high sweet voice: "It's all right."

She squeezed her lids together so tightly that she saw red sparks in the blackness.

"They're magic carpets," the voice went on, with a strange coaxing quality to it. "They can take us to France."

At that, she opened her eyes and, by the light of the moon filtering through the flimsy curtains, saw a very thin girl in white about her age with a pale, somber face and long hair that streamed over her shoulders like black water. Thinking about it, many years later, she was certain that girl had been a ghost—perhaps of another frightened child who'd once lived in the remote, creaking house. But her new friend, whom she called Naomi, came to seem more real to her than anyone except her mother.

Helen would sometimes interrupt their conversations. "Who were you talking to?"

she'd demand. "How many times have I told you not to play in the airing cupboard?" She'd retidy neat stacks of sheets and towels, looking anxious and cross as she waited for an answer.

"Phoebe," Celia would fib, pointing at her doll, sensing it was the right thing to say. She'd made a crucial discovery: the person closest to her no longer knew what went on in her head. But why, she wondered, did her mother find talking to Phoebe, with her dead blue eyes and rigid pink lips, more acceptable than having fun with Naomi?

It wasn't until Priscilla and Bet came into Celia's life when she was sixteen that Naomi faded back into the house as if she'd never been: one of its hidden voices, or perhaps one of hers.

CHAPTER FIVE

Everyone kept secrets then. It was not having them that was the exception.

Note. No date.

The worst crime you can commit is to turn your back on someone you love.

Scrap. No date.

"Nothing ever happens," Ella had taken to grumbling once supper was eaten because, all of a sudden, she no longer seemed to find the company in the kitchen amusing. In 1938 youth had started slipping away like an unwrapped sweet. She'd get up from her chair and go to the window and stare into the empty darkness where the pines moaned and swayed, as if she still expected a handsome prince to appear.

But Celia would look past Ella's brawny back straining the seams in her blue-and-white striped dress, and her black hair rolled into an uneven sausage, and her feet in lace-ups, twitching as if she longed to be asked to dance, and see what she couldn't: a little tableau of the rest of them reflected in the glass. They were Ella's future, she'd think a little sadly, even if she didn't want to recognize it.

There was less joking and less gossip among the staff now: a new solemnity to reflect what was happening in the outside world. Mr. Peters would hold forth for hours on the political situation, getting cross with himself when he lost his thread; once—to general but respectful amusement—he referred to "the threat of appeasement and the futility of fascism." "You mark my words," he'd reiterate, as if Cook and Helen and Ella and Celia, trapped in the kitchen with him, night after night, had any choice. He was right about the inevitability of war, of course, but couldn't possibly have predicted the great change on its way to their isolated stretch of shoreline, or that three of them would soon leave the house for good. Most surprising of all, a dashing princelike figure *was* going to appear out of nowhere and scoop one of them up— only it wouldn't be Ella.

By the end of 1943, that bleak seashore and surrounding marshland had been appropriated by the navy and the military and invaded by an army of young men and women. And yet, at the same time, the area had become as cut off as the island on the horizon, impossible to penetrate without a permit. Whereas previously the only sounds had been the lapping of waves and the cries of gulls, there was now an ever-present hum of low-flying aircraft, though there were no known landing strips in the vicinity. Covered jeeps puttered up and down the coast road all day long. The stony beach scattered with white cuttlefish and tangles of dark seaweed was now parked with massive sections of concrete that groups of men conferred over in somber, intent huddles. Something enormous was happening but nobody knew exactly what, because each person's part in that complicated jigsaw puzzle was so minuscule. And besides, they'd taken a solemn oath never to divulge what information they possessed. Even the locals, who'd spent their whole lives there, felt anxious and out of place.

When war was declared in 1939, Ella was the first inhabitant of Far Point to join up, weeks before Albert Falconbridge was reluctantly enlisted into the army. They said you could take your pick if you volunteered, she explained excitedly to the kitchen, and she had her heart set on becoming a Wren. Out of her hearing, Cook remarked that the uniform must have had a lot to do with it because dark navy with touches of white was very flattering for someone overweight. But the general opinion was that Ella was setting her sights too high. It was girls like Hermione Falconbridge who had the real choice, Mr. Peters commented sourly, and the war wasn't going to change that.

The next volunteer was Cook (who, to general amazement, turned out to be only forty-three). She was accepted by the munitions factory in Southampton, where Ella ended up, too—thus proving Mr. Peters right. But Cook was delighted and she looked quite different as she left. "Almost pretty," Helen whispered to Celia when they were alone together. "Almost," agreed Celia, thinking of the smart green two-piece Cook had worn, but also the freshly powdered dark shadow on her upper lip.

However, at close to fifty, Helen was too old for meaningful war work, and besides, how would Lady Falconbridge—recently widowed—manage with no servants at all? No wonder she hated war, which had brought madness and ruin. And now, instead of resting on the reputation she'd built up as a housekeeper, she'd suddenly been landed with all the cleaning and cooking, too. But at least Lady Falconbridge showed appreciation at last. She seemed angered and bewildered by the desertions. "I don't know what more they expected," she said over and over again, as if Cook and Ella had been treated like queens, instead of being expected to sleep in tiny bedrooms without heating and eat margarine instead of butter and drink watered-down milk.

She was taking the loss of her husband hard. Mr. Peters swore he'd heard her call "John! John!," as she stumbled through the pinewood in her head scarf and fur coat, but he might have made it up to illustrate a pet theory that the less happy you'd been with a spouse, the more deeply you grieved, and vice versa. It was rubbish of course, thought Helen. When her own husband had died, she'd grieved only briefly but would never have described her marriage as happy. The truth was, widowhood was grim from any angle. She watched with sympathy as Lady Falconbridge kept up rituals and standards while the invitations dwindled away. It was like a game of spillikins. Remove a crucial stick, the man of the house, and the whole edifice of social life collapsed.

Then one day, smelling sour from loneliness, Lady Falconbridge pushed through the green baize door in search of company. Her son Albert was bad with money, like his father, and never stopped demanding it. Perhaps she could only have made that humbling admission to someone like Helen, who understood her world while having no place in it. "Be strict with Master Albert; it's the only way," Helen advised, thankful her Celia was such a good girl. Once Lady Falconbridge asked: "Who helped *you* when you lost your husband?" Though she didn't wait for the answer, it was as if she'd finally become aware of Helen as a fellow human being. "What a pretty girl you are!" she'd sometimes exclaim at the sight of Celia, as if taken by surprise. "You and Albert and Hermione must get together next time they're home." The war was blurring class barriers. Everyone remarked on it.

The house limped on, more tatty every year, and Mr. Peters, furious that he was too old to fight, was obliged to destroy the beautiful formal garden he'd spent his life on and turn it into an enormous vegetable plot to aid the war effort. But he kept his bees going, despite rationing. He gave up having sugar in his tea and tried to forget about his sweet tooth, and hoped for honey to come, like dreaming of an end to the fighting.

When she left school at sixteen, Celia started helping him with the digging and hoeing and planting. As the days grew shorter, the two of them established a pleasing father-daughter relationship, their thoughtful conversations measured in white vapor. Mr. Peters seemed upset on Celia's behalf that her hands were ingrained with earth and blotched by chilblains. She was only young, she should be having the time of her life, he grumbled on her behalf, as he watched her chip away at frozen earth. But she was quite content. The job allowed her to daydream without interruption, and living half in the real world, half in an imaginary one had become a habit. It explained her poor marks at school in everything except English.

Mostly, she daydreamed about the people she'd read about in the novels Lady Falconbridge now allowed her to borrow from her library—wonderful stories by the Brontë sisters and Charles Dickens, but also more contemporary fare from authors like Georgette Heyer. Lady Falconbridge belonged to a book club and parcels would arrive at regular intervals. She derived pleasure from selecting suitable titles for the guest bedrooms, just as she'd once enjoyed arranging the flowers before they disappeared from the garden; but nobody came to stay at Far Point anymore and often Celia was the first person to read a new book. She loved the way it cracked faintly when first opened; the aspirinlike smell of fresh paper.

"Sooner or later you'll have company

your own age," said Mr. Peters, as if looking into a crystal ball. He was right. Adventure had arrived in that backwater. She
could feel a fresh energy in the air, as if
someone was gently nudging her awake.

She met Priscilla and Bet when delivering
a couple of crates of carrots to Island View,
a beautiful grand house with famous gardens farther along the shore which had
been requisitioned by the navy some time
before. Mr. Peters had said he was happy
to transport the crates in his ancient van
as usual, together with a consignment of
potatoes, but she'd insisted on strapping
them to the back of her bicycle. "I need
the air," she told him, even though she
was outside all day long. Beneath her thick
sweater, she was wearing a clean pair of
the dungarees that had become her uniform, and her long hair was tied up in a
turban. She wobbled along the slippery
shore road, passing groups of young men
who whistled appreciatively and made re-
marks. Once, humiliatingly, she lost her
balance and was forced to dismount and
pick up some carrots that had tumbled off.
    "That were no accident," remarked one

of the young men, and they all laughed, but Celia maintained a stony expression, as if being noticed and commented on was the last thing she'd wanted.

It was rumored that whatever mysterious thing was in the offing, it was being orchestrated at Island View. It was said that the owners were now living in a pocket tucked away in the west wing and the rest of the elegant rooms had been turned into offices and dormitories. As she wheeled her bicycle through the iron gates, Celia could see for herself that the place hummed with activity. There were a dozen new-looking wooden huts dotted around and there no longer seemed to be a tradesman's entrance. Both doors to the house were wide open and a constant traffic of men and women poured in and out. She stopped, uncertain which way to go.

Two girls in navy bell-bottoms were perched on a wall overlooking an overgrown sunken garden, drinking mugs of tea. One was dark and stocky with a broad laughing face more interesting than pretty; the other was like a little doll with lovely pale skin and a fleece of auburn hair pinned in an untidy roll.

"You're wasting your time on that man," she said.

"Says who?" retorted the dark girl, producing a tobacco tin.

What made Celia linger was not the conversation but the unlikely pairing. The redhead spoke in an elaborate strangulated drawl; the dark girl sported a rough local accent. They were close: she could tell from the way they nudged each other and shared the same homemade cigarette.

"You know perfectly well you're causing talk."

For some reason, this made the dark girl beam even more.

"Nobody's going to want to marry you, Bet," the redhead went on crossly as she passed the cigarette over.

"We're not all on the lookout for husbands, Priscilla."

"You could have fooled me!"

Then they both seemed to become aware of Celia, who was mortified to have been caught eavesdropping.

"What's with the carrots?" the dark girl asked. Even this seemed to amuse her.

Celia explained where she was from.

"The wedding cake! I seen it from the water."

"Bet!" said the redhead very sharply. But the dark girl went on smiling as she flipped the fag end away and held out her hand.

They were Wrens, which, according to Mr. Peters, meant they'd been born with an unfair advantage. This was patently true of Priscilla, though not of Bet, whose father was a postman in Southampton, it turned out. She'd volunteered early, like Ella, but had been luckier or, more likely, made a better impression on the selection board. Celia thought that Cook had been right about the uniform. They looked casual yet glamorous, and very grown up.

"See you," said Bet nonchalantly as they got up to go; and Celia decided that, when she got home, she'd suggest to Mr. Peters that she deliver all the vegetables from now on, even if it meant several trips a day. "We should be saving petrol," she'd say and envisaged him fingering his purple earlobe as he acknowledged the logic in this. "I like doing it," she'd go on, before he could tell her she was only a lass and spuds weighed a ton.

She turned up the next day and the next, discovering that if she timed it right, she'd find them ensconced on the lip of the sunken garden, enjoying a break.

"*There* you are!" Priscilla would exclaim, very much as if they'd been discussing her—but they were always nice. Perhaps it flattered them to be courted so shamelessly: to have someone who listened so attentively as they squabbled and gossiped, and who laughed at their jokes even if she found them incomprehensible. It was Celia's first glimpse of the way proper friends interacted, and also how real girls talked. Her only experience was gathered from the local school, where she'd been regarded as an oddity, and Ella, several years her senior. Like Ella, Bet and Priscilla talked mostly about food and men; though there wasn't nearly enough of the former at Island View, there was an unusual surfeit of the latter. Pretty well every other subject was out of bounds. Someone had put the fear of God into Priscilla, but Bet, who was a lot less discreet, explained it was because they'd had to sign the Official Secrets Act.

They could admit to loving the job, though. Known by the men as "water hens," they were boats crew, which explained why they dressed like sailors. They wore whistles around their necks and, when it rained heavily, oilskins with matching sou'westers. Very occasionally, out of Priscilla's hearing, Bet would let drop a snippet of information that hinted at the pattern of their days, like grumbling about having to scrub out a boat after numerous seasick men had endured a stormy night crossing in it. She and Priscilla slept six to a room in bunks set up in the old servant quarters, and Priscilla said she'd never met such dishonest, foul-mouthed girls. At first, she appeared overprivileged and shallow, and Bet hard-bitten; but that was before Celia discovered Priscilla's secret acuteness and Bet's vulnerable heart.

Early in 1944, with the country still in winter's grip, Lady Falconbridge was visited by a local volunteer in charge of billeting and informed that half a dozen army officers would shortly be arriving at Far Point.

Celia heard it from her mother, who was making a stew out of surplus turnips and

swedes, tossing in whatever dried-up fla-
vorings she could find in the cupboards.
The job suited her cross and put-upon
mood. Now there'd be more people to
cook for and more housework, not to mention soothing Lady Falconbridge, who was
behaving as if *she* was the injured party.

"You'd think she'd welcome the company." Helen mixed in a spoonful of very
old dried-up mustard, tasted the result,
and shrugged. After more than a decade
at Far Point, she'd absorbed some of the
attitudes of a servant, expressing resentment where she could get away with it.
The food (never a strong point, even when
Cook was still around) had become atro-
cious. She added: "She's worried about
her paintings and the good furniture. She
wants them stored in the stables for the
time being. Can you tell Mr. Peters? She'd
like it done as soon as possible."

"Why doesn't she put the officers in the
stables?" Celia retorted sassily. She was
gobbling a jam sandwich, tolerating her
mother's flat, cardboardlike bread but relishing the sharp sweet flavor of one of the
last remaining pots of Cook's damson jam.

She hadn't eaten since early in the morning, and as usual, the fresh air had made her ravenous. Frost had crisped the grass and iced each black twig. Even the sighing of the sea was muted, as if the cold had slowed the waves. But at least the kitchen was warm. She'd begun lighting the range for her mother before leaving to work in the garden and was gradually becoming familiar with its temperamental nature. Sometimes she'd park herself on its top, like claiming a prize, though her mother would frown and, though reluctant to mention the word "hemorrhoids," mutter about ruining her health.

"That jam's for the dining room!" she was now reminded.

Her mother went on: "I've tried to tell her she's been lucky to get away with not having evacuees. We all have."

Celia disagreed. It might have been fun to have children in the house, ripping away the veil of gloom that had fallen since Sir John's death. Lady Falconbridge had been spared evacuees only because of the high security of the area. Officers were different.

"We'll just have to put up with it," her

mother concluded, as she turned her attention to pudding and started flinging ingredients into a bowl randomly, without using the scales. "I do miss Cook's treacle sponge," Lady Falconbridge had remarked wistfully the day before. Ever the good servant, Helen had taken note, but on her own terms.

Bet studied Celia in her bold, inquisitive way. "Beats me why you're wasting your time with us."

Celia thought of the six officers, who must have arrived at Far Point by now. Some shyness had driven her out of the house, though her mother had urged her to stay and lend a hand. Though she thought about men most of the time now, the prospect of half a dozen up close was alarming, especially when her only real experience had been limited to Mr. Peters. She muttered, "They're probably all middle-aged and married."

"Well, that's how some people like them," said Priscilla pointedly.

Bet was having an affair with a married man. Almost more shocking, she was perfectly open about it. He worked on one of the many boats moored in the river, where their assignations took place even though it was forbidden to sneak out after night fell. Bet claimed she wasn't alone—some of the other girls had even composed a bittersweet song about illicit, short-lived affairs called "Thanks for the Memory." She didn't believe in regrets, she said, with a sly glance at Priscilla. "When I'm eighty, I'll only have to think 'Doug, January 1944' and it'll all come back. The smell of the sea, and the spray on my cheeks, and him wrapping us in his coat and the boat rocking around in the water. . . ." She gave Celia a cheeky smile, inviting her to share the joke. "I'll have my own little library of memories."

"And I'll have a husband," said Priscilla, putting her in her place. "Mine, not someone else's."

The minute the officers arrived, Lady Falconbridge regretted her decision to store the good stuff. They had beautiful manners and were exactly the kind of people she'd have welcomed as guests. Her glance flickered unhappily over the pale squares on the walls, the dark patches on the parquet floors, and she muttered a fib about spring-cleaning. Once she and Helen were alone together, she asked her to arrange with Mr. Peters to put everything back as soon as possible.

"It'll be like having half a dozen Alberts around," she enthused. Relating this to Celia later, Helen commented, quite acidly for her: "Without the debts and worry."

One of the officers, a little older than the rest, was particularly charming and, to add to his glamour, had been decorated. Lady Falconbridge straightaway earmarked him for her daughter, Hermione, who was nursing in London but expected on leave within the next fortnight. It was only a shame, she'd remark afterward—jokingly, of course—that, on his first evening at Far Point, someone hadn't stopped that absolute dreamboat from wandering down to the beach.

Celia dawdled on the way home, though conscious she should be helping her mother. When she reached the last bit of shoreline before the house, she sat on a recently installed bollard and gazed out to sea. Two new jetties had suddenly appeared. She watched them pointing at the orange sun sinking into the island in the distance—but surreptitiously, because you never knew when or if you were being observed, these mysterious, uncertain days.

It was six o'clock and getting chilly. She was still in her dungarees, and as usual her fingernails were full of earth. No chance of a bath, she thought: she knew just enough about men to be confident they'd take all the hot water. She was easing herself off the bollard when she heard a pebble rattle behind her.

Frederick would later claim that when he caught sight of her sitting on the beach, hair edged with rosy light by the last shafts of the sun, he promised himself, "I shall marry this girl." Before she'd even turned round! It was most uncharacteristic. Besides—he said this more than once—he wasn't looking for a wife.

As for her, she saw a tall, exceptionally handsome man with dark glossy hair and deep blue eyes, thirteen years her senior. He could only be one of the officers whose bed she'd helped make up that morning. She smiled tentatively.

He responded with a flash of fine white teeth. "Hermione?"

It was a perfectly reasonable assumption. He knew Lady Falconbridge had a daughter because one of the first things she'd said to him was, "You must meet my Hermione." But she hadn't mentioned that another girl lived in the house.

Celia smiled back, while shaking her head.

"I thought you lived up there," he said, indicating the big white shape encircled by pines: a property bound to impress any young man.

Celia paused, putting off the moment when the admiration in his eyes would be replaced by embarrassment. "I do."

If he was taken aback to learn she was the daughter of the middle-aged, careworn servant who, half an hour earlier, had ushered him into the house, he didn't show it. But, as time went on, she couldn't shake off the conviction that she'd deceived him: taken advantage, without intending to, of his susceptibility. It didn't help that, for all her new affability, Lady Falconbridge seemed to think so too.

"I can't believe I'm getting married," Celia told Bet, happy to catch her on her own at Island Point and enjoying a roll-up on the lip of the sunken garden. Ever since her engagement had been announced, Priscilla had treated her rather as Lady Falconbridge did, with a sort of grudging admiration. Bet wasn't like that. Celia sensed real kindness beneath the wildness.

"We all know you're a dark horse, Celia!"

"Don't, Bet!" Celia was watching the gulls dip over the steel-colored sea and thinking how much she'd miss that familiar sight. Even dear old Mr. Peters had behaved as if there'd been an element of calculation on her part. As for her mother, she'd reacted with an odd mixture of triumph and humility. A stranger at the tiny engagement party might have been forgiven for assuming it was beaming Lady Falconbridge who was the mother of the bride, not the dumpy woman in a dark dress who kept a watchful eye on the refreshments.

"What are you? Seventeen? Bless!"

Bet had been at the shoe polish again, which meant she had a date with one of her married men. Her eyelashes were sticky black from blinking into the tin; and there was more polish drawn in impressively straight lines down the back of her bare legs (which meant Priscilla had lent a hand with a paintbrush, ticking her off all the while). Celia hadn't the nerve to practice these austerity tricks herself. Besides, she sensed Frederick wouldn't like it. He disapproved of Bet. More surprisingly, he hadn't welcomed Priscilla, either. Celia was very much afraid that, once she left Far Point, she might not see these good friends again.

"I'm so lucky," she told Bet. As the fiancée of a now prized guest, she was no longer permitted to eat in the kitchen, which meant she had to sit at the dining room table and be waited on by her own mother. To add to the discomfort, Helen didn't object. As she bent to offer a dish, their eyes would meet for a second, shame and awkwardness encountering only loving pride. Still more significantly, Celia had been moved to the Falconbridge side of the house. She now slept in the Chinese Room: so called because of the hideous green and gold dragons with chipped red tongues that adorned the headboard of the bed. But it had a wonderful view of the sea, plus three new novels on the bedside table that Lady Falconbridge had chosen especially for her. Frederick's bedroom— the Blue Room—was just along the corridor, though she'd not been invited in.

Bet whistled. "Lucky! I'll say!"

"And I don't *really* mind about not getting married in church."

Bet was looking at her very quizzically as if she didn't believe a word of it.

"The thing is . . ."

"What?"

"He might get killed." Celia looked at her friend imploringly, as if begging her to disagree.

But Bet nodded without expression. They were in wartime, after all. What she said next was shocking: "You don't have to marry him." She added, in case Celia had missed her meaning, "You can still have him."

Celia blushed and looked away. After supper the night before, she and Frederick had gone for a walk in the dark pinewood, where, as usual, he'd kissed her as if she were precious and fragile. But moving away, he'd lost his balance and tumbled backward onto a bed of pine needles and bracken. They'd laughed and she'd dropped down beside him and they'd kissed some more.

Bet went on. "There's ways not to get yourself up the duff, you know." She added with an oddly grim smile: "So they say."

Celia went even pinker and couldn't meet Bet's curious affectionate gaze. In the darkness, mouth to mouth, breathing in her soon-to-be husband's heady scent of Brilliantine and tobacco, her usual shyness had evaporated. But his reaction to what had been entirely spontaneous behavior was appalling. "No, Celia!" he'd said very sharply, like ticking off a dog, and they'd returned to the house in silence. He'd appeared not to notice the tears coursing down her cheeks, the gleam of her white handkerchief in the dark.

She was bewildered. All her knowledge of love came from the novels she'd read. Men were masterful and predatory, and—though they'd never discussed sex—her mother obviously agreed. She was very subdued these days, as if fearful of saying the wrong thing, but she'd stare at her anxiously as if cautioning that, until a wedding ring was safely on a finger, promises shouldn't be trusted. But Frederick wasn't like that. He might even break off the engagement now.

Bet could explain. Who else knew so much about men? "He doesn't want to," she muttered. But it wasn't precisely true. Part of him had very much wanted to, as if the smell and feel of her had tripped a switch over which he had no control. But that thrilling passionate force had lasted just a few seconds. And after he'd buttoned himself back into his familiar affectionate but controlled self, he'd appeared to despise himself, too.

"Doesn't want to what?"

Celia went even pinker. "*You* know!"

Scarcely a beat passed before Bet reacted as if this was a common problem: "Right!" Then she asked, "He's what, twenty-nine?"

"Thirty."

"He must have had other women."

"He has." At the beginning of their walk,

Celia had steeled herself to ask. After all, didn't she have the right, as his fiancée? But Frederick had hesitated before replying distantly, "No one to concern you."

"And?"

"He doesn't want to talk about it."

"Right," Bet repeated, frowning.

Celia could sense her exasperation: "Won't make love! Won't talk! What's the *matter* with the man?" "I love him," she muttered because what else was this feeling of helpless enslavement? People never stopped telling her how lucky she was; and she knew she wanted to be married because she'd seen at first hand the loneliness and humiliation of life without a man.

"What did he mean, telling you he wasn't looking for a wife?" Suddenly, Bet sounded relieved, even amused. She'd solved the puzzle. "He thinks there's two sorts of women." She made a face because she knew very well which category she fell into. No wonder Frederick was so unfriendly when she was around! "He'll be fine once you're married. Trust me!"

Something was troubling Celia far more, but Bet was the last person she could talk to about it. Soon she and Frederick would leave Far Point for good, and he'd warned her several times, very meaningfully, to prepare for an entirely new life. But she was only seventeen. How could she bear to do without her friends, let alone her beloved mother?

CHAPTER SIX

You asked for my memories of that time, but I'm not rightly sure I should be telling you this, even all these years later. Silly of me probably—but so long as Priscilla never finds out, here goes.

One evening in 1944, I sat in the garden at Island View, sharing a smoke with a lad who was being sent across the Channel that night. That's all it was—a shared smoke. He was only twenty-two, but he'd been trained to set mines and he told me he'd have to swim underwater once they dropped him off in case the night patrols spotted him, and he was scared silly of drowning. He shouldn't have said any of it, of course. I can see him now—his skin all fresh and pink as if he hadn't

even started shaving—and hear the excitement in his voice as he told me about the girl he loved, almost like he was drunk, only we had no alcohol. It was as if he had to leave a record of his feelings with someone—even a stranger like me—because he knew he was going to die. I never saw him again, but since I turned eighty I've thought about him every day. Perhaps it's he who doesn't allow me to forget. Is it possible the dead do that?

Letter to C. from Bet Parker,
dated February 26, 2004.

Bud broke the shocking news to Guy in an e-mail. It said: "Guess what, my dad's having an affair! His girlfriend's six years younger than me!!!"

He responded instantly, not fooled by the jaunty exclamation marks, concentrating on being practical. "We'd better talk about this asap. How are you fixed for tonight?"

So here they were now, discussing everything except the shocking infidelity that had blown her family apart.

"More fish?" Bud asked, though there was still plenty on his plate.

"Delicious," he murmured. "If only I'd known, I wouldn't have had lunch."

She couldn't cook. Her father—who prided himself on being honest—would have pointed out that the fish was over-done and the potatoes nearly raw. But Guy wasn't like that, which was all the more reason to appreciate him. As usual, he had dark rings under his eyes. But for her e-mail, he'd probably be asleep by now. Poor Guy, whose working day started with the dawn. No wonder his private life was so unsatisfactory. But their whole genera-tion worked too hard, as their grandmother had frequently pointed out. "What's hap-pened to dancing and nightclubs?" she asked, honestly bemused when they laughed and laughed.

Guy had offered to take her out to dinner—mostly because, as she couldn't help but be aware, he dreaded coming to Brixton in his prized new car. He never criticized the way she lived, but his wary expression said it all. He disliked Brixton's scent of lawlessness; the incessant wail of police sirens; the fact that the front door had been jimmied open and inadequately repaired since his last visit. However, he behaved impeccably, as if he were visiting Belgravia, not even commenting on the drifts of dead leaves on the communal stairs (caused by a long-running dispute about cleaning with the other tenants). But she couldn't have discussed her father's affair in a restaurant. It felt too raw. She needed the comfort of the cozy, tidy little flat she was so proud of. "Why you want to be saddled with a mortgage . . ." her father had puzzled, as usual making her feel middle-aged. But she needed security. Guy understood. He loved his family but wanted to be different from them, too.

Putting off the moment of truth, casting around for a harmless topic, she said brightly: "Well, I think it's good news that someone wants to write a book about Gran." But she was thinking of her father, of course. Could it be that he was merely rattling at the bars of his marriage as a warning to her mother not to take him for granted (though when had she ever)? He tested every relationship, as Bud had learned most painfully as a child. Staying at Parr's one Christmas, he'd made out that her adored kitten, Stripy, had been eaten by her grandmother's dog in the night. He'd hidden Stripy in the garage and left its collar, together with a snipped-off wisp of fur, in the dog's basket; and then he'd watched as she became horribly distressed. He'd ruined Christmas for the entire family. "Only a joke!" he'd protested after finally owning up. Would this turn out to be another?

"Lovely fish," said Guy, putting down his knife and fork.

"Sorry about the bones."

"Didn't notice any," he insisted, even though she'd just watched him pick two from his teeth. Then he said: "So go on about the woman who wants to write the book."

"She told Mum and Margaret she'd like to look at Gran's stuff. But Margaret doesn't seem to trust her."

"Does she ever trust anyone?"

It was true. What an extraordinarily difficult person their aunt was, with a kind of bitter contrariness that distorted every judgment. "She's a living warning never to marry for money," Bud observed rather unkindly.

"As a matter of fact," said Guy, "Dad's not in favor of the book either. He says the family's had quite enough publicity."

"Really?" She was remembering the strange and awful time preceding the funeral. "Reptiles," her uncle had called the journalists who'd telephoned or turned up at the door day after day; and the photographers had been "those infernal snappers." But when the attention had died away, he'd seemed to miss it. "He liked being on TV, didn't he?" she said, remembering him asking them one by one how he'd done, as if he'd been interviewed on his own merit.

"Did he?" asked Guy, as if he'd not considered this before.

"I think so," said Bud cautiously. They never criticized each other's parents, which was another reason why she felt able to confide in him about Whoopee.

"What's your mum's attitude?" he asked very gently.

At this mention of her mother, tears welled up in Bud's eyes. Anyone else might have ruined things with a rush of sympathy, but Guy waited patiently, looking down at his hands as if willing her to compose herself.

"She liked the journalist."

"I see."

Silence fell. She heard a heavy vehicle trundle past in the street below and waited for the window frames to rattle in their sockets a second later. She seldom drew the curtains because it had become an evening pleasure to watch lights flick on in the surrounding flats and houses, paint pictures of the relationships between distant and diminished figures. But maybe they, too, were being observed. What conclusions were being drawn from the sight of a young man and woman so obviously engaged in a difficult conversation? That an intimate relationship was coming to an end?

Then she saw Guy edge his cuff back very slowly from his wrist and snatch a glance at his watch.

"It's only nine!" she protested immediately.

"It's okay!" he soothed. Then he seemed to make a decision. "Does your father intend to leave home?"

She stared at him. "He says he hasn't decided yet."

"I see. And in the meantime?"

She burst into tears. "Sorry!" she said,

as she gave way to the burden of being treated as a confidante by both parents. She mopped her eyes with a piece of paper towel, very grateful Guy was still keeping his distance. "On the one hand, I have Dad telling me how dreadful he feels, *but* . . ." As she repeated her father's justifications, a strange thing happened: she felt herself mimicking his preening self-satisfaction, hateful though it had been. " 'I am sorry, Bud, I know this is difficult for you all, but I'm still young, biologically speaking, and I may never have an opportunity like this again.' He's in his fifties, Guy! He's not thinking about anything except his feelings—what an amazing thing has happened to *him*. He keeps telling me how wonderful this girl is! How much I'd like her! Then I get poor Mum crying on my shoulder. She phones all the time. It's getting really difficult. Yesterday she got me out of a meeting. Goodness knows what they think at *her* work. If she loses her job . . ."

"Spud . . ." Guy began.

Bud made a face because, as Guy should know, her brother Spud lent his presence to the family when requested but remained unmoved by their dramas. In this sort of situation, he was about as helpful as a closed box.

"I think it would be good if Mum could get away for a bit."

"I agree," said Guy instantly.

"She's due some leave. If she took a week off work and went down to Gran's, she could get on with the sorting."

"Good idea."

"It'll be lonely. But it's got to be better than being at home, wondering if he's going to turn up, hasn't it?"

"Much."

"If Margaret went too, they'd only argue."

It was settled. She would encourage her mother to leave the family home and go down to Parr's, while her father sorted out his feelings on his own.

She accompanied Guy to the front door, as usual affecting not to notice the mess in the stairwell. She wished he would stay and talk. She felt the evening was ending on the wrong note. She wanted their old easy relationship, not this desperate neediness, this pressure on him to put everything right. "How's life otherwise?" she asked.

He shrugged as if to say "what life?" and she guessed yet another girlfriend had got fed up with taking second place to his work. Love was for the young, wasn't it? But where was the time?

"You?"

Bud made a face. Though she'd grown up watching a very contented marriage, she found herself drawn to men like her father, which didn't seem a recipe for happiness. Like Guy, she was currently single. Sometimes, she wondered if she'd grow old on her own, cocooned in her little flat, relying on cocoa and hot-water bottles for comfort. But having seen what had happened to her mother, it didn't seem too awful a prospect, just for the moment.

They were outside by now, and Guy's attention had shifted to his beautiful new car, gleaming under the lamplight. She guessed he was checking for possible damage—tires slashed, polished surface scored with keys, windscreen wipers twisted off—but he managed the inspection very casually even though she sensed his relief that the car was untouched.

"So you'll phone your mum first thing tomorrow?"

"Will do," said Bud cheerily, before waving him off. But as she shut her front door, she was filled with gloom. Her mother hadn't spent a night away from her father for decades. She was entirely unequipped for solitude.

CHAPTER SEVEN

For years and years, I aimed too low. I know that now. But it's hard to hold onto the faith I have been given that it's in me to write something good. It's like being in a room with a locked trunk. Everything I need is in that trunk, and all I have to do is get inside it. And some part of me also knows that the minute I give up in despair and leave the room, the trunk will spring open.

Notebook, circa early 1990s.

"We were really really happy!" Sarah insisted, blotting her tears with a damp ball of paper towel. "I know I'm not imagining it."

"Of course not!" Jenny Granger soothed. She added, "Besides, you know about happy marriages, Sarah. You grew up in one."

Sarah nodded, though conscious that the relationship Jenny had read about in the papers was very different from the one she remembered. Her real parents were moving further and further away, the subtlety of their personalities buried under a mountain of clichés. It must be a common experience, she reflected, when the press became involved. They'd been happy—of course they had—but in a normal, human kind of way. "I have to remember Daddy's exhausting energy," she thought resolutely. "And that vagueness of hers could be jolly irritating." After his stroke, the relationship had changed, as it was bound to, but the press had painted a one-dimensional sentimental picture of that, too. The truth was that because his brain had been affected, her father had not been an easy patient, and this had been very hard for her mother. Nevertheless, the two of them had become touchingly close. He depended on her utterly—you could see it in his eyes—and she put his happiness far above her own.

It felt very cozy in the old sitting room where they had kept each other company

evening after evening for so many years:
he absorbed in one of the military biogra-
phies he'd loved, or staring at her from his
wheelchair when he could no longer read;
she dreaming up plots and people as she
darned socks and replaced buttons. Rain
pattered against the windowpanes in sudden bursts, and the fire crackled every so
often as if adding its own incisive com-
ments on unfaithful husbands.

When she'd first heard tires crunching
over wet gravel outside, Sarah had believed
for a wonderful moment that Whoopee had
come. She'd flung open the front door, already smiling tremulously, to be confronted
by this almost stranger getting out of her
car. "I say, are you all right?" she'd asked in
a voice so full of compassion and understanding that it had undone Sarah completely.

Sarah did wonder briefly why Jenny
hadn't telephoned first, because the house
could so easily have been empty. Had she
driven past on previous occasions, watching for a parked car in the drive and lights
in the windows? It was not a comfortable
thought. But Sarah put it aside because it
was such a relief to have company in this

place she'd grown up, where the old beams and floorboards creaked by night and occasionally she could have sworn that she heard her mother's soft cough.

At first, as the story unraveled, they drank tea. Then at a quarter to five, unable to hold out any longer, Sarah asked, "Would you think me awful if I had a whiskey?"

"Not at all," Jenny responded with her sweet smile. "Sensible." But she turned down a drink herself.

She was almost unrecognizable from her last visit. She'd discarded the little-girl look, opting instead for a calf-length skirt and tailored jacket, and her long hair was pinned up in a bun. The sophisticated style made her appear younger, not older. Sarah found herself wondering if she often changed her style. Had she been all in black for the funeral of a woman she'd never met? Was that why she'd passed through the company unnoticed?

As usual, alcohol cheered Sarah and loosened her tongue—and so what if she was repeating herself! After decades of being married to a warm free spirit like Whoopee, she'd forgotten how inhibited her siblings were. She knew they were deeply concerned about her, but in Robert this had started to show itself as a kind of helpless anger (almost as if he found her grief an embarrassment) and Margaret had just announced there was nothing to be gained from further discussion. Sarah knew it wasn't fair to go on testing Bud's loyalty: even in her misery, she could appreciate that. But Jenny was a confidante from heaven: listening very intently, remembering everything, occasionally asking a direct question in her soft, girlish voice and astounding Sarah with her insight.

"What is your husband *really* like?"

"Whoopee?"

Jenny smiled. "That can't be his real name!"

"It's not," Sarah whispered. "It's Derek."

"But he wants to be a Whoopee." The mockery was very gentle. "If you were asked to sum up Derek in one word, what would it be?"

"Different," Sarah responded without hesitation. "I come from a very conventional background," she explained.

"So I understand. Even so, your mother

was a highly unusual woman. You must always have been aware of that?"

Jenny's attempts to bring the conversation back to Celia were beginning to annoy Sarah and she ignored this latest one. "To be honest, I think my husband is as unhappy as I am."

"Oh tush! Is *he* pale and wan? Is *he* in floods of tears?"

"Well, no," Sarah agreed, remembering Whoopee's air of creamy self-congratulation.

"Led by their dicks," Jenny pronounced, like reading her thoughts. But then she leaned over and touched Sarah's arm and inquired in a very much softer way, "Sorry, have I shocked you?"

"No, no!" protested Sarah, though it wasn't true. Jenny had such a demure air about her.

"I mean, really! Breaking it to you he was having an affair the day after your mother's funeral!"

"It was awful," Sarah agreed, though, strangely, this hadn't occurred to her before.

"Typical! He wasn't thinking of you at all. Don't get me wrong," Jenny went on. "I love men. But one can't take them seriously!"

Sarah stared at her.

"They're a different species. Rather like deep-sea squid, I always think, because they're dangerous, and they inhabit a strange dark world without morals, and they're ruled by primitive impulses."

They had a good laugh about that and Sarah realized that it was the first time she'd smiled for days, which made her appreciate Jenny's company all the more. "I never took him for granted," she assured her.

"I'm sure you didn't. I'm sure you were a wonderful wife." Jenny went on thoughtfully: "We can believe we know someone through and through. But do we really, even in the happiest of marriages? I wonder, how well did even your mother and father *really* know each other?"

This time, Sarah pouted like a resentful child.

Jenny glanced at her. "You know," she said with her sweet smile, "it's coming back to me now. I saw the two of you together in this very room, after the funeral. Your husband's a very tactile person, isn't he?"

Sarah blushed. She hadn't forgotten the shock of feeling Whoopee's warm hand on her bottom as they were conversing with a particularly stuffy neighbor; the struggle not to react as he painted a convincing picture of his work as a clinical psychiatrist.

"You were trying not to laugh."

"Oh, always!" Sarah responded enthusiastically. "He made everything such fun!" Since his affair had come to light, she'd tried very hard to hate her husband, but now she remembered the passionate early days—the two of them so close that their damp skins clung together—and tears came to her eyes. Unlike her sister Margaret, who'd married a rich man she didn't care for, Sarah had married entirely for love. She had to defy her parents (which was dreadful for such a dutiful person), because right from the start they made it clear they considered Whoopee unsuitable. "They're snobs," he retaliated, and infatuated Sarah went along with it, even though she'd never felt her mother was class-conscious (unlike her father). She put up with the disapproval of her siblings, too; and she joined in with Whoopee's mockery of the family, though for years she'd subscribed to every value they lived by. She worked hard to support everyone.

She gladly accepted doing without luxuries. Love was all they had, which made it all the more terrible that he had flung it so carelessly away.

She drank more whiskey. "Could you . . . ? Did you . . . ? What I mean is, what did you think when you saw us together?"

"That he loved you," Jenny responded without hesitation. Then she corrected herself: "He still loves you, however badly he's behaving. I expect he's told you so, too, even if he claims he's not"—she made quote marks in the air with her index fingers—"'in love' with you anymore."

Sarah stared at Jenny wonderingly. How did she know so much? "Do you think he'll come back?"

"Oh, husbands always go back." It was only later that Sarah remembered the way she put it: as if, for all her empathy, she'd been listening to the story from a different angle. Then she glanced at her watch, as if suddenly aware of the passing of time. "I've a favor to ask. Could I see your mother's study?" She went on hastily. "Just a peek, I promise. It would mean so much to me to have a picture of where she worked.

Because if you're selling the house, it'll all be gone soon, won't it? That special place where she created her magic."

Sarah didn't hesitate. "I don't see why not."

"Really?" Jenny seemed extraordinarily pleased.

"Remind me, won't you?" said Sarah, thinking she'd take Jenny up there when the time came for her to leave, which she hoped wouldn't be for some time yet.

"Now would be as good a time as any, wouldn't it?" said Jenny, already rising to her feet.

"So she never had a study when your father was alive," she observed as she followed Sarah up the stairs. They passed faded wallpaper and worn carpet treads and chipped paint, all of which she appeared to find extraordinarily interesting.

"Mummy didn't need one then."

"But she'd been writing for years, hadn't she?"

"It was different after Daddy died."

"Oh?"

"She had all this time, suddenly."

"So she was lonely?"

"Not exactly . . ." Sarah broke off. The fact was, sometimes when they'd come to visit, they'd found their mother strangely exhilarated, almost as if they had interrupted an invisible party.

Jenny answered the question herself. "Of course she wasn't lonely because she had all her wonderful characters for company."

They'd reached the landing outside the study.

"Right at the top of the house," mused Jenny, as if finding significance in this, too.

"It was just a spare room," said Sarah, as she took a key from her pocket.

"So you keep it locked?"

"Mummy always did."

"Is that so?"

Suddenly, Sarah regretted agreeing to this. Unhappiness was having a strange effect. In her miserable, intoxicated state, she found herself wondering if her mother's gentle, mysterious spirit was still behind the locked door. Would it flee in dismay if a stranger were admitted, especially one so piercingly interested? But it was too late for second thoughts.

She heard Jenny catch her breath as the door swung open. What had she expected? Almost certainly not this shabby, unbelievably untidy little room, where millions of words jostled for space: words shut in books, words scribbled on scraps. As Sarah was thinking about this, a clothes moth fluttered up from the old blanket in the corner where Oscar used to lie, and in her oddly heightened state, a picture came to her of a swarm of print streaming from the room, with nobody the wiser. "It was her place," she said, shamed by the dust dimming the surfaces, the cobwebs hanging from corners. "She didn't even like the cleaning lady coming in."

But to her surprise, Jenny announced contentedly, "It is exactly what I expected." She went on: "I think this room is proof of the wonderful freedom of the mind. Your mother led a very protected life, didn't she? But she used her imagination to transcend it."

"She did?"

"Well, yes. She wrote about things that couldn't possibly have happened to her." She shook her head as if she still couldn't believe she was there. "After your father's death, she went to some strange places."

She seemed to have forgotten her promise only to look: she was touching things very lightly and hesitantly, but as if gaining confidence all the time—a book here, a pile of papers there. "I'm surprised she wrote on a computer," she observed, eyeing the Dell on the desk.

"I'm not sure if she did," said Sarah. "She went on using notebooks and bits of paper. I'm pretty sure she couldn't type properly. I'll have to ask the children."

"Was she on the Internet?" Jenny asked, brushing the dusty computer keys with a finger.

Sarah nodded, happy, for once, to be informed. "The grandchildren taught her how. Apparently she picked it up right away, which is a lot more than I did!"

"I suppose there were publishers in different countries to e-mail, fans, people like that."

"I've never thought about it."

Then Jenny said: "You could always check."

"Sorry?"

"They're probably still in there. All the messages she ever sent and received. That's the thing about computers. Unless you know what you're doing, it's hard to delete things completely."

So there were even more words in the room, and a decision would have to be taken on every one.

She must have shown her dismay because Jenny observed: "It's a huge responsibility you've been left with." She paused. "Where's your sister, by the way?"

"It's difficult for her to get away," said Sarah.

"More difficult than for you?" Jenny asked very softly but pointedly.

Sarah said nothing, though it was true that Margaret was selfish.

"It would be such a privilege if you'd let me help." Jenny sounded so wistful, as if this was an impossible dream. And then she said something really odd. "In this sort of situation, you can sometimes get to know someone better than when they were alive. That can be very comforting, I assure you."

CHAPTER EIGHT

Dear Celia, many thanks for including me in a most successful and enjoyable evening. I have it on good authority from my sister, who drove ambulances for the Red Cross (and consequently can change a punctured tire in two minutes in pitch darkness) that there is no greater terror than holding a dinner party. May I say that you acquitted yourself with considerable grace? Your husband is a fortunate man. Yours very sincerely, Martin Spencer.
Letter dated August 28, 1946, postmarked Hanover. Found among a mass of miscellaneous papers.

On August 15, 1946, Celia set sail from Tilbury on the SS *Empire Trooper,* as part

of "Operation Union," which would unite
wives and children with British occupation
personnel in Germany. Frederick had been
sent out there almost as soon as the war
ended, and since then they'd had to survive on short periods of leave, the last of
which had been nearly three months before.

They had no proper home, as yet,
though the long-term plan was to find a
permanent base in England. In the meantime, she would have preferred to stay with
her mother at Far Point, but Frederick had
made it clear that he wished her to live
with his parents in Wiltshire. She understood why, of course. Brought up on the
wrong side of the green baize door, she
humbly acknowledged she had a lot to
learn.

For company on the long sea voyage,
she had Aphrodite Barclay, whose husband, Simon, a childhood friend of Frederick's, was also based near Hanover. It was
a wonderful coincidence, they both agreed.
It was the first time they'd met and they
were getting on well, despite a ten-year
age gap. "We were awfully happy for Frederick when we heard about the marriage,"

Aphrodite told her. She came from an army family, and her pleasant unmade-up face bore an expression of sunny stoicism passed like a torch through generations of women. It had been her mother's idea to name her after the goddess of love, Aphrodite explained with practiced good humor.

After the ship had docked at Cuxhaven on the northwest coast, the two of them were given yellow flags, then guided to a yellow-tagged train bound for Hanover, where they found that cigarettes and sweets and magazines had been thoughtfully provided in their carriage. They exchanged pleased glances as they settled into comfortable corner seats. After the grinding austerity of Britain, it felt wonderful to be so spoiled.

They were enjoying lunch in the restaurant car and slowly approaching the first big town when they saw the children lining the tracks. Pitifully thin and dressed in rags, they mimicked the women, stuffing invisible food into their own mouths, faster and faster as the train passed. Celia immediately put down her knife and fork, but Aphrodite shrugged and continued to eat her sausages and mash with enjoyment.

There were more shocks when they reached Hanover and saw the full effect of hundreds of Allied bombing raids. That once beautiful city and its exquisite buildings had been reduced to a sea of rubble, and in its formerly leafy parks, even the stumps of vanished trees had been chiseled out of the ground for fuel. Over all lay a gray mist of dust and a stench that never entirely dispersed. It was both dismaying and impressive to see how the traumatized population was adapting. People were crammed into every available living space. Smoke drifting from pipes protruding from the rubble indicated that whole families existed in cellars somewhere beneath; there were even people living in rooms left suspended in teetering ruins and reachable only by ladder. Here and there, lines of washing straddled the ruins, like flags of surrender or brave pretenses of a normal life.

Frederick had said none of this in his letters home, of course. But once he and Celia were reunited, he told her a little about the still worse situation he and his regiment had encountered a year before. The wrecked bridges and blocked waterways and tangles of twisted metal that had once been railway lines; the precarious masonry that meant patrols had to keep to the middle of the road lest their marching feet set off fatal vibrations; the public clocks that no longer functioned; the ten thirty curfews that shrieked like air-raid warnings; the lack of water and electricity and gas. But as he never failed to remind her, if victory had gone the other way, they would be the suffering ones.

As it was, they'd been allocated a house with elegantly proportioned rooms and a lovely big garden. However, it had not come without cost. It was the property of the Braun family, but now all six of them, three generations, had been crammed into the cellar, leaving their lovely eighteenth-century dining room table and their Bechstein grand piano in the care of strangers. Friends of Frederick billeted in another German home had reported finding damask table napkins embroidered with swastikas; but he agreed that the Brauns seemed decent enough people. Just because they'd been caught up in the cruelty and madness didn't mean they supported it, he suggested magnanimously. Indeed, it was his idea to engage

Frau Braun to clean her own house, in return for a nominal sum; and in the same spirit, he decided it could only benefit everyone if Herr Braun was encouraged to continue cultivating the fruit and vegetables in his own garden.

Celia found the situation deeply uncomfortable, for all sorts of reasons. But after only ten days in Germany, she was establishing a tenuous friendship with Frau Braun, using sign language and a small English-German dictionary. With Frederick's approval, she'd asked her to help with their first dinner party.

All might have been well if Aphrodite Barclay hadn't decided to drop in unannounced on the morning of the party, to which she and her husband had been invited. "Thought you could do with some moral support," she explained, but it was more probable she was at a loose end, like so many of the wives out there. It was the first time she'd seen the house and its lovely garden, and it straightaway became obvious that the quarters she and her husband had been given didn't compare. "Nice!" she kept saying, in a clipped kind of way. But when Celia explained the situation with the Brauns, she observed: "At least we don't have to put up with that."

"Come and look at the food," Celia suggested eagerly in much the same spirit as she might have asked Aphrodite to admire a newly acquired picture. The evening before, Frederick had brought home a big joint of pork, together with extra butter, sugar, and flour to make a pie. It was black market food, of course, bartered for cigarettes—but justified, he explained with a laugh, when one's commanding officer was coming to dinner.

The two young women headed for the big old-fashioned kitchen, kept immaculately clean by Frau Braun, who'd come in earlier to clear away breakfast and, as usual, remove the used coffee grounds to recycle for her own family.

"Frederick invited the regimental chaplain," Celia told Aphrodite. "He's called Martin Spencer."

"Oops! Have to watch our language, then."

"Frederick says that's why he asked him!"

She was displaying the meat when there came a soft knock at the back door and Frau Braun entered with her usual timid, anxious air. It didn't go with the raised voice they sometimes heard coming from the cellar. Herr Braun and his old parents seemed crushed by war and their own failures. Even the children, Fritz and Ilse, were unnaturally quiet.

With pity, Celia would contrast the German couple's fractious relationship with her own. Bet had been right, of course: Frederick was made for marriage, and so, she now knew, was she. She no longer thought about pretend people in books, following them long after their stories had ended because she couldn't bear to let them go. Memories of passion slowed her movements and clogged her brain. Didn't he suspect how the hours dragged when he was gone? Had he never noticed how she watched his strong beautiful hands, and sometimes shivered with her own imaginings? While her husband spoke of the minutiae of his day she thought only of the night to come.

Now she smiled at Frau Braun, preparing to make an introduction.

But Frau Braun was staring at the pork with an expression of terrible longing. Soon she would have to rub salt over that substantial, yielding fatty flesh before putting it in the oven. Then the delicious smell of roasting meat would gradually fill the kitchen and float through the windows open to the garden, where it would drift back down to her family crammed into the cellar.

All this Celia understood in a flash, and was appalled by her own lack of sensitivity. Impulsively, she scooped up a pile of rations delivered by the army's official trading outlet, NAAFI, the day before—tins of sardines and corned beef and even a couple of bars of chocolate for the children—and pressed them on Frau Braun. She'd give her any meat that was left over from the party, too, she decided. From now on, she would find every way she could of helping the family.

Frau Braun shook her head in disbelief; and then, tears coming to her eyes, she started to smile. But that was before Aphrodite spoke.

"I don't believe this!" she hissed. "Have you forgotten Coventry? They're lucky even to be alive!"

No translation was necessary. Instantly, Frau Braun replaced the tins and the chocolate on the table and turned and left the kitchen. She didn't look at Celia at all. It was as if, in that moment, she regained all her dignity as the true owner of the house.

"Well, good riddance," said Aphrodite and the German woman surely picked up the venom in that, too.

"How could you, Aphrodite?" said Celia, who was frightened of most people. Quite apart from the guilt and dismay, she had a problem on her hands. "I'm going to have to cook the dinner myself now," she said, "and Frederick's so anxious for this party to be a success."

It was a moment before Aphrodite reacted, so what came next couldn't have been entirely impulsive. "Oh don't worry," she said. "He's not expecting you to live up to *her*."

"Who?"

Even then, Aphrodite could probably have extricated herself, but Celia would come to understand she was too angry. It made no difference to her that the army had lifted its original edict not to fraternize with Germans. She was from a family of soldiers, and unused to compromise. "Oops!" she said. "He hasn't told you, has he?"

"Hasn't told me what?" Celia faltered.

"Oh my lord!" said Aphrodite, gathering up her handbag and cardigan. "Forget I said anything!"

When Frederick arrived home, just in time to change into a dinner jacket and prepare the drinks, it was obvious that he scented trouble straightaway. But there was no time to talk because his commanding officer arrived, punctual to the second.

As for Celia, she relived that evening for years, though the only scrap of conversation that came back to her was Frederick informing the company, "My wife was brought up in a beautiful house on the south coast." But she could remember her own terror, and wanting to be sick, and Aphrodite's mixture of contempt and self-righteousness whenever their eyes met. But there was no shortage of alcohol to jolly things along—there never was at army gatherings—and the food was all gobbled up even though the pork was dry and tasteless from overcooking and the pastry for the fruit pie was pale and soggy and the custard was like glue. It was a wonderful evening, everyone kept saying. It only confirmed what Celia had absorbed as a child living among servants: appearance had little to do with reality.

She'd guessed the truth at least two hours before her husband confirmed it. There had been a previous wife. Beyond that appalling fact, she knew nothing.

"Damn Aphrodite!" Frederick exploded. "She had no right to tell you about Katherine!"

They were outside by then, and Celia thought of the Brauns, all packed into a small damp space for the night, hearing raised voices and speculating about a handsome older husband and a fearful young wife.

She'd learned something—a name. It had slithered into her innocent young life like a poisonous snake. Now she understood the reason for not marrying in church. There had been a painful divorce.

The guests had stayed unnaturally late. After their fulsome thank-yous had faded into the night, Celia had fled the house, too. Frederick had followed, and now they were standing at the far end of the garden by the Brauns' vegetable patch, which had a glut of ripe tomatoes. The bursting intensity of their aroma brought tears to Celia's eyes: somehow she hadn't expected German tomatoes to smell exactly like the ones Mr. Peters had grown at Far Point.

"You're cold," Frederick observed, removing his dinner jacket.

She shook her head, though she was shivering. She'd caught a glimpse of herself in Frau Braun's gilded, cherub-adorned mirror on the wall by the front door: no longer radiant and dreamy-eyed but shockingly young and ashen-faced. Was that why Martin Spencer, the regimental chaplain, who'd turned out to be funny and indiscreet, had pressed her shoulder as he left?

"I insist." Frederick was already wrapping her in his jacket. He went on, sounding strangely formal: "I don't know how much Aphrodite told you."

"Nothing! She wouldn't't!" She was remembering that mixture of slyness and apprehension, the way Aphrodite had clammed up immediately after dropping her bombshell.

"Ah!"

She guessed he was relieved to be able to tell the story in his own way. Would he reprimand Aphrodite for what had at best been thoughtlessness, at worst malice? Knowing how greatly he prized courtesy and detested confrontation in personal relationships, she doubted it. He was more likely to avoid his old friend's wife from now on.

A fearful thought struck her. "We are married, aren't we?" she whispered, remembering the fate of one of her favorite heroines, Jane Eyre. Her wedding ring had belonged to his paternal grandmother. Hidden inside was "For G., forever, E." *G* was Geoffrey, apparently, and *E* was Elizabeth. It had never occurred to her to ask for it to be re-engraved. She'd felt only honored. But now it occurred to her that Katherine, who'd surely been offered the same ring, must have rejected it. Then she thought of a worse scenario: Katherine *had* worn the ring and, after the breakup, had been required to return it to the family. Celia pulled it from her finger for the first time since her wedding and moonlight glinted off it like telling tales.

"What?" He sounded astonished. "Of

course we're married! Speaking of which, you'll drop that if you're not careful and then we'll never find it!"

"It was hers, too, wasn't it?"

He said with a frightening hint of temper: "How dare you suggest such a thing!" He added more equably: "Katherine still has her ring."

Though this puzzled her, she let it pass. "What was she like?"

He failed to reply. Had she offended him by being too direct? The truth was, even now he intimidated her. He was so much older, so much more experienced and socially accomplished, where she only felt shy and gauche.

"Katherine," she prompted in a whisper, and thought with a strange envy of Frau Braun, who might no longer love her husband but would never be disappointed by him.

"Katherine," he repeated, and something happened to his composure. "Excuse me," he muttered. He came right up to her and she felt his hands tremble as he searched the pockets of his jacket. He was so close that she could smell the Brilliantine on his hair before the acrid whiff of nicotine drowned it out. He was a disciplined smoker, but this was his second cigarette since leaving the house. "She was . . ." She'd never before witnessed that handsome and confident man struggle for words. Pity almost impelled her to excuse him from this ordeal, but she waited with a sickening mixture of dread and impatience.

"I don't know how you begin to describe someone," he said eventually, sounding lost and helpless.

"Beautiful?" she suggested, though it was agonizing.

She heard him draw on his cigarette and, in the silence of the night, it sounded like a prolonged kiss. "I suppose people said that about her, yes," he agreed in a measured kind of way.

A part of her noted that it was clever of him to attribute the opinion to others. She was remembering what he'd told her soon after their meeting on the beach: "I love your shy but direct eyes and your generous mouth and your wise forehead." No mention of beauty, though.

"Look," he said, "this is all very unfortunate. . . . I *was* going to tell you about her when the time was right."

She wanted to believe him. And it was true that there had been little chance to talk because, though they'd been married for nearly two years, they'd been separated for most of it. Then she remembered how, after moving to Far Point, her mother had never spoken of her father again, so it would come to seem to her as if she'd only ever had one parent. If a woman like her mother could shut off the pain of the past, how much more likely was a professional soldier to do so?

"I'm wondering if there's anything to be gained," he went on. "*We're* all right, aren't we?"

"I need to know what happened," she insisted with uncharacteristic fierceness. She decided to think about him describing them as merely "all right" later.

"Very well," he agreed eventually. "But then let that be the end of it."

She nodded in the dark.

"Do I have your word, Celia?" he demanded.

"I promise."

"I never want to talk about this again."

"I promise."

But he was clearly finding it very hard to

begin. She knew his contempt for people who "whinge on about themselves," as he put it, and guessed how greatly he must hate having to relive his humiliation before her, of all people.

She decided to help him. "How did you meet?"

A second or two passed and when he answered, his voice had changed. It had become gentle and pleased, as if a spell had been cast all over again. "The first time I ever saw her was at Oxford. She was crossing a lawn, and I asked someone who she was, and he said, 'Don't you know? That's Katherine Cooper-Seymour. Everyone's talking about her.'" He hesitated, as if words couldn't begin to convey the effect on him. "And that was pretty much it."

"I see."

"I couldn't believe it when she chose me!" he marveled in that eager, boyish way as if he'd been taken so thoroughly back to the past that he'd momentarily forgotten all courtesy and tact.

"She was clever then, too," said Celia, trying to make a joke.

"Well, obviously!" Suddenly his mood

flipped. "*I* wasn't, though! I should have known, shouldn't I? I should have guessed!"

Silence fell in the dark garden and once more she took pity on him, as if she'd become the older, protective one. "Where did you marry?"

"Ah!" As she'd hoped, his voice had lightened again. "The church in the Devon village where Katherine was brought up. It was a lovely service, a beautiful day. It really seemed as if . . ." His voice tailed away. After a moment he resumed briskly: "I'd been commissioned by then and I was raring to go." Then he said something strange for such a practical man: "Is it possible a part of us knows what's going to happen?"

"What do you mean?" she asked, very puzzled.

Suddenly her hand was grasped with such strength that she almost cried out. "She wanted to travel," he said, "and she loved the sun. But she was afraid of going to India."

It was the first time India had ever been mentioned. Obviously he'd been posted there, soon after the marriage. It must have been where everything had collapsed. To add to the humiliation, had his rival been a colleague, or even a friend?

"The rest you know."

"I told you! I don't! I didn't even know you'd been in India."

"Ah!" he said, as if he'd be content to leave it at that.

"She left you."

He murmured something, and a second later there was the flare of another match and she thought how that proud man must hate it being spelled out.

"Where is she now?" she asked fearfully, because what if Katherine realized her mistake and came to reclaim him? She felt sick, even contemplating it.

"There, of course." He seemed astonished.

"Still in India? What's she doing?"

"*What is she doing?!*" He'd gone from quiet humiliation to fury, without changing gear. "What in hell do you *imagine* poor Katherine is doing? What would *you* do in a grave?"

Celia was so shocked that she couldn't speak.

"You didn't know she was dead?"

"I told you! Aphrodite said nothing!" she repeated, her voice shaking with terror.

He must have believed her because he calmed down, and even apologized. However, now the moment had come, he seemed unable to tell her more than the bare facts. One minute twenty-two-year-old Katherine had been laughing and full of life; almost the next, she was interred in a foreign grave. Years later, he sounded as if he still couldn't comprehend it. Because of the heat, the funeral had to be held within twenty-four hours (he related this almost coldly, though his voice trembled), and once that was over he'd completed the posting, before returning to England nine months later. Then he fell silent like someone utterly spent, and she couldn't bear to inflict more questions on him.

It was up to her to imagine what had been left out. Katherine must have died of cholera or some other tropical disease. It happened in such harsh climes. She thought of hope put away like an unused wedding present; nobody to hold his hand at the hastily arranged funeral; his first dreadful return to an empty house. But, knowing his character, he would have rejected compassionate leave. He'd have assured the army and everyone else he was fine, and, to add to his tragedy, they believed him.

"When the war came along," he said eventually, "it was a blessing for me." He laughed without amusement. "Frankly, I didn't care if I lived or died. That's probably why I ended up with a Military Cross." But after a moment, his voice softened. "Then I met you . . ."

"Chapter two," thought Celia, with a strange disconnected flippancy. "It seems to be a habit with him, picking a wife at first sight. Perhaps it's because he's already decided what he wants—first a beautiful, brilliant girl everyone will envy; then someone shy and ordinary he can control. . . ."

Suddenly she shivered with recognition because, give or take a few details, she was in another favorite novel—a worldwide best-seller devoured on the sofa in the library at Far Point. Here was another handsome, much older widower, another unequal marriage haunted by a charismatic first wife. And she might as well have been an orphan, like the girl in the book, because of the way she'd been separated from her mother. True, there was no fabulous Manderley in this version, just his parents' freezing, inhospitable house in Wiltshire, where nobody had seen fit to enlighten her about Katherine, either.

"I know it was wrong of me not to have told you. As I said, it *was* my intention when the time was right. For the record, I'd vowed never to marry again." He gave a deep deep sigh, then he seemed to rouse himself. "But that evening on the beach at Far Point, everything changed. You were so young and fresh. I only had to look into your face to know you could never deceive me. I know I've hurt you, but please understand—I believed I was acting for the best."

"But when I asked . . ." Her voice faltered. "When I asked about other women, you said there'd been no one important."

"I did," he admitted, sounding deeply ashamed.

And then it dawned on her that he had not actually said he loved Katherine. Furthermore, if he'd been so happy, why had he vowed never to marry again? He could have had any girl he wanted, but instead he chose the daughter of a servant, as shy and humble as the second unnamed Mrs. de Winter. "'I only had to look into your face to know you could never deceive me'"—an odd thing to say, in the circumstances. Had Katherine, like Rebecca de Winter, shown her dark side, once married? Suddenly it seemed perfectly possible that sooner rather than later he'd explode with the shocking truth: "You think I loved Katherine? I *hated* her!"

A breeze stirred the air. She heard it rattle in the trees at the end of the garden as if the leaves were applauding her.

Then he cleared his throat and told her quietly, "Katherine was an angel. But sometimes one's only hope of survival is to walk away and not look back." He paused. "You asked for the truth. Now we must put it behind us and concentrate on the future."

It wasn't possible. Katherine's shadow lay between them now. To make it still worse, she'd learned nothing. Obviously, Katherine had been wonderful and adored. But had she been fair or dark, tall or short, slight or voluptuous? Was her voice whispery and childish or husky and assured?

At dinner in the evenings, had she striven to amuse him, all the time fearing she wasn't interesting enough? Or had they discoursed seriously, as intellectual equals? Most painful of all, had she been passionate?

"Please!" he begged. "We've talked about it now. You agreed that would be the end."

She thought, strangely distanced: "It *is* the end, but not in the way he thinks. How can it be anything else?"

Then the moon glided out from behind a cloud and the big lush garden took shape, though without color, as if seen through dirty water. He looked exhausted, with his hair falling over his forehead, but she could think only of the next time he'd touch her and the next, and wondered dully if he'd felt the same helpless desire for Katherine. She'd never been more vulnerable and frightened: as powerless as a reader turning a page. She could see now that infatuation had blinded her from the start. Katherine had always been part of the marriage. It explained the lost, anguished look on his face sometimes, his sudden upsetting silences. The difference now was that his first great love had been acknowledged. In the space of minutes, Katherine had become so real to Celia that she fancied she could pick up a faint thread of musky perfume in that cool foreign garden. And she believed she could sense triumph, too, as if the ghost of the other woman had been waiting very patiently for this moment.

CHAPTER NINE

**When I return to that familiar house in
dreams, I'm a trespasser. Everything is
the same except for the extra room. If I
were to draw a map, I could place it exactly, halfway between the two stair-
cases, one carpeted and silent, the
other bare. The door is always locked
and I hear moaning behind it and I am
very afraid.**

Written on the back of a lunch menu
from the Coq d'Or restaurant,
Stratton Street, Piccadilly, dated
September 30, 1946.

"It *was* fun, wasn't it?" said Priscilla, and
for a moment she seemed the same girl
who'd sat in bell-bottoms in a cold garden,
warming her chilblained hands on a tin

mug of hot tea while the sea stroked the shore just out of sight. Then she settled her mink wrap around her shoulders and touched her diamond engagement ring, as if taking an inventory. A waiter presented her with a bottle of wine, and she tasted it very expertly before giving him a curt nod.

Bet beamed at the waiter to compensate for Priscilla's imperiousness. She was behaving abominably, thought Celia, considering what the lunch must be costing. But it was Priscilla's fault. Had she lost all sensitivity? Was she deliberately setting out to show that, now the war was over, she and Bet had nothing in common?

It felt surreal. England was almost as ruined and bankrupt as Germany, but here the three of them were in one of London's top restaurants, the Coq d'Or, eating steak and mushrooms at four shillings and six-pence apiece and drinking the finest claret.

When Celia had telephoned Priscilla and Bet to say she'd returned to England to see her mother, they'd been delighted. They all decided to meet for lunch, though Priscilla had insisted on a condition: "My treat." But they were still out of breath from hurrying down Piccadilly from the Café

Royal, where they'd eaten the first course of oysters.

"*Everyone* lunches on the hoof," Priscilla kept assuring them, as if that excused the inconvenience. And it was true that on the way to Green Park, they'd met a group of her friends spilling out of the Ritz. "Isn't this fun?" they'd shrieked before heading toward Mayfair and Claridge's. As Priscilla explained, it was a way of getting round the rationing laws that prohibited spending more than five shillings per person on food in any one restaurant. "How else can one have a decent lunch?" she'd demanded ingenuously, and seemed not to hear when Bet protested that you could get an excellent three-course set-price menu for well under five shillings at Lyons Corner House. She seemed very nervy for someone who'd just become engaged, but there was no time to talk properly because when she wasn't greeting friends she was looking at her watch and fretting about the next table. Soon, they were due at the Café Anglais, where she'd assured them the crêpes were sublime.

She seemed very much at home in these top restaurants. "You should have seen the *broche*," she said, making a strange guttural sound in her throat. "It means a 'spit.' It was just over there. Before the war, there were dozens of chickens, going round and round on it. We used to drop in and watch, just for the fun." She gave a tinkling laugh. "It was as good as going to the cinema!"

"I don't go to the pictures to see dead birds!" scoffed Bet, trying to catch Celia's eye.

The rich food stuck in Celia's throat. She'd longed for a taste of the old fun and camaraderie. But this was like having to watch one more precious thing destroyed.

Then a man at a nearby table exclaimed very loudly and angrily: "Damn and blast! There's a maggot in my spinach!"

The restaurant went ominously quiet.

A man at the same table clicked his fingers: "Waiter!" But just as the offending plate was about to be whisked away, he said loudly: "I say, my good man, what is the meaning of this shocking discrimination? Bring me one of your finest maggots forthwith!"

A gale of laughter swept the room; even

the staff joined in. It was so silly. They must all have appreciated it even as they wiped away tears. But a year after the end of the war, the euphoria had evaporated and London was still in ruins. No wonder they reacted so hysterically.

"Cheers!" said Bet. She went on, sounding gruff and awkward, "Thanks, Priscilla."

"I only meant to spoil you," Priscilla explained, as they clinked glasses. "You don't know how I've missed you." Her fiancé was called Rupert Wardley and he was a viscount, which apparently meant that one day, when he became an earl, she'd have to get used to a new surname. The wedding wasn't for months, but all her time was taken up with dress fittings and making lists of guests and presents. "I'd no idea it was so complicated getting married. Even if I wanted to, I couldn't call it off!" She added more soberly, "I think my mother would kill me."

"Priscilla?" said Bet, all of a sudden very stern and anxious.

Something happened to Priscilla's pretty face. Her eyes filled with panic and her mouth trembled. But even as she seemed to be struggling to express herself, the moment passed. Besides, as she'd just informed them, her mother was already planning the flowers. "Roop and I are a good team," she said, like reciting tables. After that, she glanced at her watch, and Celia guessed that the whole expensive, disjointed exercise had been designed to scupper any chance of a proper conversation.

Bet sighed and turned her attention elsewhere. "I'm surprised Frederick let you go, Celia."

"Well, she missed her mother," said Priscilla. She giggled. "Remember that evening when we went to Far Point? Such a hoot, having to use the tradesman's entrance! I dined out on it for months. How is she, by the way?"

"Fine," said Celia brightly, because to admit to anything less would be to risk breaking down in tears. What was the point of the lunch, when nobody was being truthful? If only they knew this whole trip was an act of defiance!

She'd found the beach deserted once more, but evidence of the long occupation was everywhere: the concrete lookouts set along the low cliff; the iron jetties built to help send off an armada so massive that, for one extraordinary day, it had really seemed possible to leap from one deck to another and reach the other side of the Solent without touching water. More ominously, there were newly painted signs pegged along the beach warning of the possible presence of mines. She remembered how, as a child, she'd stamped on sticky brown sashes of seaweed to pop their pods. If she tried that now, an enormous explosion might be the last sound she ever heard.

During her absence of almost a year, the house had deteriorated. Some of its white paint had flaked off, and the gate dragged badly (just as her mother had once predicted). There was a reason for this. She'd learned from letters that Mr. Peters had suffered a heart attack and the doctor had forbidden him to work.

She paused at the lime tree in the courtyard where she and Frederick had once posed for engagement photographs. Her mother had been entrusted with the camera. "Smile!" she'd urged quite unnecessarily. A moment later, she'd captured

Lady Falconbridge hastening out of the house, bearing a bottle of prewar champagne. But nobody had taken a picture of her disappearing through the tradesman's entrance soon afterward to prepare lunch.

Celia slapped the tree's crusty trunk, like chiding it for being a party to a deception. There was no way Katherine hadn't been in Frederick's thoughts that day. It was only strange that the magic of photography hadn't picked her up: a beautiful woman on his other side, soft hand laid possessively on his arm. Celia envisaged him in the big house in Germany, alone except for the Brauns in the cellar, conjuring company out of emptiness. Of all people, she knew how easy it was. "Katherine," he'd call softly, just as, long ago, she'd summoned her imaginary friend Naomi. A moment later, he'd hear a soft step and then would come Katherine, his dead wife, forever beautiful and beloved.

"Darling!" Helen hastened out of the tradesman's entrance, wearing her old blue-and-white—striped apron.

Celia fell into her mother's arms and cried and cried.

"My precious child," Helen murmured,

hugging her close. She smelled different—like old lard mingled with sour milk—and her body no longer yielded plumply to the touch. It couldn't be the same apron, either, Celia found herself thinking, because now the strings were wound twice around her waist. "There!" said Helen briskly, and Celia noticed that the skin under her eyes had become bluish and puckered.

"Are you all right?" she whispered very anxiously, for hadn't her mother's letter given her the courage as well as the excuse to leave Frederick and Germany? "I am not too good at present," it had read, "but I daresay that with God's help I shall survive."

"Of course I am!" Helen assured her a little crossly, as if someone else had penned those words.

"You're sure?" Celia persisted, because it was unthinkable that anything could happen to her mother.

"Yes, yes, yes!" And now it was Helen who looked anxious as Celia felt herself being scrutinized very closely.

Then Lady Falconbridge emerged from the house, beaming goodwill. Wartime and loneliness had cast a spell. Though the two women continued to address each other as "Helen" and "Lady Falconbridge," they dined together in the warm kitchen every night now. "Two eggs are better than one," Lady Falconbridge liked to say, as if expediency alone accounted for the change. But two eggs had created a delicious soufflé. "It's such bliss not to be spied on by those dreadful servants anymore," she once confided, as if Helen cooked and cleaned for her out of friendship.

"Did you know Priscilla was so rich?" Bet asked, as she and Celia threaded their way through the crowds in St. James's Park on the way to her digs, where Celia would stay the night.

"Well, I knew she was different," said Celia, remembering a story of Priscilla's about being robbed as she slept. How many other Wrens had worn expensive pearls under their nightdresses?

Bet stopped to roll a cigarette from the same pale green Capstan tin she'd once carried around in boats. "We won't be invited to that wedding," she predicted. "That's why she kept telling us it was 'up in

Scortland' and 'mostly fam'ly.' And did you see how she behaved when we bumped into her friends? You'd have thought she didn't know us!"

"She loves you," said Celia sincerely.

"On her terms," Bet amended, though she looked gratified. "Well, *I* couldn't do it," she said as if she, too, had the option of marrying an aristocrat with a vast estate.

Once, she'd walked as briskly as a soldier, but now she seemed curiously aimless and apathetic. She stared at the ducks on the newly refilled lake. "It all seems so long ago, doesn't it? Like a different life."

"It does."

Bet began to reminisce about the war but in a grumbling puzzled sort of way, like remembering a disgraceful but irresistible lover. "Being stuffed into that stinking dormitory with girls who were robbing us blind when they weren't keeping us awake with their snoring. Being woken at dawn and ordered to scrub out boats in the freezing cold and rain. Once that bitch of a petty officer made me do it three times before she was satisfied. We were always famished, too. And put in fear of our lives if we so much as breathed a word about what we were doing. We were kids! What did we know?" She gave a deep deep sigh. "I know it was the war. I know it was cruel. I know we're lucky to be alive. But . . ." It was as if even she, with her audacious spirit, couldn't bring herself to admit it. Would life ever again be so good?

Celia was watching a couple exchange lingering kisses on a bench. They looked at each other so tenderly and intimately, but she knew about secrets now—those dark hidden surprises. She had said nothing to her mother about Katherine. But Bet would tell her what to do. Maybe, given her independence of spirit, she'd advise her to leave the marriage for good.

However, Bet was still talking about the war. "Remember how wonderful everyone looked in uniform? Men were men then!"

"You could always go back to the Wrens."

But Bet insisted, shaking her head, "It wouldn't be the same." She added, "Perhaps *I* should get married," but she sounded as if the prospect depressed her.

They reached the other side of the park and crossed Westminster Bridge, pausing every so often to lean over and watch the river coiling in dark and mysterious cross-currents beneath. There was more rubbish than ever caught up in it, flotsam and jetsam shunted back and forth by the tide, like a metaphor for the thousands uprooted by war. From the bridge they had a fine view of the damage inflicted on the city: whole streets sliced through, as if a child had carelessly knocked over lines of bricks, patches of burned-out buildings like dark stains.

"Is this it now? All we can look forward to?"

But Celia wasn't listening to Bet anymore because she was worrying about her mother again.

"Skin and bone," Mr. Peters had agreed gloomily. "But she won't see the doctor and Her Ladyship goes along with it." He added absentmindedly, out of long habit, "Bless her!"

Celia had stared at him, terrified. This was typical of her mother, who always behaved as if the human body was an embarrassment—and self-centered Lady Falconbridge, too, for all her late-flowering affability.

"Them two rattling around up there, not getting any younger. . . . Tap dripping in her bathroom, *now* she tells me." He seemed gratified to be kept in the picture but also ashamed—as if the bad heart that prevented him from changing a washer in the big house was a slur on his masculinity. "Blast this ticker!" he exploded, pounding his chest. Then his expression softened. "Look at you! Proper married lady! Seems only yesterday I'd hear you chattering away when I were working that garden. 'Who you talking to, miss?' I'd say, and you'd hold up your dolly—Phoebe, weren't it? Could've swore I seen a black shadow skipping alongside you once. Give me the fright of my life before I seen it were a trick of the sun. Now look at you!" He beamed with pride. "Your mam thinks the world of that husband of yours. 'He's so handsome in his uniform,' she says. 'They'll make him a general any day.'"

"What's wrong with her?"

"Women's trouble?" he'd suggested delicately. Then he shrugged, because the truth was he knew as little as anyone else.

It had felt strange to be visiting his cottage with her mother's blessing. In childhood, it had been forbidden territory, though her mother would never explain why. "He's a man," was all she would say—as if even kind, fatherly Mr. Peters might behave unpredictably on his own territory.

Lacking his attention, the garden had become a jungle and a fig tree sprawled over his corrugated iron roof like a vast green spider. Inside, the air was suffocating, its unpleasant sweetness intensified by the heat blasting from a rusting paraffin stove. She'd looked at the tightly shut windows and the brittle fly corpses scattered over the sills, and remembered his love of sea breezes, and marveled that a man so particular about the look of a shrub or a plant could endure such squalor. Then she felt the dead and endless silence and imagined being trapped there, day after day, with his dog Sparky long gone and only a collection of stained old mugs bearing likenesses of the royal family for company. But he still had an opinion on everything. The Germans were filthy Huns and murderers and he'd wondered out loud how she could stand it, living there. Even so, he appreciated it was her duty to be with her husband. They all did.

What would he say about a war hero who had lacked the courage to mention a previous wife? "He thinks of her all the time, Mr. Peters—I see it in his face. Sometimes I say something and he frowns and I know he's comparing us. Or I'll speak and he won't even hear me because he's thinking of her. She's started coming between us at night, too. But he won't talk about it, and I can't ask because I promised not to. And there's something else . . ." But in the end, all she had said tearfully was, "I don't know what to do."

He'd seemed under the impression they were still talking about her mother. "You're here now, ain't you?" Then she had felt the touch of his big rough hand. "Best medicine in the world, family."

"It must have been hard, leaving," said Bet. Her little room was freezing and she had been attempting to light the fire for some time. But although the gas kept popping away expectantly, the matches died the moment they were struck. "Nothing works," she grumbled.

"It's only for a night," said Celia. No wonder Bet was depressed, she thought. This was a terrible place to live. A tiny low-ceilinged room in a run-down part of London, it looked onto a brick wall and had a single gas ring and a shared bathroom that stank. One wall looked as if someone had once punched a hole in it, then carried out an unsuccessful repair. There was a narrow divan bed with a clump of lumpy, stained old cushions, which Celia assumed the two of them would sleep in later.

Bet shook her head, smiling. "Don't be daft! I wasn't talking about your mum—I was talking about that gorgeous husband of yours. Catch me leaving a man like that! I should be so lucky!" As if in response to this mention of Frederick, the fire ignited in a sheet of quivering, almost sexual blue flame. "You hungry?" She was talking too much, like she'd been doing ever since they'd left Priscilla. "Silly question!" she said, because even though they'd just eaten lunch in three of London's finest restaurants, there were years of hunger to make up for. She heaved open the window, wedging one shoulder under it while she removed from the sill outside a small, discolored packet wrapped in newspaper and a covered bowl. "Kidneys!" she crowed. "And dripping!"

"Remember you asking me if Frederick had had other women . . ." But even as Celia was struggling to bring this out, Bet started talking about herself. "I'm always so careful," she said as she peeled the foil from a bottle of Hirondelle.

Celia stared at her, puzzled. She was remembering how Bet had jeered at Priscilla's caution during their years as Wrens, when they'd been surrounded and outnumbered by men. "What are you keeping it for?" she'd mocked. And once, when Priscilla had retaliated with uncharacteristic coarseness and called her a tart, she'd laughed and said, "Life's for living!"

"I am careful," she repeated, shaking her head. "I was!" Clearly she was troubled; but she couldn't resist a joke. She poured the inky wine into a tin mug and tasted it with precisely the same frowning pretentious expression Priscilla had assumed at lunch.

Celia was beginning to understand now. As a married woman, "being careful" had only one meaning. Frederick said it often—

"You are being careful, aren't you?" He was very anxious to postpone having a family until they were properly settled. He'd made her go to the doctor to be fitted with a pessary.

"I'm nearly three weeks late," Bet admitted.

"The father . . ."

Bet made a face.

"You have told him?" Celia persisted.

Bet shrugged. "He's his own family to think about, hasn't he?"

So nothing had changed. Celia thought of the dozens of unattached men who'd passed through Island View, none of whom Bet had seemed to notice. Once Priscilla had described her as her own worst enemy, and Celia had pondered the cliché and decided that it was precisely Bet's contradictory nature—the astringency balanced by warmth—that made her such wonderful company.

She was more critical now. She remembered all the wives who'd been deceived and betrayed. She even thought: "No wonder Frederick didn't want me to go on being friends with her."

"Your family . . ." she began.

Bet shrugged. "What about them?"

"Do you love him?" Celia asked, frowning. She saw from the big alarm clock ticking away on the mantelpiece that it was early still. If she left now, she could catch a train from Waterloo and arrive at Far Point while it was still light. She could join her mother and Lady Falconbridge as they sat at the table in the warm kitchen, drinking cocoa. She thought with strange longing of the company of those old-fashioned women who'd only ever been with one man.

Bet actually laughed. "What's love got to do with it?"

"You have to tell him."

"Could be," Bet agreed with another mirthless smile, "'cause I can't do this on my own."

"Do what?"

Bet shrugged. "I'll have to get it seen to, won't I?"

Celia knew what Bet was talking about because, once married, she'd been let in on the suffering of women, including the horror of childbirth, of course. But Bet didn't seem distressed, as if abortion was no more traumatic than having a tooth pulled. Then she confounded Celia. Perhaps she recognized that their friendship hung by a thread. "What am I doing to myself?" she whispered. "Oh, Celia, you're so lucky, and I'm glad."

"No!" Celia protested, thinking that at last the opportunity had come to talk about Katherine.

But Bet was obsessed by her own situation. She didn't even like the man, she said. He was a selfish pig—"Aren't they all?" It was the first time Celia had seen her cry and for a long while the tears got in the way. "You're so lucky, Celia! You expect people to be good."

"No," Celia insisted, but it was useless.

"Can't believe I'm here again," said Bet, and more tears rolled down her cheeks.

"Your family . . ." Celia reminded her once more.

"You can forget *them*," said Bet. She seemed convinced that if she went home pregnant, her parents would turn her away. "No choice," she concluded, slugging down the grainy crimson dregs of the Hirondelle.

"Where will you . . . ?" Celia began.

"Don't ask," said Bet with a bitter little smile. She added briskly, with a frown: "Done."

"Well, I'm glad you told me. Really, I am."

Eventually, they settled top to toe in the divan bed.

"I'm not saying anything to Priscilla," Bet warned.

Celia thought of Priscilla, who still closed up like a mussel when asked what she'd done in the war yet seized on tittle-tattle about anything else. She squeezed Bet's foot in a silent promise, feeling as if a knot had been tied between the two of them. "Bet," she whispered, preparing to pull it tighter. But Bet had fallen asleep, exhausted by all the emotion.

Celia was beginning to understand there was good reason why she'd been prevented from telling her story. Fate meant her to return to Germany and Frederick. Even her mother (who hated the thought of losing her) had started to ask when she was leaving. Frederick was a fine husband with a splendid future—everyone said so. And there was another more pressing reason for going back. Despite her pessary, she was nearly four months pregnant—something she hadn't dared tell Frederick and now felt unable to reveal to Bet.

The flavor of that night stayed with her

for a long time—the two of them young and pregnant and scared. As it turned out, Bet was right to call her lucky. Often Celia would reflect that, had their situations been reversed, she would never have known her Robert and learned about a different kind of love.

CHAPTER TEN

**MY PLANS FOR THE FUTURE,
BY ROBERT BAYLEY, AGED
EIGHT YEARS, TWO MONTHS,
THREE WEEKS, AND FOUR DAYS.
When I grow up, I am going to be a millionaire. I will give some of my money
to charities. I will buy myself a helicopter and a yacht and I will have a private
zoo and chocolate cake for every meal.**
Found in a box with other family
memorabilia, old school reports, etc.

Looking very spruce in cavalry twills and a
sweater, Robert was experimenting with
the Apple computer Guy had given him as
a retirement present. He was well aware
of his son's motives and shocked to have
so much money spent on him; but he was

being seduced by the computer's brisk efficiency. It was made for lists.

1. Close hot water shave every day, regardless of plans.
2. Clean smart clothes, ditto, ditto.
3. Help Mel more in the kitchen. Take cordon bleu course with view to more dinner parties?
4. Sort rubbish properly.
5. Learn to play bridge.
6. Eat less cheese.
7. Spend more time with sisters.
8. Make start on memoirs to keep brain ticking over.
9. Put kibosh on book about Mummy. We have had *quite enough* attention as a family.

There was a screamingly obvious tenth resolution, but as usual he pushed the Miranda problem to the back of his mind. He knew he was behaving badly and this made him even more miserable.

It was half past nine on the first day of his retirement and—in a panic now that he'd finished with the list—he decided to work out a proper budget. Money was an

increasing concern, though Mel kept telling him they were perfectly comfortably
off. He objected to "perfectly comfortably."
He wanted fun. What if he lived to be over
eighty, like his mother? How far would their
income stretch then? And now, to add to
their problems, they'd acquired an elderly
pet, which would almost certainly lead
to astronomical vet's bills. The price of
dog food was a revelation. "It might even
come to the three of us dining on Tesco
Choice Cuts," he reflected somberly. Still,
it pleased him to have Oscar lying under
his desk. After all, during her last years, his
mother had spent far more time with the
animal than with any of them. He was gratified that it seemed to prefer his company
to Mel's.

"Daft old thing!" he said, patting the dog's
head.

What else had he achieved so far that
day? Besides spending quality time with
Oscar, he'd polished his shoes, cleaned
his teeth with dental floss the way Mel was
always nagging him to, and employed several cotton buds in a useless attempt to
clear the wax that must be bunging up his
left ear: though he had a problem hearing

properly, he refused even to consider the possibility that he might be going deaf.

Suddenly time was sliced into two distinct parts—then and now. During the "then" period—a respectable but unremarkable career in the army—he'd enjoyed a measure of authority but never enough time. Now that had been reversed. Even so, he noticed that on this first morning of his so-called life of leisure even the familiar act of shaving took longer. He cast another look over the list he'd just spent more than half an hour composing and saw it as a mess of senile ramblings. The fact was, as a man in his sixties, he'd woken up with no idea how he was going to spend even the next week. He was so overwhelmed by self-pity that when the telephone rang he didn't pick up. He couldn't cope with his son Guy (or anyone else) asking him how he was doing, with the nagging implication that he should be considering some kind of voluntary work. He hadn't ruled it out—he'd been brought up to believe in public service—but definitely wasn't up for it yet.

After a minute or so, there came a soft tap at the door. It was Mel, of course, who always knocked, being considerate and courteous. He knew she understood how he felt, though he'd confided very little. That was the thing about a good marriage: you didn't need to spell things out. At least he'd achieved that, he told himself, although since Miranda's shocking announcement, he and Mel had been going through a miserably disconnected patch, and they hadn't discussed that either.

"I'm not interrupting anything, am I?"

"Quite all right, my love!" he assured Mel, closing his computer. He managed to appear both welcoming and abstracted, a man disturbed in the middle of important business though happy to see his wife. As usual, her sweet protectiveness was deeply comforting. Sometimes he'd shiver, remembering the parade of uncaring blondes who'd preceded her. He'd fallen in love with Mel after their marriage, not before, and thanked God for his good instinct.

"The phone," she informed him unnecessarily. "It's Rodney Cartwright."

"Ah!" He'd been expecting this call from his mother's solicitor about the will. He passed his hand over his face from brow to chin, like preparing it for serious business. There'd be no real money left because of the constant drain of nursing bills over more than twenty years. Furthermore, it was possible that his mother had amassed debts that would eat into any future profits from the sale of the house. Women were bad with money, he reminded himself, and she'd never shown much interest in it. Even so, she'd fiercely rejected any offers of help. He understood it had been about maintaining independence. "Very important for old people," he reminded himself gloomily.

"I'd better take it," he told Mel, already picking up the phone.

"Robert?"

"Rodney! Good to hear you!"

"I wondered if you and Margaret and Sarah would mind coming into the office one day this week? We've things to discuss."

"Of course!" he agreed enthusiastically, even though his mother's will had to be pretty straightforward. He wondered briefly why the solicitor hadn't spelled out the details in a letter. "Silly me!" he chastised himself with a sardonic smile because the whole world was bent on making a fast buck. What did country solicitors charge?

Probably the bill for the three of them quite unnecessarily traveling down from London in order to spend an hour or so at Rodney's office exchanging platitudes before being told the obvious (with a cup of tea and a couple of limp digestive biscuits thrown in) wouldn't leave much change from five hundred pounds. The clock was ticking even now on the solicitor's desk. "All right for some," he thought grimly. "Obviously I've spent my life in the wrong business." But he said extremely amiably: "I'll have to check with my sisters and get back to you." He explained: "Sarah's down at Parr's, sorting out stuff."

He rang off as soon as he decently could. They'd go in his car, he decided, since he considered both Margaret and Sarah to be poor drivers, and have lunch in a pub on the way. It would be an excellent opportunity to put one of his resolutions into practice. He found himself looking forward to a day out. A project. Suddenly life appeared brighter. But then a photo of Miranda's laughing face caught his eye and he was overwhelmed by despair. Until now, every step of his beloved daughter's life had brought him such pride. What had possessed her?

As it turned out, the journey a couple of days later wasn't enjoyable. His sisters bickered all the way, even during lunch, which he paid for. But they'd never really got on, apart from a short-lived truce at the time of the funeral. Sarah's obsession with her marital problems was certainly trying, but Margaret wasn't helping. Her way of disagreeing was to fall silent, which just encouraged Sarah to repeat herself.

"I know Whoopee loves me," she insisted. "I know I'll always be the most important woman in his life. He's not going to throw everything away, is he?"

"Of course not," Robert muttered from the driver's seat—even though, for as long as he'd known him, his brother-in-law had professed to despise what he called "people who live safe little bourgeois lives."

But Margaret just pursed her lips and stared out of the window.

"What are you saying?" was Sarah's panic-stricken reaction.

But Margaret wouldn't answer that, either.

"My beauty," their father had called Margaret when they were all young, and Sarah had been "funny one." Contemplating his sisters more than half a century on, Robert saw that Margaret now looked much like any other woman in late middle age and Sarah had temporarily (and unsurprisingly) lost her sense of humor.

It was a real relief to escape from the car.

Welcoming them to his plush, modern office, Rodney Cartwright twinkled with goodwill. He asked if they'd had a nice trip down and they murmured enthusiastically. And then he inquired after the rest of the family, even though he'd seen them at the funeral only three weeks before. In return, he was assured with more beaming smiles that everyone was in excellent health, thank you very much, and doing splendidly. Nobody informed him that Whoopee had left the marital home and Miranda was pregnant by a stranger's sperm found on the Internet.

"Ah well, better get down to business," he said once his secretary (who they'd also known for years) had brought in a tray of tea and some exceptionally nice chocolate biscuits. Even so, he seemed reluctant to begin and they thought they understood why. He was a family friend and, for all his skin of professionalism, must dread being the purveyor of bad news. He was going to tell them there was nothing left.

For Sarah, this would be particularly bleak. She and Whoopee had always been short of money, though he'd affected not to care. If he set up permanently with his girlfriend, the family house would have to be sold. Robert had told Sarah that he wished he was in a position to help. In truth, only Margaret, married to a rich man, would be untouched by the contents of the will.

"I must congratulate you all," Rodney Cartwright told them, "on having such a very talented mother."

They hid their impatience. What they didn't appreciate was that, despite years of talking about money to grieving families, today was a new experience for the lawyer. Much as he liked them, some devil in him enjoyed prolonging the suspense.

"Disaster," Robert informed Mel when he got home. He caught sight of his face in the mirror that hung over the fireplace in the sitting room and thought he looked uncannily like his mother's old dog: mournful, resigned, though receptive to any affection that might be going. "Huge debts. Vast. There'll be nothing left. It's even worse than we feared."

Mel let out a horrified gasp but instantly recovered, just as he'd known she would. "We'll manage," she assured him. "It's not the end of the world."

"Isn't it?" He kept his head down, as if he couldn't bring himself to look into her anxious eyes.

"Of course not." He could hear the effort she was making and almost kissed her. "We're so lucky, really. We have all the things that matter."

"Have we?" he asked dully.

"Of course! A lovely family life and good health and, and . . ." Surely she couldn't be about to mention Miranda's baby?

"SURPRISE!" he bellowed, making her jump just like he'd done at the funeral service. He produced a bottle of champagne from behind his back. Then he seized hold of her and waltzed her round the room. "Hooray!" he cheered as he popped the

cork. But he made her drink a whole glass-
ful before he explained.

Mel couldn't take it in, so he kept repeating the facts.

"No debts at all. *Au contraire!*"

"You can't be serious!"

"Nearly two million squidaroonies in the
black. You'd better believe it, my love!"

"That includes what you get for the
house?"

"Nope! Mummy made serious money
since Daddy died! She must have easily
made back whatever his nursing bills came
to. And that's not the end of it by a long
chalk because now the books are selling
all over the shop. Of course, there'll be inheritance tax—but even so! It means
Sarah doesn't have to worry, whatever that
ass Whoopee decides. And Margaret will
have a bit of money of her own, which has
got to improve her temper. We're rich, Mel!
Good old Mummy, God bless her!"

"This is awful!"

It was his turn to be shocked. He gog-
gled at her. "Huh?"

She enjoyed her moment, too. Then
she informed him: "I've made us a horrible

dinner. Leek and potato pie. I'd started an economy drive."

"Give it to me," said Robert solemnly.

"What?"

He snapped his fingers. "Do as you're told, woman!"

She obeyed, giggling, and he dumped the pie in the trash bin.

"You and me are going out to dinner, my love, and bugger the cost." He turned to Oscar. "And you, old chum, will be having a plate of the finest filet steak tomorrow."

"We have to phone the children!"

His beaming goodwill faltered momentarily and she thought sadly how, until so recently, Miranda had been the second person he'd always wanted to share any good fortune with. Then he pronounced: "Tomorrow. Tonight is for us, my love."

"How clever she was!" Mel marveled as they left the house hand in hand.

"A very superior female," Robert pronounced, with the air of one talking about a rare species indeed.

"But we never asked her about her books. I feel awful now!"

"Watch out!" he said, steering her away from a pool of vomit on the pavement. Then he pointed out reasonably, "She never talked about them either." His own indifference had stemmed from the conviction that writing about pretend people wasn't a serious job. But he was obviously going to have to rethink this. Fiction could be extremely lucrative. Instead of making a start on his memoirs, as he'd planned, he decided to take a crack at it himself. A thriller, set among the higher echelons of army personnel? Steamy, yet authoritative . . . it could be a best-seller.

"Your mother was a very private sort of person, wasn't she?" observed Mel thoughtfully, as they reached the restaurant.

"Hallelujah to that!"

CHAPTER ELEVEN

This is how it starts—I think "what if?" It's assuming a kind of control, I suppose—though, as it goes on, my characters surprise me, and that's when it becomes wonderful. Graham Greene's "splinter of ice in the heart" thing is wrong—for me at least. Being able to talk to those who understand this strangeness is like becoming fluent at last.

Written in notebook, no date.

The day after the visit to the solicitor, when she was alone, Margaret settled herself on the elegant sofa in her sitting room and at last started reading one of her mother's novels. She felt it was owed, though she didn't need the money like Robert and Sarah.

Perhaps it was the title, *A Good Man,* which impelled her to pick up that particular book. She approached it with low expectations. It was, after all, women's fiction, though she understood from the obituaries that, by the time it was written, her mother had progressed from romances to family dramas. But to her surprise, she found a well-constructed plot and a good deal of wit and compassion. She was enjoying it so much that she actually forgot who'd written it—until, on page fifty-four, she was brought up short by a speech. She read it three times, with mounting embarrassment and anger.

"For years I've been on my best behavior. I've offered tea and handed cake while you fixed me with your shining eyes but didn't see me at all. Is life a tea party? You think you're the expert on love, but do you know how it feels to want to crush the stupidity from a girl? Erase the brainwashing by some uncaring bastard who's made her want torment, not tenderness? Oh, Mary, how I ache to show you a different kind of spoiling."

Margaret recognized that man upbraiding a girl for her failure to notice him. Not through the words—Charles had never spoken to her like that—but because of some unmistakable resonance in the character. Here was her husband talking without guard, rather as he might express himself if he were a foreigner.

The girl was foolish, self-destructive, incapable of recognizing a good man. And as if it wasn't upsetting enough to find this in a novel written by her mother, Margaret identified a definite sympathy for the Charles character. She flipped back to the beginning of the book and discovered that it had been published in 1982; and yet only a few years later, when asked for life-changing advice, her mother had taken a very different line.

Margaret was reminded of the evening the real Charles had proposed. How would she have reacted if he'd behaved in the same angry, passionate way as the character in the novel?

"This is as good as it gets," he'd announced with quiet satisfaction after the last delicious course had been eaten; and with a shiver of apprehension, she realized the evening wasn't just about celebrating her birthday. This was something he'd waited very patiently for: the moment when he judged that the balance between them had at last started to shift in his favor.

It was November 29, 1989, the day she turned thirty-six. Despite her protests, Charles had insisted on booking a table for dinner at a Michelin-starred restaurant on the Thames. As they drank champagne and enjoyed the food and admired the lights twinkling off the dark river, they exchanged smiles as if to reassure each other that silences didn't necessarily mean a couple hadn't enough to talk about.

By then she'd known Charles, who was approaching forty, for nearly eight years. During that time, he'd treated her to numerous such excellent dinners as well as trips to the theater and opera and ballet, and she'd progressed from feeling compromised by his generosity to taking it for granted. He could certainly afford it and very occasionally, perhaps to reassure her, would point this out. Besides, she knew she was beautiful. And so she'd allowed this clever, successful man to indulge her while knowing she could never find him attractive.

He treated her with a kind of mournful respect, and she'd come to accept that, too. He was shy, she told herself, not appreciating that it would have taken supreme confidence to make a move on her.

He wasn't her type. But her type had failed her. It made this birthday very bitter. Somehow, she'd become middle-aged without having properly grown up. She had no husband or children and was without a meaningful career. She felt baffled by her own mismanagement, hollow with failure and terrified of what lay ahead. She fantasized about a man who would rescue her and yet had never considered Charles for the part.

But something was different about him tonight. She sensed impatience and even a kind of levity. "This is as good as it gets." But what had he meant, exactly? That she'd reached a stage in life when she could no longer afford to be choosy? If so, she'd glimpsed a flash of unkindness in him for the first time. It was more comfortable to decide that it had been a personal pat on the back. Yet at the same time, she understood he was letting her know that he wasn't going to wait any longer and, suddenly, the prospect of not having him in her life was very bleak.

"Yes," she agreed, laying down her knife and fork and feeling deeply apprehensive.

He'd rescued her from her life, certainly. But he was the wrong man and no amount of wishing or pretense could make him right. What she had not foreseen was the damage she would inflict on herself.

How stupid she'd been! From where she was now, thirty-six seemed so young. There was no doubt that Theo and Evie had turned out to be the real passions of her life. But women could have babies well into their forties. And they could manage it solo like her niece, Miranda, was demonstrating, only one generation on. She cursed her own fear and laziness; but, most of all, she blamed Charles for exploiting her moment of vulnerability. There was no pity for him. He'd got what he wanted, hadn't he?

"Can I have a day or two to think about it?" she'd asked.

"By all means. One day?"

"Two."

Charles had consulted his gold Rolex.

"So that means—Friday." Then, for the first time since they'd known each other, he put his hand on hers and she let it stay, alarmed by the way it trembled.

The next day, she paid a surprise visit to her parents, hoping that being in the presence of a marriage that had survived for nearly half a century might push her toward the right decision. Friends hadn't been much help. "You can't fake it," one had counseled, though another had suggested rather shockingly, "If it doesn't work, you can always get divorced."

She found her parents having tea in their sitting room in the company of the resident nurse, a man of about fifty called Steve, while the television burbled away in a corner, pictures flashing across its face, like a reminder that an exciting world raced along in tandem with this sickly, stagnant one. The house where she'd grown up was now fitted with ramps and hoists and manned by strangers; and her once vigorous father was imprisoned in a wheelchair, with limbs that trembled and twitched as if he never stopped hoping to climb out. However, her mother treated him with the same tender consideration as always. She'd caution visitors not to patronize him, stressing that his mind was as active as ever, even though he could no longer speak—as was his sense of humor, she would add, though he never smiled anymore. She'd become the keeper of his glorious past: the one who made sure caregivers and nurses understood that this silent invalid had once commanded whole battalions.

Her life had narrowed too, but she didn't seem resentful. Margaret was struck by her radiant prettiness in old age. She was wearing a soft blue jumper that intensified the color of her eyes, very clear and intense against her fine pale skin and cloud of white hair. Although she'd always been much closer to her father, Margaret could only admire the wonderfully positive way her mother had coped with a dreadful situation, even though she'd blamed her to begin with because she was so shocked and unhappy that she had to blame someone. She felt bad about it now. Her father had been in this state for over twenty years even though the doctors had originally forecast that he would not survive more than six months. It was a testament to the power of love, people said.

"I'll leave you to have a natter," said Steve as he started stacking the tea things. He snatched up the last Jaffa cake and stuffed it into his mouth. "Naughty but nice! Want me to switch off the telly?"

"Leave it, why don't you?" said Celia pleasantly, though coolly. "The news will be coming on soon."

"She must have her news!" He was piling on the familiarity, punishing her for continuing to insist on being addressed as Lady Bayley, though the general (unable to protest) had become Fred. "I'll turn the sound down, shall I?" But he seemed reluctant to leave. "Time for a change?" he speculated out loud, lifting the blanket to expose a bag of treacle-colored liquid that rested on the step of the wheelchair. Nothing happened in this house, Margaret reminded herself, keeping her temper. He was afraid of missing out.

As soon as the door had closed, her mother asked very anxiously: "Is everything all right, darling?"

"I'm fit as anything," Margaret reassured her, understanding that, in this place of sickness, good health was prized above all else.

"Thank heavens for that!"

She saw her mother's expression change, becoming first curious and then strangely knowing, and was overcome by panic. She gripped the arms of the chair she sat in. What was she thinking of, coming to her parents, who knew nothing about her private life? She was going to ask for life-changing advice while keeping them in ignorance of the backstory.

She found herself announcing abruptly: "I'm thinking of getting married."

She couldn't look at her mother, so she concentrated on her father instead, remembering with sadness how wonderfully expressive his handsome face had once been.

"His name is Charles Lisle. He's a lawyer—a QC, actually."

"We've met him," said her mother, to her surprise.

"I didn't think you'd remember." She'd brought Charles to a big family party once, wanting the supportive presence of a man and thinking he'd pass unnoticed.

She thought she detected a reaction in

her father, like a tic. Perhaps he was congratulating himself: "At last one of my daughters has made a real catch."

"He has a house in Chelsea. He's two years older than me."

Her mother spoke: "He hasn't been married before?"

A strange sound came from her father—a kind of strangled moan. But her mother ignored it.

"No, never."

Her mother frowned and her eyes wandered to the television in the corner. There was a shot of enormous crowds, a choppy sea of blue flags, an excited commentator. "I wonder why not . . ." But she sounded as if she wasn't concentrating anymore.

Then Frederick sneezed several times in swift succession and immediately she found a clean handkerchief and tenderly applied it, and Margaret was reminded of how she'd always been made to feel in their company. As the child of a happy marriage you were cursed: shown a role model you could never hope to achieve and simultaneously shut out.

She said a little testily, without thinking of the consequences: "He was waiting for me."

That got her mother's attention. "Waiting?" She rose and switched off the television, though the news was still playing. Then she stood with her back to it while Margaret crouched in her chair, looking down at her lap, feeling the full force of that searching gaze.

"Do you love him?"

"He's been very good to me," Margaret replied.

"Darling?"

She heard the concern in her mother's voice but resolutely kept her eyes on her father. She told herself the real person was still there, somewhere behind the clenched, angry façade. "He's generous," she assured him. "And kind."

She heard her mother sigh—she who had enjoyed the luxury of marrying the only man she'd ever loved. It was as if she regretted what she was about to say, but felt obliged. She put a hand on her husband's shoulder as if to remind herself of all the happiness he'd given her. "Generosity and kindness are wonderful, of course, but they're not enough on their own. I don't believe marriage should ever be entertained unless it's for love."

"It's all very well . . ." Margaret began angrily.

"Of course you want a family," her mother agreed, though this hadn't been said. She continued to caress her husband and then she closed her eyes for a moment, as if imagining the emptiness of a life without children and grandchildren. "I understand that, darling, believe me I do. . . . But marriage is too hard without love."

Tears filled Margaret's eyes. This was worse than unfair, but her mother wasn't finished.

"Love can happen to anyone at any time. Truly. And when it does, you'll know. Don't settle for anything less, I beg you." Her tone had become dreamy as if she'd begun to weave a romantic fiction. "The darkest and blackest of times can become the best, and you'll relish that golden moment even more because of having endured the other." Her eyes shone. "One should never forget it. Never never never!"

Suddenly, Margaret's father let out a desperate moaning sound and scrabbled at the arms of his wheelchair and seemed to attempt to lunge forward, and even started pressing his bell as if he wanted to stop the conversation in its tracks. She believed she understood. This was a rare tussle of wills. Her father wanted her to take this chance but feared her mother would jeopardize it. "Life's not a storybook!" he used to tease—even though, once upon a time, he'd behaved exactly like a romantic hero.

It was settled. She was not going to behave like one of her mother's heroines. She wanted a child before it was too late. She would take the advice of her father (who'd not uttered a word) and surrender her life to a man whose physical presence made her flinch.

However, it now seemed that her mother had believed Charles worth loving, after all.

There were more shocks in store. Margaret flipped through the novel at increasing speed, missing all subtlety. She believed she could identify more characters, in spite of details and descriptions having been changed. Here was a son entering the same profession as a charismatic and successful father and suffering paralyzing crises of confidence; a besotted wife laughing off the hurtful pranks of her husband.

And her mother had *intended* this to be read. . . . Margaret thought with real apprehension of the mass of notes and diaries and letters clogging up the house. What awful surprises might lie in wait?

It was clear that a biography was out of the question, even if it meant standing up to the whole family. She knew she could count on the support of her husband. But there was no comfort in it. He was, after all, Charles.

Something strange was happening to her. She was beginning to question the picture of her childhood held up for the world: the devoted parents, the thrill of glamorous, exotic holidays. The truth was that she'd barely seen her father as a little child and almost as soon as he returned, she was packed off to boarding school at the age of five. No wonder, she thought bitterly, that she'd married the wrong man.

CHAPTER TWELVE

My dear Celia, You were very brave at the funeral. I thank God you have a family to sustain you. Your mother was so proud of you. I want you to know how greatly I valued her. It is shocking to feel the emptiness at Far Point, especially with Peters gone too. It seems I am the only one left from our happy little household. Please remember that you and Frederick are always welcome, and little Robert, too. You are in my thoughts and prayers, dear child. With great sympathy and sadness, Edie Falconbridge.

Dated February 25, 1947. Found in prayerbook, together with remains of white pressed flower (carnation?).

The winter of 1947 was the bitterest in living memory, exacerbated by a shortage of coal from the pits. It meant that in the big cities, with gas pressure reduced by three-quarters, the blue flames that flickered across gas fires like restless ghosts never blossomed into crimson warmth and electricity regularly blinked off altogether. People went to bed fully clothed, wearing knitted balaclava helmets, and water pipes froze up, making it impossible to keep clean and inflicting even more misery.

But for Frederick and Celia, now living in Surrey with a tiny baby, that time was the saving of their marriage. It brought out the courage and resourcefulness that made him such a fine soldier and showed her his real quality as a man. There was no room for anyone else, least of all the spirit of dead Katherine, who'd never borne a child or known the anxiety of caring for it in such harsh circumstances. Looking back, Celia would often wish that she and Frederick and Robert could have stayed frozen in that uncomplicated life forever.

Snow had started falling at the end of January, flakes peeling ever more frantically from a lowering, yellow-gray sky. In the countryside, it blocked the roads and sealed up the houses as if intent on turning them into tombs, isolating whole families for weeks. But at least there was no shortage of wood for open fires, or food, either, provided you could force a way through the drifts. Then, said Frederick (describing it like an ambush), all you had to do was keep very still and watch, and after a while, your eyes adjusted to the blinding white canvas, the unearthly light, and you could identify movement against it: animals and birds sampling the freezing blankness with a kind of cautious dismay. Years later, Celia would remember being bound up in a woolen shawl with Robert, nipples tingling from the pressure of his tiny greedy mouth, while, outside, the crack of rifle shots, muffled by snow, echoed around the valley. Frederick was an excellent marksman: he invariably came home with a rabbit and, if they were particularly lucky, a pheasant or a partridge too. After she'd cooked them a meal, they'd eat it in the warm kitchen, drifts pressing against the windows, as effective as blackout curtains. It was the only time in their marriage she could remember Frederick being happy to live informally.

But now, in early March, the spell had been broken. Drops of light rain were blistering the immaculate complexion of the white landscape and icy blossoms were sliding off black branches and melted snow was trickling down the roads and at last Frederick could return to work.

"If you're not careful," he told her, "he's going to get used to that." For the first time in weeks, he was dressed in a suit: tall and fit, standing with his back to her, sleeking his dark hair at the dressing table with a couple of silver-backed brushes. She saw him smile in the mirror at the two of them reflected behind him: she in a thick flannel nightdress, Robert suckling at her breast. Then he put a dab of Brilliantine on one palm, rubbed it briskly against the other, and passed both hands over his head, fixing the businesslike look.

"I don't care if he does," Celia whispered, looking down at her tiny baby, and a tear fell on his shawl.

Frederick's face softened in the mirror. He came and sat on the bed. "Chin up, old girl," he urged, offering the fresh handkerchief he'd just selected. "I'll be home in no time."

"If only . . ." she murmured.

"I know," he said, but she thought she detected the first hint of impatience, a longing to be back in the world of men. She'd gone over and over the grief about her mother, and touched on the guilt, too, and he'd listened and offered as much comfort as he was able. If only Helen could have lasted a little while longer. If only she could have held her first grandchild. If only they'd seen her more often. But she had died as stoically as she'd lived, knowing it would be just her luck that when that longed-for moment came and her family was around her once more, she'd be shut away in a box.

Frederick stroked Celia's head. Then he told his tiny son with a show of fake sternness: "You look after your mother properly now."

Celia managed a smile. She was remembering what Helen had said on learning she was to become a grandmother: "When you hold your firstborn, my precious, you'll understand *real* love." It was the closest she had ever come to admitting that her own marriage had been a disappointment.

But in Celia's experience, love was limitless. Having Robert to care for had actually improved her relationship with Frederick. It seemed he wanted to be loved but not obsessively needed, even if he occasionally hankered after the girl who'd shivered as she watched his hands. Her flight from Germany was never mentioned now. She'd returned to a different man, contrite and very anxious, who seemed delighted when told they were expecting a child. Did all marriages operate like theirs, mutating so swiftly from despair to bliss that you started to doubt your own memories?

And now there was the house, like a promise of years of family happiness to come. It was off the Portsmouth Road, but you'd never know it, Frederick would say. There was much work to be done because the house needed extending and the garden was rough and unformed. Another advantage, he'd remind everyone, was that it was less than an hour's journey from London and the Ministry of Defense. It was only a pity about its rather ridiculous name—Parr's. Who had Parr been, anyway? Nobody seemed to know. But changing the name of a house seemed almost as drastic as breaking up a marriage.

A vehicle splashed into the drive and stopped with the engine running and Frederick went to the window and exclaimed: "Postman!" It was an exciting moment: their first visitor, as well as their first post, for more than three weeks. Then he was off, springing downstairs in his socks.

He returned with an armful of letters and sat down again on the bed. "Strange," he said, frowning at one of the envelopes. "Wrong name, right address. Florence de la Tour. Sounds like the owner of a dress shop!" He tossed the letter to one side, ripped open a telephone bill, sucked in his breath. "I say, this is a bit steep. Have you been talking to your friend Priscilla again?"

Celia didn't answer.

Frederick glanced at her, sensing unease. "It's all right!" he reassured her. "I *want* you to stay in touch with Priscilla." He paused. "And Bet, of course." He sorted rapidly through the rest of the post, put most of it aside for later. "Time I was off." He fitted on his highly polished shoes, stood up, dropped a kiss on her head, and covered the frail curl of Robert's hand with his own enormous one. "Hail and farewell." Then he took the letter addressed to Florence de la Tour and tucked it into a pocket.

"What are you doing?" asked Celia anxiously.

"I'll drop this in at the post office on the way to the station."

"No, wait," said Celia. "I know who it's for." She'd anticipated that letter for weeks. But what with Robert's premature and complicated birth, followed almost immediately by the death of her mother, it had gone out of her mind. Now, most embarrassingly, she was going to have to make a confession. Robert had fallen asleep and she buttoned up her nightdress, searching for the right words, though there was no easy way to say this. "When we were in Germany I wrote something."

"Oh?" He was thinking of the working day ahead, only half listening. She understood that he'd set aside his tenderness for them for the time being, like depositing a precious possession in a safe. "What sort of something?" he asked, putting on his jacket.

"A story," she whispered. Too late, she

could see the folly of what she'd done, and now everything they'd gained during this private, precious time was threatened.

She had his attention. "You wrote a story?"

She nodded. "Well, more of a novel, really. . . . I didn't say anything because it was nothing—just something to occupy myself with. I mean, I never expected . . ."

"In Germany? When?"

"The afternoons, mostly. I had a lot of time."

"Go on." He sounded grim. Was he aware of the extent to which the other wives had ostracized her, after word had spread about the shocking overtures of friendship she'd made to her German servant? She was remembering the loneliness and that strange decision to write out the jealousy because there'd been nobody to unburden herself to in that foreign place, least of all Frederick. "I hate you, Katherine!" she'd scrawled across the first page of a notebook, and then she'd written "Celia Bayley" half a dozen times like reminding that threatening spirit who was Frederick's wife now. But then something had happened. As day followed day, a story had begun to take shape, as if, without even being aware of it, she'd absorbed lessons on plot and character from all the books she'd devoured in the library at Far Point. Very soon, her notebook became as important to her as her imaginary childhood friend, Naomi, had once been. She was often frustrated by her own lack of skill; but even so, all that solitary striving was occasionally lit up by extraordinary satisfaction. "You look pretty," Frederick would say when he returned home, as if he sensed some difference. "What have you done today?" But she hadn't enlightened him—clearly another mistake—and now could no longer relate to her strange burst of independence.

"And then—I don't know why—I sent it to a publisher." She'd hesitated for days before wrapping her handwritten manuscript in brown paper and sending it to Gollancz in London, who'd published some of her favorite books. "They weren't interested," she muttered, more ashamed by the minute. "And nor were any others." She added, more to herself, "I don't know what got into me." But it wasn't quite true because she'd continued to send the book to publisher after publisher, as if a separate and hitherto unrecognized part of her was strangely confident, even arrogant.

"Let me get this right," he said. "You wrote a book, in secret, and then sent it to not just one publisher but several—without telling me?"

Celia looked down at sleeping Robert, unable to meet her husband's eyes. In the long silence that followed, she felt the weight of his disapproval. It never occurred to her to charge him with hypocrisy: remind him how he'd doctored the truth, encouraging their new friends to believe her background had been safe and privileged. "No one wants to publish it," she repeated, thinking of the seven other rejection letters hidden away in a drawer.

"Did you do this under your own name?" he asked suddenly.

Celia shook her head. "Of course not!" She indicated the envelope. "I invented one, didn't I?"

"Ah!" He understood now. "Well, that's something," he said, sounding relieved. There was no need to explain. The army didn't welcome unconventional wives. He retrieved the letter from his pocket. "You'd better open it."

"Later, maybe."

"Do it now," he said firmly, as if he wanted to wrap up this strange display of rebellion for good.

Celia obeyed him, knowing what to expect. They'd enjoyed reading her manuscript, but it wasn't for them. If they were nice, they might go on to wish her luck placing it elsewhere; but this seemed unlikely since they hadn't bothered to return the manuscript, though, as usual, she'd enclosed a sheet of fresh brown paper and string and even a stamp. "Oh!" she exclaimed, completely taken aback.

He took the letter from her but, as she watched anxiously, his handsome face remained quite expressionless. "Bravo!" he said when he'd read it.

"I can always say no." However, she was quickly adjusting to this astonishing development. Someone actually wanted to publish her novel! How could she bear it if Frederick took her at her word?

"Wouldn't hear of it!" But there was no real enthusiasm in his voice.

"Really?"

"Of course not!" Then she understood that he was determined to behave well. It was like his decision not to discourage her friendships with Priscilla and Bet or separate her from her mother (though, sadly, that had come just too late). It touched her that he'd made such efforts to change. He tapped the page like making a point. "They say you've got talent."

So she had noted to her secret delight, but she made a show of dismissal. "It's just a romance."

He'd expected no more. Even so, she sensed a measure of new respect. Suddenly, he was indulgent and full of affection. "You're a clever little thing, aren't you?"

"Am I?"

He stroked her hair. "Fancy my wife publishing a book!"

"You really don't mind?"

He shook his head. "I'm proud of you." He paused, became thoughtful. "But let's keep this to ourselves, shall we? I think it's for the best."

"Of course!" she agreed with feeling. The thought of Aphrodite Barclay or any of his other friends reading it made her shiver.

"Well, I must have a look at this master-piece of yours," he went on as he picked up his car keys. But she knew him well enough by now to be confident that when he came home, he'd find something more important to claim his attention.

When he'd gone, she held Robert against her shoulder to bring up his wind, relishing his soft dependence. "You won't remember any of this," she murmured against his downy, milky-smelling hair, "so I'm going to do it for you. Tomorrow I'm starting a diary. I'm going to describe exactly how strange and dangerous the world became and how your wonderful father kept us alive, day after day. I'll be your eyes and ears, my darling, until you're old enough to remember everything for yourself. And maybe I'll tell you that this was one of the best days of my life as well as one of the saddest."

CHAPTER THIRTEEN

Is writing about being shy—telling without having to say it? And who is it really for? Now there's him, it feels selfish. Sometimes I wonder if writing is necessary at all when I can create something so perfect. I love him so much it hurts. I love the fact that he needs me. Most of all I cherish the absolute certainty that I know him.

Written in diary, started soon
after birth of Robert.

"You're really sure you liked it?"

"I've told you I did."

"You don't have to be polite. Honestly."

"I know that! I said it made me forget my troubles." Bet smiled. "Celia, someone wants to publish it!"

"Sorry to be so pathetic," said Celia. "It's just that somehow I never imagined anyone reading it."

"Why write it, then?"

But Celia hesitated even though she knew she could trust Bet and had decided that today was the perfect opportunity to tell the whole story at last. "For something to do, I suppose," she found herself saying. "I had a lot of time on my hands in Germany."

"Weird," Bet commented. It made Celia feel anxious and vulnerable but she had to agree. Other wives with time on their hands took up dressmaking or knitting, though she wouldn't have expected such a liberated person to point this out. Writing a book was a deeply personal business— especially for someone like her, who found it difficult to articulate feelings. Had Bet been shocked by the passion she'd found?

With Frederick's blessing, Celia had gone up to London to meet the man who'd written to tell her his firm wanted to publish her novel. As she'd sat in his office, blushing at the compliments, he'd given the opinion that the book was "a little melodramatic— we need to tone that down a bit" and "a trifle purple in passages" (though that might have been a joke). Otherwise he'd behaved rather like Bet: as if he couldn't quite believe the person who'd written it was a decorous young wife and mother so shy she could barely speak.

Bet had arrived for lunch in a dusty old Ford lent by a friend—a good one clearly, because she was a famously bad driver. As a matter of fact, she confessed straight-away, she'd bumped the gatepost on the way in. "Don't worry," she soothed, "it's only a bit of paint. Frederick won't even notice." And then she unpacked the pre-cious carbon copy of Celia's handwritten manuscript (freckled with fresh tea stains), a wooden giraffe for Robert, and a box of dates. She was barely recognizable as the prickly resentful girl who'd turned up at the Café Royal in a shabby old coat and un-polished shoes, determined not to enjoy herself. She wore a pink cotton dress with a tight belt that showed off a nice new waist, and she'd treated herself to a fash-ionable bubble cut.

It was a perfect day in early June and they were settled on an old tartan rug spread on the lawn, eating a picnic lunch under the copper beech tree. It was a lot more comfortable than being in the house, where builders had started extending the kitchen and there was dust everywhere. "Sorry to miss your hubby," Bet had said, but they both knew it wasn't true. These days, Frederick made an effort with Bet for Celia's sake, but they were too different to get on. Besides, she was still single in her mysterious way, and they lived in a world of couples. He would become elaborately courteous in her company, which made her awkward to the point of rudeness.

"Don't get me wrong," Bet went on, picking up a piece of corned beef in her fingers, "I couldn't put it down. Where'd you get the idea from, anyway?" But before Celia could respond, she answered her own question. "Cyril's the image of Frederick, isn't he?"

"Is he?" Celia managed to sound as if it was the first time this had occurred to her.

"Oh, I know he's blond, not dark. And he's not in the army, like Frederick. But he's dishy as heck, isn't he? Older than Alice, too. Matter of fact, she reminds me of you." This was accompanied by another sly, inquisitive glance.

"Oh, really?"

"Only child, shy, no father," Bet went on, like ticking off a checklist.

After a minute, Celia conceded, "I suppose there are certain similarities. You write about what you know. But it's nearly all invented."

"Hmm." Bet seemed unconvinced.

The baby lay on the rug, blinking up at the sunlight slithering through tiers of shiny bronze leaves that rattled softly in the faint warm breeze and sent elongated shadows dancing across his face. He wore a white cotton bonnet and a blue romper suit. Every so often he'd smile and frown in quick succession, as if still working out the difference, or fling out his plump, creased legs in a spasmodic, uncoordinated way, and Bet would break off from whatever she was saying and murmur almost tearfully, "Oh, bless!"

"Any news?" she asked suddenly.

"I phoned her last week."

"And?"

Celia shrugged. Now based permanently in Scotland and ruled by an exclusive calendar, it was Priscilla who was doing the cutting off. But sometimes, during increasingly rare telephone calls, Celia would pick up a thread of uncertainty beneath the brittle recital of race meetings or shoots or grand house parties and remember her face crumpling at the reunion lunch. "Actually," she said, "*he* answered. We had a bit of a chat."

Bet looked interested, because neither of them had met Priscilla's husband, Rupert. As she'd predicted, they'd not been invited to the wedding. "And?"

"Sort of what we expected," said Celia, making a face. Despite his immaculate manners, Rupert had sounded like a buffoon.

"At least there's the baby," Bet pointed out. For Priscilla was newly pregnant and seemingly delighted though she'd said, rather mystifyingly, "If only one didn't have to go through that other stuff."

They fell silent, listening to wood pigeons murmuring in the trees and Robert snuffling and murmuring nearby, and Celia thought, "This is all so precious and it should be enough." But the book nagged, like someone tugging at her sleeve.

"If there was something you didn't like, you can tell me, honestly."

Bet tickled Robert's cheek with a strand

of grass. She kept her eyes on him as she spoke. "Only thing I thought was, would Alice have married Cyril if she'd known about the ex-wife? *I* think it'd be more like Cyril not to tell her about Nina at all. Then it'd come as a real shock when she turns up out of the blue with her suitcase."

Celia held her breath, but Bet carried straight on.

"Cheeky bitch! Who'd she think she was, anyway? Real dog in the manger, 'cause when she had him she didn't want him, right? Going with all his friends—not even behind his back! She was like Rebecca, wasn't she? Oh, I *loved* that book! I couldn't feel sorry for him, though. He's such a drip! Okay, she turns up with some sob story, asking to stay, but why does he go along with it? Poor Alice. She wants to do the right thing 'cause all she wants is to be a good wife, but all the time Nina's plotting to get rid of her. It was great when you sent her packing, Celia. Cheers for that!"

"Well, it was Alice really." Celia blushed. It sounded so foolish; and Bet was right, of course—Alice was herself. She couldn't explain to her friend how strange the process of writing a novel was: how, once you breathed life into your characters, they acquired a strange independence. Their voices spoke in your head; in the end you felt as if your only real job was to record them. "Did she feel real to you? Nina, I mean?"

"I wanted to smack her," Bet confirmed in a heartfelt kind of way. "Where'd she come from, anyway?"

Celia thought of the monster she'd created: a promiscuous manipulative girl who wasn't even that pretty. It gave her a pang sometimes to remember an unlucky bride buried far away in India. But, at the time—those lonely, confused months after returning to her husband—rewriting Katherine had been the only way to live with her ghost. Nina was an amalgam of all the villainesses she'd ever read about. She was also herself behaving badly, as she never had and knew she never would.

However, once again, some deep shyness—or an abiding sense of marital loyalty—stopped her from revealing the truth. Part of her wondered if it was even necessary because Bet was so quick and smart, more than capable of disentangling hidden messages, as every one of her questions had demonstrated. "I will tell her," Celia thought.

"Priscilla thinks you're a dreamer, but I always said you were sharp." This was typical Bet—direct but warm. "What does Frederick think?"

"He's been wonderful."

"I bet he's proud as punch." There was an unmistakable little question mark. She was still waiting to hear that Frederick loved the book.

But Celia wasn't going to admit he hadn't read it because that would seem like another betrayal. If Bet was confused, so was she. She was proud of her book but deeply apprehensive; anxious to show loyalty to her husband yet terrified she'd done the opposite. She said: "Bet, I wanted *you* to read it, but I've decided not to say anything to anyone else. Not even Priscilla."

"Is that why you wrote it under a different name?"

"It's difficult with the army."

"Oh, sod them! Be proud of yourself!"

"Frederick's career's important. I have to consider it." She added, being truthful for the first time, "Anyway, I like the anonymity. It means I can write what I want."

"So this isn't the last Florence de la Tour?"

Celia shook her head. It was the first time she understood that she hadn't only written a book. She'd become a writer.

Bet had news of her own, but she kept it until the very last minute, even as she was saying good-bye to Robert. "Say ta-ta to Auntie Bet." She seized his fat little foot and kissed it while his sweet toothless smile flickered on and off. "Oh, bless! Shall I eat you? No, I know—I'll steal you. When your mummy's back is turned, I'm going to take you home with me. Yes, I am!" Then she picked up her handbag and informed Celia, sounding very matter-of-fact: "By the way, I'm getting married."

Celia stared at her. "This is very sudden."

Bet blinked and nodded as if she could only agree.

"Why didn't you say?"

"I'm telling you now, aren't I?" However, Bet gave the odd impression that she hadn't known either, until a moment before.

"What's his name?"

"Jack," said Bet after a moment. "He's called Jack."

"How long have you known him for?"

Bet shrugged. Then, relenting, she admitted: "He was on boats, too."

"Well, that's wonderful!" Celia enthused, wondering why she'd never heard of this particular boyfriend before. "When?"

Bet looked a little shifty. "I'll have to ask Jack, won't I?"

"You must bring him down."

"Okay." She cast a last doting glance at Robert. "Little love," she crooned. Then Celia observed her shut her eyes and cross her fingers, like making a wish but fearing it might never come true.

CHAPTER FOURTEEN

This baby business is doing such damage, and it worries me dreadfully. But in spite of all Robert's huffing and puffing, I know he'll do the right thing in the end. "All change is preceded by chaos." I think I never was told anything more profound.

Diary entry. Recent. Whose baby?

A month after retiring for good, Robert was still responding to all telephone calls in curt office fashion. When his daughter, Miranda, rang, he was relaxing in his sitting room over a covert second whiskey and thinking about Paris.

"Bayley."

"Dad!"

"Miranda?" Caught by surprise, he re-

acted with all the old pleasure. Then he remembered that he was furious with his
daughter and had been snubbing her for
weeks. "Ah, Miranda," he amended, sounding cold and disapproving.

"This isn't a bad time, is it?" He could
hear the effort she was making as if, every
single time, she hoped he'd be different.

"As a matter of fact," he informed her,
even though there were at least twenty
minutes to go, "we're just about to have
supper."

She gave up—he could tell from the
sudden deadness in her voice. "Is Mum
there?"

"What does she expect?" he thought.
The two of them had always been so
close—partly, he believed, because they'd
shared the same values. But he'd been
wrong. In very dark moments, he saw her
decision to get pregnant by a total stranger
as a personal attack.

"Can I speak to her?"

For a second, he hesitated, because
something about this worried him. Then he
said, "Just a minute" and, without putting
his hand over the receiver, bellowed: "Mel!"

His wife hurried into the room in her apron.

"Miranda," he informed her coolly and watched her damp down the rush of plea- sure and assume a neutral mask for his benefit. "Bang goes our peaceful supper," he thought, blaming Miranda, even though it was he who would ruin the evening with frowns and silences. He knew how much all this was upsetting Mel, but he refused to back down. He wasn't even going to permit her to talk to their daughter in private.

Mel said "Miranda?" Then, as she lis- tened, her composure fell away. "When?" she asked anxiously.

"What is it?" Robert hissed, but she waved a hand at him to keep quiet. It seemed Miranda had a lot to say, and though Mel frowned and chewed her lip as she listened, she continued to murmur soothing re- sponses like "I'm sure" and "Don't worry" and "That's the important thing."

Alarmed, Robert seized the telephone. "Miranda?"

But it was her turn to do the punishing. She said: "Give me back Mum, will you?"

He left the room in a fit of pique, but for once Mel paid no attention, and by the time he returned a few minutes later, the conversation was over.

"Well?" he demanded with a kind of savage amusement.

"She started bleeding."

He stared at her.

"She got herself to hospital all on her own! She must have been terrified!" This came out in a kind of wail, as if for once Mel found it impossible to mask her real emotions. "They think they've stabilized things for now, but she needs complete bed rest." She glanced at him a little doubtfully. "I've told her she can't go back to her flat, with no one to look after her."

To his astonishment, he found himself agreeing instantly. "Of course not!"

"I've said she must come here."

Again he didn't hesitate. "Quite right! And?"

"She said yes."

"Ah!" There seemed to be something in his throat. His eyes were pricking, too. The worst of it was that as he cleared his throat and blinked, he could sense Mel observing him very tenderly, as if, despite all the sulking and bad temper, she'd never doubted his goodness of heart.

If Miranda lost this baby, he was thinking, then the family could return to normal.

No shame (because none of their friends had been told) and, very soon, no more blame. So why wasn't he relieved? To his astonishment, all he could feel was sadness. It was because only now could he admit that he'd never seen his daughter so happy. She was a strong character, and if she lost her baby, she would survive; but perhaps she would never again smile in that triumphant ecstatic way.

He cleared his throat once more. "I'll go and collect her, shall I?"

"Of course not, darling," said Mel (who knew perfectly well that he'd helped himself to more whiskey while she was in the kitchen). Her tone was brisk and practical. "I think there's enough supper for three." She added, "It might be a good idea to phone Guy and put him in the picture."

From the moment Miranda walked very slowly into the house, chalky pale and supported by her mother, the house began to recover its old peace.

Was Robert nudged to take up Miranda's supper tray, or did he suggest it himself? However it came about, he found himself very happy to be rat-tat-tatting on the door of her old bedroom like he had years before when she was a child. "Do not come in unless invited," an old hand-written poster had read.

"Enter," she replied just as she used to, and he felt ridiculously grateful.

She was sitting up in the single bed, reading an old paperback she must have found in the bookcase and dressed in a revealing nightgown he recognized, with some embarrassment, as Mel's. Her serious bespectacled face and pregnant, newly voluptuous chest looked as if they belonged to two different women, as if she was taking part in a real-life game of Heads, Bodies, and Legs.

"No time to pack," she explained with a faint smile.

"Ah well," he said a little sternly, as if apologizing for Mel, even though he knew perfectly well that the flimsy, lacy nightgowns she ordered from catalogs were entirely for his benefit.

"Miranda, Miranda," he thought, remembering that the name meant "extraordinary, to be admired." He loved her quiet cleverness, and thought her beautiful in her pale, harelike way. And yet as far as he and Mel knew, Miranda had never had a significant relationship. Was it because she worked too hard? Was too independent? Had neglected her femininity? Then Robert frowned as he remembered something his mother had once said: "We can never really know what goes on in another's heart." Could it be that Miranda had a whole romantic history none of them were aware of? Once, when she was in her early twenties, he'd found her sobbing on her bed (though he'd tiptoed away for both their sakes). She deserved a good husband, but why hadn't he made an appearance yet?

"Daft," she said, abandoning her book; he noted it was *Five Go Off to Camp* by Enid Blyton. Once she'd loved the Famous Five, just as he and his sisters had. She'd treasured her collection of Barbie dolls, too. He wondered where they were now: that gaggle of tiny pink plastic women with pudding basin–shaped bosoms and articulated waists and glistening nylon hair. For at least half a dozen birthdays all Miranda had wanted was more over-the-top outfits for them, more minuscule tacky items of furniture. How strange that such a clever, successful woman had once regarded Barbies as role models.

"How are you feeling?" he asked as he set down the tray. There was no wine because Miranda had given up alcohol the moment her pregnancy was confirmed. But Mel had laid a rose from the garden beside the plate, which made her smile.

"Better," she said, but he saw her cross her fingers. "So long as I take it easy."

"Well, you can do that here. Very quiet here." He was gabbling. "Can't fault the quietness, apart from the occasional mating fox. All that matters . . ." He stopped, suddenly anxious about where this was leading.

Miranda saved him. "I'm being horribly spoiled."

"And so you should be."

She smiled at him properly, and he smiled back, realizing just how much he'd missed their tender interaction. Then she put a hand to her mouth, horrified. "I just remembered! You and Mum were going to Paris this weekend!"

"Don't you worry about that."

"You *are* going?" When he didn't answer,

she insisted, "You *must*. Listen, Dad, I won't hear of you putting it off! I'll be fine. Really!"

"Now, you listen to me," he said very firmly. "Paris will still be there next month or even next year."

"But you've bought the tickets! And what about the hotel? They're not going to give you a refund this late! Oh, Dad!"

"We can afford it," he maintained, even though he'd been looking forward to the treat for weeks and hated to waste money. The truth was, a secret part of him felt guilty about being rich—or at any rate enjoying it.

She couldn't speak. But she touched his hand. After a moment, she asked, with seeming irrelevance: "Any idea what Mum did with my Barbies?"

As he closed the door behind him, he felt happier than he had for weeks. Though the baby hadn't been mentioned, he'd been aware of it throughout and now found himself trying to visualize it. Tiny, of course, but already recognizably human, with a big head, its legs and arms folded into its comma of a body. Its eyes would be closed and its mouth set in a fatalistic line as if equally accepting of life or death. "But *I* care?" Robert realized, to his astonishment. The baby had to live because it was Miranda's. Bugger that unknown father, he thought: it had half her genes, too. And how could she, who was so thoroughly good, fail to instill her quality into any child?

"Little tyke," he murmured, making a face. He didn't even know if this first grandchild of his was male or female, but it occurred to him that Miranda must because, at her age, she'd have been scanned, for sure. The whole family probably knew, too. He decided to ask Mel very casually over supper. Then he grinned suddenly. He'd just realized there was no need because Miranda had as good as told him the sex of the baby herself.

CHAPTER FIFTEEN

In my limited and not very interesting experience, writing comes from anguish; but I'm not a good writer, though I always hope to become a better one. And then there's that peculiar thing of striving to be honest in fiction, even if one can't bear people to know what's going on in one's head in real life.

Notes. No date. Poss. 1960s?

Dusk was falling as Bud walked along the lane to Parr's. It was a Saturday afternoon and she was arriving unannounced, worried by her mother who had sounded unnaturally cheerful on the telephone. Both parents were spinning off into different forms of madness, and yet as a child—unlike most of her peer group—she'd never once feared they'd break up. To have that profound sense of security shattered, even as an adult, was extraordinarily upsetting and, furthermore, had caused her to look at her father in a new light. She was no longer prepared to indulge the image he'd cultivated of a man of brilliance held back by bad luck and a refusal to compromise. To her dismay, she had discovered he could be weak and unkind, and though she still loved him, she was finding it hard to like him. Furthermore, she'd begun to suspect that his affair had gone on longer than he claimed, because for all his talk of caring nothing about others' opinions, he had made an exception of his mother-in-law. The timing of his confession—the day after her funeral—was beginning to seem significant.

"Oh, Gran," mourned Bud, because there was only one person she longed to talk to about this horrible confusion. As she approached the house, she told herself: "If I want this enough, it can happen." After all, Celia herself had suggested that communicating with the dead was no less magical than sending a fax to the other side of the world (for so it seemed to a woman

born in 1927). "I'll give you a sign, if it's in-
humanly possible," she had joked, and
added: "You're blessed with imagination,
my darling. With imagination, comes freedom." Mindful of those words, hoping to
trick time, Bud now tried to imagine this
was just another visit to her grandmother.

First would come the excited barking of
Oscar on the other side of the front door,
then her grandmother's voice soothing him
and the tap of her stick on the stone flags.
And after the double welcome was over—a
close embrace from Celia, a nudge on the
knees from Oscar—she would become
aware of the familiar smell of comfort food
drifting from the kitchen, chicken pot pie or
macaroni and cheese. Though Celia's
white hair would be neatly coiffed as always, she'd be wearing her cozy, trodden-
down old shoes. At supper, Oscar would
sit just by Bud's chair, watching the passage of every mouthful, and her grandmother would say, "Don't feed him, darling,
it only makes him worse" (even though it
was obvious the dog was used to tidbits).
And then, when the time was right, they'd
start to talk: or rather, Celia would listen
most attentively while Bud unburdened

herself. She would be deeply saddened by the marriage breakup, of course, but resolutely diplomatic. She'd say: "I know how hard this is for you, darling, but try not to judge your father." By this time, Bud was so carried away that she could almost hear her grandmother's warm, troubled voice.

It couldn't last. The house was unlit and forlorn. For a moment, she feared her mother was out, but then she spotted the family car parked in the garage alongside her grandmother's old Volvo, which was permanently grounded now and so encrusted with bird droppings that it looked as if it had been in a snowstorm. This was odd in itself because there was scarcely room for two cars.

However, though she rang the bell several times, her mother failed to appear. She banged on the knocker but there was no response. Then a terrible picture came to her of her mother unconscious on a bed, an emptied bottle of pills beside her. She flapped the letterbox and screamed through it: "Mum! Mum!"

To her astonishment, the door opened immediately, as if her mother had been hiding behind it all the time.

"Darling!" she exclaimed, looking simultaneously flustered and delighted. "How on earth did you get here?"

"I walked from the station." Bud went on: "Who were you expecting, anyway?"

"No one."

Bud gave her mother a sharp look.

"Well, if you must know, I thought it might be that journalist who wants to write the biography," Sarah admitted. "I couldn't imagine anyone else who'd turn up without warning."

"But you liked her, Mum!"

"I did."

"Huh?"

"It's different now," Sarah muttered; and within minutes, she explained the reason for her change of mood. Whoopee had started sending affectionate text messages.

"I think he wants to come back," said Sarah, and she smiled as if she'd been given the most wonderful present in the world.

"What exactly does he say?"

"I'm not sure I should be talking about this with you, darling . . ."

Nor was Bud, but she could see it was going to happen anyway. Who else was her mother to talk to? Who else knew Whoopee so well? Even as Bud struggled with feelings of embarrassment and distaste, she could appreciate all this.

"Darling Crinkle, you are sant," said the first text message.

Bud frowned.

"I think he means 'saint,'" said Sarah.

"Right." Whoopee's dyslexia was a closely kept family secret, and one of the reasons he was so proud of Spud for becoming a poet. He was expert at avoiding situations where he'd have to write, unless Sarah was around to correct his spelling. Bud wondered what his new young girlfriend thought about it—or was it possible she hadn't discovered yet? She also wondered why he hadn't telephoned instead. Was he testing the water or just avoiding answering tricky questions about his affair?

"Bare with me!!!" the message ended, and Bud made a despairing face because there had to be some boundaries.

"It's a joke," her mother hastened to explain. "It's what telephone operators say when they put you on hold. 'Bear with me.' It's one of his pet hates."

The other message said simply: "We

shoud plan trip" and ended with a row of
x's.

Bud was beginning to have a nasty suspicion. She realized that although, in theory, nobody was talking to Whoopee
anymore, it was quite possible he was in
touch with her brother. Spud would enjoy
going against the family. He might even
have written a giveaway poem about the
surprise inheritance—a sparse and bilious
rant at privilege.

But even as she was pondering how best
to warn her mother, she was confounded.

"I know perfectly well what you're thinking, darling," Sarah informed her with a
smile. "Of course Dad knows about the
money."

"He does?"

"I told him myself!" Her mother sounded
more triumphant than ashamed. "And do
you know what? If that's what it takes for
him to come back to me, I don't care!"

Much later, after her mother had gone
to bed, Bud telephoned Guy on her mobile in the garden, where she couldn't be
overheard. "Now I've heard it all!"

"Sad," Guy agreed, and she heard him
yawn.

"I just hope," said Bud with feeling, "that I never ever humiliate myself like that."

"Can't see it." Then he suggested: "I think you should stay the weekend. Keep an eye on her."

But Bud had no intention of wasting time talking about her father—or rather, listening as her mother went on and on about how he'd never meant to hurt them and the girl was to blame. Immediately after breakfast the next morning, she announced they must get to work on the sorting of the house. "I can't believe you haven't started!"

She decided they should begin with the attic and work their way down. "How much is there up there?"

"No idea."

"You mean, you haven't even looked? What have you been *doing* all this time?"

"Thinking," said her mother as shamelessly as an adolescent.

The attic could only be accessed via a trapdoor with a flimsy, pull-down ladder. Once her eyes had adjusted to the gloom, Bud began to realize the scale of the task ahead of them. There were countless boxes and at least half a dozen ancient bulging suitcases bound by leather straps. A woolly carpet of dust covered everything: obviously nobody had been up there for years. "What's it all *for*?" thought Bud, who prided herself on living in the present, tearing up the past as she went along. Letters barely existed for her generation, who had infinitely less laborious and swifter ways of communicating. As for diaries, who had the time now?

All this paper! It was as if her grandmother had lived only to write; and yet she'd had a successful marriage and three children and six grandchildren, and lasting friendships, too. She'd worried about the junk, certainly, but there'd been a far greater priority. "The minute I open my eyes," she'd once confided, "all I can think of is getting to my desk." But even if she'd been willing to sacrifice her work, climbing that ladder had been out of the question. And so she'd procrastinated until, one day, death had pounced.

Bud blew the dust off a box and unfolded its dirty cardboard leaves. Inside, there was a tightly packed mass of old letters and diaries. She opened a diary at random. "Played grandmother's footsteps

with the children," she read in familiar writing in the space for September 16, 1961.
Bud smiled as she reflected that had been
written long before Celia had become a
real grandmother. A black-and-white photograph was tucked into the box, too. It
was a formal portrait of a young woman
with a sweet narrow face reminiscent of
Miranda's. Her hair was styled in a simple
chignon and she wore a plain black dress
and drop pearl earrings and stared a little
defensively into the camera, as if she
wasn't used to having her picture taken.

"That must be your Great-Grandma
Helen," said Sarah, looking over Bud's
shoulder.

Helen was the relation who'd died
before any of her grandchildren or great-
grandchildren could meet her. But they
knew about her through Celia's bedtime
stories. Far Point had come alive for them
then: that beautiful white house by the sea,
where the wind moaned in the pines and
waves lashed the shore all night long.
"Were there any ghosts?" Bud had once
asked, and Celia made up a story especially for her about a thin pale girl called
Naomi with long black hair streaming down

her back, who walked the windy corridors in search of scared children to comfort. However, Great-Grandma Helen's personality had been shadowy and indistinct, which was quite odd because every one of the servants was a sharply defined character. There'd been a fierce female cook with a mustache, Bud remembered; a maid who'd dreamed of romance, and a gardener who'd loved the sound of his own voice. But the star character was the housekeeper, a wonderful woman, who—in a favorite story—once fought a triumphant tug-of-war with a savage dog for a leg of lamb.

There were strange pieces of junk buried among the paper. A dirty old handkerchief with pale brown stains on it; a tiny wooden vial painted with flowers that had obviously once contained a very sweet scent; a single battered and bent unfiltered cigarette; and strange red and white tassels on silky strings that seemed to serve no purpose. There were theater programs and restaurant menus and school reports and even a white linen napkin with a crimson crest embroidered on it. But Bud noticed that the paper in all the boxes had begun to yellow and turn brittle, and the ink was fading away. One box was suffering badly from mold, and mice had reduced the contents of another to shreds. Margaret was still talking about destroying all this, unread, but suddenly Bud understood: they'd been given a last chance to catch the past even as it was sliding away, to obtain answers—in her grandmother's distinctive voice—to some of the questions they should have asked when she was alive. Because, however thoroughly you felt you knew someone, there were always unanswered questions.

"Listen," she said urgently to her mother, "this is precious. But there's no way we can sort through it all on our own. Oh, Mum, why don't we tell that biographer to go ahead? Gran *deserves* to be remembered, doesn't she?"

Then something thrilling happened. One moment, the stale and dusty air was quite still; the next, a gust from nowhere ruffled the leaves of an open notebook. To Bud, it meant only one thing: her grandmother's spirit lived on and was confirming that she wanted her story told and remembered. She shivered and glanced at her mother, sure that she'd seen the significance, too.

"I think you're right," said Sarah. "But to be honest, I'd rather have nothing more to do with that woman. I'm embarrassed, to tell the truth. You see, she got me at a bad moment and I talked to her about Dad. You wouldn't mind dealing with her, would you, darling? I say, there's a bit of a draft up here."

CHAPTER SIXTEEN

I'm efficient and capable. P. just told me so! When darling F.'s home, I pretend to be dreamy and feeble because he does long to be in charge; and so we shiver and the children jump to attention when he speaks. I'll do anything for love!

Note in diary, November 5, 1956.

At half past eight one morning, when Celia was still in her dressing gown and cutting toast soldiers for her children, she received a telephone call from someone she thought had disappeared from her life for good.

"How's that divine husband of yours?" was Priscilla's first question once they were past a flurry of excited greetings.

"He's away," said Celia. She put a hand

274 over the mouthpiece and said sternly,

over the mouthpiece and said sternly, "Don't play with them. Eat them."

"Darling, I have *the* most enormous favor to ask."

"Go on." Celia was hoping she'd be brief because two-year-old Margaret had disappeared, which could only mean she was up to mischief. The day before, she'd tipped a bag of flour down the lavatory; and a week before that she'd stuffed a small marble up her nose, which meant Celia had to bundle Robert and Sarah into the car and take them to hospital, too. Accidents always involved the whole family when Frederick was away.

"I was wondering if I could stay for a few days?"

"Of course!" Celia agreed with pleasure. "As long as you don't mind the children."

"Angel!" Priscilla exclaimed. Then she asked a little anxiously: "How many are there now? I've lost track."

"Three, can you believe? There's Robert, of course, who's nine now; and Sarah; and my little one, Margaret."

"No!" said Priscilla. Then: "Oh, darling! It's all my fault! I'll explain everything."

She saw the surprise in Priscilla's face once they'd stopped embracing.

"Oh, Celia," she exclaimed, examining her very thoroughly with her sharp green eyes, "you've grown up!"

"What does she expect?" thought Celia, amused, because ten years had passed since that strange disjointed lunch just after the war, and she was a busy mother now with a lot more confidence and a wonderful marriage, even if she didn't see Frederick nearly often enough.

Priscilla was as slender as Celia remembered, but her skin had lost its beautiful pale luminosity under too much makeup and the old laconic self-possession had given way to a kind of desperate vivacity.

"What fun! We're slumming!" she enthused, when it became clear they were staying in the kitchen. In the winter months, it was by far the warmest room, thanks to an iron range that threw out a constant blanket of heat. Beyond the closed door, drafts whistled along the corridors and ice etched flower patterns on the inside of windowpanes. However, when Frederick was there, the family was expected to behave as if they hadn't noticed, and even take all meals in the bone-chilling dining room. The truth was, he scared the children. He was at home so little, yet expected absolute obedience, especially from his son, Robert. And it would never have occurred to any of them to laugh when he referred to the larder as "the cold room."

Priscilla had left her marriage. She didn't know where else to go, she said, because "everyone up there knows everyone else, and you're the only person who . . ." She shrugged a little apologetically, with a charming smile, and Celia understood that she was the perfect bolt-hole, being tucked in the sticks and the wife of a professional soldier. As Priscilla must have hoped, she had her all to herself—apart from the children, of course.

"Sure I'm not being a nuisance?" she kept asking as she huddled in her mink coat on the chintz sofa Celia trundled from the sitting room into the kitchen when Frederick was away. She lit one cigarette after another while Robert and Sarah fidgeted self-consciously at the kitchen table with crayons, stealing glances, and Margaret dragged a chair to the sink so she could switch on the taps and flood the floor and reclaim the attention.

"I do admire you, darling," Priscilla said, when she discovered there was no nanny. "What a dear little pudding," she commented about Sarah, and, touching Margaret lightly on the head, "this one's going to be a beauty." But she had no real interest in the children. She only wanted to tell her story, filling in the detail the way Robert was even now dotting birds across a swath of blue sky on his sheet of rough paper.

"Have you ever had that feeling when you're being driven so mad by someone you think you're going to explode if he utters one more word? And you think you'll die if he touches you?" She answered the question herself. "Of course not, darling! You married the love of your life."

Joining the Wrens had been extraordinary for a girl like her, she explained. One minute, she was waiting perfectly happily to be married off, like everyone else; the next she was being given real responsibility and meeting the kind of people she would never have met normally (she touched Celia's hand a little apologetically as she said this) and having more fun than she'd believed possible. But, once the war was over, her mother behaved as if it had never happened. Though the chance of a debutante season had gone, she was still determined to arrange a good match and deaf to Priscilla's protests that she couldn't marry a man she didn't love.

"That day at lunch," Priscilla went on, "I was *this* close to running away. You never guessed, did you? Oh Celia, you're so lucky never to have felt like that!"

In the end, she'd given in, of course, because she could see that nothing had changed. All that exhilarating freedom and democracy had been an illusion. "Girls like me . . ." she began. For uneducated, upper-class girls, marriage was presented as the only option. "I did try," she claimed and Celia imagined her chattering, empty life and the growing despair. "That's why I stopped seeing you and Bet. For some reason, darling, you're the only people in the world I can't lie to." She let out her mirthless laugh. "Funny, isn't it?"

Inevitably, an affair had come along, in the shape of a neighbor called Giles French, long married and a notorious philanderer. Priscilla gave a tremulous smile. "I don't regret it, darling. Not one bit. I never knew that—" (she glanced at the children and spelled out the word) "—s-e-x could be so . . ." Then her voice died away as if "divine" couldn't begin to sum up the wonder of being with a man who knew how to give a woman pleasure. After Giles, "things sort of staggered along," as she put it, until the outburst that had indirectly brought her south. "I blew it. No going back. But d'you know, it's all rather thrilling in a funny kind of way. At least I can be me."

It appeared that in a moment of extreme exasperation—"nothing more grisly than an over-s-e-xed man who hasn't got a clue"—she'd admitted the affair to her husband who, in an uncharacteristic display of decisiveness, had ordered her out of the house.

"What about Giles?" Celia asked.

"Well, I wasn't the first and I won't be the last," said Priscilla, which turned out to mean that, demonstrating a time-honored pattern of behavior, Giles had scuttled back to his wife. She still hadn't taken it in, she admitted. But she seemed more thrilled than upset.

"So maybe I won't have a bean," she went on, making an amused face. "So maybe my parents will never speak to me again . . ." She raised her coffee cup in a toast to recklessness and her old friend, who seemed perfectly happy living in a very modest way. She kept the worst until last: "He's threatened to take Archie."

"That's terrible!"

"It is," Priscilla agreed much more soberly. "I adore my little boy. But he can't, can he?"

"I don't know. I'll have to ask Frederick."

"Oh, would you, darling?"

"Next time we speak."

"Where exactly is he? I forgot to ask."

"Somewhere out east."

"I say, he's not involved in this frightful Suez business, is he?"

But Celia appeared to have been struck by deafness. It happened whenever anyone asked her about Frederick's work. "I thought we might take the children out before it gets dark. There are some beautiful walks round here."

On the walk, stopping constantly to minister to Margaret, who wailed if she was strapped into her pushchair and created even more of a fuss when taken out of it, they saw a tall man with a brown Labrador and immediately Robert and Sarah started jumping up and down with excitement.

"Who's that?" Priscilla asked.

"Michael Oldham," said Celia. "He lives in the cottage down the hill. He's a commercial artist."

"And that's Bovril," Robert added, pointing at the dog. "He eats spiders."

"Looks promising!" Priscilla hissed.

"He's no good at unblocking sinks," murmured Celia, remembering a plumbing disaster a few weeks back and a pleading telephone call.

Then it was time for introductions.

But after shaking hands with Priscilla, Michael Oldham turned and said to Celia, "I need your opinion on something. When can you take a look?"

"Sometime next week?"

"Next week it is." He smiled at her. "I'll look forward to it."

After he strode away, Priscilla asked coyly: "Was that code?"

"Sorry?"

"Darling, I saw how he looked at you!"

"He only wants to show me a drawing!"

Priscilla gave her tinkling laugh. "Of course he does!"

Later, as she put the children to bed, Celia thought about her neighbor. It had been a pleasure to have the occasional adult conversation with someone who appeared to like her and value her opinion, but it had never occurred to her that he found her attractive. It terrified her that Priscilla could question her fidelity. It was obvious that in future she'd have to be cold and off-putting to Michael, which was sad because it could be lonely at Parr's without Frederick.

The following morning, Priscilla stayed in bed until eleven and used all the hot water for her bath and then she picked up the telephone and summoned Bet for dinner. Listening to her gushing, intimate way of talking, Celia pictured Bet's reaction at the other end and thought, "She'll never come."

However, soon after dusk fell, headlights wobbled into the drive and Bet's car jerked to a stop with a series of awful grinding noises. She hadn't brought her husband, though Priscilla had urged her to. Celia

wasn't surprised. Jack didn't bloom in company and, faced with Priscilla's over-the-
top style, might not have uttered a word all
evening. He was big and handsome, a little
younger than Bet. It seemed he'd loved
her for years: an honorable man, unlike
her old collection of married scoundrels.

Robert and Sarah were waiting at the
window even though, moments before,
Sarah had been grumbling that Bet didn't
like them anymore. Her strange new coldness didn't fit with their memories: the
pouncing on them for kisses, the games
and presents.

When they rushed to open the front door,
she told them sharply: "Watch it! I just had
this coat cleaned!" She ignored Margaret—
a difficult feat—but seemed pleased enough
to see Priscilla. "We meet at last!" she said
when they'd finished hugging.

"You look well, darling," Priscilla told her
emphatically, "very."

"You mean, fat," said Bet with a laugh.

It was true she'd put on weight; but, for
Celia, this was less remarkable a change
than the sadness that was beginning to
color her whole personality. She'd guessed
the reason, of course. At the same time,

the pretense had to be kept up that it was Bet's choice not to have a family. But her infertility was driving them apart. Celia knew it was only because of Priscilla that she'd come at all.

But the children showed no tact. They shadowed her like dogs. "I know what s-e-x spells," Sarah confided in a hoarse whisper and, when Bet's attention was elsewhere, confidently fished through her bag. But even after three bars of chocolate had been found, Bet seemed just as cross.

"You haven't any of your own, have you?" Priscilla inquired, and Celia froze.

"No!" said Bet with a savage laugh. "Who wants the responsibility?"

"Go and play," Celia ordered the children. "You've half an hour before bed."

"We want to stay here," said Robert.

"Well, you can't," his mother told him.

"It's cold in the nursery," Sarah pointed out very reasonably.

"It'll be cold in your bedrooms, too." Priscilla added under her breath: "Run along and play now."

But Robert stood his ground. He was bold in a houseful of women.

"I don't think they know how," said Bet, sounding amused.

"We do!" Robert protested indignantly.

"Don't believe you."

A moment later, the children slid from the room. And soon the women heard a series of strange grating, whirring sounds in the distance as if all the clockwork toys in the nursery had been simultaneously wound up and let loose.

"Remember all the married men?" Priscilla marveled after Bet had driven herself back to London. "Remember all that fornicating in boats that was going to keep her warm when she got old?" She let out a shrill laugh. "Can you *imagine* it now!"

Celia was remembering Priscilla and Bet in the garden at Island View—back to back, bickering gently as they shared a cigarette, the affection between them as visible as the mist rolling in off the sea. All these years later, she understood that the friendship could only have happened in wartime even though, in one respect at least, they had more in common now. Having once deplored Bet's obsession with sex, Priscilla had come to appreciate its power.

However, if she'd hoped to impress Bet, she was disappointed. Bet wasn't the slightest bit interested in hearing about Giles French's skill as a lover. "But you have a child!" was her immediate reaction. "How *could* you have abandoned him?"

"It's only temporary," Priscilla had protested. "And he's got Nanny. And I've every intention of going back for him once I've sorted things out."

"Might not be so easy," Bet had pointed out grimly. "You were the one to leave, remember? *And* you've admitted adultery."

Priscilla had hesitated, as if trying to control herself. But it was no good. "Is this really you talking?" Disappointment made her cruel, because of course she'd guessed what made Bet so sour. "Anyway, what do *you* know about being a mother?"

Celia had intervened at that point. "I'm afraid Bet's right. If your husband's as angry as you say, he's not going to give up your son easily."

"Archie," Priscilla had said with a catch in her voice. "That's what he's called— Archibald Arthur Edward George. And I love him more than you could possibly understand, Bet. But I'd rather die than go back to my marriage." Then she'd informed them both bleakly, "You're *so* lucky, not to know what that feels like."

CHAPTER SEVENTEEN

My darling, It was wonderful that you managed to get through just now; so good to hear your dear voice. Forgive me for bothering you with Priscilla's worries at such a time and thank you for coming up with such a helpful suggestion. I just want to reassure you that everything's shipshape and the children are being angelic. I long for you to come home.

Letter to Frederick on rough unheaded paper, undated, but almost certainly written when his battalion was serving with the Anglo-French forces in Suez. Unfinished. Kept for some reason, though never sent.

"He's a peer, isn't he?" said Frederick. "Unfortunately for Priscilla, that might work in his favor. After all—sorry, my love, I've forgotten the boy's name . . ."

"Archie," Celia supplied. "He's called Archie."

"Thank you. After all, Archie's the son and heir. I suggest she find herself a good lawyer."

His voice sounded strained over the crackly telephone line, but as usual they were unable to discuss what really concerned them both even though there was a running national debate on the rights and wrongs of the Suez invasion. It was bad taste for newspapers to run headlines like "Law not War," thought Celia indignantly, when so many men were risking their lives. But she knew that even if she had Frederick in their warm bed, he would never discuss work. He was a soldier first and a husband second, and like every other army wife, she'd learned to accept it.

"Do you know anyone?" she asked, aware she was pushing him.

"Who?"

"A lawyer. Sorry, darling. She's in a bit of a state. I do so want to help if I can."

There was a short silence during which she was made acutely conscious of his impatience and the inappropriateness of asking anything of him at such a time. But perhaps he guessed what "a bit of a state" really meant; or maybe he was reminding himself of his vow to encourage her friendships; or even thinking that the quicker Priscilla got herself sorted out, the sooner she'd leave. He said: "Look in my desk. You'll find the key under the frog paperweight. In the first drawer down, there's a blue file right on top. The telephone number of our lawyer is in there. He's the only person I can think of who might know of a good divorce person. The *blue* file," he repeated before his voice faded out.

Celia went back to the warm, quiet kitchen and, brimming with love for her husband, snatched up a sheet of the children's drawing paper and started scribbling him a letter of thanks. It was eleven o'clock: that longed-for slice of peace midway between breakfast and lunch. Priscilla was still in bed and, as it was a Saturday, all the children were playing outside in the frosty garden. She could hear the crunch and patter of their Wellington boots, the predictable bursts of squabbling and those occasional ominous silences that always cut into her concentration. Was it wrong to consider this her time? The truth was, work gave a sense of identity. "I am a writer," she'd remind herself as she stirred a malodorous bubbling stew of washing on the stove; "I am a writer," as she hacked a spade into frozen earth in search of elusive potatoes. Writing had yielded such rewards: six books in nine years and an independent, though tiny, income—and most important of all, a new confidence. She had to concede that poor dead Katherine, now long forgotten, had done her a real service.

But writing was still furtive and unacknowledged. She'd decided not to tell Priscilla about it—though, like teasing, she'd put one of her books, *She Loved to Love,* beside her bed. "I say, a penny dreadful!" had been the amused reaction; but Priscilla was far too obsessed by her problems to read. Sadly, Bet had been right: her husband, Rupert, had turned vindictive. Priscilla hadn't spoken to Archie since she'd left because the servants up in Scotland— "People I've been perfectly nice to for years!"—were obeying orders not to put her through. She was trying to be positive, but yesterday she'd stared into her powder compact at her tense reflection and wailed, "What's to become of me?" And after that, she'd buried her face in Archie's school scarf, snatched up as she left Scotland, and sobbed and sobbed. It no longer smelled of boy, but of Helena Rubinstein powder and Chanel No. 5 and Woodbines.

Though Celia was longing to start work, that image of distress kept returning to her. She mustn't be selfish, she told herself sternly. The letter to Frederick had been put aside for finishing later, but she delayed opening the kitchen drawer, where her precious notebook was kept, and set off for his study, next to the equally unused sitting room.

It amused her that he kept his desk locked. He was quite right, of course, even though he had no idea how naughty the children could be. This was where he kept important business like bank statements, records concerning the house, birth certificates, and so on: the reason he had a study and she did not. But there was no sense of grievance. She found the warm kitchen with its big wooden table an ideal place to work. Sometimes late at night, when the house was dark and quiet and she could scribble away uninterrupted, she'd reflect on Frederick's absolute lack of interest in her writing. He never asked about it. Perhaps the importance of his own job made it impossible to take hers seriously. Or perhaps he feared her strange difference from other wives and still worried that she might embarrass him, even though she'd demonstrated that she understood the rules. Maybe it was just as well he wasn't interested. If he knew that she occasionally worked right through until dawn, he'd say: "This is not acceptable, Celia. The children are your priority now."

The blue file was precisely where he said, on top of a pile of others. They trusted each other. So once she'd found what she was looking for, why did she linger? It wasn't as if it was comfortable to stay in that room, where the air was so chilly that even after her gasp of shock, her last contented breath was still visible, like a puff of smoke.

Priscilla emerged from her bedroom just in time for lunch. As usual, she was absurdly elegant for a day in the country, with a silver fox fur looped around her shoulders, its dangling plastic snout and glass eyes ensuring the children kept at a safe distance, though her cloud of lovely perfume seemed to send out a different message. Normally, she launched into her own problems, but today she inquired anxiously, "Is everything all right?"

"Of course!" Celia tried to smile. "Margaret woke me in the night," she lied.

"That's funny. I didn't hear her. Sure you're all right? You look white as a sheet." Then Priscilla looked fearful. "I heard the phone earlier." She stared at Celia, biting her lip. "It's not—bad news, is it?"

"Frederick's fine. That was him, actually."

"Thank God! But, darling, I've never seen you so . . ."

"Actually, I have some good news," said Celia and, just as she hoped, as soon as she started explaining about the divorce lawyer she'd found, Priscilla was distracted.

She'd been wrong about the first wife. Katherine hadn't been forgotten at all. Suddenly it was horribly apparent that as the years had rolled past and she'd relaxed into her marriage, Katherine had been

Frederick's equivalent of a notebook in a drawer, his own secret passport to the world of what-if.

It had been a fatal impulse to look through the rest of the folders: buff-colored for the house, green for matters financial—and yellow, the color of the sun, for Katherine. But there was nothing written on the yellow folder to warn her. There were half a dozen photographs inside of the same tall, dark girl, who was quite different, of course, to how Celia had imagined. But she recognized the background in every picture as the estate in Wiltshire where Frederick had been brought up: its ugly imposing house and formal gardens. Obviously, this was how he wanted to remember his first wife—in the safe English world where she should have stayed. Celia wondered how often he opened that folder. Was it every time he sat down at his desk? Or did he save the pleasure for when he felt crowded by his children and bored by his living wife? There were no letters or other mementos. "Beautiful," he'd said of Katherine, but unforgettable was infinitely more dangerous.

Celia had studied the photographs for a

long time, trying not to picture the expression of the one behind the camera. And since she no longer trusted her husband, she'd searched for her marriage certificate (kept in a red folder at the very bottom of the pile) and found the word she'd failed to notice on her wedding day twelve years before: "widower." He'd taken a big risk there. And then she remembered the expression in his eyes and understood that it couldn't have been tender lust, after all.

Priscilla was still anxious, unsatisfied. "Darling, are you quite quite sure you're all right?"

"Honestly," said Celia. "Just exhausted." She added, "You know how it is," which was a little ridiculous, since Priscilla had a nanny to look after her own child.

"You and Frederick . . ." Priscilla began very tentatively.

"Mmm?"

"You are all right, aren't you?"

"Absolutely," Celia assured her, forcing a smile.

Priscilla studied her as if still uncertain. Then she said: "Of course you are! I don't know what I'm thinking!"

Celia thought: "I have the perfect marriage. Everyone needs to believe it, for some reason."

Priscilla rushed on, sounding very relieved: "Oh, darling, of all the marriages I know, yours is best. It's what we all hoped for—still do, actually! Thirty-one's not *so* ancient, is it? I can't imagine how it must feel to come home to someone you love. By the way, darling, when *is* that wonderful man of yours coming home?"

CHAPTER EIGHTEEN

Last night I dreamed I was young. When I took off my clothes, I could glory in my body again and it was all for him. He was young, too, like a brigand. He said, "I have waited so patiently, my love."
Notebook entry. No date, but shakiness
of writing indicates extreme old age.
Idea for one of the later novels?

Jenny Granger heard the shuffling steps well before there was a smudge of movement behind the panes of stained glass, and then shallow, wheezy smoker's breathing just the other side of the front door while she felt herself thoroughly scrutinized through a security pinhole. She assumed what she hoped was a friendly, nonthreatening expression; and, as she waited, she thought of everything she knew about Bet Parker.

It was four months since she'd first talked to Celia's daughters and just three weeks since she'd gained access to the treasure trove of memorabilia in the empty house. She was still flushed with triumph, though she had to concede that the Bayley family had made it easy for her. She'd noted the tensions at the funeral: the chasm of ice between Margaret and her husband, Charles; something tormenting Robert (clearly a control freak) and his wife, Mel. It was ironic that the only one who appeared really content had turned out to be the vulnerable chink. Jenny had no qualms about the way she'd manipulated Sarah. Straightaway, she'd scented an intriguing story behind the clichés as well as the chance to advance her career.

She'd been of two minds about this visit because she would have preferred to carry on working at the house while she had the chance. But the fact was, she'd made a couple of rather surprising discoveries and it seemed politic to bounce them off someone outside the family. As one of Celia's oldest friends, Bet was ideal.

Her name appeared again and again in diaries and letters. Her personality jumped out of that huge, disintegrating mass of paper—intelligent, no-nonsense, big-hearted, but with a hint of sadness. Jenny was still working out Bet's narrative: trying to paste together the gaps between established fact and ambiguous fiction. She knew Bet was a widow, but she was sniffing at the wartime promiscuity, guessing at the anguish of childlessness. "Never trust a writer," she'd reflected soberly more than once. But Celia had made friends with Bet before becoming a writer. And besides, Jenny was beginning to comprehend that a very deep kindness had gone hand in hand with professional ruthlessness. She could relate to that.

Waiting patiently on the step, she remembered a snatch of description from Celia's 1947 diary. "Bet looked so pretty and happy, all in pink. I've told Robert he's entirely responsible for that marriage. I pray that this time next year she'll have a baby, too." She found herself oddly sentimental, wishing that glowing young woman could open the door. She was discovering the helpless sadness of the biographer:

you traced lives from their beginnings, knowing how they'd end, and yet still you hoped to change them.

And now Bet was eighty-six and her husband, Jack, was long dead. This Victorian terraced house in Clapham had been too large for two and must overwhelm Bet now. Jenny wondered why she hadn't moved to a more manageable property. Was it out of nostalgia for happier times? On either side there were newly installed York stone steps, freshly laid black and white tile paths, but Bet probably felt there was no point in paying a builder to smarten up her house. After all, how many years did she have left?

But despite having discovered so much about Bet, Jenny still couldn't be one hundred percent certain which of the two ancient women she'd noticed at the funeral would open the door. She was putting her money on the overweight one who had eaten and laughed with such remarkable gusto but every so often looked bereft and fragile. However, there was just a chance Bet had been the skinny one with the strangled diction and wandering eyes and bleeding magenta lipstick.

"Driver's license," a rough voice demanded, immediately dispelling any doubt. And only after it had been pushed through the letterbox and examined at length was Jenny admitted.

Bet had a plump tabby cat tucked in her arms. She wore a shapeless woolen tube of a skirt and a beige cardigan. Both garments were lightly stained and a pair of smeared spectacles bumped against the shelf of her bosom; but she smelled very pleasantly of soap and toothpaste, as if efforts had been made to maintain cleanliness. She looked cross and put-upon, even though the appointment had been arranged.

"Thank you for agreeing to this," said Jenny warmly, extending her hand.

Bet ignored it. Still clutching the cat, she turned her back and stumped through the hall to a dark sitting room at the back. Jenny followed. There was nothing modern here, either. She imagined the interiors of the houses on either side: decorated much like her own, with oak floors and uplighters and granite surfaces in the kitchen. Here there were fitted carpets with old rugs spread over them, and standard lamps that cast a dim dusty light over photographs of children arranged on every surface. But there was no time to wonder why, though the faces were oddly familiar.

By this time Bet had plonked herself in a flaking brown leather armchair that looked as if it had once been her husband's. Jenny appropriated an uncomfortable low sofa opposite, trying to avert her eyes from the flash of purple thighs spilling over beige support stockings. "I *am* grateful to you," she reiterated.

Bud scowled. "Be grateful to Bud," she said in her rough, gruff voice that seemed not to fit in the gracious world of the Bayleys.

"What a wonderful girl!" Jenny enthused. She liked Bud, from the little she knew of her. More to the point, Bud championed the biography. In fact, it was she who had arranged this meeting.

"She is." Bet gave a wintry smile. Then she blew her nose and scoured out her nostrils very thoroughly, inspecting the handkerchief before tucking it back into her sleeve. "Well, get on with it," she said ungraciously. Obviously no tea or coffee would be offered.

"As you know, I'm writing a biography of your friend, Celia Bayley," Jenny began.

But Bet immediately interrupted. "Would she want that? I don't think so. Very private person. Wouldn't like it one bit."

Jenny said gently, though firmly: "I'm afraid she's become too famous. Someone's going to do it."

Bet scowled. "People aren't interested in the old." There was no self-pity. It was a statement of fact.

"She doesn't deserve to be forgotten," Jenny protested.

"She'll be remembered by everyone who loved her."

"But she was a great writer, too!"

"Really?" Bet pondered this as if for the first time. "Didn't like the early ones much," she pronounced. "Always thought she could do better." Suddenly she smiled, managing to give an astonishing impression of youth despite the nests of wrinkles around her eyes and the tombstone teeth. "I think she was just different. An old person writing about sex? That's tricky, isn't it? "'Specially when it's old people that are at it. Could have been revolting." Another joyous, disturbing smile. "But she made it beautiful. *That* was her special gift."

Bet was right, thought Jenny, a little taken aback that someone else had managed to define Celia's appeal so precisely. "As you know," she began, "the family have granted me access to all her papers, for which I'm enormously grateful. They've kindly given me a key to the house, too. I've been there for the past few weeks, reading and making notes." She added, watching Bet carefully: "I have to say, it's been extraordinarily interesting."

To her relief, Bet responded heartily: "I can imagine!"

So it didn't look as if she'd be springing any surprises on this formidable old bird. She consulted her notebook. "You and Celia Bayley and Priscilla Forbes-Hamilton first met in 1943."

"Correct. Over a crate of carrots." Bet flashed another ecstatic smile, but almost immediately it faded and she gave a deep deep sigh. "Strange times," she pronounced with another hawking sniff and seemed about to go through the handkerchief routine once more.

"That was at Island View on the Solent, which had been requisitioned by the navy. I believe you and Priscilla were both Wrens."

Bet shot her a sharp glance. "Correct," she agreed after a moment.

"And Celia was living nearby with her widowed mother, at a house called Far Point."

But this time, Bet failed to respond. She was staring down at her cat, which was purring loudly as it kneaded her thighs, just out of sync. No wonder her skirt was full of pulled threads.

Jenny decided to get straight to the point. "Look, I'm aware they didn't own that house."

"And how do you come up with that?" Bet sounded very fierce.

"It's not difficult to find out these things." Jenny went on very smoothly and confidently: "There are records."

But in this particular case, fate had conspired to cover up much of the evidence. She'd deduced that Celia and her mother had arrived at Far Point sometime in the mid-1930s and, by rights, the official census records, taken every ten years, should have established the relationships in that house. However, to her frustration, it turned out that, because of the war, no census had been taken in 1941; and then she discovered from a letter that Helen Farmer, Celia's mother, had died in 1947, four years before the next census was due. However, a subsequent search through Land Registry records had proved helpful. It appeared that during Celia's growing up, Far Point hadn't belonged to Helen Farmer at all. It had been owned by a Sir John Falconbridge, who'd purchased it in 1932, and, on his death ten years later, it had passed to his wife, Edith (in whose possession it remained until 1960). It looked very much as if the Falconbridges had been relatives of either Helen or her husband, Richard. They must have taken in Helen and her little daughter, Celia, which seemed to indicate that after the death of Richard in 1930, the family had fallen on hard times. However, Jenny needed all this to be confirmed.

But to her very great astonishment, Bet announced: "So she was the housekeeper! So what?" Then she let out a hearty whistle, as if it was a relief to have it out in the open at last. "Did she have a choice?"

Jenny almost stopped breathing with excitement. When she could think coherently, she realized that this fresh scenario made sense. No wonder Celia had known quite so much about life below stairs, as she'd demonstrated in an early novel, *She Waited for Love.* Then, quite suddenly, Jenny remembered something else Sarah had let slip that day she'd called at the house, soon after the funeral: "Daddy once mentioned an all-purpose housekeeper who'd stayed." Not only was Celia the child of a servant, but there'd been a deliberate cover-up! It was a dream breakthrough, but she managed to keep her cool. She nodded without expression, as if Bet had only substantiated what she already knew. And then she waited because professional interviewing had taught her the extraordinary power of silence. It induced nervousness, which almost invariably made people gabble.

It seemed that, for all her intelligence and individuality, Bet was no exception. She launched into a defense of her friend, confirming what Jenny already suspected. And whenever she paused, Jenny looked blank and unhelpful and let the silence stretch, and concentrated on memorizing the information that was leaking out like water from a spluttering tap. (She seldom took notes or used a tape recorder, having learned this caused self-consciousness.)

"It was Frederick who insisted it be hushed up, not her. . . . Let's face it, he was a bit of a snob. Probably couldn't help it, the way he was brought up. Oh, grand, very grand! But she wasn't going to expose him as a liar, was she? Least of all to their children. That was Celia all through— loyal to a fault." Bet paused, might have stopped for good if Jenny had broken the spell. "It wasn't even as if her mother was a real servant—but it was that or the poorhouse. . . . They never mentioned the father, though Celia did once tell me he'd been wounded in the Great War. Reading between the lines, I think he went doolally— probably shelled. They never get over it. It was a look in her mother's eyes, poor love, as if she'd been through hell. . . . When he died, they were left with nothing, though they didn't bleat about that, either. They never were bleaters, bless them. Those two were close as close, but after Frederick came along, well . . ." She shrugged.

"Celia would have done anything for him, as you'll have gathered. He didn't take to yours truly either when we first met. Thought I was a bad influence, so that was me out of the picture, too." Bet made a comical face, as if in old age she could only concur with Frederick's opinion of her much younger self. "It was hard on her mother, though. He was coming round by the time Robert was born—oh he was a decent man at heart—but then the cancer got her. It was very quick." She bit her lip, as if remembering the intensity of her friend's grief. "And after that, well . . ." She shrugged her beefy shoulders. "You never met Celia, did you?"

"Alas, no," said Jenny very sincerely. She thought she understood what Bet was getting at: for the sake of her beloved husband, Celia had done an impressive job on herself. She was remembering a recent press photograph—the old patrician features beneath a sculpted nimbus of white hair. Also, a passage from one of the tabloids (no doubt a source of pride to the hack who'd written it): "Celia Bayley was the quintessential general's wife, with a cut-glass accent that brought to mind generations of cucumber sandwich teas eaten with daintily crooked fingers on bowling green lawns." Perhaps with time, even Celia had come to believe in the myth.

They'd progressed smoothly enough to the next matter Jenny wanted to raise. "He was a lot older, wasn't he?"

"Twelve years, thirteen . . ." Bet was really chatty now (somehow, it never failed to surprise Jenny when this happened). "Well, she was a child when they met—a very young seventeen. The gap between them narrowed in time, of course. He just got better-looking. Men!" Bet let out a strange barklike noise. "I know what *I'll* choose to be next time round!"

"I've seen photos. He was sensational."

"Oh yes!" Bet sighed. "Best-looking man for miles—and, remember, we had half the navy to pick from." She chuckled. "Clever little thing, Priscilla said. But Celia wasn't like that. She was as gobsmacked as everyone else." She flashed her wonderful, youthful smile. "I love that word, don't you?" She was barely recognizable as the grumpy old woman who'd answered the door.

"No wonder she started by writing romances," said Jenny. A comely servant's daughter barely out of the nursery had caught the eye of a handsome, aristocratic army officer. As Sarah had observed with such unwitting accuracy the first time they'd met, it had been "pure Mills and Boon."

"Mmm." Bet looked into the distance as she stroked her cat.

"And then the way she cared for him for all those years at the end," Jenny continued encouragingly. "A true love story . . ." If only, she thought, she could access the memories spooling in Bet's head: her lifetime's take on the shy young girl who'd matured into a famous writer. She seized advantage of the relaxed, nostalgic moment. "Interesting there was no mention of the first wife, Katherine, in the obituaries. What a tragedy! They were only married for five minutes!" She was staring down at her notebook as she said it, reminding herself of the details. Katherine Elizabeth Bayley, née Cooper-Seymour, born 1915, married August 1935, died January 1937. Once again, it had been Sarah who'd pointed her in the right direction with the casually dropped snippet that her parents had married at Caxton Hall. And after a routine trawl through the records had yielded the surprise of a first wife, there was more to come: Frederick had omitted to mention Katherine in his entry in *Who's Who.* However, there was no doubt Celia had known about her because the marriage certificate clearly stated Frederick Bayley's marital status as "widower." But why had she kept that from her children, too? If anyone could explain, it was Bet.

The next thing Jenny was aware of was a crash. Bet must have risen to her feet very suddenly and, in so doing, tipped over a small table. The cat had vanished. "Get out!" she shouted.

"What?"

"Now!" She was trembling with anger. There'd be no more smiles; she looked every year of her great age now.

"I'm sorry?" Jenny was honestly confounded.

"I should think! Scum!"

"Look," said Jenny, "I'm sure we can . . ."

But Bet cut her short. "Fuck off!" she roared as she fumbled for her stick. Unbelievably, she started whacking it in Jenny's direction.

"There's no need for that!"

"I said fuck off!" Bet took another swipe, lost her balance, and toppled back into her chair.

"I'm going right now," said Jenny, grabbing her notebook and handbag.

The next minute she was out on the street. It was a long time since she'd been treated like that, and she was surprised how shaken she felt; but there was also a growing excitement because she now knew her instinct had been right. There was a real story bubbling away beneath the seemingly decorous surface. Why else had Bet flown into such a rage? So the first wife was a taboo subject. . . . Could that indicate scandal as well as tragedy? Come to think of it, hadn't Celia Bayley written about a promiscuous, heartless ex-wife in her very first novel?

Just half an hour before, Jenny had welcomed the revelation that Celia's childhood had not been privileged, after all. It rendered her far more sympathetic and seemed to fit with the endearing person full of self-doubt she was discovering in diaries and notebooks. But it was now beginning to appear as if Celia had absorbed the worst

characteristics of the upper classes: snob-
bery and deviousness, and maintaining a
sort of absurd secrecy for its own sake.
Jenny could feel herself taking a step back,
which was probably no bad thing for a
biographer.

She was sorry to have upset Bet,
though, because she admired her valiant,
uncompromising style. If things had gone
differently, she'd have asked another question: or rather, felt her way around it, while
watching very carefully for a reaction. For
some reason, yet to be discovered, a happily married young woman had started
penning escapist fiction. But Jenny was
beginning to scent a stranger development
much later: some emotional sea change
so great that it had transformed Celia into
a real writer. Had that good-looking husband of hers everyone maintained was so
devoted become entangled in a serious
love affair? Was that it?

The answer must lie somewhere in the
house and as long as she could keep the
family sweet, she was confident of finding it.

CHAPTER NINETEEN

You can leave your children to be looked after by someone else. You must never do it with a husband.

Piece of dialogue from *She Loved Him.*

Dear Celia, I was surprised by your request to say the least. As you know, I have a job that is quite demanding of my time. However, after talking it over, me and Jack have agreed we can help out for the time being. I hope the children are easy about this. We understand your need to go to Nigeria with Frederick, but in our view, Margaret is far too young for boarding school. . . .

Part of letter from Bet Parker,
dated June 1958.

Was blood relevant? Bet thought not. From
her long perspective, friendship was the
true thread of life. Though an only child
without issue, she'd considered herself
half a matriarch for decades now. She and
Celia had fretted about Robert's tendency
to overwork or the very different problems
of the girls (as they went on calling them,
even when they were over fifty) and rejoiced in the grandchildren. Her first task
of the New Year was always to copy a slew
of birthdays into her new diary, because it
would be unthinkable for any of the family
to turn sixteen or twenty-six or even sixty
without receiving a parcel containing a
piece of ethnic jewelry, a pair of embroidered Turkish slippers, a nifty gadget for
slicing avocados, or some such painstakingly chosen gift. With Celia and Frederick
both gone, she felt her responsibilities
acutely; so she kept quiet about the pain in
her knees and the frightening breathless-
ness. She must live forever—she'd made
the decision at the funeral, hence the fre-
netic energy that had so impressed everyone.

Usually she would have looked forward

all day to dinner at Robert's house. But this time she felt sick with apprehension. "I'd rather not talk on the phone, darling," she'd informed him. "It's family stuff. Important."

He'd reacted with his familiar endearing blend of courtesy and enthusiasm. "Sounds intriguing, Aunt Bet! What an excellent excuse for a dinner party!" But, of course, he had no idea what was to come.

"We share everything, don't we?" Celia had once commented happily. But it turned out they hadn't. Bet was still reeling from the revelation of a dead first wife. To think that her best friend had kept something so monumental from her! She couldn't remember being so hurt. No wonder she'd laid about that ghastly journalist with her stick, and what a pity she'd missed her. God only knew what effect the news would have on the children. And she was very much afraid they weren't going to welcome the truth about who'd really owned Far Point, either. "Oh Celia!" she thought, with a kind of tender exasperation. "How could you have? I know you were protecting Frederick, as usual, but the children would have understood—especially once they'd grown up. *They* knew he wasn't a god!"

But she was cross with herself, too. She cringed as she remembered the way she'd run on to the journalist, whose name she'd already forgotten (though not her sly ways). She should never have agreed to be interviewed. She'd only given in because Bud had begged her to: Bud, who'd been closer to Celia than any of the other grandchildren.

She was so miserable that she didn't notice how unusually warm and well-lit Robert's house was in spite of the familiar typed labels pinned to every switch and knob: "Please put out light." "Please turn down thermostat." "Energy is limited."

It seemed that a chunk of unexpected money could unhinge the most principled of men. "Economic crisis? What economic crisis?" he joked as he dispensed champagne (the real stuff, not the usual Cava), though he moved swiftly on before the fizz had a chance to die down. But Bet could only think that very soon he was going to regret wasting all this generosity on her.

Unusually, she was the last to arrive. Margaret and Charles were there, of course. So was Sarah; but, to Bet's dismay, Whoopee was among the party, too. She found

Sarah's fragile happiness very painful to behold; but remembering the way Celia had steadfastly refused to criticize Whoopee, however badly he'd behaved, forced herself to greet him courteously, though inwardly she fumed. "He has no shame. I don't believe he's given up that girl. He's come back because of the money, and as soon as it's spent he'll be off."

Whoopee was still a very attractive man but, when young, he'd been irresistible. Peering at him through her failing eyes, Bet was remembering their first encounter all those years before.

"Thank you for coming!" Sarah had whispered at the front door of Parr's, enfolding Bet and Jack in a passionate joint hug. She looked anxious—perhaps because she'd momentarily left Whoopee alone with her parents. It was the first time anyone outside the bubble of their love affair had met him. She'd told Bet very passionately that everything depended on the evening going right.

"Dear oh dear!" was Bet's first thought, because although she'd never seen Sarah look so lovely, he was in a different class altogether, as handsome a man as Frederick, though blond rather than dark. "Chippy," was her second reaction, for he was without a tie, though Sarah must have indicated that it was required. "I know it's silly," she'd have said in her shy way, "but that kind of thing matters to Daddy."

Whoopee—introduced by his real name, Derek—told them all straight off that his father was a butcher. "Nothing wrong with that," Bet, the daughter of a postman, reminded herself; but he made such a thing of it. He said blood didn't bother him because he'd seen so much of it as a child. He went into detail about the deliciousness of tripe and pigs' trotters. He talked and talked, with a worrying glint in his eyes as if he was enjoying a private joke at the Bayleys' expense, and Bet saw the anger in Frederick build and freeze and thought, "He's never going to allow this marriage."

Jack had doubts, too, but they both agreed that they'd never seen Sarah so happy.

"He's young," he ventured as they drove home.

"That's true."

"Early days." Jack paused. "Plenty of time to find his feet."

"That's true," Bet repeated, because Sarah's young man hadn't yet settled into a proper career.

"She's set on this, love. It'll break her heart if . . ."

"You're right." They were as one. "I'll have a word with Celia," Bet promised. And next day she did, knowing it would be filtered through to Frederick in an acceptable form.

"If you try and stamp on this, she'll be all the keener," she warned her friend. "Let them be and she could come to her senses. But he loves her, Celia. Jack and me are certain of it."

They'd been wise not to condemn the match. There were practical worries, certainly. But until so recently, Whoopee made Sarah exceptionally happy, lightening her serious, dutiful nature and encouraging her to flower. That had been a wonderful home to visit, Bet reflected: full of affection and laughter, even if money was scarce.

Not like Margaret's house, she thought

sadly, noting the silences between her and
Charles, the cold indifference they no longer bothered to hide for family. And yet not
so long ago, she and Jack had convinced
themselves Margaret was going to be happily married, too.

How odd it must feel to know that beauty
was the first thing people noticed about
you, Bet had reflected on Margaret's wedding day. It must be like transfixing them
with a blinding light, knowing they'd never
even hear you if you said something stupid. In her late thirties, wearing a cream
silk suit and a gardenia in her dark hair,
Margaret was still spectacular and loving
the attention.

Bet had watched the years pass as that
beautiful girl failed to marry. Who was she
waiting for? Had Frederick so shamelessly
indulged her that she was spoiled for all
other men? Thank goodness, Bet thought
at the wedding, that she'd come to her
senses—hopefully in time to squeeze out
a baby—because it was obvious that
Charles adored her. She needed to be
adored. And it would suit her to be rich.

"You're a lucky man," were Bet's first

words to him after the ceremony. She meant it. She'd known Margaret since she was a tiny child and prided herself on understanding the depth of feeling beneath the spoiled and uncaring façade. She was remembering little arms locked around her neck, kisses that seemed as if they'd never stop. That scrap had been packed off to boarding school before she could even read! And then, when she was a vulnerable teenager, she'd seen her beloved daddy felled by that dreadful stroke. No wonder she'd found it hard to sort herself out.

Bet had never seen such a smile. Charles was almost handsome, she thought, now the anxiety had vanished. She understood that it had been there right up until the moment when Margaret said "I do."

"I know," he said, looking at the shiny new ring on his finger. "And I promise you, Bet, that I'm going to spend the rest of my life making sure she doesn't regret this."

But it hadn't worked, thought Bet very sadly twenty years on. What was best: a marriage to a loose cannon like Whoopee who gave you years of happiness before humiliating you or an unhappy one to a thoroughly decent man you couldn't love? It was too complicated for Bet, who, almost haphazardly, had married a good man she'd come to adore. Thank God for Theo and Evie! At least Margaret and Charles had been blessed in one truly important respect.

They were all essentially polite people. Even so, Whoopee must have picked up the suspicion and resentment. He began to talk to Sarah intimately, though loud enough for everyone else to hear. "Did you know, Crinkle, that your breasts are different shapes?"

"Are they?" Sarah sounded coy though uneasy, as if she welcomed this attention but was silently pleading with him to defer it until they were alone together.

"More champagne," Robert boomed. It was a measure of his deep embarrassment that he offered again so soon, and so was the way that he filled glasses to the brim.

Whoopee continued, undeterred. "Yes, my love. Your right one's shaped like a pear and the other's a melon—one of those little stripy jobs we sometimes have with Parma ham."

The family was perfectly aware that this was a deliberate assault on them, but they felt unable to protest because on the face of it Whoopee was behaving like a loving husband. That was the worst part. It was a typically cynical and manipulative piece of behavior, thought Bet. Mel appeared in the doorway just as he had both hands on Sarah's breasts and was speculating out loud which one he preferred. Bet couldn't look at Sarah. Was she, too, imagining him making a private and far more hurtful comparison?

"Dinner," Mel announced, before bolting back into the kitchen.

It was Robert's first attempt at cooking a meal, he reminded everyone, and it wasn't a disaster, thanks to Mel. She'd whispered to Bet that it had been necessary to point out to him that if he made cheese soufflé for the first course and chocolate mousse for the last, each person would end up eating the equivalent of three eggs. She'd cleared up his mess, too, and, though he didn't know it, seasoned the meal properly when his back was turned. But she beamed like a proud mother as he doled out steak and kidney pie with roast potatoes, followed by trifle with whipped cream.

"Stuff cholesterol," he advised his guests. Then he bowed his head and became deeply serious for grace, while Whoopee's lips twitched with amusement, as usual. "For what we are about to receive," he intoned, "may the Lord make us truly thankful."

However, Bet was unable to enjoy any of it. She looked at the three people she loved most and could only think that very soon they'd never trust her again.

Her closeness to Celia's children had started when she was thirty-five and free-falling in despair after her third and final miscarriage. She had not told Celia about those lost babies. As for her long-ago abortions, they were like a dark stain on her soul. A silence fell between the two friends that stretched and might have become permanent. But then, suddenly, there was Celia—who'd sworn never to be parted from her children—writing to inform her that she was accompanying Frederick on his next posting to Nigeria. This apparently meant

that when the summer term ended, someone had to collect Robert and Sarah and
Margaret from their boarding schools and
put them on a plane for Lagos. As if that
wasn't enough, once the holiday was over,
the whole thing would have to be done in
reverse. It was presented as a favor that
couldn't be turned down. It ignored the fact
that for years and years, Bet had shunned
Celia's children and didn't get on with
Frederick. She said yes, of course. "What
else can we do?" she demanded crossly of
Jack.

It didn't stop there. The army would pay
for the children to go out only once a year,
which meant that for the remaining two
school holidays they were obliged to go to
Frederick's mother in Wiltshire. Bet orga-
nized that, too, until six-year-old Margaret
announced they'd rather stay with her. "It's
not right," Bet grumbled to Jack, who responded with a smile and a pat on the
hand. With his blessing, she gave up her
job and became "Aunt Bet." Her warmth
was exactly what the children needed,
along with the efficiency. She and Jack
even moved to a more spacious house in
Clapham (though they told everyone it was

because Jack wanted a garden). Those were wonderful times. And meanwhile, out in Africa, Celia played the dutiful wife and, without doubt, missed her children dreadfully. A great friendship was like a great love affair, Bet had once reflected, in that you never needed to spell out why you loved that person. Understanding shimmered between you like a ghost.

Breaking the news to the family turned out to be just as terrible as she'd feared. She resisted the temptation to point out that it had been their mistake in the first place to sanction a biography (as she'd have told them if they'd only asked). It was obvious that any halfway competent journalist was going to lift up a few stones. Privacy didn't exist in the twenty-first century, she reminded herself—unaware that it was entirely through her indiscretion that Jenny Granger had discovered the truth about Celia's background. She shivered as she contemplated her own mistakes being picked over. Thank God she'd never been famous!

"The filthy reptile!" Robert exploded.

Bet flinched. "I do realize how difficult

this is for you, darlings." She'd known the truth about Far Point all along—she'd just admitted it. So why should they believe her claim to have been as shocked as them by the revelation of a first wife? She searched the faces around the table and found dismay and embarrassment in all but one.

"Who asked her to shovel muck?" Robert continued, by now very pink and cross.

"My wife did express her misgivings, if you remember," Charles reminded everyone in his fussy ingratiating way, but Margaret ignored him, and Bet noticed that, too.

"Makes my blood boil," Robert went on, and Bet wished he hadn't put it quite like that because she could almost hear the blood churning in his veins. Frederick had had high blood pressure, too, as none of them could forget.

"We'd better get the key back," said Sarah in a small voice.

He reacted with almost comical dismay. "What?"

"Bud did ask you," she reminded him.

"Tell me I'm dreaming! That reptile's been rootling through Mummy's things?"

He'd forgotten all about giving his consent. Either that or he hadn't taken in the implications. Bud had caught him at a bad time, what with the worry about Miranda; and of course it had never occurred to him that there might be family secrets. "That's it! We're getting the locks changed tomorrow, first thing." He was blinking and twitching with stress.

Only Whoopee seemed happy, and Bet knew why. He'd trumpeted his working-class roots for years while claiming to be patronized. Now the tables were turned. His smug, amused expression said it all: he was as good as them—better in fact, because he was no hypocrite. He licked his knife ostentatiously. He was even planning a joke—and so what if it exposed his dyslexia? He'd just shown Bet the notice he'd scribbled to pin up in the hall for Robert to find later: "Stuff globel worming, I'm ok."

Then Miranda made a late entrance. "They said you'd be here, Aunt Bet!" she exclaimed with real pleasure.

"Look at you!" Bet exclaimed, enfolding her in a fierce embrace. The time had long since passed when it had been anguish to be anywhere near a pregnant woman. Besides, she was keenly anticipating the first great-grandchild. It was such a relief that Robert and Miranda were reconciled, though she wished Celia could have lived to see it. And she'd have loved the way Robert had become so involved: far more than he'd ever been with Mel's pregnancies. Medical terms like "elderly primi gravida" tripped from his lips. He might have been having the baby himself.

"So," said Miranda, tucking into her food, "what's the goss?"

But nobody answered; and with a sense of doom, Bet realized they were all waiting for her.

However, Miranda seemed remarkably unfazed once she'd heard the story. "I daresay they had their reasons," was her only comment. Then she asked Bet to try and remember every scrap of what Jenny Granger had said about her grandfather's first wife. "Katherine," she repeated with a tender smile, like welcoming the shade of that tragic young woman into the family. "Poor Grandpa! He was really young, too. He must have believed his only hope was to pack it away. I can understand that." Her voice trembled because she was very emotional these days.

But Bet still couldn't understand why Frederick had concealed his first wife (or far more hurtful, why Celia had colluded with him). Where could the shame be in a young death? But fond as she'd eventually become of Frederick, she'd always seen him as something of a cipher. It had always mystified her why he insisted on keeping up the myth of Celia's grand background. After he'd gone, Celia could have told her about Katherine, surely? They'd shared everything else, hadn't they?

"Then he met Gran, thank goodness, and they lived happily ever after."

Bet smiled at Miranda. It was going to be all right, she told herself. But that was before Robert spoke—ill at ease though determined.

"Just one last question, Bet . . ." Not "Aunt Bet," this time, like stressing she wasn't real family. He sounded frighteningly detached. "Is there anything else we should know?"

"Any more skeletons in the cupboard?" Whoopee was very drunk by now, and it was obvious Sarah would have to drive them back. He put on an exaggeratedly upper-class accent: "Do tell! I'm consumed by curiosity! Any prison sentences?" He cast a sly glance at Miranda's stomach. "Any bastards?"

Bet ignored him, like everyone else. Memories were returning, unprovoked and stinging, like insects batting into her face at night. A day in 1944 when newly engaged Celia, clearly upset, had confided Frederick's refusal to make love or, far more significantly, discuss any previous romances. Celia on a surprise visit from Germany, plainly even more anxious, but she'd been obsessed by her own problems. ("I was about to have another abortion," Bet recalled, wincing.) And finally there was that surprising first novel about a troublesome ex-wife. All these years later, Bet understood that Celia *had* confided the secret, probably in the only way she could. It wasn't Celia who had failed as a friend, she acknowledged miserably.

All marriages took time to settle in, but Bet was in no doubt that Celia's had turned out to be a good one. She was remembering the terrible time immediately after Frederick's death, and Robert's SOS call. "Please come, Aunt Bet. She won't eat, she won't talk. We don't know what to do." And

Bet had instantly packed a case and was about to leave the house when Robert phoned again. "There's no need," he'd said, actually laughing with relief. "She's going to be fine." At the funeral a week later, Celia had shown inspiring strength and dignity. Thereafter, writing had sustained her, as she'd once admitted to Bet—lightly and without fuss.

Could there be other secrets to upset the children? Some memory was nibbling at the edges of Bet's consciousness, but she couldn't put her finger on it. That was what happened when you were old. And then suddenly the missing thought would appear at the most inconvenient time, when you were in the supermarket or talking about something else: like a price popping up on an old cash register. She decided to consult Priscilla because running through her apparent foolishness was a strange streak of intuition. She'd rattle on about trivia, but occasionally she'd let slip an acute observation as if a hidden clever part of her had been watching and listening all the time.

"If there *was* anything, I'd tell you," she assured Robert and the girls. She was remembering Frederick and Celia at the end, like a pair of old entwined trees. That handsome, once vigorous man had come to depend on her utterly, following her with fierce unblinking eyes. But throughout his long illness, Bet had never once heard her friend complain. Once, she'd even wondered if Celia welcomed the chance to show the extent of her devotion. No wonder so many people saw that marriage as an example of perfect love.

CHAPTER TWENTY

She was like a devil, twining herself around him, doing her best—or worst—to lure him. Sylvia felt the pity of the other women, but found it more amusing than upsetting. She knew Humphrey would never betray their special bond. The foundation of her happiness rested on the certainty that this supremely clever and attractive man loved only her.

From *Her Special Hero,* published 1959.

Celia hadn't expected the boldness of Africa, like an overly made-up opinionated person who refuses to be ignored. One minute she was following Frederick out of the dark little transfer airplane at Abeokuta; the next she was met by a wall of heat and an explosion of brilliance and—when her senses could take them in—the sweet scent of frangipani blossom mingled with the stench of sewage: an experience as simultaneously beautiful and distressing as Africa itself.

Twenty-three years earlier, in 1935, another woman—beautiful and clever—had stepped into just such a hot, alien environment. In the Stratocruiser on the seemingly endless flight to Lagos, stopping at Frankfurt and Rome and Tripoli and Kano to refuel, Celia had noticed Frederick's abstracted expression, his long silences, and understood with a familiar ache that he was tuning in to old emotions and hopes. She was the mother of his children, but she felt forgotten in the seat next to him. Having made the painful decision to sacrifice watching Robert and Sarah and Margaret grow up in order to be a good wife she finally understood that Katherine would never go away and, furthermore, that now, more than ever, he'd be tempted to compare them. However, one good thing could come out of her sacrifice (which was, after all, commonplace among army wives): Bet could revel in the company of children at last. "I'll never be jealous of her," Celia vowed on that flight. "Pray God, I won't."

Frederick's job at the station involved helping to prepare the Nigerian army for independence. Celia's was to support him at all times and play hostess at the many dinners and cocktail parties considered an essential part of a high-flying soldier's career path. It was daunting for someone shy. She was well aware that Katherine would almost certainly have managed better, but they never discussed this. In fourteen years of marriage, they'd had just one conversation about his first wife.

They were given a spacious house set in a big garden kept unnaturally fresh and green by a battery of gardeners. In recognition of Frederick's seniority, it was on the outer rim of the compound with superb views over the savannah and the desert beyond.

The best thing about life in Nigeria was being waited on, according to the other wives, but it continued to make Celia uncomfortable even after Frederick pointed out that it was their servants who should be grateful in such a poor country. There was no sign among the staff of the sly mockery she'd grown up with. Any tension seemed to derive from tribal differences or the pilfering the other wives said was inevitable. And yet every time she went into the bustling, noisy kitchen to talk about menus it made her homesick for Far Point.

During her first week, Sam, the Yoruba cook, brought two live guinea fowl for her to inspect. Under the impression that they were house pets, rather like the two birds of paradise kept as regimental mascots, she admired their spangled gray plumage. "Sweet," she told Frederick, and he kept a poker face until they turned up, plucked and roasted, on the lunch table.

Sam would make sponge cakes with the flour that was kept in a locked cupboard (just like Lady Falconbridge's olive oil had once been), and shepherd's pie and, as a rare treat, steak and kidney pudding. Meanwhile, peanut stew or palm nut soup bubbled away pungently on the stove, trumpeting the deliciousness of African food, which, for some bizarre reason, the Europeans refused even to try.

Sometimes Celia longed to take her

notebook in there and work at Sam's table heaped with yams and plantains and okra. Instead, she wrote furtively in her bedroom whenever there was time, which felt a little like having an affair except that Frederick knew about it. The deal had never changed: she was permitted to continue with her writing so long as it didn't interfere with more important duties and she told no one. Meanwhile, back in England, Bet was still the only person to receive inscribed copies of the books. She never commented. Perhaps, thought Celia, she didn't read them either. No wonder she felt like two women: the decorous soldier's wife and the spinner of romantic stories for an unknown audience.

But without her writing Celia could never have endured that time. There was so little to keep the women occupied: no children to care for and only a certain amount of bridge games and parties and picnics to organize or attend. There was a fabulous, exotic world beyond the compound, of course, but a surprising number of women chose never to explore the bush and its animals and birds. They behaved as if they were on an island: a little piece of England that had been shipped over, along with favorite pieces of furniture and fine china.

Dinner was over—four stodgy courses served by William, the Hausa houseboy, in his immaculate white uniform and gloves. The Wedgwood plates and the gleaming silver cutlery and the exquisitely laundered linen napkins had been cleared away. And now, after their half hour of important, uninterrupted male talk over brandy and cigars at the long lustrous mahogany table, the men had rejoined the women, and the strains of "Oklahoma" played on the windup gramophone were drifting through the mosquito screens into the steamy night.

It was like dozens of other evenings—or so it seemed until about ten o'clock, when one of the Bayleys' guests started behaving extraordinarily inappropriately.

Her name was Milly Noonan. She was newly arrived in Abeokuta and, it seemed, unaware that the main priority for junior wives was to avoid attracting attention. But she was younger than the others, and far prettier, with long dark hair and skin as milky and luminescent as Priscilla's had once been. Even her dress of clinging silver lamé seemed attention-seeking to the other women, who'd removed themselves to a watchful, disapproving distance.

"Oh, for God's sake!" she was heard to exclaim. "How can you all stand it? Let's at least have something we can dance to!" Then she rose from a sofa and started rifling through the neatly arranged pile of 78s under the anxious scrutiny of William, whose job it was to select the music (invariably show tunes from *Oklahoma!* or *The King and I* or *Carousel*).

"She's drunk too much because she doesn't care," thought Celia. "She's bored to death with her nice but dull husband, who's terrified that she's just ruined his prospects but still can't keep his eyes off her." She could feel the electricity from the other wives and knew she must intervene: find some pretext to remove Milly while protecting her dignity and that of her husband. And after she'd recorded the guests and the menu and the flowers in her hostess book, she'd pencil a line through the Noonans' names. Gossip traveled fast here. They would not be invited anywhere after this.

"Frank Sinatra!" exclaimed Milly, sounding happier. She seemed oblivious to her husband, who was following her every doomed move like a man in a trance.

But a part of Celia was enjoying this because it was so novel, in that stuffy, insular environment, to see anyone behave spontaneously. Milly was so young—and she'd only articulated her own secret feelings. How *did* they all stand this unnatural life?

Then she noticed that William was staring at the empty doorway as if he'd seen a ghost—though soon afterward she understood that one of the junior servants must have come to the drawing room with the intention of attracting his attention. A moment later, William was gone, too, and Milly had taken over the gramophone and the sound of "Bewitched, Bothered and Bewildered" filled the room, that singular sophisticated mastery of syrupy lyrics surmounting the hiss of the needle, the crackly recording. She started swaying in her clinging silver dress. But however greatly the men were tempted to dance with her, Celia knew none of them would. She might as well have painted a black cross on her forehead. To compound her bad behavior, she increased the volume, drowning out their favorite conversation about how the country was likely to fare post-independence.

But just as Celia was about to suggest to Milly that she might like to powder her nose in one of the grand bedrooms upstairs, William was back, hovering silently by her side, waiting for her to notice him.

"What is it, William?"

"There is a messenger outside, madam."

They were the words every mother out there dreaded because they could only mean bad news from England. International telephone calls had to be booked hours in advance, so if anyone living in the compound needed to be urgently contacted, headquarters would get a message to the army mess, and a runner would deliver it in person.

Later Celia had no memory of the messenger. All she could focus on was the brown envelope she was handed. Standing there in the warm night, she knew this was punishment for abandoning her children.

She ripped it open. "Sarah had successful operation for burst appendix yesterday, no worries," it read. Succinct and positive—typical of Bet. She and Jack must have received a call from the school and, knowing them, had dropped everything to drive to the hospital where Sarah had been taken. Bet had probably held her hand as she came round from the anesthetic, whimpering and disoriented, and murmured words of love and comfort. For a second, Celia experienced visceral jealousy. "They're *my* children!" she thought. Then she pulled herself together. "Thank God for Bet!"

William was hovering in the background: too well trained to ask questions, too human not to show concern.

"My daughter Sarah's been ill. But she's going to be all right, William, thank goodness, and that's all that matters."

"God bless you, madam," he responded with a flash of white teeth.

Sometimes Celia wondered what the servants made of the strange cold practices of the Europeans, whose children were sent out like parcels once a year, then dispatched back, pale and sobbing, the paper scrumpled, the string all loose. "It's only for a few years," she'd remind herself, even though these were crucial years as far as the children were concerned and she had no real idea how long they'd stay in Africa and Frederick might even be posted elsewhere immediately afterward. And then she'd think of Priscilla, who'd lost her only child for good after her divorce (with her own servants testifying that she was an unfit mother). Frederick was right: the aristocracy lived by different rules.

She knew he must have been worried by her absence and was anxious to reassure him. She felt as if hours had passed, but to her surprise the same tune was playing as she hurried back to the big drawing room. She saw the figures, slightly distorted through the etched glass in the door panel: a man and a woman dancing in perfect accord, the woman like a glittering silver snake, dark hair tumbling down her back.

"She can laugh but I love it, although the laugh's on me . . ." Strangely, it took a second or two to absorb the identity of the other dancer. It was because he was the last man Celia had expected. Though Frederick had a good sense of rhythm, dancing wasn't considered appropriate for a top man, especially after a formal dinner party, and quite apart from her unseemly behavior, Milly was the wife of a very junior colleague. Celia noticed that the other women were regarding her in a hateful new way, as if it pleased them to discover that her husband, apparently so upright and devoted, was just like all the rest. If only they knew! Looking at Milly's pale incandescent skin, the curves of her body in her silver dress, Celia thought, almost amused, "He's blind to it all. He's never seen anyone but Katherine."

"Bewitched, bothered, and bewildered am I . . ." She must fill in the details for herself: Milly, all of a sudden horribly sober and dismayed that she'd blown her husband's chances; Frederick, meticulously courteous, taking pity on a foolish girl and repairing the situation as only he could. Yes, she thought, that must have been how it happened. As the dance ended, she smiled at him, thankful he could be relied on to do the right thing. But he was looking down at Milly with an expression that was half frowning, half fascinated, as if he had just been asked a completely unexpected question and was still pondering his reply.

CHAPTER TWENTY-ONE

The soil is clammy and dark unlike this fine red dust that I fear will lurk in my hair and clothes forever, and the cool garden smells of wood smoke and leaf mold and even the birds are quieter. Inside the house, butter lies softening on the kitchen table all day long because there are no servants to notice and put it away, and when the children and I return home after searching the beechwoods for chanterelle mushrooms, we spread it on toasted crumpets for tea. . . . Oh, how I long for all this even though I know I shouldn't because of F.

Diary entry under October 15, 1960.

Two years had passed, bringing a thrilling promotion and a move up-country to the military base at Kaduna. And suddenly the school holidays had come round again and the idle gossiping wives were transformed into anxious mothers, as if a cord that had lain slack for ten months had suddenly been pulled taut.

Now that their children were, at the most, half an hour away, they dared to remember the soft hedgehog feel of a recently shaved nape, the press of perfect skin, but instead of sharing this swell of emotion, they complained about the heat, as usual, as they sweltered under the corrugated iron roof of the airport building at Kano. In keeping with her status as senior wife, Celia used a proper fan. The others stirred the air with old copies of *Vogue* and, in the case of a woman who prided herself on her superior intellect, *Encounter*. All of them were anxiously consulting watches. For ten and a half months, they'd survived on stilted letters written under the scrutiny of school matrons and horribly expensive three-minute Christmas day telephone calls that were so keenly anticipated by both sides that nothing of importance was ever said or remembered. But now they pictured the interior of the jet plane coming ever closer: the serried seats of beautifully behaved children dressed in shorts and T-shirts under the winter clothes they'd left England in, money belts clasped round their waists. It was strangely unrealistic of them because, on previous occasions, when the doors had at last opened, a rabble of children had come roaring out. Furthermore, a mother who'd ventured inside the plane in search of a forgotten satchel had reported an indescribable mess. She finally understood, she said, why the air stewardesses always appeared so exhausted.

"It's late," one of the women observed unnecessarily.

Celia glanced at her own watch and felt faint because this was all too much—first the love and now the fear. She thought of her children in a massive two-decker Britannia jet held up only by air currents. She once suggested to Frederick that the three of them should fly out separately, but he told her fondly not to be absurd. Flights to Kano were infrequent. If the children flew out one by one, the last would be obliged to go home almost straightaway. She agreed, of course, because by now she'd learned that the only way of conveying anxiety to a man trained to dismiss it was to make a joke of her own weakness.

"Ahh . . ." A collective gasp went up because someone had spotted a tiny blob in the brilliant blue expanse of sky. And soon they all heard the whine of the jet engine, like that of a separate, invisible plane following on behind. Then it was a matter of silent prayers before the terrifying thump on the runway, the scream of the wind as it tore against the flaps that shot up on the wings.

"Ahh!" the women gasped again, this time with relief because the landing had been successful and now the jet was trundling briskly toward the airport buildings. There was still the flight on the much smaller (and riskier) airplane bound for Kaduna, but they could face anything now that they had their children.

Like all the other mothers, Celia was convinced she'd recognize her own immediately. However, in ten months, Robert had grown at least four inches and Sarah had put on weight. Only seven-year-old Margaret was unmistakable, with her oddly mature little face, her cloud of dark hair, her singular grace and beauty.

The day the children arrived was always a success. They were delighted to see their parents and thrilled to be in Africa, with its exotic animals and birds, where their every wish was anticipated by a retinue of smiling servants. Then reality kicked in. They'd been turfed out of their real home and packed off to strict, uncomfortable boarding schools so their parents could enjoy this wonderful life all year round. They started behaving less well on about day three, though never to their father. That would have felt like showing disrespect to a king.

Frederick said: "What are the plans tomorrow, darling?"

"I thought we'd go riding. Take a picnic. They say it'll be cooler."

"Good, good!" said Frederick. "Margaret will love that."

The children had gone to bed and, as usual, the two of them were enjoying a nightcap on the veranda, catching up on the day, discussing any problems or anxieties. Beyond the mosquito screens—out there in the mysterious warm dark, where fireflies drifted like dying embers—they could hear the faint cracking of branches as if huge beasts were stealthily encircling their nice house full of servants and perhaps even contemplating smashing through the stout fencing that bound the green oasis of a garden. It was a comfort to know the compound was well guarded at night. You felt the murmur of danger all the time, and not just from elephants and hippos and poisonous snakes. There were dark stories of murder and robbery in the forest. And everyone in that compound was warned not to stop if they became involved in a traffic accident involving a Nigerian, especially in a town or village.

Celia said: "Darling, I think it would be a good idea if you could spend some time with Robert. Just the two of you."

He glanced at her and heaved a deep sigh. Having the children was splendid, but he couldn't drop everything just because they'd come out for the summer holiday. The army was a tough game, even at his level: you couldn't take your eye off the ball for a second, and she, of all people, should appreciate this. All of which he conveyed without uttering a word.

Undeterred, she continued: "He feels you're disappointed with him."

"Has he said that?" he inquired very sharply.

"Of course not!" she soothed. More marital tactics: plant an idea, then retreat, allowing him to deal with it in his own time without loss of face. She knew he was a good and fair man. She also understood that he loved his son, though he seemed incapable of showing it.

In effect, Robert had two fathers. For ten and a half months of the year, one of them listened to him and laughed at his jokes and cuddled him when he was upset. For the remaining six weeks the other (who shook hands when they met) demanded too much and expected to be obeyed. Robert had picked up Jack's gentleness, his way of considering a question long and carefully before responding; but this seemed to madden his real father. "Spit it out!" he'd urge, drumming his fingers. Robert tried hard to please him, even boning up on his passions. "So how exactly did Monty keep the initiative in North Africa?" he'd asked at dinner, which had temporarily done the trick, though his father had reprimanded him for showing insufficient respect to Lord Montgomery, a national hero. He was thirteen now and making the awkward transition from child to adult. Should he emulate the man he loved or the one for whom bands played and whole battalions marched? Sensing uncertainty, his real father became even more exasperated.

The girls were confused, too. Sarah played the fool and overate. Margaret stamped her foot and shrieked when thwarted.

Celia concentrated on packing the holiday with treats and expeditions, while edging as close to her children as she dared. Her servants could never have guessed from her cool, composed demeanor how deeply she was suffering: aching for embraces yet terrified of rejection. There was no time for explanations or adjustments. When Margaret sobbed for Bet, there was nothing to do but sympathize. It was Bet, of course, who would pick up the pieces once the holiday was over, and become even more loved in the process. It was so hard not to feel resentment, despite all her good intentions.

"Margaret worries me . . ." But while Celia was still wondering how best to phrase this, Frederick murmured, "Little minx!" in a voice dripping with tenderness. Earlier that day, he'd spent at least an hour instructing Margaret on how to saddle up a horse, though any one of the grooms in the compound's stables would have been delighted to do it. Celia told herself that this love for his youngest child was something he couldn't help. He called her "my beauty," whereas Sarah was "funny one" and Robert was "Mr. Plod." Like weary actors, the two eldest dutifully played up to this pigeonholing while Margaret pirouetted in the spotlight.

"What about you? What are your plans for tomorrow?"

"Oh, I have to fly down to Abeokuta for the night. Did I not mention it?"

"In the children's holidays? Whatever can be that important, darling?"

He didn't answer because he never discussed work, as she really should know by now.

Celia had no idea if Milly Noonan was still in Abeokuta. Once she'd wondered if that unhappy, self-destructive beauty was the real reason for the move to Kaduna. In this hot unnatural place, gossip fed on itself and it became almost irrelevant whether or not there was any substance to it. But clearly the army didn't believe he'd been foolish enough to risk his career for the wife of a subordinate. He was a general now: a big fish in a small pond.

As Phil, the new houseboy, had forecast, it was slightly cooler by the following morning.

Frederick left very early in a chauffeur-driven car for Kaduna's tiny airport, where the pilot of a light plane had waited all night to fly him south to Abeokuta. The house relaxed and Celia let the children sleep on until nine. But when they discovered why, they seemed only hurt that yet again, their father had put them second.

Celia watched Sarah consume all four eggs John, the cook, had scrambled (expecting only a third to be eaten); then three of his delicious warm rolls, slathered with Keiller's Dundee marmalade flown out from England; then mangos and bananas picked that morning from the trees in the garden. "Darling, we'll be eating our picnic lunch soon," she murmured, striving to appear more gently amused than critical.

Sarah looked surprised and even a little hurt. Of course she'd eat lunch! When had she not eaten everything that was put before her?

By contrast, Margaret played with her food, treating it as a bargaining tool. She'd eat a mouthful of egg but only if she was allowed to ride the beautiful gray mare Frederick had warned them all was unreliable.

"Darling, you know that's out of the question."

"Daddy *said* I could!" She was working herself into a fury. Celia marveled that even when her face was red and contorted, she still looked more beautiful than any child she'd ever seen.

"Liar!" said Robert quietly but savagely, as if he'd had enough of Margaret getting all the attention and now that his father was absent he felt free to say so.

How would Bet have defused this? Celia tried for distraction. "Look!" she said, pointing at a troop of mongooses running across the lawn. "Daddy swears the same one is always leading them—Captain Mongoose, he calls him."

"They all look the same to me," said Robert. However, Margaret slid from her chair, a roll in hand, with the intention of feeding the mongooses. When they took fright and shot into the undergrowth, she let out a piercing scream. This was the cue for Sarah to imitate a mongoose. She dropped on all fours on the lawn and tried to scamper, but she was too plump. She collapsed, giggling and showing her knickers. At this point, Phil entered to ask if more tea or coffee was needed and stopped short, a hand over his mouth, more fearful than amused, as if picturing the general's reaction.

When he'd gone, Celia said impulsively: "Do you remember when Priscilla came to stay with us at Parr's?"

Immediately Sarah lay still and Margaret stopped crying. Celia knew it was a risk to mention the house where they'd been born, which had lain empty throughout the posting to Africa. However, for the first time since they arrived, she sensed a softening in their attitude. Perhaps they were remembering that at Parr's they never questioned her devotion.

She went on talking. "Daddy was off somewhere. It was long before we got central heating and we lived in the kitchen. Priscilla was always staying with us— remember? And she was fun when she'd had a drink or two. We used to play charades. Once you had to act out 'collaborate,' Robert. You took a piece of coal from the scuttle, which was clever."

A look of pleasure flickered across her son's face as if he wasn't used to praise, and she had to rein back the impulse to hug him.

"Did I?"

"Absolutely," said Celia in a composed way, "and you know why I know? Because I wrote it down in my diary. I decided I would remember everything for all three of you until you were old enough to do it for yourselves."

"That's silly," said Margaret in her baby voice.

"*You* may like to know, miss, that when you were two you pushed a marble up your nose and we all had to take you to hospital."

"That was really daft," Robert observed.

Margaret was fingering her nose as if contemplating doing it again.

"What have you done with them?" Sarah asked very casually.

"What?"

"Your diaries."

"They're at home," said Celia, relishing this first real conversation since the move to Africa.

"Where?" Sarah was picking at a piece of scrambled egg on her shirt with an expression of intense concentration.

"Parr's, of course."

Celia observed her two eldest children exchange a covert glance. It was painful to read them so easily. Could it really be true that after such a long absence Parr's was still their real home?

"Which room?" Robert asked, sounding eager, as if already anticipating their return—pushing open the front door that would stick with damp, breathing in the house scent of old wood ash and dried flowers, checking if there was still a mouse nest under the stairs, pulling off the white sheets that shrouded the furniture like sleeping ghosts. What special place had she chosen to keep the diaries safe? The big desk in his father's icy, unused study, kept locked for as long as any of them could remember? Or the secret drawer of the high hard double bed in his parents' room looking onto woods and fields, from which, according to family lore, his father had once shot a rabbit and, in his excitement, forgotten to open the window? No, it had to be the kitchen, where the four of them had once kept warm and been so close.

Celia hesitated. "They're in a trunk in the attic."

"Oh . . ." Immediately Sarah's voice went dead, and Robert walked stiffly out into the garden as if he wanted no more of this.

It was useless to tell them the truth: that she'd put her precious diaries somewhere they could never get stolen or mislaid. They'd made up their minds. The diaries had been packed away to gather dust because they were seen as unimportant and inconvenient. They could relate to that.

Margaret's baby voice returned. "Daddy said you wrote books."

Celia hid her surprise. "Did he?"

"Not *real* books," Margaret explained, and Celia recognized her husband's amused, indulgent tone as surely as if he'd spoken instead.

"I should have lied," she thought. "It's not as if I can't do it." She'd lost them now. They were still there in body, being over-polite or playing the fool or, in Margaret's case, winding up into a tantrum. But their real selves—their hopes and fears—had scurried off as decisively and completely as the troop of mongooses.

Much later, she concluded that this must have been the moment all three of them decided never to read her books. It was their way of consigning her to the attic, metaphorically speaking.

Rain was beating down ever faster, though the monsoon season had yet to start. Then Celia woke up and realized that it wasn't rain at all and someone was knocking on her bedroom door.

With awareness came terror, because being roused in the middle of the night could mean only one thing. Then she re-membered that for once the children were under the same roof. The relief was enormous. She put out a hand to reassure her husband on the other side of the bed before remembering that it was he who was absent.

Phil was outside, looking young and scared. The major was downstairs, he announced, lowering his eyes as she stood in front of him in her decorous cotton dressing gown.

"The major?"

Hastening down the wide staircase, she saw Hugo Devereux, Frederick's aide-de-camp and close friend, waiting in the hall below in full uniform complete with rank insignia, and immediately knew what had happened. There'd been a plane crash and Hugo had come to tell her Frederick was dead. Everyone talked about the risks the pilots took, the strange wildness that entered into them once they zoomed into the huge empty sky. They flew so low that passengers could watch through the cloudy Perspex windows as the plane's shadow scanned the tawny ground like a vast bird of prey.

But, even with this dreadful realization, she could spare a little pity for Hugo. Poor Hugo, who adored Frederick and would flirt with her in a respectful sort of fashion. His blond good looks were visibly melting away in this searing environment where hard drinking was the norm. There was a piece of bloody cotton wool stuck to his chin. Did army protocol also dictate that a man must present himself freshly shaven to break bad news?

But to her astonishment, he said, "There's no need to worry, Celia."

She stared at him.

"There's been a minor accident," he told her. "Very minor," he added, and she smelled the gin on his breath. "Frederick's going to be home a couple of days late."

She had to sit down because her legs had started to shake. "He is coming home, then?" she managed to ask.

"But of course!"

"I thought you were going to tell me his plane had crashed."

"Oh no!" He actually laughed, but she guessed it was out of nervousness. "Never fear, Celia!"

"What sort of accident, Hugo?"

He hesitated. "He'll tell you about it himself."

"Tell me it wasn't a car accident!"

"It wasn't a car accident," he agreed. Then he frowned, almost as if conscious of a missed opportunity.

"He *is* all right?"

He made an obvious effort. "Absolutely! Spoke to him myself just half an hour since."

She stared at him, very puzzled.

He seemed to realize his mistake. "He didn't want to wake you, Celia. That was the thing."

"Hugo!" Celia exclaimed, trying to engage his sense of humor. "What *is* all this?"

He hesitated. "It's no good asking me." He gave an elaborate shrug. "What do I know?"

It wasn't true. His eyes slid away from hers and she sensed the sweating panic just below the surface. She saw him dousing his face in a basin of cold water, shaving with a trembling hand, chivying his hungover reflection: "Get a grip, man! This is important!"

She was beginning to understand. Whatever mysterious thing had happened in Abeokuta, her husband's career was under threat. Had this nocturnal visit been Hugo's idea? Or was he obeying his superior, Frederick, who also happened to be a close friend? She believed she understood the significance of the uniform now. It symbolized courage and duty and loyalty. She was an army wife being warned that very soon all those qualities would be put to the test.

CHAPTER TWENTY-TWO

Fanny had decided that a good marriage was like a patchwork quilt. Her own was made up of all sorts of scraps which, when put together, created a warm and comforting whole that those who weren't married always envied. They never understood the faith and hard work that had gone into it, or reflected on the true meaning of "patchwork."

From *Love and a Family,*
published 1975.

Men didn't like clever women, Priscilla had once confided to Bet. It was in wartime when, everywhere she looked, she saw girls brought up like her doing tough, intelligent work and even being entrusted with national secrets. More than six decades

on, when there were no men left, she gave
the impression of being sillier than ever.

Only a lifelong friend like Bet could appreciate that the foolishness had always
been a mask. Priscilla, who could so easily
have collapsed with grief after the loss of
her son, had for more than thirty years,
and with great success, run a charity for
ex-servicemen. She never spoke of Archie
now and no one outside her old circle of
friends even knew she was a mother, let
alone, in time, a grandmother. She viewed
other people's families with studied detachment, and Bet's lifelong preoccupation with
Celia's with a kind of indulgent amusement.
If she missed having a family, she certainly
wasn't going to admit it. Bet could only admire her gallant spiky spirit and feel all the
fonder of her.

She should have known what to expect
when she broke the news that Frederick
had been married before. One of Priscilla's
tricks had always been to pretend she
hadn't heard (which was easy now that she
could pass it off as deafness). She carried
on talking about the fun to be had in London immediately after the war. It was hob-
bling through Piccadilly, that old playground

of her youth, that set her off, along with much grumbling that the pavements felt softer then.

"D'you remember the three of us lunching at the Coq d'Or?"

"Of course," said Bet, making a face. She always forgot how loudly Priscilla spoke, the embarrassment of her exaggerated accent. "And a couple of other places besides," she muttered.

"Never thought about money then," grumbled Priscilla. Then she went into a predictable rant about the rudeness of the twenty-first century. No one opened doors for you anymore or offered their seats, though they'd plenty of energy to hiss at you in the street for wearing the old fox fur stole that kept your neck warm or damn you as a racist for using words you always had, like "golliwog." The week before, she said, a man whose foot she accidentally trod on had called her an ugly middle-class old bag, and she'd drawn herself up and pulled her stole around her and said "Don't you dare call me middle-class!"

They were sitting in the Royal Academy having tea—Lapsang souchong for Priscilla, Assam for Bet—and rich slabs of chocolate cake. When Bet had phoned to make a date, Priscilla had suggested very brightly, as one who kept abreast of cultural affairs, "We should take in the Byzantine icon exhibition." But the minute they'd successfully negotiated the steps, they headed, without conferring, for the downstairs café. All around them, other old people were animatedly discussing what they'd seen: "That wonderful fourteenth-century virgin and child from Thessaloniki!" "The sheer detail of that gold leaf!" Bet was thinking that if they couldn't summon up sufficient energy to look around the exhibition, at least they wouldn't go away uninformed. But culture wasn't the point.

"We should have guessed there'd been a first wife," said Priscilla, demonstrating that she'd been listening all along. "He was years older than Celia, wasn't he? Oh, I know it was wartime, but I often wondered why they didn't marry in church."

Bet decided to get straight to the point. "Priscilla, if that journalist woman comes calling, you mustn't let her in."

Priscilla frowned, as if it might be nice to get a visit from a stranger, especially if they could talk about Celia; and Bet reflected that she was probably lonely, despite the determined filling up of time: the carousel of bridge evenings and drinks parties.

"Sly piece," Bet went on. "Lot older than she looks. Little whispery voice. And if she rings, you put the phone down on her immediately."

Priscilla looked almost distressed. "Oh, I don't think I could do that!"

"Bugger manners!" Bet exploded. "I'm worried what else she might dig up. This is an emergency, Priscilla. The two of us must put our heads together, for the sake of the family."

It was the right mixture of urgency and flattery. Priscilla ate a piece of cake with her fingers, disdaining the fork Bet had provided her with. Then she sipped at her tea like a bird.

"There was a time when Celia and I lost touch," Bet prompted. "Must have been the early fifties. But *you* saw a lot of her round about then, didn't you?"

Priscilla blinked and looked lost, as if, despite all her steely intentions, it still hurt to remember that period when she'd believed she could reclaim her son. "Yes," she agreed eventually, "after I ran away from Rupert, I often stayed with her. Frederick was always off, though she'd never say where—and quite right, too. We played box and cox. The minute he got back, I had to make myself scarce."

Bet thought: "So she never saw them together either." She said: "How did she seem?"

"Busy," said Priscilla. "No staff, you know. But I do remember her being upset one morning. She'd had a phone call. My dear, she'd gone white as a sheet but would insist it was nothing." She shook her head as if dissatisfied with herself for not probing further.

"Oh, well . . ." Bet decided there was little to be gained here. She eased her shoes back on under the table and looked around for her stick. "Are we up to this exhibition?"

Then Priscilla observed with a little frown: "I always thought Frederick was too young to retire."

"Was he?" asked Bet, uncertain where this was going.

Priscilla looked vague and amused.

"What was he when they married? Thirty? And that was in 1944. So in 1960, when they left Nigeria, he must have been, what?"

"Forty-six. He didn't retire. They were always coming home after independence." But even as she said it, Bet thought: "That's what Celia told me. But Priscilla's right. It was too early."

"Should have gone right to the top," Priscilla went on in the same guileless, chatty way. "He kept his gong, though, so he couldn't have blotted his copybook too badly."

Bet threw her a sharp look. "And a good job at the Ministry of Defense for a while and a respectable pension at the end," she pointed out.

She'd come to prod Priscilla's memory in the hope that a look, a conversation, would take on fresh meaning after all these years. But—wouldn't you know?—at the mention of Africa and that nudge of scandal, something tripped in her own brain. A memory of collecting the children from the airport after the last summer holiday they ever spent out there (only nobody knew that, then) and a story they'd told.

"Guess what happened to Daddy?" Margaret was obviously bursting to get in first. She had bagged the front seat, naturally. "Duchess," Jack called her because she always got her way.

Bet was in the usual panic about driving. During the war, she'd been a cool operator of boats and cars and, once, for a fabulous ten minutes (courtesy of a lover), an amphibious tank. Had six years of living with death—feeling the beat of its wings in every frame—caused her subsequent collapse of confidence? Jack didn't know the extent of it or he'd have stopped her from driving for good. And to make this particular ordeal even worse, the car was packed with people she loved.

When Margaret spoke, Bet was trying to edge into the inside lane and thinking, "Why does everyone always have to be so angry?" She noticed that Robert and Sarah had gone very quiet in the back, but the pattern was familiar by now: first the holding back and later the bitter tears. An exhausting evening lay ahead, but come tomorrow the children would start to adjust. Bet felt almost tearful herself as she anticipated all the hugs and confidences to come. She was conscious that passing drivers must automatically assume she was the children's mother, and this made her acutely happy. Then she reminded herself of the need to concentrate.

"There was this leopard cub someone had rescued from the bush," Margaret continued in an important, excited voice.

"What, darling?"

"You're not listening, Aunt Bet!"

"No need to shout, darling. I am. Just trying to get us safely home." She glanced into the side mirror, checking that nobody was coming up too close behind, which always spooked her. "You were telling me someone had rescued a sweet little leopard cub," she said, forcing a smile.

Margaret's voice rose to a scream. "I didn't *say* that! I didn't *say* it was sweet! It tried to kill Daddy!"

That got Bet's attention all right. "Is this true, Robert?" she asked. "A leopard tried to kill Daddy?" But the lapse in concentration was nearly catastrophic. She failed to take proper account of a lorry merging with the inside lane from a slip road. She braked and the children lurched forward, shrieking. "It's okay, darlings," she said. "Sorry, darlings."

However, nothing could distract Margaret. "Why are you asking Robert? It *did* try and kill Daddy!"

"I'm not sure about kill," Robert replied in his cautious, self-conscious way. "More like attack. It was when he went away to Abeokuta." He pronounced the name very precisely, as if he'd taken pains to get it right.

"In a little airplane!" Margaret shrieked. "When he came back, he had claw marks all down his cheek."

"Where it had raked him," Sarah elaborated, enjoying the drama. "There were scabs where the blood had dried. He said he didn't do anything. It just went for him."

It was a shocking tale. Bet thought how ill-judged of Frederick, usually so sensible, to have approached a leopard as if it were a cat or a dog. After that, she nearly missed getting onto the wooden flyover at Chiswick, and when she tried to correct the error, she was hooted and shouted at from all sides. By the time she'd recovered from that horror, they were almost home. And somehow or other, Jack never got to hear about the leopard and perhaps cast a more cynical, male eye on the episode— and Bet had to wait nearly half a century before Priscilla said something that jiggled the bits and pieces into a shape that made perfect sense.

A picture came to her, plucked from no-where but so convincing it had to be true. Frederick's handsome face bearing the livid marks of fury but also a look of stern defiance, like someone simultaneously re-vealing a secret and denying it. It made Bet tremble to imagine her own husband subjecting her to an expression like that. But she decided the story of the leopard was not something she wished to share with Priscilla. Even all these years later, it would feel like betrayal because Celia had never said a word.

Next thing, she became aware of Pris-cilla studying her, head cocked on one side, almost as if she'd been listening to this interior monologue throughout.

"Very, very few men are faithful," she pronounced. Then she sighed, and Bet looked at the old wandering eyes, the thin hair scooped up into an unsuitable scarlet comb, and felt their long connection, like the press of a frail bony back against her own upholstered one. "Something happened in Africa," Priscilla continued, as if there could be no argument. "Might've been the end of them. But if you ask me, it gave that marriage a second wind."

"D'you think?" Bet responded, though she too had noticed a change after Celia and Frederick returned to England. They'd "evened out a little," as Jack had put it in his predictable but comforting way. Frederick had been "less full of himself," whereas Celia had "come into her own." She'd reclaimed her children, too, of course, which Bet had been dreading. But Celia had encouraged the bond that had been established, sharing them like the thoughtful and unselfish friend she was.

Priscilla nodded sagely. "Infidelity's not always a bad thing."

Bet couldn't agree, but resisted the temptation to say so in case she distracted Priscilla.

"Last time I saw them, he seemed afraid to let her out of his sight . . ."

"Mmm." Bet could remember that, too.

"It was the day before it happened, you

know. I couldn't believe it later, when I heard. He looked so well. Dishy as ever—I remember thinking 'men have all the luck!'—and he couldn't keep his hands off her. Darling, I didn't know where to look—he actually pinched her on the bum! And she was like a girl again. So sad . . ."

For a second, Bet saw Sunday after Sunday with the Bayleys, a parade of lovely memories. The dead came back to life and sunlight shimmied through the fluttering leaves of a copper beech onto a white tablecloth and the laughter never stopped. But then a long shadow had fallen over the family. At the age of only fifty-four, Frederick had suffered a massive stroke. He'd lived on for an astonishing twenty-two years (out of sheer willpower, everyone said, because he couldn't bear to leave Celia), before dying in 1990, very soon after seeing Margaret married.

"I felt dreadful," said Priscilla. "I mean, I thought if only I'd stayed the night, it might not have happened."

"Oh, I don't think so," Bet murmured and tried not to smile as an image came to her of a blood clot frozen in its stealthy passage to Frederick's brain by Priscilla's chatter.

"I wanted to, you know. But I got the feeling he couldn't wait to be alone with her." Priscilla glanced at Bet. "Funny thing, sex," she went on, and a couple of elderly men at the next table stopped chatting and studied their catalogs. As if that wasn't embarrassing enough, she gave a gummy lipsticked beam and announced: "*I didn't have a proper orgasm till I was forty-nine years old.*"

She pronounced it "oh-gesm" in her strange upper-class way and Bet hoped (without much confidence) that the old men hadn't understood. She studied her watch ostentatiously. Five to five. If they left now, they could avoid the rush hour, and she'd be home in time to feed her cat.

"*Thought* I had," Priscilla went on, seemingly oblivious to Bet gathering up her handbag and checking she hadn't mislaid the bright orange plastic wallet containing her Freedom Pass. "But when the real thing came along it hit me like an express train." She let out a cackle. "Best sex of my life, though he was no good."

Bet had long ago forgotten the library of erotic memories she'd invented to torment Priscilla. She was thinking: "It's disgusting when old women boast about the lovers they've had." She inquired crossly: "What's this got to do with anything?"

Priscilla looked mischievous. "What do *you* think?"

"You tell me," said Bet curtly because now the old men weren't even pretending not to listen.

"That day I had lunch there, Celia looked like she'd woken up," said Priscilla.

Bet couldn't help being interested because the happiness of her own marriage had depended on a very deep sense of security. She doubted she'd have liked it if the sex, always so tender and satisfying, had entered a startlingly erotic phase. It wouldn't have been Jack. More to the point, it would have worried her. If Priscilla was right, there was even more reason to pity Celia. How tragic to discover truly wonderful sex with your husband, only to have it almost immediately snatched away.

"Think about it," Priscilla advised, sounding smug and authoritative. Then she unclasped her bag, took out a somewhat tarnished silver compact, and studied her reflection. The sight seemed to depress her. When she next spoke, she sounded meek and ordinary—nothing like the witch whose insights Bet had hoped would help her get back into the good books of the family. "Is it too early for a drink? I do long for a martini. How's the Ritz these days? Have you been lately?"

CHAPTER TWENTY-THREE

How can a place be so uplifting, yet so melancholy? I sit under the sprawling ceanothus tree and listen to the bees murmuring in its fluffy blue blossoms while the wind whips up the sea like egg white and the bell on the buoy tolls a warning before the pine trees start bending and moaning in the wind. . . .

God, what appalling drivel! I know I can do better. Somehow I must try and forget every cliché I've ever read, approach this from a different angle.

From notes for *Under the Moon,* 1972.

"And you know what the very worst thing about all this is?"

Bud knew Guy probably didn't care, but

she'd been trying to draw him into conversation ever since they'd left London. It was a Sunday morning and obvious that he was thinking longingly of his bed, where he should have been recovering from the working week instead of creeping down the M3 as part of a long procession heading south. But she refused to feel guilty, reminding herself that this trip was important for him, too.

She was trying to imagine her grandmother as a little girl, to pick up on her feelings seventy-six years before like straining for notes of music long after they'd died away. There'd been no motorways then, just winding empty roads. Not like now when ranks of cars advanced down the tarmac like an endless shining army. But Celia and her mother had almost certainly traveled to Far Point by train. "I was a dreamer," she'd said, often. Bud pictured her in 1933, in a smocked dress and plaits, dreaming and smiling as she looked out on poppy fields fluttering with butterflies, untidy haystacks, and occasional thatched cottages. Perhaps her mother hadn't warned her what kind of life awaited them. Perhaps, right up until the last minute, that little girl had believed they were moving to their own house. Much later, she'd talked about the buses from Southampton that used to deliver her to Far Point. But surely, on that first occasion the Falconbridges had sent a car to the station to welcome the new housekeeper and her daughter?

Bud heard Guy sigh, as if making an effort. "So what is the very worst thing about all this?"

"It's not the thought of that woman going through all Gran's private stuff."

"No?"

"Well, that's bad enough," Bud conceded. "I mean, what possessed us to let her into the house when we didn't even know her?"

"Your mum said she was nice," Guy pointed out.

Bud snorted. "Nice? She just wanted to get us on her side."

Jenny Granger had shown a different side of her nature when she'd given back the keys to Parr's, as requested. Did Bud know that before moving to Far Point, her grandmother's home had been a little two-up two-down in Tooting, shared with a violent, shell-shocked father? Not a hero of the Great War, as the family had been led to believe, but just one more pathetic casualty of that legalized slaughter. "I gather it was hell for them," she'd said with a phony gush of compassion, before giving a last twist of the knife. "If you don't believe me, ask Bet Parker."

Guy suppressed a yawn as he took the right-hand fork for Winchester. "You still haven't told me."

"It's not feeling that she doesn't belong to us anymore. It's not finding out Bet knew the truth all along . . ." It wasn't even Jenny Granger saying, with a practiced mix of charm and determination, that it made no sense to shut her out because information about Celia was in the public domain now—which apparently meant that, even if they didn't let her write the biography, someone else would. When Bud eventually answered her own question, she was close to tears. "It's being afraid that maybe the person I loved so much didn't exist."

She was being overly dramatic. But the hurt was all the more because of her closeness to Celia. That person everyone had believed to be so honest hadn't been straight, even with her, and now the chance was gone forever to find out why. That was the real reason for this expedition. They were going back to when the significant part of their grandmother's story had begun: seeking out the place where a little family of two had washed up all those years ago, long long before the lies.

The beach they were heading for was well documented in histories of the D-day landings. But after its brief moment of glory, the desolation and silence must have settled once more, the only evidence of that perfectly executed wartime operation the concrete watchtowers dotted along the shoreline, the peeling signs warning of buried mines, the occasional rusting jetty. They now knew that Lady Falconbridge, the real owner of Far Point, had lived on there, alone and without servants, until her death in 1960. What a wonderful name the house had, Bud remarked to Guy. It suggested a place way beyond the range of e-mails and mobile phones—an impossibility these days.

"There'll definitely be a family there now," she went on, imagining shouts and laughter echoing through the house and its wonderful garden sloping down to the sea; bathing expeditions and scary games in the pinewood. There were no proper photographs of Far Point in the albums, just tantalizing glimpses—like part of the thick, ridged trunk of the lime tree where Celia and Frederick had once posed for engagement pictures and a section of the house's white façade against which a well-dressed middle-aged woman (Lady Falconbridge, for sure) had flourished a bottle of champagne.

Guy disagreed. "It's a big place, isn't it? It's more likely to have been turned into an hotel."

"Whatever. We'll talk our way in. We'll tell them our grandmother lived there as a girl." She added quickly: "But not who she was."

They'd become wary of celebrity, tired of the inevitable reaction. Soon their grandmother might be forgotten by the outside world, but for the moment she was "the eighty-year-old who wrote about sex" or "that old woman writer in all the papers"— never someone who'd been private and human and beloved.

A picture postcard view was laid out before them: the sun glinting off a ruffled sea, a long low mass of dark island on the horizon, the shore snaking away to their left. On a cold but sunny weekend in early 2010, the place bustled, with happy families in place of serious young men and women from the forces. There were cafés strung along the shore and even a Mr. Whippy ice-cream van. But this cheerful scene was oddly dispiriting. Suddenly, Guy and Bud longed for the bleak and stormy place their grandmother had once described.

"Do you think Gran and Grandpa ever came back?" she asked.

"Whatever for?"

"Anniversaries?" she suggested, with-out conviction. Of course they hadn't—it would have meant confronting their lies.

Her phone was beeping. She frowned at the number displayed. "Theo. That's the fourth or fifth time he's rung this morning."

"Shouldn't you answer?"

"What for? Hang on, he's left a message. . . . 'I have something very important to tell you, Bud. Please pick up.'"

"Well, shouldn't you?"

"No, Guy," said Bud, like explaining

something elementary. "You know Theo. He only wants to boast about some exam result."

They were passing a set of big iron gates, an avenue lined with beech trees, an imposing property in the distance, a sign that read "Island View Retirement Home." They exchanged glances. It had to be the house where their grandmother had first met Bet and Priscilla, which meant Far Point was very close.

They dawdled impatiently along the coast road, waiting for the waves of day-trippers to part, anticipating their first view of the big white house set in a thicket of pines that their grandmother had described so many times.

Any minute now the road would wind round a bend and up a hill away from the sea. In fact, Far Point should already be visible. But beyond a rusty barbed-wire fence, a jungle of brushwood terminated in a ragged rhododendron hedge. Above that was only empty sky.

"We've got it wrong," said Bud. "It must be the other end of the shoreline."

"No, this is right."

They left the car in a pay-and-display

parking area. As they walked up the hill, they were silent, tense. They were remembering their grandmother's stories about the buses that had delivered her from Southampton station to the beach, the short walk to the house. "There was a big wooden gate a hundred yards on the left. It dragged on the gravel and Mr. Peters, the head gardener, never got round to mending it. It was one of the sounds of Far Point, like the wind in the pines and the shush shush shush of the sea."

These were no pines anymore. And instead of a gate there was a rusty corrugated iron barrier topped with a tangle of more barbed wire and a peeling notice warning, "Keep Out—Patrolled by Guard Dogs." But directly adjacent, mocking this empty threat, was a big ragged hole in the hedge with bits and pieces of litter caught on the foliage, as if people went in and out all the time.

Once through the hedge, they understood why. An enormous rubbish tip took up the entire space and all around, a ferocious tangle of nettles and brambles pressed in. And yet, according to their grandmother, the gate had once opened directly onto a courtyard dominated by a spreading lime tree. To their greater dismay, there was no sign of the house. Then they saw that there were bricks and broken planks and slates and even shards of marble all jumbled up in the rubbish as if someone had taken a vast sledgehammer to the whole edifice. There were also discarded refrigerators and television sets and even an old computer—not to mention disgusting items like twists of used lavatory paper and discarded condoms. Near at hand there was an insistent buzz of flies, but down below, masked by the noise of people, the sea washed rhythmically against the pebbled shore exactly as it must always have done.

"Why did we come?" asked Bud, almost in tears.

"I should have Googled it," Guy responded with a helpless shrug. Photographs taken from the air might have forewarned them, tracing the foundations of that once imposing house and even picking out the rotting stumps of fallen pines. They understood the back of it had faced south, but in their state of shock they felt unable to work out which direction that was because the beautiful house and garden had vanished completely, as if they'd never existed.

"We'd better go," said Guy, already jingling his car keys.

Bud had other ideas. South must lie in the direction of the distant cries coming from the beach. They found a couple of stout branches and started to beat a way through the brambles until they found a patch of ground with a view of the shining sea and the mass of island beyond. Then Bud started rummaging in her bag. "Keep looking ahead," she advised Guy. "Try to imagine none of the stuff behind us exists." She produced a copy of the novel containing a description of Far Point, *Under the Moon*, which she'd brought along to make an amusing comparison, never imagining how precious it would be. She opened the book at a passage she'd marked and began to read out loud.

Their grandmother described approaching the place for the first time, but from the viewpoint of a small child. Pushing open a heavy wooden gate that dragged; enjoying the crunch of gravel underfoot; gazing up into the green umbrella depths of a huge lime tree that shaded the whole courtyard;

entering a door in a wall that led to a rose garden and circling a magnificent house; discovering a white façade so brilliant in sunlight that it hurt the eyes, and green shutters, and a veranda that clung to the base of the house like a wrought-iron snake, and a sloping lawn that ended in a flowering rhododendron hedge beyond which was the gently heaving sea. They could have sworn they heard the mournful bonging of a bell on a buoy, so precisely and beautifully was it described. And that was before she took them inside the house.

When Bud had finished reading, Guy said, "I wonder if it really was quite so wonderful. It's not mentioned in any architectural reference books, you know."

"Does it matter?" She felt she'd had a revelation. Being in this broken place and hearing that lyrical description, it seemed to her that she comprehended the point of fiction. It was a myth that it was only for readers. For writers, it was a way of repairing broken dreams. They created a world to compensate for one they feared they were excluded from, or had lost forever.

Guy blinked at her as she strove to explain. Then he moved his shoulders up and down and waggled his neck from side to side, as if trying to limber himself up to get into a different mind-set. But she knew it was no good. This time, her dear cousin had no idea what she was talking about.

Out of frustration, she answered her phone the next time it went off. As soon as Theo began talking—his tense anxious voice clacking down the line—she started paying attention.

"What?" asked Guy, noting her concentrated expression.

"Of course you were right to phone me," she told Theo very gently and kindly. "Of course you're upset." Then she put her hand over the phone and hissed: "Now *his* father's only gone and left his mother, too!"

CHAPTER TWENTY-FOUR

How lucky I am that nobody is ever going to tell me it's time to stop writing. How could I endure life if I could no longer slip into that strange country where all dreams can be realized and all disappointment can be rewritten?

Written in notebook. No date.

That Sunday in early June 1968, Frederick made Celia tea in bed, which was a habit he'd got into since retiring. By the time she gave him breakfast in the dining room an hour later, he'd patrolled the garden to check that every plant and shrub passed muster and chivied the barometer until the needle stuck at "set fair," even though it was obvious from the cloudless deep blue sky and the absence of any breeze that it was going to be a wonderful day. Through the open french windows, they could hear insects massing in the lavender, the complacent roo-coo of pigeons, and the strangely human cough of a heifer in a distant field.

"How lucky we are!" she murmured, thinking that she'd never again take for granted living in a country where heat was celebrated and everywhere she looked was fresh and green. As if this perfect English summer's day wasn't gift enough, the whole family would be there for lunch, and so would Bet and Jack.

"Indeed," Frederick agreed, as he sliced the top from his boiled egg. He wasn't really listening. He was scanning the headlines of the *Times,* which he would read thoroughly later. Enoch Powell's speech on the danger of Britain being flooded by immigrants was still causing ripples. Though Powell had been sacked from the opposition government for his inflammatory views and roundly condemned, Frederick had some sympathy for him—"and I'm not alone," he'd claim. At a dinner party they'd attended the night before, he talked about Africa in depth, putting the case for imperialism. He was much respected in that safe and wealthy place. They were a popular couple.

He was in such a good mood that he couldn't even pretend to be cross with Margaret for being late for breakfast again. She chipped at the house rules, and because she was his favorite, she got away with it. It didn't stop her from grumbling. Living in the country was dull dull dull, she complained. Just as soon as she could, she was going to follow Sarah to London. She made it sound like a threat even though, so far, Sarah had never caused her parents the slightest trouble.

The family had been back at Parr's for almost eight years. A formal photograph of Frederick and Celia, taken in Kaduna, was prominently displayed in the sitting room where visitors could absorb the medals and diamonds, the suggestion of hovering servants just outside the frame. "You must miss it," they'd say, and, like actors responding to a cue, Frederick and Celia would exchange smiles before shaking their heads in unison. Just once, Frederick had departed from the script and confessed, "Not any more," indicating that in the weeks and months after leaving Africa, he'd secretly grieved for that life.

The people they socialized with were at his stage in life, not hers—the men about to retire, if they hadn't already, with wives in their fifties and, often, grandchildren. None of these friends had been told she wrote on the side. But she was on her fifteenth romance and making enough money to pay for holidays and a new car, though she managed this very tactfully. Frederick appreciated these luxuries, but never referred to their source either.

She treated Africa with similar sensitivity. Had her husband really risked so much for the wife of a subordinate? No admission had ever been made. However, Celia would occasionally remember the deep scratches on his face with something like gratitude because people often remarked on their closeness these days.

Margaret had been asked to lay the table under the beech tree but predictably vanished at the crucial moment.

"Let me," offered Bet, who was looking festive in a bright yellow sundress.

"You've only just got here!" said Frederick. "Sarah can do it."

"No, I'll call Margaret," said Celia. "She can't behave like this."

"It's okay," Sarah assured them all extraordinarily amiably, even though she'd only just arrived, too, and she and Margaret were usually at odds.

"You look pretty, love," said Bet. "What's up?"

"Nothing." Sarah seemed shifty but pleased. Bet often complimented her on her looks, just like she'd tell Margaret she had a good brain if she would only use it, and Robert that he was going to make an excellent soldier (which was not an opinion shared by his father).

"Nothing?" Bet smiled at her husband and so did Celia because she loved the way her friend coaxed words out of that deeply shy man. "She looks pretty as a picture, doesn't she, Jack?"

"She does indeed," he agreed, looking at Sarah in the same fond, inquisitive way. He had a nice soft voice with a hint of West Country burr. He was wearing his Sunday clothes—cream trousers with knife-edge creases and a navy blazer with shiny brass buttons—whereas Frederick was in old corduroys and a moth-eaten jumper. But it was Frederick who appeared perfectly dressed for the occasion. He'd kept his figure. He was marvelous-looking for his age. Everyone said so.

And then Robert roared into the drive in his sports car, with a new beautiful blonde in the passenger seat. He looked reckless and dashing, the image of his father. "Anyone who didn't know him would think he was a heartbreaker," thought Celia tenderly, waiting at the open front door to welcome them. She saw the girl, who was introduced as Vanessa, look at him wonderingly as if all of this—a lovely family, the house and its pretty garden—was an embarrassment of riches.

And then Frederick turned on his mischievous lethal charm, and Celia was reminded of the way he played competitive sports with Robert. "It's good for him," he'd insist to justify never letting him win, even if it meant pushing himself to the limit. But she decided that if he started the usual cross-examination about Sandhurst, she'd change the subject (if Bet didn't get in first).

When Margaret finally joined the party, Jack murmured "duchess," as usual, and Celia saw Frederick wince, even though he'd been known to say, "Margaret will marry a duke." He didn't like it, either, when Bet encouraged the children to call her "aunt." Fond as he'd become of Jack and Bet, he'd never get used to their difference. "I'm not sure they'd fit in," he'd say if Celia suggested inviting them to meet their friends. It was a good thing Jack was so shy—Bet said he'd sooner face torture than a dinner party—and she herself seemed quite content to be compartmentalized. As Celia well knew, it was the family she loved.

Margaret was fifteen and her body had all of a sudden caught up with her beautiful, oddly wise face. She had a proper bosom now and a little waist and long shapely legs, and a mesmerizing effect on men of all ages, including her father, who indulged her shamelessly. "Poor love," Bet would say, implying beauty was a burden—though how would she know?

After lunch, the young ones started playing croquet. It was a game Frederick excelled at but this time, to Celia's relief, he left them to it. He and Jack sat in deck chairs in the sun reminiscing about the D-day landings, which they'd seen from opposite ends of the spectrum: Frederick as an officer involved in strategy, Jack running one of the boats. Frederick did most of the talking, while Jack puffed thoughtfully at his pipe. Whenever he said anything, Frederick would exclaim "Good man!" like making a mental note to recommend Jack for promotion. But twenty-three years on, Jack was the one still in work.

Celia and Bet cleared away—another Sunday lunch tradition. It was cool in the kitchen, with its big dresser cluttered with mismatched china, its humming fridge. And at last there was a chance to discuss family matters, like picking up a piece of shared knitting.

"Robert's in good form," Celia observed. She added, as if the flirting had passed her by, "Vanessa's a pretty girl, don't you think?"

"If you like that type."

"You can't deny she's pretty!" Celia went on after a moment, "If you ask me, there's a lot to be said for arranged marriages."

"He wants someone sweet and kind

who'll understand him," Bet agreed. "When he's good and ready, he'll make the right choice. I know it."

They smiled at each other and Celia noticed wiry gray threads in Bet's dark hair. "I'm glad I'm not young anymore," Bet maintained, though she still wore brightly colored tops that showed her upper arms and skirts that were too short for her, even in the late sixties.

"Then there's Sarah," said Celia.

"Seems she's already found herself a boy."

"Really? She's not said anything to us."

"I was coming to that, love. She wants to bring him home."

Much as Celia welcomed Bet as part of the family, it hurt when the children confided in her. Sarah must have whispered the secret out in the sunlit garden. "I'm in love, Aunt Bet. But, please, I need you to put in a word to the parents for me . . ."

"His name is Derek," said Bet. "Sarah thinks he's God's gift."

"Well, I'm sure we've nothing to worry about," said Celia. "She's such a sensible girl."

The conversation could have stopped there. Instead, because Celia was struggling to subdue her feelings of jealousy, she found herself saying something she hadn't really intended to: "By the way, I've joined a writers club." It wasn't as if she didn't know what kind of reaction to expect. Bet had always been funny about her work: it was the only real way she could fault her as a friend. For twenty years she had sent her signed copies of every book, but apart from brief thank-you notes, Bet never commented. Celia was used to her family's lack of interest, but she expected more from Bet. "It was my publisher's idea," she went on. "It's the Romantic Novelists Association."

"Right!" said Bet in a tone of such instant comprehension that it cut Celia to the quick.

"He thought it would be good for my career," she went on, feeling more and more defensive. "He says it's important to circulate. So anyway, I went to a lunch. It was a bit scary on my own, but I really enjoyed it. It was wonderful to talk to people who were doing the same thing. It made it seem almost normal. And they'd read my books, too." She hesitated. "I've sort of made friends with three of them."

All Bet's attention appeared to be taken up with searching for coffee cups in a cupboard, but Celia went on talking.

"One's called Mary Truefast. She jokes about it. 'It's all true,' she says, 'because I know about love; and I'm fast—I turn out three a year.' She wants to set a book behind the Iron Curtain and they're planning to go to Prague next month and they've asked me to join them. It's only for a week. I must say, I would like to, but husbands aren't invited, and I can't very well leave Frederick behind." She laughed. "He never wants to go anywhere, these days. He says he doesn't know why anyone does when they can live at Parr's. I'm only forty-one, Bet. That's not old, is it? I feel I know so little about the world."

There was a shriek from Margaret from outside: "I *didn't* push the ball! You're the cheat, Robert! Why's everyone so mean to me?"

"Little madam," Bet commented with a fond smile as if her thoughts had never left the children. "I forgot to ask how her exams went . . ."

It was only afterward that Celia understood that she'd been listening all along
and, like the very best of friends, noting
what hadn't even been said.

CHAPTER TWENTY-FIVE

We're having a wonderful time, but we're all feeling a bit bemused and, truth to tell, disappointed in an odd sort of way. But this is only the first day . . .

> Entry in notebook marked,
> "Notes for Mary."

We are off the map. So far as the rest of the world is concerned, our tragedies have not even happened.

> Scribbled piece of dialogue from
> different notebook. No date.
> Note for novel?

Frederick and Bet were at loggerheads, but indirectly and very gently, and it both amused and touched Celia. Each was anxious not to be seen as either selfish or bossy, while maintaining they were only thinking of her. Frederick had insisted he was quite happy to be left, though he couldn't resist adding, "If it's what you really want." It was going to be jolly hot, he pointed out, and she'd miss the church fête. But when Celia relayed that to Bet she laughed and said: "Will he be any happier if you go in winter? And is the church fête going to be any different from last year, or the year before?" She also said very much more seriously, "You've just the one life, Celia. Take this chance. It's only for a week."

She made the trip happen. When Prague proved impossible because of a sudden influx of curious foreign visitors and consequently a dearth of accommodation, she was the first to point out that there were plenty of other suitable countries to visit in that part of the world. And, though she hated to leave Jack, she insisted on moving into Parr's to take care of Frederick and Margaret. If it hadn't been for her, Celia would never have set off for an obscure part of Eastern Europe in July 1968 in the company of three other romantic novelists. And if it hadn't been for old guilt to do with Africa, Frederick might have made sure that he won the argument.

For almost all her adult life, Celia had been accustomed to thinking of herself as the less interesting half of a couple. But suddenly she found herself with three women who behaved as if men were superfluous. There was Sandy Pritchett, ginger-haired and witty and opinionated, who smelled like a full ashtray; and Mary Truefast, who was shy and earnest as well as the plainest woman Celia had ever met; and Jane Pargiter, who'd left a husband at home, too, but seemed more indignant than guilty. "I wash his socks, don't I? I cook his meals!" Once Celia tried to imagine Frederick part of the group but could only see him crouched by a window staring out, like a cat trapped in a room.

"We've made it, girls!" crowed Sandy, as the plane thumped onto the runway.

Roles were falling into place. Sandy was organizer and team leader; Mary, who'd done preliminary research for her book and was by far the best informed, would be their guide; Jane was in charge of finding suitable places to eat; and Celia would be an extra pair of eyes and ears for Mary. They followed the businessmen off the plane in pairs: Sandy with Mary, Jane with Celia.

Celia had envisaged a hotel to match the sweeping romance Mary planned: a former palace (a relic of a vanished monarchy), a grand staircase and enormous old-fashioned rooms with balconies overlooking a formal garden and a tinkling fountain, charming and attentive staff. Instead, they'd been booked into a big purpose-built hotel in the center. But the rooms were very clean and spacious and comfortable enough in an unstylish sort of way. Celia duly noted the yellow-and-white–patterned wallpaper that didn't go with the red-and-blue–patterned carpet; the weak overhead lighting that trembled when it was switched on; the bathroom down the corridor they were expected to share, the thin towels, the mingy block of unscented soap. But, all in all, the women were delighted, especially as the hotel was extraordinarily cheap by their standards. The only annoyance was the surly, unhelpful manager, who spent nearly an hour registering them at the hotel desk, poring quite unnecessarily over the stamps in their passports. But at least he spoke minimal English. He told them breakfast would be available between seven o'clock and nine o'clock in the dining room.

"Time for a drink," said Sandy as they all gathered in the room she and Mary were sharing, which adjoined Jane's and Celia's. It was time for a fag, too. They'd only been there for half an hour but the room already stank of smoke. Mary had opened a window and they could hear the whining stop-start sound of trams in the distance. The city had an excellent transport system, she informed them. When they started exploring the following day, there'd be no need to take taxis. Then Jane wondered out loud if that was why there were so few private cars, though they'd seen some on the way from the airport.

"This reminds me of school," said Sandy, with a fond smile, as she produced a bottle of gin purchased at Heathrow. There were no glasses, so they had to pass it from mouth to mouth. "Any brilliant ideas about dinner, Jane?"

Jane had done her homework and they

headed for a restaurant two or three blocks away from the hotel. The streets were quiet and clean, Celia noted on the way, with no litter and certainly no beggars. She also observed that although the people they passed were cheaply dressed, some of them—particularly the young girls— exhibited real style and were beautiful in a dark, lush kind of way. But the population en masse seemed curiously detached, as if a group of foreign tourists held no interest.

The restaurant, which had a cozy folksy decor, turned out to be even more pleasing than the hotel. The only real problem was communication and, though Mary had brought along a phrase book, they were laughing too much to pronounce the phonetic spelling and ended up pointing at the menu and hoping for the best. The food took a long time to arrive, but they were all in such a good mood that it didn't matter. They passed the time reading out some of the phrases, which had been badly translated into English: "Have you one and a half diopter glasses for shortsight/longsight?" and "Do you have a disengaged table?" They couldn't imagine needing to use this last phrase, as all the other tables in the restaurant were free. But, as Mary reminded them, it was a Monday night.

The food was delicious: far better than in an equivalent British restaurant. It turned out they'd ordered long meatball sausages with fried mushrooms; and the salads that accompanied them were fresh and tasty, as was the soft white bread. There appeared to be no wine list but, after an energetic display of sign language from Sandy, the waiter brought small glasses of colorless spirit so raw that it burned their throats.

When the ridiculously small bill was presented, Jane said it for them all: "Well, if this is communism . . ."

It wasn't what they'd been led to expect. It was true that on the way from the airport, their taxi had passed blocks and blocks of hideous concrete flats seemingly dumped haphazardly like piles of giant matchboxes, as if no consideration had been given to those who'd have to live there. But the center was different. Instead of ruin and decay, anarchy on the streets and nothing but soggy dumplings to eat,

they'd found a perfectly adequate if not
luxurious way of life, a city that seemed extraordinarily well run, and no obvious signs
of unrest. Mary pointed out that it was far
safer than London. According to the official guidebook, crime was almost nonex-
istent. Furthermore, there were no listening
bugs in the rooms, said Sandy, who put
on an amusing performance of searching
under the beds and feeling beneath the
tables and chairs; and no sinister men in
raincoats following their every move, either.

Celia found all the women so interesting in their different ways, so generous
about each other's work and serious about
their profession because, observed Sandy,
"we've a lot of fans out there." She wondered what Mary would end up writing.
The fact was, she couldn't imagine setting
a romance here. The country had turned
out to be too dull, in the nicest kind of way.

Jane had bagged the bed by the window. She was going to have the first bath,
too, and she'd covered the dressing table
with pots and bottles because, unlike
Sandy and Mary (and Celia herself), she

wore quite a lot of makeup. After meals, she would take out a compact and powder her nose and touch up her lips.

Celia smiled as she searched for cold cream in her sponge bag. "This is really fun."

"Oh, they always have fun!" said Jane with strange meaning. She whispered: "They've been together for years."

It was a moment before Celia understood.

"I think it's sweet. Sandy's always been—" Jane hesitated, seemingly too embarrassed to spell it out. "But Mary wasn't, till she met Sandy. It was a *coup de foudre.* She left her husband for Sandy. She told me once she'd never even considered being with a woman before. She just fell in love. I *like* the idea of love having nothing to do with looks or age or even gender. Love striking out of the blue because you recognize the beauty and purity of another person's soul."

Celia couldn't help being a little shocked, but she had to admit that, as a definition of true love, Jane's description couldn't be bettered.

———

Mary had unearthed a bizarre fact: the city had a mausoleum containing an embalmed former dictator. After two days of checking out the obvious sights, the women decided to take it in, especially as they were planning to visit the former tsar's palace, now a museum, which was directly opposite.

By eight o'clock in the morning, the heat was already shimmering off the asphalt. Over breakfast—fresh white bread cut in chunks, good coffee, cubes of delicious creamy, salty sheep's milk cheese, and tomatoes cut in quarters—Mary read to them from the official guidebook. They were going to view "the father of the nation": in other words, she said, consulting her own research notes, the dictator who, from 1946, was entrusted by Stalin to impose Soviet communism on that previously democratic country, before dying a few years later in somewhat mysterious circumstances. Then she frowned and Celia guessed what was coming because Mary's characters had pursued them all over the city. "I could have Roderick spotting Lara there for the first time . . ."

"Go on," Sandy murmured encouragingly.

"Not hot like this. Winter. Then I can

cover everything with lovely thick snow. More snow falling, horse-drawn sleighs with jingle bells. . . . Do they have an equivalent of Father Christmas, I wonder? Roderick visits the mausoleum as a tourist. Lara's working there as a guide. She's just left school."

"Death as a metaphor for stifled hopes," said Sandy suddenly. "Not a guide—a guard. The job's a punishment. Her father could be a dissident. But you can skate over the politics, of course."

"Genius!"

They exchanged delighted smiles and Sandy even suggested a title: *Love Comes In from the Cold.* Celia couldn't imagine how marvelous it would be to have that kind of support and encouragement for one's writing. It was all the more remarkable because the women were technically in competition.

The big wide street was paved with distinctive yellow stones, and the mausoleum was a long two-storey building with a balcony. This was where all the parades took place, Mary informed them—and, for a

second, they saw block after block of uniformed men marching in perfect synchro-
nized time to solemn music from brass
bands, blank young faces turned as one
toward the mausoleum, and the party
leaders watching from the balcony, the
whole city coming to a respectful halt.

There were two soldiers in long khaki
coats and caps decorated with what looked
like pheasant feathers goose-stepping
past the mausoleum, sweat glistening on
their expressionless faces. More soldiers
stood like statues at the entrance while
uniformed guards controlled the queue,
which was composed mostly of young children, obviously on a school outing. Sandy
was the only one of the foursome who
wasn't a mother, but that didn't stop her
from initiating an animated discussion as
they waited in the hot sun. It was obscene,
the others agreed, to encourage children
to look at a corpse. And to think that the
authorities encouraged it!

All the while, they were being edged
forward by the crowd following on behind.
It would be a relief to get inside, said Mary,
because of course the mausoleum would

be heavily refrigerated to slow decomposition. After all these years, she went on chattily, the dictator's hands had almost certainly been replaced by wax ones. Then Sandy suggested with a wink and a nudge that probably other bits of him were wax, too.

Just then, one of the guards spoke very sharply to her.

"Pardon?"

He made a gesture. She must remove her hands from her trouser pockets immediately.

"Bloody cheek!" Sandy spluttered, still jingling coins, and the guard moved very close, glowering into her face.

"Just do it, love," said Mary, looking deeply apprehensive.

Suddenly they were no longer relaxed and amused. They could see now that they'd been lulled into misapprehension: mocking the customs of this alien world without even bothering to lower their voices. The cold reality was that this was a police state and they were four middle-aged foreigners who were unprotected and far from home. Their passports could be taken away. They might even end up in jail.

To their very great relief, however, the guard's intense, over-the-top fury evaporated. It was as if scaring them had been satisfaction enough. His attention shifted to a group of children, one of whom had apparently shown gross disrespect by sucking a boiled sweet.

"Psycho," muttered Sandy, though too softly for him to hear.

But Celia was beginning to panic. She'd momentarily forgotten her terror of death. Now, like lifting a black curtain, she started to remember her mother's funeral and that dreadful initial sight of her coffin. As they were herded down a dark passage, she felt the first breath of icy air and panic rose up, threatening to suffocate her.

"I can't!" she told the others. But even as they hesitated, they were being swept along. Any minute now it would be too late.

"Wait, I'll come with you," said Jane quickly.

"No, I'll be fine. I'll meet you back at the hotel."

"Are you sure?" Jane seemed touchingly concerned and responsible, almost as if she'd started to think of the two of them as a couple like Sandy and Mary.

But Celia was already battling the tide of children, forcing her way back to the entrance. The guards seemed to register her panic. Perhaps they feared she was about to vomit and defile that revered place, because none of them tried to stop her.

Outside, the sky had darkened and drops of rain were beginning to fall. Every so often, a large black car with little curtains drawn across the back windows swept past, strikingly shiny and new, in contrast with the rusting old cars they'd seen on the main road on the way from the airport. This was the seat of power, Mary had told them. Celia could see the red star gleaming on top of the politburo building just down the street.

"I should get away from here," she thought, feeling very conspicuous and remembering the frightening behavior of the guard. Besides, it was raining harder and harder, soaking her nice dress, threatening to ruin her expensive sandals and good leather shoulder bag. The hotel was some distance away. She should find somewhere to shelter as quickly as possible. She began to run in the direction of a distant maze of side streets, suddenly horribly anxious and lonely, as if the years had fallen away and she was young again, but with none of the advantages.

CHAPTER TWENTY-SIX

It's not always the people we love most who can bring us the greatest unhappiness. Entry in notebook. No date.

Something peculiar was happening to the family, as if Celia's death had caused them all to reassess their lives. Margaret's husband, Charles, so long-suffering for so many years, had just announced that he wanted a divorce; and now Margaret was thrown into turmoil and couldn't understand why. She went over and over the way it happened, though it meant losing the true intonation of a voice or the real message of a look. It was like searching for a dropped key in the dark.

———

All through their marriage, he'd stayed late at the office, and she had never objected. After all, it paid for the grand London house, the holiday cottage in the Dordogne, the fine education enjoyed by their children, and all the other privileges of the rich. However, on this particular weekday evening, he surprised her by taking her to a play she'd expressed an interest in and, after that, her favorite restaurant.

Glancing at him in the darkened theater, it was obvious he was enjoying the play more than she. It was the same at the restaurant, where he ate with a better appetite. She noticed the other diners glance at him curiously, as if wondering who he was, whereas she, once so beautiful, felt herself passed over, invisible. None of this improved her mood.

"Shall we walk?" he asked as they left the restaurant. "It's a beautiful night."

But she treated the suggestion as if it didn't deserve an answer even though a separate part of her had noticed that there was indeed a marvelous clear sky and a clean sliver of moon. It might have been nice to walk home—with a different man.

However, even she had to admit that Charles was a kind and thoughtful husband, as well as a wonderful father. They both spoiled the children, as if the tenderness they couldn't show each other had to come out somewhere.

She heard him sigh, and then he hailed a taxi.

Back at the house, unusually, he suggested a nightcap.

She responded a little ungraciously, "If you insist," but fetched glasses and the whiskey.

When they were settled, he cleared his throat, seemingly out of nervousness, before asking: "Do you know how very much I've always loved you?"

She declined to reply. It was because, with some dismay, she thought she now understood what the evening had been about. It had all been a prelude to sex: that tentative yet proprietorial touch on her hip, a single kiss snatched like a forbidden chocolate, and then the passion, because that anxious serious man had always been passionate. It hadn't happened for a long time, but sex often dwindled away at this

point in a marriage, or so Margaret understood from other wives. Some of them
even griped about it.

"Do you?" he persisted.

She nodded with a stern frowning expression, as if it was nothing but a trial to
be adored.

"Good." But he sounded strangely detached and, a moment later, revealed why.
"I've something to tell you, Margaret. I'm
leaving you."

She felt nothing, to begin with—neither
relief nor anger, just blank surprise. "I see,"
she managed to say.

He went on, sounding genuinely concerned: "I appreciate this is something of
a shock, but I'm sure you'll come to see
it's for the best. Can you honestly say
you're happy with me?"

She wasn't going to lie to him because
she never had. But as she looked around
the pretty and very comfortable room they
sat in, she reflected that, in so many ways,
she'd excelled as a wife. Besides being a
gifted homemaker, she was a gracious
hostess and an accomplished cook; and
none of their friends knew about the icy

empty heart of the marriage because she'd made a point of being loyal, too. Her mother had provided a fine role model of how to be a good wife, but occasionally Margaret would wonder where she'd learned to be such an accomplished deceiver.

Charles made a half-bitter, half-amused face. Clearly, he hadn't expected a reply.

"Who is she?" Margaret found herself demanding because there was only one reason why a man coming up to retirement would want to leave his lovely house, his comfortable life. After all, hadn't she watched her brother-in-law, Whoopee, fall prey to the same vanity just a short time before?

He hesitated before admitting with a strangely touching mixture of embarrassment and dignity: "There is no 'she.'"

She stared at him. She knew he was telling the truth, but instead of relief, she felt a strange dismay. She got up and refilled her glass without offering him more. "I should go to bed," she thought. But she heard herself say coldly: "As a matter of fact, I've been thinking along the same lines."

"Really?" To her chagrin, he appeared more curious than wounded.

"Ever since Mummy left me that money."

"Ah yes!" he said, somehow giving the impression that her inheritance had been a factor in his decision. "And the children are older now."

"Don't tell me you've thought about *them*!" she lashed out, before she could stop herself.

"Of course I have," he said with the utmost seriousness. "Their welfare has been my prime consideration. But now that they're both away at school, I don't think this is going to affect them too much. Do you?"

The next day, Sarah became Margaret's favorite company. She knew why, of course. Hadn't she so recently been left, too? So she listened as Margaret talked about Charles in much the same anguished obsessive way that she had talked about Whoopee and kindly forgot that when she'd needed help, she'd been shown only impatience. But Margaret's agitation puzzled her because the marriage had never seemed happy. And why was she quite so interested in how Whoopee had come to return?

"Well, I don't know anything," she said,

"but it did surprise me when you married him."

"Did it?"

They were in an expensive Italian restaurant. Unlike Margaret, Sarah had a job, so the only time they could meet privately was during her lunch hour. She was discovering the people and props of Margaret's life—the obsequious waiters, the well-dressed women seemingly exhausted from shopping and visiting art galleries, the trolleys of rich desserts that all looked and tasted the same.

"You were always so secretive growing up. I got the feeling you never brought your important boyfriends home. And Charles was so . . ."

"Dull?" Margaret suggested, sounding oddly hopeful. She'd barely touched her food but was working her way through a bottle of wine on her own.

"I was going to say serious."

"Whoopee always acted as if he was the most boring man on the planet," Margaret pointed out a little crossly as if she only wanted to hear bad things about Charles.

"He was probably jealous," Sarah responded. She was more critical of Whoopee these days. The ecstasy of winning him back was starting to fade. It had been a shock to discover that, despite a lifetime of railing against the rich, money was important to him after all. And was love really love if it depended on who was able to offer the most?

"Men never left me alone," said Margaret, seeming to change the subject. "Sometimes I thought that was why I was sent to boarding school."

"We all were," Sarah pointed out, and she nodded, smiling, at a waiter hovering with a bowl of Parmesan cheese. "And you know it was because Daddy was in the army."

Margaret ignored this. "Once Bet couldn't drive us back after the holidays—do you remember? I think Jack must have been ill or something. So she put us on trains and asked the guards to keep an eye on us. It was the first time I'd ever been alone on a journey, but even in that short space of time a man exposed himself to me. He was old, with a bowler hat. I couldn't have been much more than seven!"

"Poor you," said Sarah automatically, though it had not been easy to be Margaret's sister. She couldn't help noticing that even now she retained the imperious ways of a beauty, fixing any man who came into the restaurant with a cool and challenging stare. But it was possible she was just doing it to annoy her.

"It got much worse later," said Margaret grimly. "When I walked down the street, men would pop up all over the place, saying they wanted to photograph me. Talk about euphemisms! No wonder Daddy exiled us to the country."

How self-centered she was, thought Sarah, though never as a mother. It was as if Theo and Evie had tapped into some pure unspoiled part of her.

"And then I met Patrick." Margaret made a face and shrugged as if to say "Now you know!"

"Patrick," Sarah repeated. She was thinking that this was the second time in as many months that a hidden character from the past had been introduced to the family. Had Patrick been as loved as Katherine?

"He was much older than me. Thirty-one or -two." Margaret paused. "I pray to God my Evie never gets involved with a monster like that."

Sarah had finished her cannelloni and

eaten her roll and butter, too. These lunches were doing her no good. She had regained all the weight she'd lost through unhappiness. But so what? And here at last was a new twist to the story.

"I'm telling you all this because it explains things. Why I only brought home the ones who didn't matter. Why I married Charles, for God's sake!"

"Go on about Patrick," said Sarah.

"Oh dear!" Margaret seemed very agitated. She actually fanned herself with one of the dessert menus a waiter had just laid on the table.

"I shouldn't," said Sarah, but she ordered a tiramisu.

"He was a sadist," Margaret told her. "Do you know what one of the definitions of a sadist is? It's someone who pulls the wings off flies not only because he wants to destroy them but because he needs to understand how they work. Patrick was like that." Then she said something strange and sad: "It was wonderful at the beginning. He was the first person who took me seriously."

"Did you never think of marrying him?" Sarah was remembering how, once she met Whoopee, all she wanted was to become his wife.

Margaret gave a painful smile and looked down at the tablecloth.

"Oh lawks!" said Sarah, genuinely shocked. "How long did it go on for?"

"Until I married Charles."

It was incredible. A beautiful girl with every man panting after her had frittered away her precious youth on someone who was already married. But Margaret had always been perverse. The secrecy and daring of the affair must have appealed to her, too.

"He was expert at controlling me. I did sometimes try to get away. But then he'd become really nice. He'd promise to get a divorce—but there was always a reason why it couldn't happen just yet. He had to get Christmas out of the way or the summer holidays. Or one of the children was starting a new school or about to have a birthday."

"The children?" Sarah echoed faintly.

"Four," Margaret confirmed. "He had three of them during our relationship— though he and his wife never had sex, of course." She said this deadpan, as if grim humor had become the only way to treat all the manipulation and deception.

But however sorry she felt for her sister, Sarah found it impossible to be completely sympathetic. After all—just like Whoopee's young girlfriend—Margaret had known her lover was married from the start.

"Oh Sarah, what a fool I was! He used to tell me we were so lucky—that it was the purest kind of love because we'd never have the chance to get bored with each other."

"What absolute rubbish!" said Sarah, thinking of the delicious familiarity of marriage. At the same time, it occurred to her that it was the kind of provocative remark Whoopee specialized in. He might even have said it to his girlfriend. Had he really broken off all contact with her, like he'd promised? The trouble was, she no longer trusted him.

"In the end, he found someone else. She was quite a bit younger than me. And he did leave his wife. And that's why I married Charles."

"Oh, Margaret!" Sarah felt very inadequate. Her sister going through all that unhappiness on her own while giving the impression she was too haughty and spoiled to love. "Did you tell him?"

"Who?" asked Margaret, sounding strangely panicky.

"Charles, of course!" When Margaret shook her head violently, she said, "You should! It explains so much." She paused, wondering if Margaret was ready to hear what she felt bound to tell her. "You know what I think? You've been punishing Charles for someone else's crime, but you're a lot more attached to him than you realize. Don't let your marriage go without a fight, I beg you."

Margaret thought about Sarah's advice for the rest of the day and the whole of a sleepless night. She was in anguish—but why, exactly? She was well aware of her own perversity. He loves me not, so I will give up all others for him; he loves me and has waited for me with exemplary stead-fastness, and therefore I refuse even to consider him romantically. Charles was a fine man, no question. But was it possible to live with a man for years and not know one's true feelings? And how could she rid herself of the deep conviction that she was not destined for someone like him?

She had adored her father and been devastated when the stroke cut him down. She'd dreamed of marrying a man as handsome and heroic as he had once been, but none of her multitude of admirers had measured up (which might partly explain why she'd picked someone as unsuitable as Patrick). However, since the truth had surfaced about the hidden first wife, she was forced to concede that her father hadn't been so perfect, after all.

She was beginning to reevaluate aspects of the marriage, too: that long partnership whose closeness everyone had remarked on. "Mummy deserves nothing but praise for the way she keeps at her writing," her father had told them when he could still speak. But the truth was that while he enjoyed the luxuries it bought for the family, he had treated Celia's work as an unimportant hobby. They all had.

By the time she married at the ripe age of thirty-six, her father had only a little time left to live. He'd come to her hastily arranged wedding in a wheelchair and watched with his fixed grumpy expression as Robert gave her away. But a tear had trickled down one cheek as if the real person—the one who'd doted on her—still existed inside the silent, clenched body. The old Frederick would have kept Whoopee in order, insisting that hardworking successful Charles be given proper respect; but, from the beginning, Whoopee got away with teasing his brother-in-law mercilessly. Had he been motivated by jealousy, as Sarah suggested?

Margaret could see now that it was Whoopee who'd never applied himself to anything and had recently been un-masked as a hypocrite, who was the real figure of fun. Was Sarah right? Should she be fighting for Charles? But now that he was on his own, suppose he found someone else? Jealousy had never en-tered their relationship—not on her side, anyway—so that couldn't be what was causing her chest to constrict, making it difficult to breathe.

CHAPTER TWENTY-SEVEN

I can't let this crush me. I have to make something positive come out of this despair, this sense of being locked away behind iron bars.

Note scribbled on back of bill from Russell and Bromley for walking shoes, dated September 23, 1968.

It was the second such meeting in a month, but as yet none of them knew what it was about.

All Robert had told his sisters on the telephone, sounding very clipped (which, from long experience, they knew meant he was in a state), was: "We need to hold a family conference ASAP." He'd asked them to convene at his house at seven that evening and suggested to Sarah that since Miranda and Guy would be present, it might be a good idea to ask Bud, too.

Charles had now moved from the marital home, but his anxious, serious presence left a definite gap. To Robert's surprise, Margaret had asked if she could bring him, but since she appeared more nervy and distracted than ever, he assumed Charles had rejected the invitation. She was taking the breakup badly. By contrast, his other sister seemed very chipper and had also come on her own. Robert found it a relief not to have Whoopee around. The last thing he wanted was jokes. What he had to tell them all was quite embarrassing enough as it was.

Unlike his sisters, he'd never met the journalist who'd raked up the muck on his father. Furthermore, once Bud had retrieved the keys to Parr's, he'd assumed she was out of the picture for good. He'd never anticipated that she would turn up on his doorstep, dressed in an elegant suit and high heels and looking quite unlike the bitch he'd envisaged.

She had a kind of bold sweetness about her, and because she stepped so confidently into the house, he straightaway took her for a friend of Miranda's. But there was no way to check because Mel had taken Miranda to the doctor. It was almost as if Jenny Granger had known he'd be on his own and fretting about his pregnant daughter and feeling vulnerable.

"Spit it out, Dad," said Guy encouragingly.

The three grandchildren were sitting together, Miranda flushed and enormous. "I'm eating for two," she'd say as she tucked into her food, but it was more like three. Her pretty legs had become shapeless sausages. Even her personality had changed. "My mind's a sieve," she'd say with a careless laugh. But once the baby was born she'd be obliged to return to work, with its harsh intellectual discipline and long hours. Tears came to her eyes when she contemplated it.

Robert went deep crimson. He wasn't sure he was up to this.

He'd been trained as a soldier in a man's world, but flinched from everyday confrontation and deferred to women. It put him at a real disadvantage when Jenny Granger revealed her true identity. By then, she had inveigled her way into the sitting room and somehow maneuvered it so he was seated facing the window and she was in shadow. Blinking in bright sunlight, he could barely make out her face, whereas she must have been able to follow his every horrified reaction.

He should have thrown her out. Instead, he'd just sat there as she flattered him shamelessly.

"You're the image of your dishy dad. Everyone must tell you that."

He'd nodded curtly, thinking what a fine mix of emotions this had always provoked.

The penny had dropped by then. The journalist was about to spring a new revelation on the family, and he'd a pretty good idea what it was. As he'd learned to his cost as a young man, his father had been an accomplished flirt. All these years later, he could concede that while his parents had been very close, that handsome, vain man might not always have been faithful.

Then Jenny had confounded him. He didn't think he'd ever been more shocked in his life.

"She's got it into her head that Mummy had an affair," he made himself tell the family. His chin wobbled with emotion. It felt dirty even to repeat it. Having striven all his life to be worthy of both parents, it was bitter to discover that they might have been less than honorable themselves.

"Mummy?" said Sarah.

"Is this some kind of sick joke?" Margaret demanded.

Both sisters looked terrified. It was as if they longed for someone to reassure them— Bet, for instance, who'd cared for them so lovingly as children and, as their mother's closest friend, surely knew the truth. But nobody had suggested inviting her. Bet was out of the picture. The whole family had been avoiding her for weeks.

"Is she saying it was when Daddy was away and Mummy was looking after us at Parr's?" Sarah demanded, wrinkling her brow. She seemed to recall a friendly, handsome neighbor. She couldn't remember his name, but his dog had been called Bovril.

"That's ridiculous!" Perhaps Margaret was remembering how naughty and time-consuming she'd once been.

"No, no!" Robert told them. "She claims it was later—in the sixties."

The *sixties*? They looked bemused because their mother had been middle-aged then. This was getting crazier and crazier.

Robert didn't look at Bud. "Somebody thought it would be a good idea to let that reptile into the house so she could snoop to her heart's content. She had three clear weeks before we rumbled her. That's how she came up with this disgusting slander."

Guy sprang to his cousin's defense: "Bud was only trying to do the right thing by Gran's memory."

Robert snorted. He'd gone quite pink.

"Calm down, Dad," Miranda soothed, and he forced a smile, remembering that she was the one who mustn't get stressed.

"Is it because of stuff she found in Gran's diaries or notebooks?" Bud demanded.

"That, too," Robert admitted.

"That doesn't mean it was true!" she protested. "Gran was a fiction writer, for goodness' sake!"

"She's right," said Margaret, thinking of the way the truth was all tangled up in the one book of her mother's that she had read.

"But during the sixties, Mummy and Daddy were never apart," Sarah announced triumphantly. "There's no way it could have happened!"

That was what Robert had thought, too. But actually he'd been wrong.

It seemed that, while exploring the house and its contents, Jenny Granger had found a whole cache of his parents' old passports, going back decades—and then she'd compared them.

For Robert, passports were more personal than diaries, more enthralling than novels could ever be. You only had to look at those stamped pages and the memories came floating back—of magnificent sights and delicious food and the strange sense of liberation you always got from being in another country. He felt real sadness when the old stiff black passports were replaced by flimsy red European Union ones. For once, he could understand why his mother had never thrown any of them away.

Jenny had taken a notebook out of her bag and consulted it. "I've established that in the summer of 1968 your mother spent a week away from your father. Any idea why she might have gone on a solo trip to Eastern Europe?"

"None." He kept a poker face while trying to dredge his memory. In 1968 he was in his last year at Sandhurst and his father had been retired for some time, living contentedly in Surrey with his mother.

"I'm convinced that something with profound consequences happened to her then," Jenny Granger told him. She seemed to hesitate for a moment, before dropping her bombshell. "All the signs point to a love affair."

"I remember!" said Margaret suddenly. "Bet moved in to look after Daddy and me. He pined for Mummy like mad. But it was a working trip! She was with three other romantic novelists. One of them had an odd name. They must have been together all the time."

"There you are, then!" Robert sounded tremendously relieved.

"I knew it was ridiculous," said Sarah. "Anyway, what can happen in a week?"

"Ridiculous," Robert echoed, but immediately afterward glanced anxiously at his sisters. It was as if some shocking idea had just occurred to him and he was very much hoping it wouldn't occur to them too.

"The main reason why I think something happened to her during that week," Jenny Granger had informed him with the air of authority he found so maddening, "is that her writing changed."

Which proved absolutely zilch, he thought contemptuously.

"That was what alerted me. By the beginning of the seventies she'd stopped writing romances and started writing about real people."

Robert had made a face because how could made-up people be real?

"Families." She wore a strange little smile. "You're better placed than me, of course, to know if she drew on her own experience. It was as if she was striving to be honest—to describe how people *really* talked and behaved."

"If my mother wrote about real people," Robert said, making another dismissive face, "it was because she'd had a reality check. My father suffered a bad stroke soon after her return. It was a huge shock for us everyone. The wonder is that she managed to write at all. She was on her knees with exhaustion!"

"Hmm . . ." Plainly Jenny had different ideas. "The fact is, her work became far more sensual."

"You mean she wrote about sex," he'd said, blushing violently.

"Writing about sex doesn't have to mean you've done it," said Bud.

Sarah and Margaret immediately murmured "Hear hear!" But they looked troubled. Obviously, they found it embarrassing and distasteful to be having this conversation about their mother.

Bud was remembering her visit to ruined Far Point with Guy, and the lyrical description of the house and its gardens that she'd read aloud from their grandmother's book and her subsequent flash of inspiration about fiction as therapy.

After the stroke, her grandfather had lived on, severely diminished, for more than twenty years. All that time, Celia must have felt as if she was in prison. Maybe, Bud speculated (because, unlike the rest of her family, she'd read every one of the novels), those tender, sensual imaginings had been her own form of escape.

It was time for supper, but they hadn't formulated a plan yet. Robert knew they were going to have to because it was clear that Jenny Granger had no intention of abandoning the biography. It seemed that fabricating this calumny against their mother had released a whole new energy. She was very anxious to return to the house, she had informed him. It was one of the reasons for her visit. She even indicated that things had gone so far that it was pointless to put up objections. It wasn't quite blackmail, but almost.

Something was troubling Sarah, and a moment later she blurted it out. "Jenny said something about Mummy's computer— that it'd be possible to access all the messages in it. And now I'm wondering if she's done that, too, and that's why she's come up with this, this . . ."

"Not possible," said Guy. To everyone's relief, he explained, "I gave Gran a password and I'm the only person who knows what it is."

"Sorted," said Robert, and they all went into the kitchen where Oscar was dozing in his basket in the corner, twitching every so often as if, in his dreams, he was reliving the best time of his life, bouncing through the long grass of the meadow at Parr's, exulting in its secret rustlings and mysterious smells.

CHAPTER TWENTY-EIGHT

My hair is thin and white and my legs are scribbled with blue veins and sometimes I forget a saucepan on the stove and the house fills with black smoke. But once I was desired with such passion that a candle scorched the wallpaper and we never even smelled the burning until it was almost too late. Oh that extraordinary time! So long as memory survives, I will always be rich.

Passage from *A Woman's Life,*
published 1994.

When she looked back on that extraordinary day in July 1968, Celia would picture the scene outside the mausoleum with strange detachment, as if remembering the unimportant beginning of a story. In a wide, hot avenue somewhere in Eastern Europe, a tearful middle-aged tourist in an expensive linen dress dashes through tor- rential rain.

In Guildford, it would have caused com- ment for sure. But here the people she passed behaved as if she was invisible. What madness had possessed her to leave Frederick and Parr's? A terrible vi- sion came to her of being back at home but still cloaked by the same invisibility— compelled, like dead Katherine, to watch from the shadows. It made her run even faster. She was primed for an accident and in a side street some distance from the mausoleum, it happened. She tripped on a cobblestone and fell heavily on one knee. By the time she stumbled into a nearby café, she was in real distress.

To make matters still worse, she dropped her handbag and some of her possessions spilled out over the wooden floor. A waiter moved forward immediately.

"My passport!" she exclaimed in panic.

He didn't understand. Following his gaze, she saw that her knee was bleeding heavily.

She scrabbled for her powder compact

as well as, to her chagrin, a packet of Imodium in case of stomach upset, but no passport. Obviously a thief had seized his opportunity and now she would never be able to return to England.

Suddenly another man was beside her. "May I help?" he asked in English.

"I seem to have lost my passport. I don't know what to do . . ." But she was already calmer. There was no mistaking the concern in his black eyes. She took in a fine expressive face that was more appealing than conventionally handsome, thick dark hair threaded with gray, a slim frame, an old but very clean short-sleeved shirt that showed off tanned and muscular arms.

"Are you not staying in a hotel?" His English was astonishingly good, with only a faint accent.

"Of course."

"And were you not obliged to hand over your passport for the duration of your visit?"

She'd completely forgotten about this. "Of course!" she exclaimed, mortified. "Sorry!"

"For what? Look, you've injured yourself! Let's do something about it."

He spoke rapidly to the waiter in his own

language, and a moment later a bowl of tepid water materialized, and a towel. By this time, he'd helped her to a chair and a table and, after another word to the waiter, small cups of dark sweet coffee were brought, together with glasses of brandy.

"Allow me," he suggested, dipping a corner of the towel into the water. There was an awkward moment when it seemed as if he was about to wipe away the blood himself but in the end he watched as she dabbed at her knee and even flinched in sympathy when quite a deep cut was revealed.

"You've torn your pretty dress, too."

"So I have." She thought: "I must look an absolute fright." But there was no way she could bring herself to take out her compact and check her reflection as Jane so frequently did. Frederick had always frowned on such public displays.

By the time she'd bound up her knee with the clean handkerchief he offered, she was anxious to escape. "You've been very kind," she said. "I'll wash this out for you and drop it back here, shall I?"

But he shook his head as if he'd done nothing special and had dozens of handkerchiefs to give away. Then he picked up his brandy and smilingly encouraged her to do likewise, and she took in her surroundings properly for the first time.

The café was small and packed, with a fog of cigarette smoke as if, in this society, smoking was almost as natural as breathing. The incomprehensible talk rose and fell like the sea: sometimes passionate and stormy; at others, tranquil and contemplative, lapping the room. Her rescuer was obviously liked here: people touched him lightly as they passed. This was a glimpse of the authentic life of the country, she told herself, an unexpected adventure to regale the women with later.

"I'd better go in a minute," she went on. "I'm with friends, you see. We got separated. I promised to meet them back at the hotel."

"Which hotel are you staying at?" he inquired.

But for some reason she behaved as if the name had temporarily escaped her.

Moments passed. Then he asked: "So what brings you here?"

"Holiday." She owed him this at least. "Well, working holiday," she amended. She went on brightly: "I'm a writer. And the friends I've come with are writers, too."

"And are you going to write about us?" He sounded amused and resigned, and instantly she felt ashamed of the mockery she and the others had indulged in, the way they'd behaved as if they were a superior species, and even her own ridiculous secrecy a moment earlier. The fact was, he'd shown great kindness to a stranger. Suddenly she found herself very anxious to impress on him that she wasn't shallow and overprivileged. Something tripped in her mind, like a fuse blowing, and words began to tumble out, almost as if another person was speaking and she was powerless to stop her.

"There's four of us, all middle-aged women. I said we were writers, but I wish I could believe it. We make up stories about innocent young girls who get rescued by handsome heroes with steely blue eyes and chiseled jaws and live happily ever after. We've come to your country because one of us wants to set a story behind the Iron Curtain. Mary Truefast is her name and she has a joke about it that she tells everyone—she even said it to the customs people. She's done all this research, but it doesn't mean anything. It's like she wants to believe she's a serious writer, even though she'll end up writing exactly the same sugary romance as always.

"She's having a passionate affair with one of the others. You'd never think it to look at them. Last night I couldn't help hearing them because their bedroom's right next door and the walls are thin and they were making such a noise. They were saying over and over again how much they loved each other. I've been married for more than twenty years, but I've never been made love to like that.

"Actually, my husband's always loved someone else. It's not his fault. Someone wonderful, but dead. It wasn't until he had an affair with a live woman that I stopped being so jealous of her. Well, he never admitted the affair, but I'm sure it happened, otherwise why did he lose his job? That was in Africa. Going there meant I had to abandon my children because it's part of the deal if you marry into the army. Sometimes I think it was punishment because of how I treated my mother. My husband was ashamed of her being a servant, you see. I ran out of your mausoleum just now because all these years later I still can't bear to think of her death.

"The only good thing that came out of Africa was that my best friend could pretend to be a mother for a bit; but now I'm very afraid my children love her more. They worry me. Do children pick up unhappiness, even when you try your hardest not to show it? Everyone has always said we're so happy, you see—everyone—and I am, mostly. But I know that my son only became a soldier because he felt he had to please his father, and he has no confidence and all his girlfriends dump him in the end. And my eldest daughter has fallen in love with a boy none of us like. And my youngest daughter has always been my husband's favorite even though we don't believe in favorites in our family, but Bet— that's my best friend—and I really fear for her because she's so beautiful and empty-headed that she's bound to get into trouble. The truth is, I feel I've failed all round. And I carry on writing books about love even though I don't believe in it anymore."

She fell silent at last. She could feel her heart pounding. Had she really said all that? Mad, he'd be thinking, as well as horribly self-pitying. He must be regretting his moment of compassion. He'd be wondering how to get rid of her, for sure—but, actually, she couldn't wait to escape.

But he didn't look annoyed or even particularly surprised. Instead he stared at her with his kind black eyes for what seemed like several minutes. Then he drew his brows together, seemingly deeply puzzled. "Tell me, what is a chiseled jaw? I have to admit, this is the first time I've come across the phrase."

She could have gone then: made a stab at dignity and left her absurd (but thankfully anonymous) confession lying on a table in a café in a foreign city with no harm done. Instead, she started to laugh and laugh until tears rolled down her cheeks. "This is ridiculous!" she managed to gasp eventually.

He was laughing, too. "Maybe we all have to be ridiculous, occasionally."

"Maybe."

"It's good," he pronounced, nodding. "Every day now, I see more people laughing like you."

"Why?"

To her consternation, his face darkened. "Don't you read the newspapers?"

Instantly her laughter ceased. Of course she had read about the attempts being made in Czechoslovakia to liberalize the communist regime. It was, after all, the reason why the women had originally chosen Prague for their trip. But now she began to comprehend that winds of change were blowing through this apparently bland and sleepy backwater of Eastern Europe, too. It explained the energy in the café, which she guessed was a meeting place for the intelligentsia.

As Celia pondered this very different perspective, a picture came to her of Frederick reading his newspaper back in Surrey while morning sun gilded the garden beyond the open french windows. He read selectively, and to a set routine: first, a taster of sport; then a big helping of hard news, but only the bits that interested him; and finally, as a sweet signing off, the cartoon and the crossword. What was happening in Eastern Europe could easily pass him by.

"Forgive me," she said.

"For what?"

"Talking about myself at such a time. I feel so embarrassed. I don't know what came over me."

His reply both soothed and worried her. "For years and years we can deny the truth, pretend it doesn't exist. But now I understand that it always finds us in the end." He held out his hand. "Alexei Simeonev. Actually . . ." He brought out the word seriously as if to make the point that he wasn't mocking her, he just liked the very English sound of it. "Actually, I'm a writer, too."

"Celia Bayley," she told him. "And I'm staying at the Balkan."

When Celia turned up at the Balkan Hotel three hours later, the three women were huddled in a tense knot in the reception area.

"There you are!" said Sandy. "We've been frantic!"

"Frantic!" Mary echoed.

"Look at you!" Jane exclaimed. "What on earth happened?"

Celia related the bare facts, editing out Alexei. After an accidental fall, she'd been trapped in a café by the heavy rain. "Luckily, people were awfully kind." She gestured at her bandaged knee. "Someone even gave me a handkerchief."

"But that storm only lasted an hour," Sandy pointed out.

"And you told me you'd meet us back at the hotel," said Jane.

"We were about to get onto the embassy," Sandy went on.

"We were," Mary confirmed.

"We didn't want to worry your husband," said Jane. Suddenly, husbands seemed to be part of the picture once more. "If we hadn't heard from you by six we were going to book a call to England," she continued, giving the impression that even contemplating this had been time-consuming and costly.

"I'm really sorry to have worried you all."

But they weren't ready to forgive her yet.

Sandy said coldly, "This isn't a holiday," even though until now she'd been behaving like a carefree tripper. "Mary has a book to write. I shouldn't have to remind you, Celia, that we're all busy working women with tight schedules."

"If you wanted to go off and explore on

your own," Mary pointed out in the same icy fashion, "all you had to do was say."

They didn't believe her story. She saw it in the cross, baffled glances they exchanged. Then she understood that, despite her bandaged knee and torn dress and rat's-tail hair, she must give off a kind of radiant difference. Something had happened. She hummed with anticipation like a young girl, and it wasn't yet tempered with the sober mistrust of an adult.

He'd had a privileged education. That was why he spoke such beautiful English, slipping up only occasionally on his idioms. He might wear worn, shabby clothes, but he had attended the finest school in the country. He began to explain the anomaly within half an hour of their meeting.

They sat in the café absorbed in conversation, but occasionally he glanced up as if a phrase in his own language had snatched at his attention, stood out from the roar of background talk, the bursts of laughter. And meanwhile, heavy rain continued to lash the streets outside. Once, the lights blinked off as if the city's electricity system had been swamped, too; when they came on again, everyone in the café cheered.

His father had been a prominent officer in the KGB. He'd wanted for nothing as a child, he told her. He lived in a nice house in a good area, and his family enjoyed regular holidays by the Black Sea. Nobody tried to deter him from becoming a writer; under that system, it was much like entering any other profession except that there were considerable rewards, provided you were productive and wrote what was required. He went along with it and eventually he owned a beautiful apartment and a Western car and wore designer suits and ate the finest food. But one day, he said, he found himself unable to write. He sat for days, then weeks, in front of a blank sheet of paper, unable even to make a mark with his pen. It was only after he tore up his party card that the words flowed once more. But he found himself writing an entirely different and dangerous kind of fiction: allegories that slyly pointed up the unfairness and brutality of the system.

He'd never regretted leaving the party, he said, even though punishment was swift: every book he'd written was summarily destroyed. The only way he could make a living now, he explained, was with a menial, poorly paid job in a shoe factory. His whole family had suffered because of his actions, he told her with an unhappy expression, and she could only guess what that meant. But even though he had not been published for years, there were whole volumes inside his head (and he tapped it, like indicating a hidden library). Words came all the time, and now he realized that one day very soon he was going to be able to sit down and let them pour out. He'd never felt such excitement.

He gave a beaming smile. "Which is best? To live like a king but see yourself turn into someone you can only feel ashamed of? Or to be like this"—he made a dismissive gesture at his shabby clothes—"and know that here"—he once more indicated his head—"you are free?"

She wasn't used to candor. She'd lived for almost a quarter of a century with a man who kept his emotions to himself and had passed that guardedness onto his own children. Even her closest friend, Bet, who came from an entirely different background, had never admitted to the anguish of childlessness. "I've always had to guess," Celia concluded. Was it her own confession, she asked Alexei, which had provoked such extraordinary honesty? No, he said, it was the time they were living through. At long last, change had arrived. "Can't you feel it in the air?" But for the mood sweeping the city, he conceded, he might have stayed at the bar, sunk in his own problems, and watched like a subhuman when she staggered in, tearful and bleeding.

Might have, he'd repeated with an unhappy look. But now he felt reborn.

"I don't know what's so funny," said Sandy.

"Nothing," Celia assured her.

"You were smiling."

"Was I?"

"You look an absolute mess," said Jane. "Why don't you go and get yourself cleaned up? Then we can decide what to do with our evening."

"What's left of it," Sandy reminded Celia grudgingly, even though it had only just gone five and there was plenty of time to have dinner wherever they wanted. Then she relented and gave her broad smile. Lecture over. Time to resume the fun.

But Alexei was in Celia's head now, blocking out everyone else.

"You're very dreamy," Sandy observed a little later as they ate stuffed tomatoes and roast chicken.

Celia made an effort. "You sound like my family."

"Well, you certainly are dreamy tonight," Mary confirmed.

"We're all dreamers, aren't we?" said Celia. "We have to be." And, just as she'd hoped, it distracted them, provoking a spirited though serious discussion about imagination and creativity, and she was freed to pore over the hours in the café and the thrilling and troubling moment in the shadows of a doorway at the end.

"Shall we meet again?"

"I don't know," she'd whispered.

"Of all the cafés in all the towns in all the world she walks into mine." He smiled as if to say, "See—even here we know about *Casablanca*," and momentarily his black eyes took on a glint of orange, but it was only a trick of the late afternoon sun. "Don't you believe in fate?"

"I'm a married woman, Alexei." But a second later she worried that she had taken him too seriously. Perhaps all the attention was mere courtesy.

"Celia," he said, making it sound as if he'd discovered a delicious new word. "Something has happened. You know that too, don't you?"

"Yes," she'd agreed, feeling simultaneously elated and terrified.

Over breakfast, the women drew up plans for the day.

"Time for a bit of culture," said Sandy, who was dressed in knee-length shorts. The money belt under her shirt made her look even stockier.

"High time," Mary agreed. She'd prepared a list of art galleries. She couldn't get a handle on her book, she'd just announced, looking disconsolate. She and Sandy had decided that it wouldn't work after all to have her protagonists Lara and Roderick meet at the mausoleum. Now they'd seen that ancient embalmed corpse, albeit bathed in soft rosy light, they realized it had no place in romantic fiction.

"Oh well," said Jane. "Books always pan out in the end, don't they?"

"Lara loves art," said Sandy suddenly. "There's a particular picture in a gallery that she adores. A woman in eighteenth-century dress with a mysterious expression. Roderick enters as a tourist, and sees her staring at it—and bang, that's it!"

"Genius!" said Mary, but more fond than excited. It was hardly an original idea. Besides, she knew all about the heady and selfish flavor of a real-life *coup de foudre*.

Celia told them she had a migraine at the fourth gallery they visited. The day had become steadily hotter and stickier. She first contemplated getting a migraine soon after lunch. She and Alexei had arranged to meet in the café at four o'clock.

But as time went on, she found herself increasingly anxious. Suppose the women insisted on coming back to the hotel with her? What if Alexei waited in vain at the café? She had to go, if only out of politeness, to tell him they must never meet again.

The women let her leave, but she felt their disapproval, their growing conviction that it had been a mistake to invite her on the trip. They were hot and exhausted, too. And if she was so prone to migraines, said Jane, why had she left her pills behind?

The same smoky shabby ambience, the same lively clientele, the same swelling and ebbing tide of talk . . . but he wasn't there. She was dismayed by her deep disappointment. He must have believed her when she'd warned him she might not be able to escape. But it was far more likely, she decided, that he'd come to see his behavior as foolish. Men did that, she thought (with the experience of only one to go by). When they left the company of a woman they were drawn to, they immediately began to distance themselves; whereas women proceeded to construct elaborate scenarios of what might happen next.

It was only yesterday that she had entered the café for the first time. She thought of herself as a very ordinary woman, yet a clever and interesting man had appeared to find her special, even exciting. He'd seemed so kind, too; but it was cruel of him to have exploded into her life like a lit firework and encouraged her to examine its dark corners, never to return.

She'd recovered her composure by the time the women returned to the hotel. And they obviously believed her migraine had been genuine because they made real efforts to be friendly.

By the end of the evening, she had almost convinced herself that she'd had a lucky escape. The things she'd told him! The memory made her blush. But at least they'd never meet again, which had to be seen as a good thing rather than a sad one. "Dear Frederick," she thought with a pang of guilt. She imagined him at hushed and leafy Parr's, where the scent of tobacco flowers would be unfurling and the pigeons murmuring in the trees, and vowed never again to feel sorry for herself.

But she must have looked more disconsolate than she realized.

"Cheer up, love," said Sandy. "It may never happen!"

Celia could only smile back. It nearly had. But she was fine. Perfectly.

When they returned to the hotel, the manager called her back as they were all heading toward the lift. "I'll catch you up," she told Jane.

There was an envelope waiting for her. "A gentleman left it," said the manager with a meaningful look.

Celia responded with blank hauteur. "I'm good at this upper-class stuff," she reflected with a certain amusement.

"What was that about?" Jane asked when she rejoined her in the room.

"Message from Frederick," said Celia, who liked to think of herself as an honest woman. She added: "Everything's fine."

Jane gave a scornful laugh. "Don't tell me—he wants to know where you keep the spare toothpaste! My husband's useless on his own, too."

She opened the letter in the privacy of the communal bathroom. Clear strong handwriting in blue ballpoint on cheap lined paper. "My dear Celia," it read, "I am so sorry. I was unable to escape work until after four thirty. I ran and ran but when I reached the café they told me you had left. Is it possible to be both sad and happy?

Sad to have missed you, but so happy that you came. I shall be there tomorrow, at the same time—four o'clock—with my heart in my shoes and in the hands of fate. Alexei."

By the next morning fate appeared to have dictated that Sandy should suffer a nasty stomach bug. Her illness effectively knocked out Mary, too, since they were inseparable. They would stay in their room the whole day, they announced. And fate seemed to step in again when, after a strenuous morning looking for postcards, followed by a lengthy lunch, Jane decided on a siesta, with a favorite Georgette Heyer beside her for later.

"I think I'll go for a wander," said Celia at three thirty, trying to sound as if she hadn't silently rehearsed this for at least an hour.

"Are you sure? It's too hot to breathe out there."

"I'll stay in the shade."

"There's nothing wrong, is there? You seem awfully jumpy."

"Nothing."

"I don't know why you've bothered to change!"

"Nor do I," said Celia, with a covert glance

in the mirror. She looked anxious, but fresh in one of her last clean cotton dresses.

"Only two more days," said Jane, contentedly opening her book. "Actually, it'll be good to be home."

He was waiting for her at the same table. It was wonderful to see his grave face crack into a delighted smile.

"Have I really caused that?" she thought. Then: "I wish I could take a photograph of him now." But if her husband came across that particular snap, what would he think?

"Maybe I've lost my job because of you," Alexei told her, still smiling.

"You're not serious!"

"Not yet. Luckily, the boss is a friend. He was a philosophy professor once."

They talked for more than an hour in the same absorbed, unguarded way as before. This time, he asked most of the questions and she found herself telling him about Naomi, the imaginary friend who'd kept her company as an only child; and the pain of leaving her beloved mother and Far Point as a seventeen-year-old bride; and the full horror of that night in Germany when she'd first learned about Katherine; and the helpless jealousy that had brought about her first book. But then something began to make her very uncomfortable. He was being silently teased: she could feel it in the sly, amused glances that were coming their way. The first time she'd turned up at the café had been chance. The third was definitely not.

"Is there somewhere else we could go, Alexei?"

He lived on the top floor of one of the blocks of flats the women had glimpsed on their way from the airport. Close to, they were even more depressing, though the muddy land surrounding them was tidy and litter-free. The lift didn't work, so they used the stairs, pausing on landings to catch their breath. "This is why I'm not fat," he joked.

As he unlocked his front door, standing very close to her, she became intensely aware of his physical presence: his fine hands, the way his thick hair fell over his forehead, his bare and muscular arms. But though she trembled inwardly, she acted like the gracious hostess she'd once been in Africa. "I thought you might be married, too," she said in a light social voice, as if she'd been looking forward to meeting his wife.

"A long time ago." His voice was very gentle as if he understood the unease and wished only to reassure her.

He'd lived like a rich man once. But now he was confined in this echoing concrete honeycomb, along with numberless others.

She expected an apartment as bare as a cell. But once they'd passed through a minuscule hall that led to a small living room, it was the wealth of books she noticed first, crammed into cheap shelves that bowed with their weight and spilling into piles on the floor. Then she took in a beautiful but very worn oriental rug and a divan bed scattered with several cushions whose covers had been embroidered with the same jewel colors of crimson and gold. There were a handful of old prints on the whitewashed walls; a single oil painting so dark that it was hard to make out; a table covered in flaking dark green oilcloth with two chairs drawn up to it, and a blue vase that had been filled with half a dozen fresh red roses.

Only after that did she notice the view. A single window gave onto an iron basket of a balcony and an uninterrupted view of the airport road, which seemed to tremble in the heat. In the far distance, a plane soared up into the blue sky. Suddenly, she understood that not only did he live in a world he was unable to escape but he was condemned every day to watch others leave freely. Had this punishment been carefully considered or come about by chance? Everything was about to change—he'd said so in the café. Even as he spoke, the old tyrannical regime was in the process of being swept away.

When she turned from the window, he was contemplating her a little sadly. "So this is how I live," he said.

She noticed something else: a cheaply framed photograph of a little girl perched on one of the bookshelves.

"My daughter, Ada," he told her. "Have I not told you about the light of my existence? But this is out of date. She is fifteen years old now. A madam, without doubt."

"Just like my Margaret!" But she doubted if "madam" meant the same to him. His daughter looked as if she did as she was told. She was dark and pretty, though not as pretty as Margaret.

"Does she live with her mother?"

He nodded. "It's better. But I see her when it's possible."

Had his wife left him after his privileges were removed? She sensed stoicism as resolute as Frederick's, but knew that whatever she asked would be scrupulously answered. It forced her to acknowledge the deep loneliness of her marriage. It explained why she was in this little apartment in a foreign city with a man she'd known for only three days. That and the attraction that shivered in the air and would have to be addressed sooner or later.

As if he read her thoughts, he plucked a red rose from the blue vase and presented it with a flourish. It was wilting in the heat, but still lovely in its full bloom.

"Walking?"

"In this heat?"

"For over three hours?"

Celia nodded, still too shaken to speak. How was it possible to feel both happiness and utter despair? She was already regretting her behavior, wishing she could rewind time and do it differently.

He was only the second man she'd ever kissed. She couldn't remember the last time her husband had kissed her with such passion, and though sex had always been fulfilling, she had long since forgotten this kind of aching desire.

But as Alexei started to pull down the zip at the back of her dress, she panicked.

"You don't want this?" His voice in her ear was very gentle.

"Of course I do!" she insisted, almost in tears but already pulling away.

He didn't try to dissuade her. He sat down in one of the chairs and lit a cigarette. As an afterthought, he offered her one, too, seeming unsurprised when it was accepted, though he knew by then that she didn't smoke.

"Of course I understand that you are married," he said eventually. "But this is not nothing. This is serious. You want to know how I know?"

She nodded miserably, rolling the unlit cigarette in her fingers—but with great care, as if she knew, even then, that it would become as much of a treasure as his blood-stained handkerchief.

"None of it feels wrong to me—it feels natural and logical. When you came into the café it seemed as if I'd been waiting for you always." He paused. "I know this is a big cliché, but often the biggest clichés are the truth. I know you, Celia. Did we already meet in some other world? I think I knew you'd feel unable to betray your husband, but actually this only makes me love you more."

She wiped away a tear. "I feel the same as you, even though we've known each other for such a short time. But this isn't just about Frederick. I have children who still need me, Alexei, and I'm afraid that if we make love now, I'll never be able to go home. But I have to—the day after tomorrow—and there's nothing I can do about it."

"Well, obviously you did some shopping." Sandy sounded very accusing.

Mary indicated the newspaper-wrapped parcel Celia was carrying. "What is that, anyway?"

"It's a picture."

They were waiting. So she undid the newspaper to reveal a small oil painting.

The women peered at it, frowning, because it was very dark. The six tiny mounted soldiers in ragged uniforms charging across a desolate plain weren't easy to make out.

"It looks very old," Jane commented finally. "Is it for your husband?"

Alexei wrote his address on a piece of the same lined paper he'd used for his letter. "Write to me," he said, adding, "It is lucky we are both writers." Then he took the painting off the wall and gave it to her, even though they'd known each other for just three days and it had kept him sane for years. It was about hope, he explained. Those horsemen had been riding across that enormous bare plain forever. "But see the expressions on their faces? See the hope?" It was keeping hope alive that mattered. He knew they'd be together again. If ever she doubted it, he told her, she only had to look at the picture.

She should have remembered Milly Noonan, that beautiful desperate girl in Africa, and the far greater infidelity of Katherine. Why hadn't she? Wasn't she entitled to snatch any happiness that came her way?

But she hadn't even allowed him to escort her back to the hotel. They exchanged a last kiss at the door and then she ran down the concrete stairs and, before she could weaken, hailed a taxi on the airport road. She cried most of the way and now she was being subjected to an interrogation because the women had decided a man must be involved. What else explained her agitation, her tear-stained face, her occasional strange smiles, her refusal to answer their increasingly pointed questions? On and on they went, but all she could think about was Alexei. She was still in his flat, breathing in the smell of roses and cigarette smoke and rewriting that final scene.

At the last moment, she had turned back. She let the empty taxi pass and climbed those endless steps and hammered on his front door. When he saw her, his sad, resigned expression changed as swiftly as it had in the café. He kicked the door shut behind them and embraced her as if he never wanted to stop. There was no hesitation this time. They undressed each other and, still entwined, moved to the divan. Then they made love, passionately and without guilt. "My darling," he said, "I'll love you forever."

But it hadn't happened, of course. And soon she'd be home in Surrey with Frederick. If she didn't have the picture and its secret message, she might start to doubt that Alexei had existed at all.

CHAPTER TWENTY-NINE

Madness . . . truth . . . beauty . . . hope . . . death . . .
> Single words scribbled in
> back of 1968 diary.

I've said good-bye to the handsome, limited men and the dull, virtuous girls— waved them off forever like sending old friends over a cliff. I know I am taking a risk, but there's no choice now because I can no longer pretend. Oh, it's so cruel!
> Notebook. Undated.

"Interesting," said Frederick, and Celia became aware that she was in their drawing room in Surrey and wondered how long he'd been watching her.

She'd let herself be pulled back to that

other world. She'd been with Alexei again, drinking in his expressive face, listening to his soft deep voice. But to what extent had she given herself away? Had her husband observed her lips move and sometimes curve into a secret smile?

"Very interesting," Frederick repeated, tapping his book, which was yet another account of the Battle of Waterloo.

"So glad," she said, selecting a dark blue sock at random from her mending basket. Remembering whole conversations with Alexei was like turning the pages of one of her notebooks, though she'd dared write down only key words that would mean nothing to anyone else. "Madness" encapsulated the one she'd just relived. For years and years, Alexei had said, his whole country had been brainwashed. But now they'd awoken to a different state of madness, which involved daring to embrace the impossible. He'd gone on to explain that it was spreading so fast that soon the people who refused to believe the world was changing would become the truly insane ones. When you lived through such exciting times, he'd added tenderly, falling in love became entirely logical.

Frederick seemed to hesitate, then he said: "You were very far away just now."

"Was I?" When she'd tucked that sock into her basket, she had never imagined she could be swept up by such violent feelings. And now here she was back in the house where she'd lived for so long, falling into its routines yet emotionally in limbo.

The sock had a hole in its heel. She sighed as she stretched it across the broad cap of the wooden darning egg that had once belonged to her mother. Darning was a dying art. Neither of her daughters could do it, though she'd tried to teach them. "Whatever for?" Margaret demanded, genuinely astonished.

"Thinking about one of your stories?"

She frowned. The hole was enormous but the sock was of fine cashmere so surely worth rescuing. "Sort of."

"Nice story?"

She shrugged, avoiding his eyes.

Then to her great surprise, Frederick asked, sounding jocular but a little embarrassed: "What's it like living with those imaginary bods?"

A short time ago, she would have welcomed this interest: the first he'd ever shown in her writing. But now she'd been in the company of three women who wrote for a living and a man whose books had been judged too dangerous to publish, and would never again feel isolated and odd.

"Crowded," she replied after a moment, because she thought it would satisfy someone who'd never written a novel.

He seemed delighted. "I can imagine!" He paused. "D'you get voices in your head? Sort of like Joan of Arc?" He frowned, a little disturbed by the comparison.

"Sort of," she agreed.

For once, they were alone in the house. Margaret had gone to stay the night with a friend and they'd had dinner and, as usual, retired to the drawing room (as Frederick always referred to it) for an hour or two. It was chilly for August but he'd opened the french windows for a dose of the fresh air he loved and they could hear a wind getting up in the copper beech. The sound of the flapping, shivering leaves temporarily drowned the faint hum of traffic from the nearby A3. He still told visitors they'd never know the road was there. The grandfather clock in the hall made more noise, he'd joke, though traffic had doubled in twenty years.

She listened to the clock's ponderous tick and became painfully aware that life was eking away. Then she thought, "Alexei wouldn't look at it like that. He'd say each tick brings us closer. I can hear his voice."

"You smiled again!" Frederick said suddenly.

"Did I?" This close attention was making her nervous.

"That sock's had it, darling."

"Has it?"

"Well," he said, very comfortably, "it's not as if we can't afford a new pair."

Soon it would be time for the news, as he was sure to remind her just before the clock geared up to emit nine deep fruity chimes. He insisted that their television (which she had paid for) be kept behind a screen. He treated it like an uninvited guest, occasionally permitting it to speak but never commending it for being interesting or entertaining. "Nice, just the two of us," he went on with meaning.

Priscilla had come to lunch that day. "What have you done to him?" she'd exclaimed, following Celia into the kitchen, eyes sparkling with curiosity. "That man of yours can't keep his hands off you. I can't say I'm surprised. You look a million dollars, darling!"

He sulked a little when Priscilla stayed on for tea. Clearly she was unwilling to go back to her quiet life, though there was a lover in the background—there always was—someone she'd insist was devoted, but who appeared mostly absent. "Lucky old you!" she'd said as she left. "You must tell me your secret sometime."

Celia knew, of course, how much Frederick had hated her going away, but she hadn't expected him to come to the airport to collect her, braving the curiosity of the other three women. He'd thanked them for looking after her; and when Sandy responded slyly (making her heart lurch), "We didn't have to," he'd reacted with blank courtesy. However, in the car, he kept glancing at her, as if conscious of some profound change but still trying to work it out. Bet noticed the difference, too, when they arrived back at Parr's. She nearly asked a question—Celia saw it in the sudden alert and fearful expression in her eyes—but then Frederick had brought in the suitcase, beaming with happiness, and Bet visibly relaxed. No one wanted to believe she could have left England devoted to her husband and returned besotted by someone else—not even her best friend, once an expert on such matters.

"How can I go back to writing about people who aren't real?" she had asked Alexei during the long tram ride to his apartment (a conversation she would later record in her diary with the single word "truth").

"Do you have to?"

"It's how I make a living," she'd reminded him, thinking of how her income had grown over the years.

But he responded very seriously: "If you write the truth, Celia, then people will want to read it."

As she abandoned her husband's sock, she knew the time had come to tell him about Alexei. She had made no long-term decisions, but with each day that passed, she was suffering more. She could make another trip; or perhaps, now that the political climate in his country was changing, Alexei could even visit her in England.

Whatever happened, she knew he was going to be part of her life from now on and reflected a little sadly that, by rights, Frederick should understand.

"My husband's always loved someone else," she told Alexei that first time in the café. "Someone wonderful, but dead." And later, she elaborated.

He seemed strangely sympathetic to Frederick at first. Unsurprised, too, because, as he went on to explain, recognizing the dead, venerating them, was part of his culture. In his country, their corpses were displayed in open coffins; photographs of them were pinned on the front doors of houses they'd never return to; food was even left on their graves. For forty days, their spirits were free to roam and say a final good-bye to those they loved. But once that mourning period was over, they were encouraged to leave the world for their own sakes, hustled gently but firmly into the darkness before they could be condemned to eternal torment. Why, he'd asked with real concern, hadn't poor Katherine been shown similar mercy?

Her husband was watching her again.

Perhaps he was struggling to formulate a new question about writing, dip another toe into her strange world of make-believe.

"Frederick, I need to talk to you," she began.

But immediately he changed the subject. "Did I tell you Robert seems awfully down?" he said. "Bet thinks that girl—Vanessa, was it?—may have given him the push. Poor chap. He doesn't seem to have much luck with women."

Celia made an effort. "I'm glad you and Margaret had a nice time with Bet."

"Very nice. Good old Bet!" He was rattling away now. "Did I tell you Jack came down for a night? He said he couldn't manage a whole week without his wife. Well, I said I could thoroughly sympathize even though he'd been good enough to lend me his. We had an excellent talk, Jack and I."

Celia nodded because of course he'd told her. She knew the sun had shone all day for the village fête. She knew a fox had taken one of the hens and Margaret had raged and wept after they'd discovered the scattered feathers. She even knew what they'd eaten while she was away—an unhealthy procession of Margaret's favorites, like treacle tart and sticky toffee pudding. Bet had spoiled her rotten, Frederick had said with a frown, as if he didn't show his special feeling for his youngest child every single day.

"Frederick," she began again, "this is important."

To her surprise, he agreed very steadily: "Yes." But then she saw him close his eyes briefly as if he knew this was coming and all that chatter had been a delaying tactic. For the first time, she acknowledged that he was suffering, too. No wonder. For days now he'd striven to converse with a woman whose thoughts were elsewhere; for nights he'd wanted to make love to a wife who silently wept in the darkness.

"Something happened, when I was away."

He made no comment, but she could feel his intense concentration, his stillness, as if everything suddenly made sense.

"I never imagined it could," she said. "I certainly wasn't looking for it. Actually, it all started with an accident."

As she told the story, she couldn't bear to look at him. Perhaps his handsome face was hardening as he listened, his eyes becoming like chips of blue glass. After all, his wife—Lady Bayley, no less—had been seen to behave with flagrant indiscretion by three other Englishwomen who were almost certainly now spreading the gossip back home. It wouldn't help, either, that Alexei was a foreigner. She thought she would welcome his anger—so much easier to deal with than his unhappiness.

She couldn't bring herself to describe the full strength of the emotional connection she and Alexei had established. "It was so kind of him to help me in the café," she said, and "we talked and talked" and "he's a writer, too" and "somehow I felt as if I'd known him for ages." But as she reached the part where she'd visited Alexei's flat, she became aware of Frederick's extreme agitation. Then the clock chimed nine times and he rose from his chair as usual but instead of setting aside the screen and switching on the television for his all-important news, he started pacing up and down. At six foot four, he was almost too tall for the low ceiling with its grid of ancient beams, but he loved everything about their house, even the drawbacks.

"I'm sorry," she said, hating to see him

so upset. She added: "I didn't sleep with him, I promise."

"What's the difference?" Frederick demanded after a moment, his voice oddly thick. "You wanted to, didn't you?"

The light was fading, but she hadn't yet switched on the lamps, and, most uncharacteristically, he'd let this pass without comment. The french windows were still open and the long curtains were starting to stagger gently in the breeze.

"Yes," she replied truthfully. "But when it came to it, I couldn't."

"I see," he said. Moments passed. Then the anger kicked in, but mixed with hurt. "Haven't I given you a good life? Aren't the children and I enough for you? Haven't we been happy?"

"All that is true." She looked at him very steadily. "But only up to a point."

"What do you mean?"

"I mean that when we first married, Frederick, I thought it wasn't possible to be so happy." She paused, remembering her old innocence and optimism. "But that was before I found out about Katherine."

Silence. Then he repeated "Katherine"

in exactly the same tormented despairing way as he had done nearly a quarter of a century earlier in a garden in Germany.

"Even now, he can't say her name!" thought Celia, but more exasperated than upset. She said: "I'll never understand why you kept her a secret from me."

He sat down in his chair and put his head in his hands as if silently imploring her to stop.

But she steeled herself. Didn't he understand that, but for his continuing obsession with Katherine, she'd almost certainly have thanked the kind foreigner who came to her aid, and then continued on her way, never to think about him again? "When the children arrived," she said, "I saw how much you loved family life. I thought you'd forgotten about Katherine, or at any rate laid her memory to rest. But then I found the photos. Oh, Frederick, that was such a terrible shock!"

"I'm not with you." He appeared genuinely puzzled.

"Those photos you keep in a folder in your desk!" She'd seldom spoken to him so sharply. "I was trying to help Priscilla with her divorce—remember? You were out in Aden and you told me where the key was kept so I could find the address of our lawyer. And then . . . I know I shouldn't have looked through your things, Frederick, but I couldn't help it."

"Photographs of whom?"

It maddened her that he was keeping up this display of innocence. "Who do you think? They were taken at your parents' place—lots of them. That's how I knew Katherine was tall and dark. Otherwise I'd never have known anything about her. That one time we talked, you wouldn't allow me to ask questions . . ."

"Ah!" His voice had become appreciably lighter.

"What?"

"That wasn't Katherine!"

"Wasn't?" she echoed, frowning.

"For the record, Katherine was small and fair." He took a moment to recover himself (because this was, after all, his beloved first wife he was talking about). Then he went on almost eagerly: "That was my sister Frances."

She stared at him, very perplexed, because she'd always understood that he was an only child too. But now she considered the matter—the girl photographed against the backdrop of his parents' estate had even looked like him. The same thick hair that sprang sideways on the crown and fell in a curl over one eye, the same strong fine features, the same entrancing smile. But straightaway she'd assumed that beautiful stranger could only be Katherine. She was remembering the awful realization that she could never ever win, then having to pretend to Priscilla that everything was all right.

"She died of meningitis when I was fourteen. She was just four years older. Ghastly business. My parents never recovered from it."

"Why didn't you tell me?"

He shrugged, looking a little hunted, as if to say, "Don't you know me by now?"

She was beginning to understand. He came from a class that abhorred displays of weakness. After his sister's death, he must have observed his traumatized parents behave as if she'd never existed. So when, less than ten years later, he suffered an even greater loss, he had a template for survival that suited the man he'd become, with his soldier's stoicism and distaste for self-pity.

"So when Katherine died of cholera out in India, nobody talked about it either!"

He glanced at her sharply as if startled by her insight. He seemed about to say something but appeared to think better of it.

"Oh, Frederick!" Celia said with a sigh, remembering the wealth of thoughts and feelings she and Alexei had exchanged during only two meetings. It seemed almost irrelevant that she'd mistaken the identity of the girl in the photos. After all, Katherine had dogged every step of her marriage, hadn't she? Couldn't Frederick imagine what that had been like? To love someone, yet always feel kept at a distance; to know, when they were out in Africa, that every single day he was wishing Katherine could have been there instead . . .

She saw him put his head in his hands again, as if he could only agree that it was Katherine—so socially accomplished— who should have been by his side. Katherine would have known how to manage servants properly: *she* wouldn't have made the mistake of treating them as equals. If beautiful Katherine had lived, he must be thinking, he would never have become involved in that crazily destructive affair with Milly Noonan, the wife of a subordinate. What glittering heights he could have reached!

"I *know* I wasn't enough for you, Frederick!" she told him, and the relief of being able to say it at last almost brought tears to her eyes.

But then he astounded her. "*Ah!*" Moments passed. She sensed hesitation, as if he were weighing up the wisdom of going further, before he said with a touch of indulgence: "*I* know what's bothering you! It's that Milly creature, isn't it?" He didn't wait for an answer. His embarrassment was obvious because he even started to stammer a little. "I know what it m-must have I-looked like, believe me, but there was nothing in it—hand on heart. I'd never betray you. You must know that!" He paused, as if wondering how best to continue without incriminating himself. "Unfortunately she got it into her head that I loved her. And when I told her not to be so absurd, the damn girl went for me like a cat!"

"Those scratches," Celia whispered. She sensed she'd been told the truth, but did it make that much difference, really? After all, the humiliation had been the same. There was no doubt that out in Africa, power had gone to his head. She was re- membering the flirting: first the scenting of an attractive woman; then the roguish chatting up, the whole process of ascer- taining that it was there if he wanted it; and finally the preening satisfaction—all without having broken any marriage vows. Poor unhappy Milly, she found herself thinking—perhaps not the only one to get the wrong idea. But Frederick might as well have slept with her because of the scandal that had ensued. She'd always known Milly was the reason they left Africa in a rush, though of course they'd never discussed that either.

He winced. "It caused gossip in a place like that. Did me no good at all. That sort of thing matters in the army." He sighed heav- ily: an innocent man nudged toward early retirement because, in the end, rumor and innuendo had rendered the truth irrelevant. All of this had been hugely difficult to talk about, and he recommenced his pacing.

She could barely make out his expres- sion in that unlit room, but sensed his im- patience to be done with this breast-baring and hand-wringing, as he'd put it. He must be hoping that now they'd cleared the decks, they could draw a line and get back to normal life. Hadn't he made it obvious how much he needed and valued her? They had a good marriage, didn't they? Everyone else thought so!

"I believe you," she told him. "But the truth is that if you *had* had an affair with Milly, I'd have found that easier to cope with than Katherine."

Instantly he stopped in his tracks, as if Katherine had laid her cold hand on him once more, and all the years of pent-up frustration and despair burst out of her.

"Katherine!" she cried. "Always Katherine! Have you any idea what it's like, Frederick, always to feel second best? *That's* what's really spoiled our marriage!"

She heard him sigh very deeply and thought, "Oh, I wish I could leave now, drive to London, catch the first airplane back to Alexei, run up his stairs, see the delight on his face, fall into his arms." As she contemplated all this, she realized she'd come to a decision. She'd been given a chance of real happiness and now understood, beyond question, that she was entitled to take it.

She'd be judged mad, of course. Mad for leaving her distinguished handsome husband and her enviable lifestyle. Mad for alienating her children. Mad for bringing down scandal on her head. And for what—an uncertain life with an impoverished foreigner with nothing to offer but himself? Leaving the marriage would be messy and painful, certainly, but at least she had her own money to ease things. It was going to be possible.

Did Frederick pick up her resolve, and also the relief? She thought afterward that he must have, because in that instant everything changed.

He said: "I didn't want to, but I can see now that I have to tell you the truth about Katherine."

He switched on a lamp and the familiar room sprang into focus—the two chairs drawn up on either side of the fireplace, the worn patch on the carpet where generations of pet dogs had lain, the photographs of the children. He was paler than she'd ever seen him, and even his movements, usually graceful, seemed uncoordinated. "Something happened in India," he said.

Celia thought: "How strange that he's used the same words as me—'Something happened . . .' But this isn't about the wonder of falling in love. This is bad!"

"An accident." He swallowed painfully, as if all the saliva in his mouth had dried up. "Katherine didn't die of cholera. I don't know where you got that idea." He gulped again. "She was killed in a car smash."

Celia stared at him as he resumed his pacing, as if forcing himself to tell the story, step by painful step.

"We'd been drinking whiskey sours. Well, *I'd* been drinking! I'd had three for her one . . ." His voice trailed away.

"Go on," said Celia after a moment, though she thought she comprehended exactly where the story was going now.

He glanced at her very anxiously, but when he began again his voice sounded a little stronger. "We were pretty happy in India. Am I allowed to say that? It was long before you and me, darling. Katherine and I were both so young and we'd just got married and we'd been sent to that beautiful place. It was so beautiful! It was like

Africa—that's why Africa always made me sad. The same magnificent crimson and gold sunsets and those wonderfully exotic birds and animals with their strange frightening sounds at night, as if they took it over then and *we* were the real trespassers . . ."

"Go on," she repeated, thinking that she'd never heard that man, who prided himself on his down-to-earth nature, speak so eloquently.

He glanced at her again. Yes, he seemed to concede, he'd got off the point, but who could blame him? He made a sustained effort, started almost tripping over his words, like a man who'd drunk too much, though he never did—not even in Africa, where heavy drinking had been accepted and even encouraged. "It was a beautiful evening. Did I say that? And I said to her, 'Why don't we go for a spin while it's still light?' We had this little car, you see—it was a real novelty out there, old-fashioned thing that it was. So few cars, and one had the roads to oneself. We'd done it before. It was the way to see really special things— like a tiger with its cubs drinking at a water hole once. 'Where's the harm? I thought. Okay, I'm a bit more squiffy than usual, but we're hardly likely to meet anyone.' And Katherine was game. She was such a good sort. You'd have liked her, darling, I know you would."

Celia thought: "That mysterious powerful beauty who haunted me for nearly a quarter of a century never even existed! The real Katherine was jolly and uncomplicated. Even her name is ordinary. It always was."

He was staring into space as if trying to comprehend how one terrible mistake could go on to overshadow a whole life. Then he rubbed a hand across his face, shivered like a dog, and gave her a beseeching look. "Can't bear to remember it," he admitted miserably. "Never have been able to."

"You have to," she told him as kindly as she could. "For both our sakes."

"Yes," he agreed, once more showing the courage she'd always admired. But he could only do it his way. "Driving far too fast," he informed her tersely. "Car spun out of control going round a bend and hit a tree. Concertinaed her side whereas I walked away with barely a scratch." He couldn't keep it up. His voice trembled. "She was dying, that poor girl, and all because of me. 'Oh God!' she said. 'Oh God!' Her face looked beautiful, there didn't seem a mark on her, but they were her last words. I saw her eyes roll back and then she was gone." He buried his head in his hands and sobbed, terrible harsh sounds as if he hated himself for showing such weakness but was powerless to stop.

The wind was shaking the poplars at the bottom of the garden as strenuously as it had once moaned in the pines at Far Point and Celia thought of the solitary child she'd been and all the years of a different kind of loneliness that had followed, until Alexei. "Oh, Frederick!" she said very sadly, "you should have told me. Why didn't you? I'd have understood."

He muttered something.

"Sorry?"

"I said, it gets worse."

Worse than the scene he'd just described? But she could feel the horror gathering in that room now. In her heightened, troubled state, she imagined it pressing closer and closer to Frederick, preparing to lift up its black veil and force him to look into its dreadful face.

"Oh God!" he said again in a voice of utter despair. "How does one even start?"

She waited. Then the clock in the hall started to chime once more and she thought with a strange disbelief, "The world hasn't stopped, after all. Everywhere around us, people must be leading ordinary lives."

"For as long as I can remember," he told her, "I wanted to be a soldier."

Celia thought: "Yes, and you had the brains and the courage and the natural authority to go to the very top."

"But if I'd been found guilty of causing an accident when drunk, it would have finished my career. The army takes a firm line on things like that." He paused. "Quite right, too."

The curtains flew into the air, as suddenly and violently as if some wild creature had launched a kick at them from outside. Then the wind relaxed its grip and they fell back into long folds once more. Celia moved to close the french windows, but he stopped her with a gesture as if his beloved fresh air was more necessary than ever now.

"I knew I was done for even as I held

Katherine's dead body in my arms . . ."
Then he stopped and stared grimly ahead
as if using all his willpower to prevent another display of emotion. When he resumed, he sounded almost brisk. "In other
circumstances, of course, I'd have been
arrested then charged. But it was such a
small world out there and the chief of police had become a sort of chum. Very civilized man, Katherine used to say—she
liked talking to him a lot. He'd even been to
dinner with us once . . ." He stopped and
glanced at her a little uneasily as if to check
whether she'd picked up his drift.

She believed she had. The chief of
police—"very civilized man"—had clearly
been a native. "A sort of chum," Frederick
had called him. Had he exploited their
tenuous, unequal friendship and begged,
man to man, to be let off the hook? Or had
the police chief offered, off his own bat,
to turn a blind eye? Perhaps none of it had
been so straightforward and a deal had
been agreed on almost before either of
them knew it. Obviously, no mention of the
whiskey on Frederick's breath had been
made in the report that must have been

required by law. Katherine's death had been recorded as an unfortunate accident, leaving him free to resume his promising career.

"Against all the odds, I got away with it." Then he muttered under his breath: "Shouldn't have, though."

Once more, Celia thought she understood. What he could not have comprehended at the time was that, despite the plaudits he'd go on to gather up and the considerable glory, the shame of that moment of terrible egotism would never leave him. When, for an entirely different reason, his career was once again threatened, he barely bothered to defend himself even though he was innocent. He believed it was long overdue punishment. It was a measure of his essential goodness, thought Celia, knowing that he'd be quite unable ever to see it like that himself.

"I wasn't going to get married again," he said. "I thought I owed that to Katherine, at least. But when I found you on that beach, it seemed like a miracle. For the first time in years, I was happy."

"Oh, Frederick," she murmured.

"Of course I couldn't tell you!" He seemed adamant. "Could you have loved me after that? It seemed better to behave as if it had never happened. At least then we had a chance."

She looked at him very sadly before shaking her head. No.

"You're telling me you *would* have loved me if I'd told you?"

"Oh, Frederick," she said, "I adored you. Anything would have been better than feeling Katherine was the only one who mattered. You were so young and you'd made a dreadful mistake and of course you should have owned up." She paused. "If you'd told me right at the beginning I'd have been disappointed in you, of course, but it would have passed. Marriages have weathered far worse."

There was nothing left to say except: "I see."

The wind battered the house all night long, rattling the sash windows and howling down the chimneys. Neither of them could sleep. Yet, despite the horror of what they'd been through, there was a palpably new closeness. They'd both been at fault in their different ways, Celia conceded. Why had they never dared talk? They could have had the perfect marriage everyone believed in. It was such a waste.

At a quarter to two in the morning, he turned abruptly in their tumbled bed and kissed her passionately and she found herself responding. But after the lovemaking, she felt only bottomless emptiness. It had taken Alexei to bring about this closeness, but she saw now that it was artificial and transitory. The reality was that since meeting Alexei, all her expectations had changed.

At three o'clock, Frederick said: "We've still so much to be grateful for. We could make a real go of it now."

"Let's talk about it tomorrow." As she turned away from him, an image came to her of a light being borne farther and farther away into the darkness. But it was his tragedy, not hers. After all, she had Alexei now.

The following day, Margaret came home: overexcited as usual, full of gripes about the friend she'd stayed with. That was the thing about her youngest child, thought Celia: everything always had to be played at top volume.

However, even Margaret noticed something amiss.

"What's with Daddy?" she asked, looking out the kitchen window.

"I don't know," Celia replied.

One of the tasks of the gardener they employed was to ensure there was a supply of suitable logs. But for some reason, Frederick had just taken this upon himself—even though it was high summer and they were unlikely to need a fire for months. Since breakfast (which he hadn't touched) he'd been splitting log after log, swinging the heavy axe above his head, smashing it down with all his force. After last night's storm, the sun had come out and it was far too hot for such exertion. But despite Celia's entreaties, he'd refused to stop.

It wasn't true what she'd just told Margaret. It was entirely logical that a man who'd always preferred actions to words would choose to deal with his anger and sadness like that. He was only using the advice he gave others—"Don't sit and mope. Get out there in the fresh air and do something physical." And after what she had told him—"I need to think about all this"—who could blame him for overdoing it?

"He's bonkers," said Margaret, but tenderly. She added very confidently: "*I'll* go and talk to him."

"Would you, darling?"

Margaret gave her a look of impatience barely masking contempt. Whatever was going on, she'd already taken sides. Now that she was a teenager, Celia found her harder to cope with than ever. She'd none of Robert's and Sarah's integral dutifulness: she was a handful and bound to get worse.

She watched from the kitchen window as Margaret approached Frederick, a vision of beauty in T-shirt and shorts. "Daddy!" she screamed at him. "Daddy, you've got to stop that!"

Dripping with sweat, Frederick at last put down the axe and Celia sighed with relief. "Good for her!" she thought. "Now she can lay the table under the copper beech and we can all have lunch; and after that I'll encourage him to have a sleep."

She turned from the window, thinking, "There's enough chicken left over from yesterday's lunch because Priscilla ate like a bird. Why don't I make coronation chicken? They both love that." She was feeling around in the fridge, wondering if there was enough curry powder in her store cupboard, when she heard Margaret shriek "Mummy!" in a tone of such terror that she nearly dropped a glass jar of mayonnaise.

Looking back on that day, as she so often did in the years that followed, she saw the sequence of events in slow motion, like something that could have been predicted and therefore prevented. She knew what had happened even before the rush to the window and the dreadful sight of Frederick collapsed on the ground, dark red in the face and twitching as if his whole body had gone into spasm. Poor Margaret was no longer bossy and confident, but hysterical with shock. Her beloved father had suffered an almost fatal stroke and she'd been forced to witness the entire thing.

With hindsight, the news item on television a couple of days later could probably have been predicted, too.

"It has just been confirmed that last night up to half a million Soviet troops and armed tanks invaded the city of Prague in Czechoslovakia. Alexander Dubček, the first secretary, who tried to liberalize the communist regime as part of a movement that became known as the Prague Spring, has been arrested. Similar clampdowns are expected in neighboring Eastern Bloc countries, where the movement has inspired demonstrations of support."

The week after that, Celia installed Alexei's painting next to the french windows in the drawing room, where she would see it every morning when she opened the curtains to a new day; and there it remained for more than forty years.

CHAPTER THIRTY

I told the bees you were dead.
Diary entry under January 10, 1990.

28.10.2009.
Dear Ms. Granger,
As you are well aware, we have made it very clear to you that we strongly object, as a family, to your proposed biography of our late mother. I am hereby formally warning you that if you carry out your threat to go ahead, based on the material you have gathered without the permission of the whole family, then we shall not hesitate to instruct our lawyer to take action.
Yours faithfully, Robert Bayley.
Pompous dick! File most reluctantly closed.

Living on alone at Parr's after Frederick's death, Celia had kept the front door open long after summer dwindled away. It was as if the house could never be sufficiently aired of the sick breath of a long illness; or perhaps she expected a visitor to wander in, along with the spiders and field mice. It was only when autumn rains began to wash over the stone flagging that she reluctantly closed the door, though she refused to lock it, even at night, which had frightened her children.

But for some weeks now, Parr's had sported new locks on the front door and also the downstairs windows; and an alarm connected to the local police station had been installed at some expense. A stranger passing close enough to notice (in other words, trespassing) might have assumed this increased security was because of the "For Sale" notice pinned to the gate, proclaiming that the house was empty. The family knew better. So far as they were concerned, ordinary burglars posed little threat.

The Saturday morning after the meeting at Robert's house, they regrouped at Parr's. It wasn't a good time, as Robert kept reminding everyone. The baby was overdue now and his house had been on red alert for days, with every flutter, every twinge interpreted as the onset of labor. Robert had already driven Miranda to the hospital twice, only to be advised to return home. But coming to Parr's had taken top priority, though it wasn't unconnected to Miranda's baby. It was about protecting the generation to come. To coin a military analogy, the family were about to obliterate the enemy's objective, thus rendering further warfare pointless. And despite the ever-present anxiety about Miranda, Robert couldn't remember feeling so exhilarated.

He drove Sarah and Margaret down, followed by Bud and Guy, while Mel stayed at home with Miranda. Nobody asked where Whoopee was. This was the second time he'd failed to show up at a family gathering, but Sarah seemed unfazed. She'd just had her long hair cut short by an expensive hairdresser. Whoopee hated it, she announced with a laugh, but everyone else had told her it took years off. The family sensed her moving toward a new independence, which they welcomed for her sake, even though they believed in marriage. Whoopee was Whoopee, they murmured, knowing what they meant. Sarah was right to protect herself.

"There are no problems, only indecisions," Robert was heard to mutter as he whisked through a roundabout, narrowly missing another car.

This favorite saying of his had always baffled the family. Didn't being robbed of all your possessions count as a problem, Whoopee had once asked, sounding innocently mystified, or getting squashed by a bus? But Robert now had the perfect opportunity to prove the truth of the maxim. He could see very clearly that the mess the family was in had been entirely caused by indecision. He had already written a firm letter to Jenny Granger. Now, under his leadership, they were going to gather up all the diaries and notebooks and letters and scribbled-on scraps and build a huge bonfire and put a match to the lot. It was true that a number of embarrassing secrets had already been uncovered; but if, as he feared, there were more bombs lurking in that mass of old paper, this would remove them for good. He'd discussed the plan with his sisters, and they were all agreed. Indecisions sorted. End of problem.

But Bud was hysterical. She'd come down to Parr's because she was still hoping to make the family see sense. She'd even offered to pay the bill herself if Robert would agree to have Celia's papers put into storage. But it was no good, and to her horror, Guy sided with him. They'd argued all the way from London. He was a Bayley through and through, she said, using their special relationship to wound him. But he was as obdurate as Robert. "All this is no good for Dad," he informed her, as if it was the only thing that mattered.

Even so, she was quite prepared to have a stand-up row. This was too important, she told herself, trying to forget how frightened everyone got when Robert became pink and agitated.

"All right?" Sarah kept asking Margaret and once Robert turned in the driving seat and asked if she was all right, too, with nearly fatal consequences for all three of them.

But he didn't really want to know—or rather, he wanted to be assured that his sister was all right (even though he could see for himself that she wasn't), without getting upset. From where he was now—happy again with Mel—marriage seemed a doddle. Once he hummed as he sped along the A3, but then Margaret's pale miserable face caught his eye in the windscreen mirror and he felt ashamed.

The house felt cold and damp when they opened it up. According to Whoopee (who'd been muttering about packing in his job as an estate agent), if you really wanted to sell a house you needed to fill it with cut flowers and the scent of freshly baked bread. "Best of all, lay on a newborn baby, but not a crying one," he advised, adding, "Miranda's bastard might come in useful after all." It was about envy, he maintained, but Sarah privately disagreed. It was to do with creating an illusion. But how absurd to believe that such a fragile and precious thing as family happiness could be purchased, along with fixtures and fittings! She now understood that it needed to be cherished or it would be gone, never to be recaptured.

Over coffee made by the women, Robert outlined tasks in brisk military fashion and ignored Bud. He and Guy would prepare the bonfire while his sisters did the clearing, starting with the attic. He knew the women had drawn the short straws, but it made him shiver to think of being anywhere near that dark cave of secrets. He was trying very hard to hold on to the memory of the mother he'd known: someone sweet and dutiful, whom he doubted had been that interested in sex anyway.

But Bud started in on him straightaway. "I don't think you've thought this through."

"What makes you say that?" Robert responded, looking grim.

"If you burn everything, you'll never know the truth about Gran."

He rolled his eyes, looking hunted.

"Don't, Bud!" said Guy warningly.

Even Sarah said, "Darling!"

"But this is who Gran was! This is her whole life!" She was shrieking at them all now. "It's like you're burning *her*!"

"Oh, don't be so melodramatic," said Margaret crossly. "It's only paper."

"It's not! It's barbaric what you're planning to do!" She burst into tears, and Robert put his hands over his ears like a child.

"It's like a medieval execution. It's as if you're going to drag her out of the house and put her on the fire and scorch the life out of her! And it's all just so you can silence her for good."

"Darling," said Sarah again, sounding really concerned this time. "It's not as if Gran didn't write all those books."

"And I suppose you'll suggest burning them next!" It was the worst insult Bud could think of. "You haven't even read them, have you?"

The two sisters climbed the ladder to the attic.

"She doesn't mean it," muttered Sarah. It was the closest she'd ever come to criticizing her daughter.

And Margaret muttered back, like defending herself: "I *did* read one of Mummy's books and I don't recommend it."

Unlike Sarah, it was the first time since childhood she'd been up to that dim spidery place, and she was astonished by the sheer volume of stuff that had accumulated—the overflowing trunks and boxes that took up every bit of space. It even distracted her from her own misery. When had their mother ever found the time to write all this? She could only remember catching her working once.

She must have been about seven or eight, and the parents weren't long back from Africa. She'd awoken from a nightmare at three o'clock in the morning and descended the stairs to the kitchen, to be confronted by the shocking sight of her mother sitting at the scrubbed wooden table and writing in a big notebook under a solitary pool of light. She'd seemed both distant and lonely, like an entirely different person, and Margaret had let out a cry. Instantly her mother had abandoned her work. She was so tender and loving. She'd even lain in Margaret's bed with her until she fell asleep.

But Margaret now understood that writing at night must have been habitual and her mother had been waiting all day for that stolen scrap of time.

"It's only stuff," Robert had told them in the car, but it wasn't true. Every one of those millions of scribbled words represented a victory. Ordinary love paled beside such dedication, thought Margaret, oddly comforted.

In the field below the house, Robert began to arrange kindling across the big
blackened circle they'd gathered around
the night of Celia's funeral seven months
before. "No point ruining another patch of
ground," he told Guy. He knew it sounded
tactless and insensitive, but the scene with
Bud had upset him badly and made him
all the more determined. They didn't shout
at each other in his family and he'd adored
his mother. He was only trying to protect
her memory, he told himself: stop the world
from picking over her life with no conception of the real person. He could see her
now, sitting in the long grass in her ancient
straw hat, reveling in her wildflowers and
butterflies. She would have been horrified
by all the attention.

"Be sad to say good-bye to those," he
murmured gruffly to his son, indicating
the enormous ash trees at the bottom of
the field. His parents had planted them in
1947, the year they moved into Parr's; and
twenty-one years later, the biggest had
crashed to the ground at more or less the
same time his father suffered his stroke
(though, unlike his mother, Robert had re-

fused to see any symbolism in it because, as he'd pointed out, there'd been a bad storm and the roots of old trees did rot).

It had lain in the long grass for weeks while, up in the house, his father moaned and twitched, as if willing himself to rise from his bed. By the time the tree was sliced up into logs, they were well into winter and the family had adjusted. That vigorous noisy man would never walk or speak again and was unlikely to last the year. "We must make it the best year," Celia told them all tearfully. But he'd hung on for more than twenty, following her with his searing unhappy eyes, as if he couldn't bear to die and leave her.

Robert had never known his grandmother. Within days of his birth, the mother-in-law Frederick had apparently found such an embarrassment was dead and the true past could be discarded. Robert had seen the "before" photos in the old albums of a dilapidated house and an overgrown garden. In light of what he'd learned, he was prepared to bet that the elegant uncomfortable decor his mother had chosen had borne more than a passing resemblance to Far Point. And by the time it was all finished, the housekeeper's daughter had transformed herself into a wife an ambitious, upper-class army officer could be proud of.

But now Parr's needed "some modernization," as the estate agent had put it after viewing only two bathrooms with charming claw-foot iron tubs but no showers and a kitchen with a pretty dresser but mismatched cupboards and a single sink. But something couldn't be fixed. Standing in the meadow where he'd once played as a child, Robert became aware of the substantial increase in traffic noise—a constant low roar like an angry sea. He decided not to mention it to Guy for the time being. What a good boy he was, he thought. It was high time he headed up a pack of his own. But he needed to find the right wife, just as he himself had eventually done.

Bud had sought refuge in her grandmother's old study. Sitting at the desk where so many books had been written, she could clearly hear the voices of her mother and her aunt in the attic above.

Her mother said coaxingly: "Talk to me."

But instead of a reply, there was a resounding thump as a full plastic bag was tossed down through the open trapdoor onto the landing outside.

They couldn't wait, thought Bud. Despite their strenuous denials, they were obviously convinced there'd been an affair. That was what all this was about, of course. And instead of confronting the problem, they were covering it up—having learned nothing from the mistakes of the past.

Though Bud didn't believe in the affair herself, she'd have forgiven her grandmother anything. Often, as a child, she'd stared at the formal photograph taken in Africa, trying to work out how the godlike man with the medals and the cantankerous old invalid could possibly be one and the same, wondering how her grandmother could stay so patient and never once lose her temper, giving out all that love and getting nothing back.

"What can I do?" she whispered, even though she could no longer feel her grandmother's presence the way she had in the days and weeks following her death.

If she didn't act quickly, it would all be gone—that vast jigsaw-puzzle record of a life that began nine years after the end of the Great War, when empire was taken for granted, and ended with men in space. It would have been such fun to piece it together: to meet her grandmother as a very young woman, when she'd only known her as an old one; to learn what sort of person her grandfather had been, before illness distorted him. And she desperately wanted to know about those parts of her grandmother's life that had only just been revealed: the childhood below stairs; the mysterious first wife. But most of all, she wanted to understand what had made her into a writer.

"I said you should talk to Charles." Sarah sounded cross because she was worried about Bud behaving so badly. Also, kind though she was, her patience had run out with her sister. Was she going to carry on being miserable forever because she was too proud to risk rejection?

Margaret didn't answer. How impossible she was, thought Sarah. She'd been given so much: the doting love of their father, and that amazing beauty for years and years, and a good husband, too, though she'd been incapable of recognizing it.

"You should!"

Margaret seized a box of letters and tipped them into her plastic bag. Then she picked up a heap of old notebooks and something slid from the bundle and landed with a faint crack on the dusty floor, shedding blackened fragments. It was a flower without a stalk that had dried to a brittle ball. It looked as if it might have been a red rose, once.

Sarah picked it up, momentarily distracted. Perhaps their father had given it to their mother a lifetime ago, when he was courting her at Far Point. In her version of events, he'd proposed in the rose garden. Perhaps he'd plucked a flower from a bed before going down on his knees. But then Sarah remembered that there'd been no flowers in wartime: the whole garden was turned over to vegetables, her mother had said. Furthermore, she couldn't envisage that practical, unimaginative man, who'd regularly forgotten anniversaries, behaving in such a sentimental way. Someone else had given her mother that rose. It was then that Sarah understood, beyond any shadow of a doubt, that her mother had had an affair.

But she didn't want to know about it. She felt exactly like Robert. So she shivered and tossed the crumbling flower away and concentrated on her sister's problems once more. "You have to do *something*!"

Margaret spoke at last—just as cross, as if Sarah was the irritating one. "Of course I've talked to Charles!"

"And?"

But to Sarah's dismay, her sister started crying: bitter, racking sobs that made her sound as if she was gasping for life.

They'd lit the bonfire, but it was still smoking and refusing to blossom into flame. Robert was conscious of Guy watching him very attentively and realized he must have noticed the can of petrol he'd brought down to the field. Robert would never have permitted anyone else to do something so dangerous, and he probably wasn't going to use the petrol anyway. But there was a side of him that was strangely attracted to risk. On the way from London, he'd broken the speed limit several times. He wasn't sensible about diet either: ladling in cream and butter, as if he wanted to provoke the same kind of dreadful incapacitating stroke he'd seen his father suffer. It was like a longing to break out of his dutiful, conventional persona and be a man who scared people rather than reassured them. That shouting at the funeral had been extraordinarily satisfying, however much Guy had disapproved.

Against her will, Bud was being drawn into the conversation going on over her head. Her mother and aunt were talking about love. She'd thought nothing could top the embarrassment of having to listen to her mother's emotional problems—especially because they involved her father—but now her aunt was casting fussy anxious old Charles, of all people, in a romantic role. And to make the story even more excruciating, it was coming out so slowly.

"And?" Sarah kept prodding. "And?" In between, Bud could hear boxes and trunks being dragged across the floor. They weren't even attending to what they were doing!

Bud knew about happy marriages and their cozy, teasing flavor, and even as a child, she had noted the chill between Margaret and Charles. But it now appeared that those two people who'd made each other unhappy for years had gone on a date. Still more extraordinary, it had been initiated by Margaret. However, she was crying so hard that it was difficult to make out what had happened next.

But the most depressing thing of all for Bud was hearing two women in late middle age talk like girls. "What did you wear?" her mother had just asked; and "How did he look when he first saw you?" And Margaret had replied: "That blue dress he's always liked" and "He didn't look *at* me, he looked through me, Sarah. Can you imagine how that felt?"

She was reliving the surreal moment of realizing with a shock that the well-dressed, presentable man sitting quietly reading a newspaper was the husband she'd despised for twenty years. It had thrown her badly, just like his air of distant politeness when he looked up and saw her. Suddenly, she wanted him back desperately.

He relaxed slightly once they got into a discussion about Theo, who was not taking the breakup well and—a bad sign—

underperforming academically. Obviously he'd decided the point of the meeting was to talk about the children.

She drank too much. It was the only way to summon up the necessary courage. And then, not daring to look at him, she told him she'd made a terrible mistake. Furthermore, she explained all about the married lover, Patrick, who had caused her such grief. And finally, she begged him to forgive her, promising that if he could find it in his heart to do so, she'd be quite different.

And then . . . She was finding the next bit really hard to tell her sister, who thought she knew her so well and was already beaming, congratulating herself on having played peacemaker.

When she had finally dared to look at Charles, that serious, careful man was trembling with joy and she began to suspect that there never had been a change of heart, just a final attempt to win her properly with an act of entirely untypical recklessness. But almost instantly, and to her horror, she realized that she didn't want him after all. Why had he pinned his entire happiness on her, of all people? Why? His unfaltering love dismayed her. It always had and there was no way she could change that, however much she might long for a conventional life.

It was the end. No man would risk his heart again after such treatment. But even as she cringed at her own cruelty, a good part of her hoped she'd liberated him at last.

"Why am I like this?" she asked Sarah through sobs. But then she started shoveling paper into bags with a set cross face as if she already knew the answer but could do nothing about it. The fact was, if you couldn't love yourself, it was impossible to believe anyone else would. And besides, she was beginning to understand that a part of her must always have divined that the marriage held up as such an example had been nearly as much of a fiction as her own.

Bud was appalled by the story her aunt had just told, but not for the same reason as her mother, who kept repeating in a horrified way, "How could you?"

Fancy cold, bitter Margaret entering into

a doomed love affair! It made her into a far more sympathetic person. Of course, she should never have married Charles, and it wasn't her fault she couldn't love him. In Bud's opinion, it had taken real courage for Margaret to behave like that.

Then she forgot about her aunt. Through the open window of the study, she could smell the first threads of wood smoke, as sharp as paint, tainting the sweet country air. Right up until that moment, a part of her had hoped the men wouldn't go through with it. But now she actually heard Guy guffaw at something his father had said, and even imagined she caught the crackle and spit of burning branches. What was she to do? Even if she gathered up all the stuff in the study posthaste, there was nowhere to hide it and, even now, Guy was thumping up the stairs on a mission to collect the filled sacks so they could be tossed on the fire.

"Guy," she began, glad to catch him on his own.

But he said with a tight, controlled expression, "Don't start." He was looking around the study as if he wasn't thinking about their grandmother at all and was simply estimating how long it would take to clear the sheets of paper strewn all over the floor, the notebooks on the desk, the boxes of scraps balanced everywhere. He even went on, sounding a little disgusted: "How could anyone work in this mess?"

"Guy, we can still stop this. Please!"

"It's all very well, Bud," he said, and she knew he was thinking of the way she'd spoken to his father.

"I'm sorry. I didn't mean to upset him. It's just that nobody seems to understand."

"They do," said Guy, looking as obdurate as Robert.

"If it wasn't for her," said Bud with passion, "this family would be so ordinary."

It was a moment before he replied, as if the truth was so obvious that he could hardly be bothered to spell it out. Then he said: "What's so wrong about being ordinary?"

The fire was going well, all the better for the dusty, brittle old paper that was being flung on it in great bundles, sending up showers of red sparks. It was beginning to send out an intense smoky heat that stung their eyes.

"How much more to go?" Robert asked Guy because a dozen sacks had been emptied so far.

"A fair bit."

"Bring it on!" Then, to his consternation, Robert saw that a photo had just fluttered into the flames. "Hey!" he shouted. For a fraction of a second, he believed he saw the faces of himself and his sisters as children, the word "proof" stamped all over them, then the image curled up and blackened and was gone. They should have thought about photographs. If Bud hadn't made such a scene, they might have, he thought, anxious to blame someone. But it was too late now.

As ash drifted over the field where he'd once played with his sisters, a sad memory returned: the first time he'd seen his parents after his father's terrible stroke. His mother was very subdued, behaving almost as if it was her fault (which was absurd); and it occurred to Robert, even then, that she'd have to give up her writing. His father needed such round-the-clock attention. If neglected even for a second, he'd press the bell attached to his wheelchair, as if the damage to his brain had swiped away all consideration, too. That shrill insistent trilling became one of the sounds of the house, yet Celia was never heard to complain. As Robert had discovered from the obituaries, it was during that grindingly hard time that she began to be a proper writer, switching her attention from unreal people to real ones living in real families, with real problems. He could appreciate the effort that had gone into that, and admire it, too. He was very proud of his mother, even if he still hadn't read any of her books.

If something had happened during that week in the late sixties that his mother had spent away from his father, thought Robert, then it couldn't have amounted to anything more than a holiday bonk, a reaction to being abroad or even getting older. Furthermore, he decided, there had to have been some element of calculation on the man's part. Why else would an East European become involved with a middle-aged English tourist? Perhaps the long-term aim had been to get to the West, he reflected, with a twinge of real pity for his vulnerable, gullible mother. After all, enough people were trying it now: claiming to be political refugees when all they really wanted was to land in a country with free housing, free medical attention, and even a fat Giro check from the social services every month. But there was no way his mother would have jeopardized her comfortable life in England, her good marriage—of that he was sure. He lobbed another mass of paper onto the crackling fire. He didn't really believe there'd been an affair, he told himself, as he prodded the mass with a stick, making sure the flames reached every bit.

More ash drifted over the field, as if someone had cast a fine dark net, and he reflected that if ever any of them doubted what their father had meant to their mother, they only had to remember the effect of his death on her. She'd become like a living corpse herself with her mournful eyes sunk in her pale face, her dreadful silence. They'd been in despair, terrified that, within a matter of days, they'd find themselves planning a second funeral.

But character had triumphed, thank God. She'd seen the sense in living, the comfort of family, and emerged even stronger;

and, with time to herself at last, she had gone on to write the books that made her famous.

However—wouldn't you know it?— Jenny Granger had tried to twist that, too: make something suspicious and scandalous out of it. "Something very odd happened to her writing after your father's death," she'd observed thoughtfully. "She wrote in a different style, almost a different voice." Then she'd made him blush and stumble for words. "What do *you* think, Robert?"

He heaved another bundle onto the fire. Damn all reptiles! Jenny Granger had even managed to destroy the special relationship he and his sisters enjoyed with Bet. Suddenly he felt very sad about that. He decided there'd been enough coldness. In fact, it made him wince with guilt to think of the anguish they must have inflicted on their beloved substitute mother who'd soothed away their miseries as children and made school holidays so happy. As soon as Miranda's baby was born, he'd telephone and make the peace. He could appreciate now that if Bet had kept secrets from them, it was because her first loyalty had always been toward their mother.

Bud was thinking that the people who bought the house would never know what a special room the study had been. When they'd swept away the cobwebs and ripped up the moth-eaten carpet and painted the walls and ceiling until they gleamed, they'd congratulate themselves on a job well done and never know that once a woman had sat in there and used her imagination to revisit beloved places and mend broken dreams and even transcend old age. So what if real love and beauty and truth were hard to find in real life? She'd create them in her fiction.

The computer looked out of place in that old-fashioned room. But it was Celia who'd suggested getting one, then asked Guy to explain it to her. Was it really true, she asked him, that it could send messages across thousands of miles that could be read just minutes later? She'd seen it in the newspaper, she said, but found it almost impossible to believe.

The computer was at least ten years old

and nobody would want it now. Bud was remembering how her grandmother had reused envelopes and string from parcels. She would never have thrown away some-one else's memories.

She'd loved the pyramid orchids that had graced the field the last summer of her life, frail pale mauve blossoms that lasted only a day or two. There'd been a glut of blackberries and sloes that year, as well. Three days before dying in her sleep, she'd gone down to the field in her ancient straw hat and picked fruit and, to the family's hor-ror, proceeded to boil up jam. Robert had asked her crossly if she was losing her mind, which returned to haunt him. But this coming summer, the fruit was destined to fall into the long grass and rot.

As he watched Guy hauling the last few sacks through the long tussocky grass, he found himself wondering if the new owners would turn the field into a tennis court, or even apply for planning permis-sion to dig out a swimming pool. He re-solved never to try and find out. Once Parr's was sold, he'd revisit it only in dreams, or stories for his as yet unborn grandchildren.

"See?" he found himself crowing. It wasn't true that he had no imagination, or his fault that his mother had never recognized it.

At least the books were left. It was amazing how many different editions there were—hardbacks and paperbacks and large-print versions and translations. It was Guy who noticed the toppling piles on the floor after being invited in by Celia to install the computer. Without a word, he'd gone out to buy materials and built good stout shelves to hold the lot.

Still seething with upset, Bud whispered, "I'm so glad I'm not like them." As if to prove it, she seized a book at random—one of the later ones, written under Celia's real name. To her surprise, it fell open at a particular page.

There was a black-and-white photograph hidden in there. After the initial shock, Bud stared at it for some time. Then she turned it over, in case there was some kind of explanation on the back.

Robert's mobile rang just as he was heaving one of the last bundles onto the fire. It was Mel reporting that at last Miranda really did appear to have gone into labor and they'd arrived safely at the hospital. Everything was under control, she assured him, and it was likely to be a long wait. She kept on repeating this in a calming tone although she must have known he was even then jingling his car keys, anticipating the race back to London.

It was Guy who stopped him. If Robert insisted on returning, *he* would drive them back. It touched Robert deeply that his son was so protective toward him, even at the expense of his relationship with Bud. But he was sure they'd be friends again soon: that Bud would understand that Guy's only motivation was to protect the family, past and present, like the good son he was.

Bud couldn't imagine taking such a photograph herself. It offended against every precept. Maybe, equally upset and disgusted, her grandmother had stuffed it into the first book at hand and then forgotten all about it. But Bud knew it wasn't so. The book had fallen open too naturally at that place. For some reason, that horrible photo had been important to her grandmother.

The hiding place proved it. She must have known it was the very last place her children would ever look.

Well, thought Bud dismally, thinking of the stacks of charred letters on the fire, they'd never know now if she had responded to the strange message on the back.

The women were coming down from the loft, murmuring about Miranda and reliving their own labors. Margaret sounded far more positive, but talking about Theo and Evie always put her in a good mood.

"It's the only pain that's worth it," she announced.

"Actually I enjoyed it," said Sarah (who seemed to have forgotten the emergency cesarean for Spud, and the weeping scar afterward).

"I didn't say I didn't *enjoy* it!"

By the time they reached the bottom of the steps, still gently competing, the real story had very slowly begun to fall into place. The date written on the back of the photo was the key. It was as if, Bud thought later, the spirit of her grandmother had suddenly flickered into being, guided her to the book, made it fall open at that particular place, and even—if she wanted to be really fanciful—seized a ray of sunlight and directed it at the numbers inscribed in glittery old ink. But her grandmother had never taken much account of "as if." Part of her appeal was that she believed in the incredible.

CHAPTER THIRTY-ONE

He has become part of me. It is the only way I can explain this strange new voice, the conviction that at last I am capable of achieving what I want to.
Diary entry, under September 9, 1990.

For obvious reasons, Bud would never forget her last holiday with both grandparents. However, before Frederick's sudden death on January 7, 1990, it had been remarkably happy, despite the resident nurse, the clutter of equipment, the nasty all-pervasive smell of disinfectant. It was Celia who made it so. Everyone had noticed the lovely enthusiasm she radiated. She should have been exhausted, so soon after Margaret's wedding and then the family Christmas. Furthermore, Frederick was more trying than ever, ringing his bell non-stop, almost as if a shameful part of him resented her happiness because he couldn't share it. (That was what Bud had heard her mother suggest to her father, anyway.) Three days after Christmas, Whoopee said: "Are you sure you don't want to come back to London with us, Budcakes? Wouldn't catch *me* staying on in the House of Usher."

Remembering that time, trying to reinter-pret it as an adult, was like finding a draw-ing done as a child. Though there was no conception of perspective, there was clarity of vision that could never be recaptured.

She'd stayed on at Parr's because she'd wanted her grandmother to herself. And once they'd waved off the rest of the family and had supper and escaped from Steve, the resident nurse, they had their first real conversation, out walking in the garden, hand in hand. It was about miracles. Celia said she knew they existed now. And just then, as if in illustration, a strange thing hap-pened: a bright light tumbled through the sky, shedding milky plumes before van-ishing into the darkness. It was the first shooting star Bud had ever seen. However, straight afterward, Celia seemed more worried than thrilled. "We must get back," she said, as if not even that beautiful New Year gift could make her forget her sick husband.

Mealtimes were torture. Frederick took an eternity to eat his food, which all had to be sieved in case he choked. Even so, Steve regularly had to spin him out of the room in his wheelchair and (audibly) clear his windpipe in the corridor outside. The night he died, about a week after the shooting star incident, they had roast chicken— which looked like sick on his plate, thought Bud. Steve spewed out clichés and repeated himself—fat Steve, who annoyed her grandmother by calling her grandfather "Fred" and raided the fridge at night and had once denied polishing off an entire apple pie even though he was the obvious culprit. There'd be a frost that night. He said so at least three times. The only relief was a silly game Bud and her grandmother had invented, which involved making him say a word they'd selected.

"Um, did you make jam last summer, Gran?" Bud asked, trying not to giggle.

"Of course, darling," said Celia. "I always do. I make it out of damsons and strawberries and . . . oh, what *is* the name for those blasted little fruits that grow wild in the hedges? It's gone clean out of my head!"

"They're black," Bud rushed in excitedly. "There are always flies on them, and brambles that prick your hands. I've forgotten what they're called, too."

"Oh," said Steve, and he stopped his spoon-feeding for a moment, "we must be talking blackberries."

And then it happened. A thumping crash as Frederick fell forward into his plate, which shattered, sending liquefied chicken and potato and leek cascading onto the floor. Immediately Steve lifted him up, but the minute he saw his slack face, all smeared with gravy, he shook his head.

"Is he . . . ?" Celia began, biting her lips, and he nodded.

Then they both seemed to remember Bud, and he grasped her by the shoulders and gently steered her out of the room—though not before she'd taken in her grandmother's expression.

Alone and badly frightened, she straight-away phoned her parents. "Grandpa has passed away," she told them because, for all the mockery at Steve's expense, the way he put things had suddenly become deeply comforting. In the same vein, she added, "He's gone to a better place." It was the only way to explain the shocking relief she'd witnessed.

She had an inspiration later as Celia was tucking her into bed. "That shooting star was warning us, wasn't it?"

"Of course it was!" Celia agreed, mak-ing her feel she'd come out with something very clever. Then she said: "Do you know what I'm thinking, darling? I'm remember-ing Grandpa how he used to be. People called him the handsomest man in En-gland, you know, and he was a wonderful soldier. So brave and strong. Do you re-member me telling you how, when Uncle Robert was very tiny, the snow trapped us here for weeks, and Grandpa went hunt-ing and kept us all alive? He's young again now and he's with his parents and . . ." she hesitated ". . . and everyone else he ever loved who died. And now he can talk to them to his heart's content and run and jump and play golf, too. Dear Grandpa. However sad we are for us, we shouldn't feel sad for him."

"Dear Grandpa," Bud echoed, a little surprised to learn that there were golf courses in heaven. The death had been terrifying. But her grandmother had made it right, just as she always knew how to do.

The next morning, Celia seemed properly subdued though very much in control. The doctor had supplied a death certificate. The undertakers had been alerted, and so had the vicar. Once the family arrived, they'd compose a suitable announcement to go in the *Times*. When they fixed on a date for the funeral, they'd have to go through the address book and phone everyone. Steve had already departed in his little blue Fiat for his next job. Later in the week, the social services would come and remove the wheelchair and the high bed with sides to it and the hoists and the ramps so the house could revert to its old and almost forgotten self.

And then the postman came and Oscar

(who'd been peacefully dozing in front of the warm range) launched into his usual imitation of a vicious rottweiler and Bud said, "Silly old dog," in exactly the same tender, exasperated way as her grandmother as she picked the letters off the mat. There were three that day: a postcard, a gardening catalog, and a big flimsy white envelope with loopy writing and funny-looking stamps. When Bud took them into the kitchen, her grandmother was making a list—working out what to feed the family for the next few days.

"I thought I'd make a big lasagna for tonight," she said. "And would you like trifle, my pet?"

"Can I have these stamps?" Bud asked.

Her grandmother glanced up, seeming suddenly wary—almost, thought Bud, as if she'd been caught doing something she shouldn't have. Then she appeared to relax and gave a lovely smile. "Of course you can!" she said.

Bud handed her the letter and she looked it for a moment before saying, "Excuse me for a moment, treasure" and then she took it up to her room.

_____

When she came downstairs again, she'd become like an old old woman. She leaned heavily on the banister, her face was ashen, she couldn't speak. Far more frightening, though, there was no sign of the strength of character Bud had always taken for granted. When she asked, "What's wrong, Gran?" Celia's lips trembled like a child's and her eyes filled with tears.

It was such a relief when, soon afterward, the family converged on the house. They were upset by her grandfather's death, of course, especially Aunt Margaret who couldn't stop crying; but almost immediately comforting order was restored. Even Bud had noticed that, however much her mother and aunt and uncle might disagree with each other, they became like one person when a crisis threatened. Uncle Robert persuaded her grandmother to go to bed and even made her a cup of tea and held her hand for a while; Aunt Margaret took over the meals, because she was learning to cook now that she was married at last; and Bud's mother made it her business to comfort and soothe her.

"Poor darling," she murmured, holding her close. "It must have been terrible for you. Why didn't you say on the phone? We'd have driven down last night."

But Bud never even contemplated telling her mother that Celia had been coping magnificently until the letter arrived. She knew, without comprehending why, that it must stay a secret between them—just like the relief she'd witnessed after her grandfather's collapse.

She clung to her grandmother, terrified she'd die, too; and when the family decided the time had come to talk about funeral arrangements, she insisted a little hysterically on joining them. But nobody could lift her grandmother out of her terrible apathy and despair: she didn't even want to discuss hymns. And then, in the midst of a cold, bare winter, that extraordinary thing happened: a rare insect was spotted, having found its way into the sitting room and settled on her grandmother's favorite picture. Some lucky impulse prompted Bud to suggest it was a spirit returning from the dead. "Mumbo jumbo," Uncle Robert scoffed afterward, but they all played along and it did the trick. Her grandmother recovered and within minutes was back to her familiar and much-loved self.

Only now, as an adult, was Bud edging toward the shocking realization that when her grandmother had bent over the moth, she hadn't been thinking of her husband at all.

CHAPTER THIRTY-TWO

You ask how I am looking. I have a strange idea in my head I am young and beautiful still but I fear that now only the "and" is true! I am too plump because I am big sugar lover but my hair is thick even if is not same color I am born with, and I have good feet with straight toes size 34.

Part of e-mail dated April 11, 1992,
found by Guy and Bud, April 15, 2010.

Back in London, Bud took out the photograph and laid it on her coffee table where she could look at it properly in her own safe and familiar environment, surrounded by the big spider plant she'd rescued from a skip, the cushion her grandmother had given her with "Never Stop Dreaming" embroidered on it, the scent of patchouli oil, and two old cigarette stubs in an ashtray (from which a visitor might infer she was a slob, but actually meant she wanted to keep the imprint of a companionable evening). To her dismay, the photograph seemed even more disgusting and offensive than it had at Parr's.

It showed a dead man lying on a bed of leaves and flowers in an open coffin. He was in his sixties, at least, and might even have been older because his face looked thin and worn. Nevertheless, someone had taken trouble over him. His long hair was carefully brushed; he was clean-shaven; he even had a white flower pinned to the lapel of his dark suit, as if he'd been prepared for a wedding rather than a funeral.

The message on the other side was stark but friendly, inscribed in careful round script, as if English was perilous territory. "Dear Celia Bayley," it read, "I regret to break terrible news my father Alexei is dead since yesterday. His heart stop sudden on street. I think was too much excitement for him. Very often we speak of you. My sincere condolences and best wishes, Ada Dimi-

trova." A date was inscribed in numerals—
29.12.89—and there was an address and
telephone number.

The understanding that had come to
Bud while she was still down at Parr's was
that this strange, distant death had occurred just ten days before her grandfather's. The address was East European,
so any communication would have taken
some time to reach England. It therefore
seemed almost certain that the photo had
been enclosed in the envelope with the
foreign stamps she'd picked up from the
mat. This was what had had such a terrifying effect on her grandmother. But why? If
Celia had once had an extramarital relationship, as Jenny Granger had suggested,
surely it couldn't have been with this
strange and very sad old man? And even if
it had happened, that long-ago trip to Eastern Europe had lasted just a week. How
could the memory of a brief encounter
have continued to reverberate with such
force?

Perhaps the man had had dozens of
friends. Maybe, even as that photograph
was taken, mourners milled around outside the frame, shedding tears. For the first

time, it occurred to Bud that the camera might not always tell the truth.

She left Parr's without revealing her discovery. She felt too distanced from the rest of the family. Furthermore, fired by anger and without asking permission, she removed another item. Sitting in silence in the back of Robert's car while Sarah drove very competently and Margaret sniffed and mopped her eyes in the passenger seat, every so often she would touch the old picture hidden in her bag. She knew her grandmother had prized it, and now it was beginning to slot into the puzzle. She also knew nobody else would want it. She laid it next to the photograph on her coffee table. How dark and depressing it was—the figures on horseback caught in an eternal prance—though, if you looked at it from a particular angle, a very faint glow was just beginning to lighten the gloomy sky.

As for the message on the back of the photograph—she reminded herself that it was twenty years since it had been sent and quite likely Ada Dimitrova had moved. And even if she was still at the same address, would she want to talk to some strange English girl—if, indeed, she could speak English at all? More crucially, did Bud really want to know the extent to which that strange old man had been connected with her grandmother? Wasn't it better to let the past be forgotten: leave it to collapse in on itself like the charred heaps of old letters and diaries even now still smoldering in the field at Parr's?

Without more ado, Bud looked up the international code and dialed the number. It rang four or five times even as she remembered guiltily that it was nine o'clock—which meant it could be eleven there, because of the time difference. It was too late to be telephoning anyone, least of all a stranger.

"Allo?" It was a woman's voice, and she sounded very irritated. "Allo?"

"Ada Dimitrova?"

A long suspicious silence.

"Are you Ada Dimitrova?"

"Yes," the woman admitted grudgingly.

Bud let out her breath, because she couldn't believe this second piece of luck. "You speak English!"

"Why is this your business?" The woman sounded a difficult customer—the kind of person who'd cut off the conversation for good once she understood what this was about.

Bud hesitated. "I'm Celia Bayley's grand-daughter."

There was silence at first, then the woman repeated disbelievingly: "Celia?" Her voice had altered completely, was warming with every second. "You are granddaughter to Celia?"

"Celia is dead," Bud explained, getting the bad bit over with quickly. "She died seven months ago."

A moment passed. Then Ada said, sounding sad and mysterious, "But I know this already." She went on, "Excuse me," and Bud heard the sound of a match being struck far far away and Ada inhaling deeply. When next she spoke, she sounded as if the cigarette had already soothed her. "You are Miranda?" she guessed. "Ah, Miranda, do you have baby now? So often you are in my thoughts."

Very surprised, Bud said, "No, and yes. No, I'm not Miranda. And yes, Miranda had her baby this afternoon. A little girl." She added: "Eight pounds, two ounces," before realizing this would mean nothing to Ada, who must operate only in kilos. She felt very detached, probably because Robert and his lot were behaving as if no one in the entire history of the world had ever given birth before. But something else was making her cautious about getting involved with that scrap of new life. She wasn't sure how she'd react: it might be like uncorking a genie and she didn't think she was ready.

"But this is wonderful!" Ada exclaimed. "Marvelous! And now I know Robert have to be truly happy." Then the sadness returned. "Oh, I wish Celia could see this, too. So often she speak of Miranda's baby— the first great-grandchild." She was silent for a moment. Then she said: "But you are not Evie! Evie is child still. You have to be Bud!"

"That's right." This whole conversation was becoming more and more surreal.

"Bud!" There was infinite delight in Ada's voice now, as if she knew very well who'd been dearest to Celia, even if she'd been too scrupulously fair to admit it. "Bud! This is wonderful surprise! Celia have told me so much about you, Bud. We were in correspondence for long time with e-mail."

She went on sadly: "When messages stop, I know truth. Well, Celia have to be eighty-two years."

And then Bud began to understand not only that a whole secret conversation had been going on for more than twenty years but it no longer really mattered that all Celia's letters and notes and diaries had gone up in smoke. She was going to learn the story of a love affair from someone who'd been in on it from the beginning. Furthermore, she would discover that Ada knew far more about Celia's life than anyone else because talking about her, retelling every truth she'd confided during the intense couple of days they'd spent together, had been Alexei's way of keeping her with him.

She was so innocent, he'd told Ada—and innocence was as much of a rarity in his world as truth. Even in the café, he knew something momentous had occurred. Everything was confided in that short time, Ada explained to Bud—every hope and fear and disappointment, beginning with childhood. Remembering all this had kept the relationship alive, and it must have been the same for Celia, too, she suggested. It was a vision of how love could and should be, she said in a voice trembling with tears.

The day before her father had suffered a fatal heart attack in the street, she went on to explain, he'd been talking about visiting England. A letter from Celia had just reached him—a real one in which she could at last write what she wanted, because the censors had stopped operating. She'd rejoiced for him that communism had been discredited, calling it a true miracle. Ten days later, with awful timing, she found herself free, too. Ada would use the word "cruel" over and over again (though it was kindness, coupled with tradition, that had prompted the sending of the photograph). But along with her acceptance of suffering as part of the human experience went a deep conviction that nothing happened by chance.

She was thrilled to hear Bud's recollections, which chimed with what Celia had already told her. Of course, the moment when Bud saw that shooting star as a child had to have been the exact same time

Alexei's heart had stopped! And what thinking person could doubt that he'd returned in the guise of a rare moth, well within the forty-day mourning period, to sit on the picture he'd given Celia and offer comfort and hope before slipping off to claim eternal peace? Ada spoke of these things with the ease of one who came from a culture thronged with ghosts. As she put it: "Next we stop believing in love!" She continued with a catch in her voice, "Those poor dear people—God rest their innocent souls," and pledged to light candles for Alexei and Celia in her local church the next day.

When Bud finally replaced the receiver, she stroked the picture, which she had yet to decide where to hang, and then she took the photograph and laid it very tenderly inside a novel her grandmother had inscribed, "To my darling Bud with love and gratitude." She would never again see it as bizarre or frightening. It belonged here from now on, where no curious stranger delving into Celia's life could ever find it. Tomorrow she'd tell the family what she'd discovered. They were going to find out anyway because Ada had asked for Robert's telephone number so she could congratulate him on his new granddaughter. Whether he liked it or not, emotional Ada, trailing her dramatic testimony like a lit fuse, was about to explode into his life, too.

Bud had learned so much. She now knew that her grandfather had been told about Alexei; and that when he suffered a stroke soon afterward, her grandmother had felt entirely responsible, hence the devoted care she'd given him for all those years.

But the affair had continued. By then, for a very different reason, any hope of liberty had been shut off for Alexei, too, so all letters had to be written in code. But it was much better than nothing; though Celia had apparently told Ada with great sadness that his letters were the only pieces of her past she'd destroyed because she couldn't risk them being found, especially after her death when she could no longer explain. But she knew every word of them by heart anyway, Ada had pointed out.

Besides, reflected Bud, continuing the story herself, Celia could revisit their love over and over again in her novels in her own secret and elliptical way. But clearly she'd found it impossible to destroy the photograph; and anyway, by the time it had arrived, Frederick was dead.

Celia and Alexei had met in exciting times and as Bet, who'd lived through the war, had once very embarrassingly pointed out, there was no greater aphrodisiac. What would have happened, Bud speculated, if they'd met again under duller circumstances? Would they have noticed or cared that in the interim they'd become old? And with time to get to know each other properly, would the penniless banned writer have found anything in common with the well-to-do general's widow with a string of commercial books to her name? Perhaps creating the illusion of perfect love had only ever been a way for two essentially lonely people to tolerate their very different prisons. "Thank God for dreams!" Celia had said, often. But dreams merely plugged the gap between hope and reality, Bud told herself very much more pragmatically.

She went to the window and felt the cold panes against her hot forehead as she looked up at the dark sky. And then she remembered that after her grandmother had recovered from the blow of

Alexei's death, she'd gone on to become a fine writer, as he had once been. What was the explanation for that? Whence had her strange new voice come, if not from him?

Bud longed to believe in magic, as her grandmother had done. She was remembering her saying it was easier in a modern age, rather than harder. "Think of the Internet!" she marveled. "Think of radio waves!" If a voice could travel through space, she suggested, who was to say it couldn't endure time, too? Soon, she forecast, it would be possible to pluck even the utterances of the dead out of the ether. She was probably right, thought Bud. In fact, the more she considered the extraordinary telephone conversation that had just taken place and the strange chance that had led to it, the more she understood that Alexei had, in effect, spoken for himself.

Just then two lights winking in tandem appeared high up in the sky and Bud reflected that if Ada had been there, she would surely have interpreted this as a sign. But it was only an airplane, of course, heading for some unknown destination. Still, Bud couldn't help thinking of how easy it would be to visit Ada in her world, and somehow, even contemplating such an adventure felt like jumping out of the life she'd always known and setting off across a boundless plain.